Praise For
WOULDN'T ⁞⁞
B
Eliza Doolitt⸳
M⟩

This clever new series stars Eliza Doolittle and Henry Higgins as amateur sleuths. A madcap, intricate mystery combines with rich historical detail, a hilarious ending, and, most of all, the author's fine re-creation of the delightful cast from My Fair Lady. Broadway fans looking for something new will enjoy this treat.
—*Booklist*

Set in London in 1913, this tongue-in-cheek series kickoff from the pseudonymous Ireland picks up where the musical My Fair Lady left off.
—*Publishers Weekly*

A charming teaming of Eliza, Professor Higgins, and Major Pickering make for an engaging light historical mystery.
—*Library Journal*

GRAINGER PRESS
www.graingerpress.com

GET ME TO THE GRAVE ON TIME
FIRST EDITION
Get Me to the Grave on Time Copyright 2016 by D.E. Ireland
Print 978-0-9981809-0-8
eBook 978-0-9981809-0-8

Printed in the USA.

Cover Design and Interior Format

MORE PRAISE FOR

WOULDN'T IT BE DEADLY, Book 1

The charming and feisty Eliza Doolittle, the masterful Henry Higgins, a Hungarian upstart, a Sanskrit scholar—all are brought together in an intriguing plot. D.E. Ireland gives us a fascinating look into a bygone world.
—Susan Wittig Albert, *The Darling Dahlias Mysteries*

In this exciting new novel, Eliza and Higgins are still nursing their grievances against each other when a murder forces them to work together. Join them in this delightful romp through early 20th century London as they try to find a killer and clear Higgins' name.
—Victoria Thompson, Best Selling Author of the *Gaslight Mysteries*

Oh so loverly to meet up again with Henry and Eliza in this ingenious mystery. All the beloved characters are here, neck deep in murder and mayhem, and the London setting is a delight. Suspects and red herrings abound on the way to a denouement that's laugh-out-loud hilarious. I hope Wouldn't It Be Deadly is the first of many.
—Catriona McPherson, Agatha, Lefty and Macavity Award winner, the *Dandy Gilver Mysteries*

I could have read all night! A delicious homage to these beloved characters--putting this classic duo in the midst of a murder is terrifically clever and authentically charming. Loverly.
—Hank Phillippi Ryan, Agatha and Anthony Award winner, *The Wrong Girl* and *The Other Woman*

We've only been waiting a century for another glimpse of this wonderful duo, and there is no better format than a juicy Edwardian murder. Higgins is his irascible, aristocratic self, while Eliza grows and evolves quickly in a world of society intrigue and danger. They make a wonderful pair of sleuths. Having now read Ireland's work I can safely say, 'By George, I think she's got it!'
—Will Thomas, *Barker & Llewellyn Mysteries*

GET ME *to* THE GRAVE *on* TIME

THE ELIZA DOOLITTLE *and* HENRY HIGGINS MYSTERIES

D. E. IRELAND

GRAINGER PRESS

"There is no subject on which more dangerous nonsense is talked and thought than marriage."
—George Bernard Shaw

CHAPTER ONE

❦

August 1913

"WHY MUST I SUBJECT MYSELF to these blasted weddings?" Henry Higgins asked. "I've been invited to four in the next month alone. Four! I swear, I would prefer murder to matrimony."

Higgins's outburst elicited groans and eye rolling from his fellow passengers in the chauffeured car. Perspiring from the summer heat, he waved his top hat before his face. "And don't think I'm dealing in hyperbole. I have a basis for comparison. After all, I've spent the past few months solving more than one murder, and been quite successful at it, too."

Eliza, who sat across from him, lifted an eyebrow. "You wouldn't have solved any of them without my help. Blimey, I've never known a man who thinks so well of himself." She turned to the older woman beside her. "Was he always like this? If so, his nanny should have tossed him out of the pram and given a swift kick to his swollen head."

Higgins's mother sighed. "You have no idea. Luckily, Henry is my youngest. If he'd been the firstborn, I'm certain his father and I would have halted any further procreation."

Although Higgins aimed exasperated looks at his mother

and Eliza, in truth he was quite fond of them. Higgins had little use for women, but he regarded his mother as unique to her species: intelligent, cultured, and capable of wielding a wicked wit. As for Eliza Doolittle, a year ago she entered his life like an unexpected windstorm. He thought teaching a Cockney flower seller to speak and behave like a lady would be an amusing lark, as well as an easy way to win a wager from his fellow scholar and friend Colonel Pickering. Instead, she exceeded their expectations by being far more clever, resourceful, and charming than they could have guessed. Higgins found Eliza a delightful companion, but he'd swallow a tuning fork before admitting it.

"In response to your question," Mrs. Higgins continued, "you're attending four weddings because for some inexplicable reason these people wish your presence at their nuptials."

"One of them is his own niece." Eliza reminded her. "Relatives have to be invited no matter how much you may like them to stay away. I showed up for my dad's wedding, even though I'd dance in the street if my step-mum dropped dead."

"Exactly." Higgins pointed at her. "You also prefer murder over matrimony."

Eliza sat up with a start. "I never said anything about murder. I'd just like Rose to choke on a chicken bone or something. I don't want her to be done away with."

He gave a gleeful chuckle. "But murder is the quickest way, is it not?"

"I say, what has gotten into you today?" The Colonel shared the backseat with Higgins, both of them facing the ladies. "You've been haranguing us about marriage since we boarded the train at King's Cross. Don't start in on murder as well."

"And don't misbehave at Minerva's wedding. She's an old family friend whom you have always regarded highly. Now put an end to this ceaseless complaining," Mrs. Higgins said sternly. "Or go back to sleep. It was a relief when you finally napped on the train."

Eliza cocked her head. "I'd prefer to listen to him say insulting things about marriage rather than hear him rattle the car with his snoring."

"The ladies are right," Pickering added. "It's too early to be cantankerous."

Higgins felt outnumbered and unjustly accused. Why in the world would anyone be pleased about having to wake at sunrise and put on a gray morning coat, striped trousers, white gloves, and top hat? He hadn't been this tricked out since Royal Ascot, and look how dreadfully that ended. Then he was forced to sit in a muggy train compartment all the way to Kent, followed by a five mile trip to St. Cuthbert's Church. What a waste of a fine summer day.

"Mother, not even you can be thrilled Minerva is marrying for the third time. And to a man nearly thirty years her junior."

"Minerva does not need my approval or counsel. She made two good marriages before this. Happy ones, too." She fiddled with the pearl buttons on her dress. "Although I do wish Mr. Farrow were older."

"I wish he possessed a fatter bank account," Pickering said. "When a handsome young man marries an older and much wealthier woman, it does give me pause."

"Why?" Eliza asked. "Beautiful young women marry rich older men all the time. Look at Freddy's sister Clara. She doesn't have more than forty quid to her name, and she's about to marry a baron. Although he's only a few years older than she is."

Higgins groaned. "Don't remind me. Yet another wedding we must attend."

"It's not the same thing at all, Eliza," Pickering replied.

"Minerva is the Duchess of Carbrey, a title and position not to be taken lightly."

"I'll tell you who's not taking it lightly. That American fellow she's marrying." Higgins liked Minerva and did not want to see any man making a fool of a sixty-year-old woman. "He goes from being an art gallery owner in Mayfair to the husband of a wealthy English duchess. Do you really imagine he's marrying her for love?"

Eliza gave him a disapproving look. "You act as if he's marrying some toothless laundress from Spitalfields. Her Grace is still an attractive woman."

"So is her money and title," Higgins shot back. "No good will come of this. Of course no good results from any marriage. Infernal institution. My advice to anyone fool enough to enter into it is that offered by Montaigne, 'A good marriage would be between a blind wife and a deaf husband.' I don't think much of the French, but I'll make an exception for Montaigne."

"Oh, you're always quoting other people when you don't have anything clever to say," Eliza said. "I'd be right embarrassed to do that. It makes you look simple."

Mrs. Higgins and Pickering laughed.

"You ungrateful monkey," Higgins said. "You don't even know who Montaigne is."

"I bet I wouldn't like him if I did."

"Well, Minerva should not be marrying anyone, least of all this American. When the vicar asks if anyone has an objection, I may speak up."

Eliza grew serious. "Don't you dare, Professor."

"Pay him no mind, Eliza," his mother assured her. "I will see to it that my son behaves. Although I hoped by now he would no longer fly into a foul mood at the mere mention of marriage. I've never understood why he has such little regard for it."

"Because he realizes no woman would ever be dotty enough to marry him," Eliza said.

Pickering chuckled.

"And what are you so amused about, Pick?" Higgins asked. "You're a confirmed bachelor, and as relieved as I am to be so. Marriage is a useless invention and you know it."

"Don't be a bore, old chap," Pickering replied. "Minerva was gracious enough to send her chauffeur to drive us from the train station."

"It's a lovely car." Eliza gazed in approval at the spacious interior and luxurious fittings.

"A Pierce-Arrow. It must have cost a small fortune to have this transported from the States." Pickering cleared his throat. "Driver, do you know how much a car like this is worth?"

When the chauffeur turned his head, they caught a glimpse of a rugged profile. "Her Grace paid over twelve thousand pounds. And the name's Luther, sir."

Higgins was stunned by such a price, while Eliza let out a whistle. "Cor, I could buy a flower shop *and* a pub in the East End with that much money."

"Minerva told me it's an engagement gift to her American groom. Rather extravagant." Mrs. Higgins sighed. "She gave it to him months ago. Of course, none of us had any idea they became secretly engaged in May. No doubt she expected her friends would disapprove. I only hope Mr. Farrow lives up to her expectations."

"A pity her expectations included marriage," Higgins grumbled. "I would have thought a discreet dalliance would have sufficed. Not another damned wedding."

"Henry, really." His mother did not approve of bad language before noon.

He slumped down in his leather seat, refusing to admit he was as impressed by the gleaming new car as the others.

This upcoming wedding was a disastrous proposition, but he could do nothing to prevent it. When the marriage ended in spectacular failure, however, Higgins would remind everyone that he had predicted it all along.

It was a burden to always be so bloody right.

Even the Professor's nonstop complaints couldn't spoil Eliza's morning. She loved to dress up, and there was no better excuse to do so than for a wedding. Mrs. Higgins reminded her that given the Duchess of Carbrey's age and it being a third marriage, the wedding would be far more modest than her first to the Duke. But it would still be the most lavish wedding ceremony Eliza had ever seen. The last wedding she attended was her father's misbegotten marriage this past spring to Rose Cleary. And that celebration ended in a drunken ruckus at the Hand and Shears Pub in Smithfield. Where her dad and Rose were concerned, she sided with Higgins. That was a marriage better left forgotten – and hopefully dissolved one day.

But the wedding of the Duchess of Carbrey gave her a lovely excuse to buy an expensive outfit, including new shoes and gloves. After her last disastrous outing wearing a hobble skirt, Eliza swore she would never put on such a constricting garment again. Yet she couldn't resist buying an ash gray hobble-skirted dress trimmed with black for the Duchess's wedding. Eliza loved its daringly low neckline and how the jacket swung open to reveal a black lining patterned with bright pink roses.

When they arrived at the church, several wedding guests milled about outside. Eliza noted with satisfaction that none of the ladies sported anything as fashionable as her ensemble. Especially since she had completed her outfit with a pink parasol and a black toque decorated with a spray of gray and pink feathers. And this hobble skirt had an extra panel sewn in so she could actually walk without taking mincing steps. The outfit cost an outrageous sum of money, but Eliza was now a woman of independent means. Not only did she give elocution lessons at 27-A Wimpole Street, she recently became part owner of a victorious racehorse. His winnings this season had already plumped up her bank account and her ever increasing wardrobe.

She guessed Mrs. Higgins spent even more on her pale green silk dress. Tiny pearl buttons decorated her crossover draped bodice, while ivory ruffles trimmed her wrists and sleeves. A green hat in the Dutch bonnet style perched atop her silver gray coiffure. Eliza admired the older woman for not only being stylish, but choosing a gown appropriate for her age.

Once their car pulled up to St. Cuthbert's, Eliza jumped out. She realized too late that she should have waited until the driver opened the door. Her excitement over this wedding was making Eliza forget all the pretty manners Higgins and Pickering had taught her. She looked at the small stone church with disappointment.

"I thought it would be bigger," she said when the others joined her.

"The trees conceal much of the west tower." Mrs. Higgins nodded a greeting to a couple who walked past. "Once we're inside, you'll be surprised at how much larger it looks."

"The church dates back to medieval times," Higgins said in his most professorial voice. "Pilgrims stopped here en route to Canterbury in the thirteenth century. And the building is made from local ragstone and flint, a dreary but expedient choice. I do wish it had a gargoyle or two to give it some character."

"Why is the Duchess getting married here? Does her family own St. Cuthbert?"

"They did," Pickering said to Eliza. "The church once stood on the Duke's property, but the Roundheads confiscated it during the Restoration."

Eliza didn't know what the Restoration or Roundheads were, but had no wish to appear ignorant by asking. "Then her house is nearby? The one you told me is called Rowan Hall?"

"One of her houses. Minerva has many, including an estate or two in Scotland. It's where she was born and raised." Higgins looked at his mother. "Near Stirling, I believe."

"Gargunnock, to be exact."

"If Minerva holds true to form, the wedding ceremony and reception will be filled with all sorts of Scottish customs and traditions. By the way, I'd choose carefully at the wedding breakfast. Only the Spaniards are worse cooks than the Scots. I nearly died from hunger when Pick and I visited Spain this spring. And it never stopped raining." Higgins cast a baleful look at the overcast sky. "I hope it doesn't rain today. These country roads will turn to troughs of mud."

"Everything will be fine, including the breakfast." Mrs. Higgins smiled at Eliza. "Following the ceremony, the cars will drive the guests to Rowan Hall. Now that is a building sure to impress you. It's nearly as big as Buckingham Palace."

Pickering adjusted his top hat. "A shame your young man couldn't join us today, Eliza.".

"He wanted to, but the London Rowing Club has a racing meet this morning. Freddy's competing in two heats. Believe me, he'd miss his own wedding before he'd skip a race."

In truth, Freddy Eynsford Hill only cared about two things: Eliza and his membership in the London Rowing Club. She was grateful the LRC distracted her adoring suitor. Otherwise he'd be constantly at Eliza's side, where he seemed to do little else but implore her to marry him. While she was fond of Freddy, she enjoyed her new life as an independent woman with a talent for teaching – and sleuthing. She refused to give it all up to be Freddy's steady companion *and* financial support. Besides, she was only twenty years old. Why rush to get married?

Higgins shot her a sly grin. "Freddy might not have been able to attend, but look who just pulled up. And in their new blue roadster, too."

Eliza didn't have to turn around. The only person she knew who owned a blue roadster was her father. When Eliza went to Higgins last year to become his student, her dad arrived soon after. He hoped to wring a few pounds from the Professor for what he believed was an immoral situation involving his only child. Not that Alfred cared what Eliza was doing – immoral or otherwise – as long as he could make a bit of money from it. Higgins had been amused by the eloquent dustman. As a joke, he recommended Alfred Doolittle to an American millionaire as the perfect lecturer for the Moral Reform League. Imagine their surprise when the millionaire did just that, paying Alfred an annuity of three thousand pounds. This windfall enabled Alfred and Rose to move from the East End to a proper middle class house in Pimlico.

Fortune smiled once again on the Cockney rascal when he spent some of his new wealth to become part owner of the Donegal Dancer, the same racehorse the Duchess of Carbrey and Eliza owned. Looking at his fancy two-seated roadster, Eliza suspected he was spending his winnings even quicker than she was.

Her father screeched to a halt beside the other cars. Alfred Doolittle hopped out of the roadster with an energy belying his fifty years. Rose exited the low-lying car with much more difficulty. Eliza was pleased to see that traveling in an open air car caused Rose's hair and plumed hat to fall into wild disarray.

Alfred raised his top hat in greeting. "Morning, ladies. Colonel Pickering." He winked at Higgins. "Governor. Aren't we all looking as fancy as the King and Queen. Bet not even King George has a car as fine as mine though. Quite a beauty, ain't she?"

"I'm impressed," Higgins said.

Rose Doolittle joined them, still wrestling with a long curl that would not stay pinned. As always, she resembled an over-baked cake with too much icing. Her red hair, which Eliza knew came from a bottle, resembled the color of ripe tomatoes today. Rose's pale skin had been whitened further by too much face powder, which made her rouged cheeks rather garish. And the beauty mark Rose normally painted on her left cheek currently graced the right. Rose seemed to move it about her face at will. Maybe tomorrow the beauty mark would appear on her chin.

"I didn't even know you could drive, Dad," Eliza said.

"He can't." Rose smirked. "Your father nearly hit two cows on the way here. And he sped so close to a postman, he knocked him clean off his bicycle." She finally pinned her hair into place. "Don't be surprised if he runs down the vicar on the way home."

"She's mad I didn't buy a car with a roof. Says this one musses up her fancy hair."

"It does wreak a fair amount of damage to a ladies' coiffure." Eliza tried to sound refined around her stepmother, knowing it irritated her.

Rose narrowed her eyes. "Don't know about any cwaffoor, but the wind tangled up my hair something terrible."

"Anyways, what are you standing out here for?" Alfred placed his hat atop his head, then tapped it twice. "I say we go inside before the best seats are taken."

A summer breeze rustled the trees overhead. Mrs. Higgins and Eliza both lifted their faces to appreciate this sudden relief from the heat. "I believe we shall wait," Mrs. Higgins said. "We traveled here via rail and a closed car. I'd welcome a few minutes of fresh air."

"Suit yourself, ma'am. But I can't say we'll be able to hold any seats for you." He pointed to the guests arriving with more frequency.

"Her Grace has reserved a pew for all six of us," Mrs. Higgins assured him.

His face creased in a wide smile. "Ain't that nice of the Duchess. Then again, she's a proper toff, she is. A fine lady with a heart of gold and a nose for the best horseflesh. Can't wait till I show her my new car. Is she here yet? I want to take her for a little spin."

"Dad, it's her wedding day."

"Are you daft, girl? I know that. Why else would I be dressed like this?"

"The bride arrives after all the guests are seated." Colonel Pickering pulled out a pocket watch from his waistcoat. "And the wedding isn't due to start for nearly an hour."

"Alfie, come on!" Rose glared at them by the church door. "There's a wind kicking. I won't have my hair fooled with again."

Alfred sighed. "When I first met Rose, she never fussed with her hair. Now you'd think she was Lily Langtry, she worries so much about her looks. It's like I said when I first met you, Governor. Middle class morality has made my life a misery." He hurried off.

Eliza looked at her friends in dismay. "Do we have to sit with them? Rose will never stop talking. And Dad is sure to sing all the wrong words to the hymns."

"I hope that's true. It may be the only way I'll get through this travesty." Higgins whipped off his hat. "That breeze does feel good. I wish they'd hold the ceremony out here."

"If I remember correctly, the curate keeps a shade garden

in the back," his mother said, "with wrought iron benches. We could take the air there for a few minutes."

She didn't have to coax them. The refreshing breeze made the prospect of sitting inside the now crowded church an unappealing prospect. Mrs. Higgins led the way, the tip of her silk and lace parasol clicking every time she set it on the paving stones. But when they reached the back wall of the church, Mrs. Higgins abruptly halted. "Is that who I think it is?" she asked.

Beyond the shade garden, the church graveyard's stone crosses and headstones marched in straight rows. A man and woman stood there in conversation.

"I believe that's the groom." Having met Ambrose Farrow several times, Eliza recognized his dark blond hair and mustache. "But I don't know who the woman is."

"Her name is Pearl Palmer." Mrs. Higgins's voice had grown chilly.

"Sounds like a stage name," Higgins said. "Is she an actress?"

Eliza, who loved to spend her free time at the cinema and music hall, failed to recall seeing that name on any theater program. "I've never heard of her."

His mother narrowed her eyes at the couple, who seemed to be engaged in a heated discussion. Both of them were waving their arms about. "She's a mannequin."

Pickering chuckled. "She looks alive to me."

"A mannequin models clothes at the more expensive salons," Eliza explained.

"Miss Palmer is far more than that," Mrs. Higgins said. "She is Ambrose Farrow's mistress."

"What?" Eliza, Higgins and Pickering all exclaimed at the same time.

"Keep your voices down," the older woman said in warning. "If you wish to watch people unobserved, the first requirement is to avoid being noticed."

"Ma'am, how did you learn Mr. Farrow has a mistress?" Eliza whispered.

"After Minerva became engaged, I made a few discreet inquiries. And too many people said the same thing. Ambrose Farrow and Pearl Palmer are lovers."

"Does the Duchess know?" Pickering asked Mrs. Higgins.

"Minerva is a woman of the world. It would not surprise me if she knew."

"And she'd still marry him?" Eliza wasn't a woman of the world and found this shocking.

"In Minerva's circle, liaisons outside marriage are *de riguer*," Mrs. Higgins said. "And she has had more than a few dalliances in her life, even while married. But one does not publicly humiliate a spouse or affianced. For Farrow's mistress to turn up on his wedding day is unacceptable."

The couple had raised their voices, but not loud enough to be overheard. Farrow grabbed Pearl's arm and pulled her close. It looked as if he might kiss her, but she slapped him across the face. He yelped in pain. Ignoring him, the young woman marched out of the graveyard.

"Pearl, don't be a damned fool! You know I'm right," Ambrose called out, but she'd already walked around the other side of the church.

"Minerva will be here soon," Mrs. Higgins replied. "If that woman dares enter the church, I shall demand Mr. Farrow remove her."

They hurried to retrace their own steps, hoping to reach the front of the church before Farrow's mistress did. But as they turned the corner, Pearl was already there, waving her arm.

"She's signaling one of the drivers," Higgins said as a chauffeur leaning against a black car lifted a hand in response. Eliza wished she could see Pearl's face, but her back was to them. She did boast a lush mane of dark hair arranged stylishly under a beribboned straw hat.

Once the car pulled up, the young woman disappeared from view into the backseat.

"What should we do?" Eliza asked as the car drove away.

"We don't know Mr. Farrow well enough to say anything to him," Pickering said.

"I'd want to know if I was the Duchess," Eliza said. "She may decide not to marry him."

They turned to Higgins, who shrugged. "Not marrying would always be my choice. But I'm not fool enough to tell a bride such a thing on her wedding day."

Eliza gently touched Mrs. Higgins's arm. "She's your friend."

"Yes, she is. But I've no idea how well she knows her fiancé. Perhaps Miss Palmer came here to beg Mr. Farrow not to marry. They did appear to be arguing so it seems as though he refused her." Mrs. Higgins looked disheartened. "Although if this fling of Mr. Farrow's is not at an end, I pray he learns discretion."

Eliza was not so trusting. Both Farrow and his mistress had been most upset; one of them had even struck the other. Higgins joked earlier about how he preferred murder to marriage. But she feared that given the right circumstances, murder and matrimony might go hand in hand.

CHAPTER TWO

HIGGINS SLOUCHED DOWN IN THE pew with a long suffering sigh. A morning wasted, when he could have finished reading The Philological Society's meeting report from Cambridge. Or if it was a tad quieter, he might have been able to resume napping. But that was impossible. As expected, guests were being assaulted with thirty minutes of bagpiping before the ceremony.

Eliza frowned at the kilted man who stood to the right of the altar. "I'd like the bagpipes more if they weren't so loud."

"More like deafening." Higgins tried not to cringe at the ear splitting wail. He shot a sympathetic look at the organist who sat motionless over his silent instrument. If the piper ever lost his breath, the poor chap might be allowed to play a few notes.

Late arriving wedding guests surged past to fill up the remaining church pews. Even without the bagpiper, there was no mistaking this for anything but a Scottish wedding. Small bouquets of purple heather and thistle looped across each pew's wooden post, while swags of Clan Darroch tartan were draped over doorways, the organ bench, even beneath the white altar cloth. Higgins doubted if even Robert the Bruce had been as proud of his Scots heritage as Minerva.

It was amazing that none of her three husbands had been of Scots origin.

"Why are weeds decorating the pews?" Eliza sneezed into her handkerchief.

"Thistle is Scotland's national flower, and heather is a symbol of good luck. The Duchess is inundating us with Scottish customs today. Including the bridal cog."

"What's a bridal cog?"

"An alcoholic drink served in what looks like a wooden bucket with handles. The bridal couple drink from the cog before they pass it around to guests." He looked at Eliza in surprise. "Didn't you notice it sitting on that table in the church vestibule? We walked right past it."

"I was too busy paying attention to the fishing basket out there."

"Another Scottish wedding tradition," his mother explained. "That one is called 'creeling'. When the bride and groom are about to leave the church, two people bar their way by holding a fishing basket tied with a ribbon. The newlyweds cut the ribbon, allowing the basket to fall." She shrugged. "It's meant to being good luck. Although I have no idea why."

"We should be thankful the Duchess isn't going completely Scottish on us," Higgins said. "Only Minerva and Farrow will drink the cog today, which means we shall be spared."

"It has a most vile taste." Higgins's mother shuddered.

"I agree," he said. "Usually she has the cog brought to the altar before the ceremony ends, and the couple drink it there. Wonder how Farrow will react to his first sip. Can't imagine he's looking forward to a warm brew of whiskey, ale, gin, and brandy. Egg, too."

"What's this about gin and brandy?" Farther down the pew, Rose Doolittle leaned over her husband. "I'd kill for a spot of gin right now. I'm sweating like a ditch digger."

"Good morning, Mrs. Higgins. Professor." A thin, middle-aged man wearing a disagreeable expression stood at the end of their pew. "Beastly hot day for a wedding. And I could have done without all this silly Scottish folderol."

Not for the first time Higgins wished his niece Beatrice had found someone other than Clyde Winterbottom to marry. Then again, Beatrice was a plain featured woman of twenty-seven. It was common knowledge in the family that she feared spinsterhood far more than a dismal marriage. A pity she had not chosen someone more agreeable than this pompous museum curator. Higgins's spirits sank at the prospect of attending their wedding later this month.

Higgins scanned the church. "Where's Beatrice? Since you're a friend of Ambrose Farrow, I assumed you'd be invited to the wedding. I expected to see my niece as well."

He sniffed. "I am Mr. Farrow's professional colleague, not his friend. And Beatrice had an appointment with the caterers at the Hotel Café Royal. She and her mother have more than enough to do preparing for our own wedding. No need to subject her to this nonsense." He winced as the bagpiper let out an especially loud squeal. "If you'll excuse me."

As a guest of the groom, Winterbottom took his seat across the aisle. Higgins was grateful for that. He had no desire to spend any time in the fellow's company.

Their chauffeur, Luther, suddenly appeared in the aisle. "Excuse me, miss, but you forgot this in the car." He held out a delicate pink fan.

"Thank you so much." Eliza accepted it from the driver with a grateful smile.

Tipping his hat, Luther walked back up the aisle. "Blimey, I'm glad the fellow has such a keen eye." She fanned herself vigorously. "It's so hot in here, we could roast chestnuts."

Alfred Doolittle mopped his damp forehead. "If that piper plays 'Flow Gently, Sweet Afton' one more time, I'll break his blowpipe in two like a stick of kindling."

"There will be an improvement soon." Mrs. Higgins gestured to the tall bearded man with auburn hair who sat on the organ bench. "Thaddeus Smith is much in demand this season at all the society weddings. He also plays occasionally at Chelsea Old Church for Sunday service."

Higgins feared Smith's talents would be lost here. St. Cuthbert's acoustics were appalling. Still, the organist gazed approvingly at the large metal organ pipes set into a stone bay above the altar, as well as the smaller ones arrayed above the actual instrument. Now and then, Smith checked the stops, his prominent Adam's apple bobbing.

Pickering leaned forward from his seat on the other side of Mrs. Higgins. "I wasn't aware Lady Winifred Ossler would be in attendance. And with a couple from India, too."

They looked up to see a finely dressed woman walk down the aisle. In her peacock blue gown, feathered hat, and silver necklace boasting a sinuous bejeweled medallion, she seemed as stylish as Eliza. Trailing after her were an attractive couple who clearly hailed from India. The coffee-skinned man was garbed in a bronze satin coat with a matching turban atop his head; the young woman walking beside him boasted similar coloring. Her exotic beauty and pumpkin-hued sari drew numerous stares, as did the gleaming gold jewelry adorning her.

When she passed their pew, Lady Winifred caught sight of Pickering and seemed startled. He nodded, and she lifted a gloved hand in greeting before entering a pew on the groom's side of the aisle. The Indian couple followed suit.

Eliza watched them with obvious delight. "I've never seen people dressed so gorgeously. The young man and woman look like royalty."

"They must be friends of Lady Winifred," Pickering replied. "Her husband is Sir Ian Ossler, a baronet and Lieutenant General in His Majesty's Army. He's been stationed with the Bombay regiment for thirteen years. When Lord Curzon was Viceroy, Ossler became one of his most trusted aides. Before that, he was posted to South Africa. Both he and Winifred were in Mafeking during the siege and have hair-raising stories to tell about their experience there."

"They sound like an interesting pair," Higgins said.

"I've been to their home in Bombay many times. They set an excellent table, and the dinner conversation is first-rate."

Higgins chuckled. "That means they spend a lot of time talking about Sanskrit."

"Indeed they do. And there are few people in the Colony who have such an appreciation for art and antiquities." Pickering looked over at Lady Winifred. "I'd heard she returned to England this past year, only our paths haven't crossed. Now I'm glad my Sanskrit conference in Bristol was canceled this weekend. We'll be able to catch up at the wedding reception." He looked up. "Here now. What's this?"

A young boy and girl dressed in red and green tartan began to march down the aisle. They held the wooden bridal cog between them. From their anxious expressions, Higgins suspected the children were worried they might drop it. The sexton waiting for them at the altar seemed just as nervous and took charge of it as soon as they reached him. Mercifully, the bagpiping ceased. The silence was exquisite.

"The wedding cog," the sexton announced in a booming voice and raised it high.

"Where's he going with it?" Eliza asked when he disappeared through a side door.

"Probably taking it to the vestry," Higgins said.

"At Her Grace's second wedding, the best man accidentally knocked it over during the vows," Mrs. Higgins said. "Minerva wants it safely out of the way until the end."

The organist unleashed a sweeping melodic phrase. Even

with the poor acoustics, the fellow managed to produce a most harmonious sound.

"Thank heaven all that bagpiping is over," Rose Doolittle muttered.

Higgins enjoyed the 'Air' from Handel's 'Water Music,' and almost crowed in delight when Thaddeus Smith segued into Bach's 'Jesu, Joy of Man's Desiring.' One of Higgins's favorites, he approved of the masterful rendering by the organist.

Eliza leaned across Mrs. Higgins. "Could you introduce me to the Indian couple, Colonel? If they're friends of Lady Winifred, she's certain to include them in your conversation. I'd love a closer look at the Indian woman's jewelry. She even has a gold pin in her nose."

Pickering smiled. "That's a symbol of a bride's purity. And the pendant she's wearing on her forehead is placed over a *chakra,* one of seven, signifying knowledge and perception."

"I've never seen such a pretty dress and veil."

"The dress is called a sari," he told her. "All women in India wear one."

Mrs. Higgins snapped open her fan. "Colonel, if I'd known you were so well acquainted with Lady Winifred, I would have invited you both to tea months ago. She's the person responsible for introducing Beatrice to Mr. Winterbottom."

Higgins snorted. "She deserves to be punished for that. Why have I never heard of her?"

"Why should you? Being an Army wife, she's lived abroad for many years. I know Winifred through her father. He and my brother were quite good friends. A pity she and Sir Ian never had children. They always seemed a most agreeable couple."

"I'd no idea she introduced your niece to Mr. Winterbottom," Pickering said. "Then again, on the subcontinent she's known as 'The Matchmaker.' Second and third daughters of good families are often eager to wed officers serving in India. Winifred has enjoyed remarkable success introducing the right woman to a suitable young man."

Mrs. Higgins nodded. "Her matchmaking efforts have borne fruit here as well. And not just with Beatrice and Mr. Winterbottom. Minerva told me that Lady Winifred introduced Mr. Farrow to her shortly after he arrived from America."

"Don't know how good a matchmaker she is, but the lady seems up to date on the Paris fashions," Eliza said. "The lace on her cuffs and collar look to be Chantilly, and authentic, too."

Higgins raised his eyes to the stone-and-timber arched ceiling. "Enough. All weddings are dull affairs. But talking about fashion will make this one even duller."

"Hush, Henry," his mother said. "The groom has appeared."

Ambrose Farrow now emerged from the vestry area to the right of the altar, accompanied by a plump, dark-haired man. Both looked uncomfortable in their morning coats. Higgins didn't blame them, especially in this summer heat. Fiddling with the sprig of heather pinned to his lapel, Farrow glanced at the door several times. Higgins wondered if he was anxious for a first glimpse of his bride – or an unwelcome appearance by his mistress.

The parish vicar, a balding man with gold-rimmed spectacles clamped to the bridge of his nose, adjusted the tippet over his white surplice. He joined Ambrose Farrow and his best man as the opening notes of Wagner's 'Wedding March' boomed from the organ pipes.

"Mr. Farrow looks quite dashing," Eliza murmured. "Only he seems as nervous as a cat ready to jump off a tall fence."

Higgins shrugged. "Aren't all grooms nervous?"

"His best man seems calm," Mrs. Higgins said. "Who is

he?"

"No idea. Probably another art gallery owner in London."

A stir in the church signaled the bride had made her first appearance. The entire congregation rose to their feet.

The Duchess of Carbrey started down the aisle with a huge smile on her face. Minerva seemed as radiant as a bride of nineteen. One would never guess this was the sixty-year-old matron's third marriage. She looked at least ten years younger, with only a few strands of gray in her ash-brown hair. And her corseted figure was still slim but womanly. Given her age and marital history, the Duchess had eschewed a white bridal gown and instead wore a forest green dress adorned with a Clan Darroch tartan sash and matching hat. Clasped in her hands was a lush bouquet of white lilies mixed with tufts of purple heather.

Before her walked the matron of honor, whom Higgins recognized as the Duchess's daughter Mary. Her buxom figure encased in navy silk, Mary appeared somber. A small bouquet of heather shook between her gloved hands. He suspected she was less than pleased to see her mother wed yet again, especially to a much younger man. No doubt the Duchess's two sons felt the same way; neither was in attendance. It could explain why a doddering white-haired and kilted Scotsman escorted the bride down the aisle. Probably an uncle or a brother.

To accommodate her elderly escort, the Duchess walked at such a sedate pace, they almost came to a standstill. Higgins glanced at the groom during this interminable march. The fellow seemed so restless, he wouldn't have been surprised to see Farrow break into a jig.

At long last the couple reached the altar. "Thank you, Uncle Angus," the Duchess said loudly before kissing his wrinkled cheek. "You can sit down now, dearest."

The old gentleman cautiously lowered himself on the first

pew to the left, as if grateful he'd made it that far without keeling over on the stone floor. The matron of honor watched Uncle Angus in concern. Higgins wondered if the family expected the old fellow to up and die during the ceremony. Exactly how old was Uncle Angus?

Once the organ's echoing notes faded away, the vicar cleared his throat. "Welcome to St. Cuthbert's. I am Reverend Robert Macpherson. As second cousin to Her Grace, I have been asked to preside over the wedding. We are gathered here today to honor the sanctity of marriage. A holy institution, one not lightly entered into…"

As the vicar droned on about the virtues of marriage, Higgins stopped listening. Instead his attention focused on the bridegroom, who grew more agitated by the minute. While the bride gazed at the vicar, Farrow kept throwing glances over his shoulder. Maybe Pearl Palmer would make a surprise appearance after all.

"I think he's shaking," Eliza whispered.

She was right. Every so often, Farrow rubbed nervously at his cheek. When he did, his hand visibly trembled. At last Reverend Macpherson turned his attention on the groom.

"Do you, Ambrose Earl Farrow, take this woman, Lady Minerva, to be your lawfully wedded wife?"

The Duchess looked at her intended groom with frank adoration. Farrow stared back at her, his mouth open as if to speak. Nothing came out. Instead he stepped back. His best man gently pushed him forward once again.. The vicar started to repeat the words, but Farrow interrupted.

"No, I'm—I—I cannot do this," he stuttered. "Forgive me, Minerva. I'm sorry."

"What—what are you saying?" Her rosy cheeks lost all color.

He took a deep breath. "I cannot in good conscience marry you."

Gasps arose from the wedding guests as the Duchess's daughter dropped her bouquet.

"It's not that I don't love and adore you, of course." His voice cracked, and he tried to steady himself. "Our difference in age—it's too much. I can't do it."

His bride stared at him. "Have you lost your mind? This is madness!"

"I can't marry you." His voice rose to a shout. "It wouldn't be fair to either of us!"

"Bloody hell," Higgins muttered. He glanced at his companions in the pew. Both Eliza and his mother looked stunned. Pickering shook his head in disbelief.

For a long excruciating moment, the Duchess regarded her groom in obvious horror and shock. "You aren't serious. You can't be!"

Farrow now ran both hands through his thick hair. Higgins suspected he might start tearing it out by the roots. "Forgive me, Minerva. But it would be wrong for us to marry. Surely you see that."

With a despairing cry, the Duchess struck him across the face with her bridal bouquet. Ambrose Farrow stumbled backwards, but there was no escape from his enraged bride.

"Scoundrel! Blackguard! Deceitful bastard!" The Duchess screamed at her cowering groom, beating him about the head until her bouquet was nothing but shredded leaves and bare stems. No one in the bridal party – or the church – dared get in the way.

"I guess I was wrong," Higgins said. "Not all weddings are dull affairs."

The church erupted into noise and confusion. Higgins, Eliza, his mother, and Pickering rushed up the aisle to help her. But Eliza doubted anything they said would comfort the distraught bride. If only Ambrose Farrow had broken the news privately to her before the ceremony. Foolish man. Eliza thought he deserved all the verbal and floral abuse he'd gotten from the Duchess. Of course, the poor woman's rage didn't last long. Once her bouquet lay in pieces, the Duchess had taken refuge in her daughter's arms and wept uncontrollably.

Uncle Angus, who'd inexplicably napped during the excitement, awoke in time to see his niece being comforted by her daughter and an obviously unsettled vicar. The white-haired Scotsman struggled to his feet. "Eh? Is she nae wed then?"

When the Duchess saw him, she fell into his embrace next and left her daughter to seek comfort from the vicar. For some reason, the bagpiper decided to play again, which only added to the din. No doubt irritated that the piper had taken center stage, Thaddeus Smith gathered up his organ music and stormed out of the church.

Eliza noticed one of the ushers sipping from a silver flask. She wouldn't have minded a drink herself. Certainly the groom needed one. Cradling his head in his hands, Farrow sat on the altar steps as one guest after the other harangued him. Meanwhile Higgins, his mother, Pickering, and Eliza kept the agitated guests away from the bridal couple. That included Eliza's father, who was spoiling for a fight.

Alfred tried to punch the groom. "How dare you insult the Duchess!"

Eliza grabbed him by the collar and held him back. "Don't make things worse," she hissed. "We don't want to turn this into a blooming brawl."

"C'mon, Alfie, let's go." Rose yanked him away from Eliza. "If there's no wedding, there ain't no breakfast neither. Which is a bleeding shame, seeing we had to pay for all that petrol to drive out here."

"All right then." Doolittle straightened his collar. "But if I ever sees that Farrow bloke again, I'll smash his pretty face. And I don't know why I shouldn't give him one good kick in the arse before I take my leave."

Like a white-haired angel, Colonel Pickering came to the rescue. "Please restrain yourself, Alfred. We don't want to upset Her Grace more than she already is."

They glanced at the Duchess, now being comforted by Higgins and his mother. Accompanied by the wailing strains of the bagpipe, the Colonel quickly escorted Alfred and Rose out of the crowded church.

Just as Eliza breathed a sigh of relief, the best man came to stand beside her. "Dreadful mess, isn't it?" he said.

"Never imagined a wedding could turn out so awful." She gave the man a penetrating look. "Did you know Mr. Farrow planned to jilt his bride?"

"Good grief, no. I never would have entered the church if I'd known. It was beastly, standing at the altar while Her Grace was humiliated. I'm mortified to have played any part in this at all. That's what I get for agreeing to be best man for a fellow I barely know."

"You and Mr. Farrow aren't friends?"

"No more than acquaintances. I own the antiquarian book-store next to Ambrose's gallery in Mayfair. We've shared a meal a time or two, and sometimes visited each other's businesses. To be honest, I was surprised he asked me to be his best man. Then he explained that most of his friends lived in America, and it seemed unkind to turn him down." He blushed. "Forgive me, I should have introduced myself. I am Milton Ellery York."

"Eliza Doolittle. Friend of the bride, although I've met Mr. Farrow a few times. I rather liked him before today. I only wish he'd acted on his misgivings earlier."

"Yes. Waiting for the vicar to speak the vows is cutting it

too close."

The aforementioned vicar tapped Mr. York on the shoulder. He gestured towards the groom, still hunched over on the altar steps. "Best get him out of here. I'm afraid one of the guests may attack him. Three have already tried."

York went to kneel beside Farrow. "Ambrose, I think it's wise to leave. I'd hate to see you hurt by one of Her Grace's friends or relatives."

"Leave me alone!"

"You did what you thought was right," he continued. "At least you had the courage to be honest. But most people here are rather angry."

Farrow groaned. "I don't blame them. I've made a damned mess of everything."

The Duchess suddenly noticed Ambrose hadn't left. She stabbed a finger at him. "Why is that cad still here? How dare he breathe the same air? Get him out! I can't bear the sight of such a scoundrel!"

Higgins threw Eliza a helpless look as he patted the Duchess on the shoulder.

Most of the wedding guests still milled about the church. Some of them wore dangerous expressions and stood too close to the altar. "Reverend Macpherson, is there anywhere in the church where Mr. Farrow can stay until the guests have left?" Eliza asked. "If he goes near the front door, there might be an unpleasant scene." She paused. "Or a lynching."

The vicar gazed at the excitable throng. "I fear you're right, miss." He turned to Farrow and his best man. "Take Mr. Farrow to the vestry and stand guard at the door. I shall do my best to disperse the congregation."

Farrow finally got to his feet, although his legs seemed shaky. He looked as miserable as the Duchess. "I can't take any more of this wedding. And it's unspeakably warm. I would kill right now for a drink. I want to leave!"

"Soon, Ambrose." York led the groom to the vestry just off the altar. Once Farrow closed the vestry door behind him, his best man blocked the entrance and kept a nervous eye on the commotion in the church.

The vicar halted any angry guests who approached. "Leave him be. It's over now, go on."

This whole thing reminded Eliza of a suffragette rally that had gotten out of hand. But with Ambrose Farrow gone, the crowd's anger lost its focus. Muttering complaints, the guests exited the church. Eliza walked over to the distraught Duchess.

"Someone should take Her Grace home," Eliza murmured to Higgins's mother.

For the first time since she had known her, Mrs. Higgins's habitual calm was shaken. "How ghastly. That awful man."

As though she had heard Higgins's mother, the Duchess cried out, "If I had my riding crop with me, I'd thrash the pig until he begged for mercy!"

Higgins wore a familiar stubborn expression. Eliza knew he was about to take action. "Send for Her Grace's car. I'm taking her back to Rowan Hall."

"Let me retrieve my parasol," Eliza said. "I left it in the pew."

He shook his head. "Best if you stay here while we leave. I need you to make certain Mr. Farrow does not show his face until I've gotten the Duchess into her car."

Mrs. Higgins touched Eliza on the arm. "He's right, dear. We'll go back with Minerva. You can follow in our chauffeured car."

With a heavy heart, she watched their departure. The remaining guests trailed after them. In only a few moments, no one was left in the church save Eliza, the vicar, the piper, the best man guarding the vestry door, and Uncle Angus. The old man had somehow nodded off again in the front pew, despite the blooming bagpiper still wailing away.

"Could you get the piper to stop, Reverend?"

"I'll try. But I may have to puncture his bag."

Eliza examined the remains of what should have been a joyous wedding. Church programs lay tossed on the stone floor while several thistle swags had fallen off the posts. A sad end for such a promising morning. She sank down on a pew. She couldn't imagine being rejected at the altar by her bridegroom. If Freddy pulled something like that, Eliza would punch him in the jaw. Then she'd let her dad finish him off. Maybe it wasn't so surprising, however. Ambrose was a handsome fellow in his early thirties, and the Duchess of Carbrey a woman nearly twice his age. Ambrose also had a young mistress who begged him not to marry only an hour before.

With the bagpiper silenced, Eliza could finally hear how quiet it had grown, both inside and outside the church. Best follow Higgins's advice and send Ambrose Farrow on his way. She signaled the vicar. Both of them walked to the vestry door, still guarded by the best man.

"Time to set our nuptial prisoner free." Reverend Macpherson opened the door.

The vicar stepped back to let Eliza enter the vestry first. Once inside the small room, she noticed several vestments draped over a wooden chest, along with a polished table holding a collection plate and communion vessels. But there was no sign of the reluctant groom.

"Mr. Farrow?" she called. Was there another way in or out? If so, she didn't see one. Then again, the vestry windows were small and made of stained glass. Given the cloudiness of the day, little light shone through. "Are you here, Mr. Farrow?"

"Good Lord!" The vicar pointed to a crumpled shape half hidden by the wooden chest. The best man gasped in shock.

Ambrose Farrow lay face down on the floor.

Eliza rushed to kneel beside the groom, who hadn't moved or made a sound since they entered. "He must have fainted. The stress of the wedding was too much."

"What's this?" York picked up a wooden object from the floor.

"The bridal cog," she said. "It held some sort of ale mixture."

"He said he was thirsty." The vicar sniffed the cog. "Given the potent contents, he may have imbibed a bit too much. He probably passed out drunk. We'll turn him over and sit him up. He'll soon recover."

But Eliza felt a wave of fear. She'd seen her father drunk and unconscious many times. He never looked like this. As if frozen, Farrow lay on the cold stone floor, one shoulder twisted, his right arm at an unnatural angle. York and Reverend Macpherson rolled Farrow onto his back.

"He's dead." She was barely able to get the words out.

"Impossible!" York shook the unresponsive Farrow while the vicar crossed himself. The best man turned to Eliza. "What happened? I don't understand. How did he die?"

However, it seemed obvious to Eliza. Someone poisoned the Scottish wedding drink.

CHAPTER THREE

❦

"AS I WARNED, WEDDINGS BRING nothing but trouble." Higgins held up the newspaper. "The headlines are filled with Farrow's death and his jilting of the Duchess."

His housekeeper, Mrs. Pearce, waited nearby. "Would you like breakfast served on the sideboard or at table, Professor?"

"Table."

"Should I bring coffee or tea?"

"Tea," Higgins, Eliza, and Pickering replied. She hurried out.

Eliza unfolded her napkin and spread it on her lap. "Honestly, you act as if every wedding ends in death."

He chuckled. "Even if no one dies during the ceremony, the bride or groom probably wishes one of them was dead soon afterward."

"How can you find any levity in what happened on Saturday?" Pickering frowned at Higgins as a maid came in with the tea tray. "Dreadful enough Farrow jilted Her Grace at the altar, but to have the poor fellow die. And all from drinking that Scottish brew in the vestry. It must have gone bad in the summer heat."

Eliza and Higgins exchanged knowing glances. "Colonel, it seems obvious the cog mixture was deliberately poisoned.

And from the behavior of the local police when they arrived, I daresay they agree." She loved Pickering dearly, but he believed most people in the world were as honest and kind as he was. Eliza knew the truth all too well. Growing up in the slums of the East End had a way of destroying pretty illusions.

"But who would want to kill the man?" Pickering protested. "No one knew what was going to happen until right before Farrow jilted the Duchess."

Mrs. Pearce laid a platter of scrambled eggs on the table. A maidservant followed with rashers of bacon and a rack of toast.

"A jealous mistress for one," Eliza replied. "In fact, she would want to kill him and the woman he was about to marry. All of us saw Pearl Palmer argue with Farrow shortly before the wedding. She actually struck him. Then she stalked off in an awful rage."

"Exactly. We watched Miss Palmer drive away before the ceremony started. The girl could not possibly have done it."

"Pick, you must try to entertain a cynical thought once in awhile," Higgins said. "Otherwise people may question your sanity."

"Farrow probably told Pearl that Her Grace wanted the bridal couple to drink from the Scottish cog following the ceremony." Eliza sipped her tea, which this morning was a tart Earl Grey. "She could have gotten there early and poisoned it. Maybe she did it in case Farrow refused to call off the wedding, as she no doubt asked him to do. If that's what happened, this tragedy could have been even worse. After all, the mixture was meant to have been drunk by both the bride and groom. Her Grace barely escaped with her life."

Pickering sighed. "I have never known anything so appalling to occur at a wedding. The Duchess has probably taken to her bed."

"She did appear to be in shock when we went to see her," Eliza said.

Indeed, following the wedding debacle, Eliza and Pickering found the older woman sitting in her front parlor, oblivious to everyone.

"Minerva turned pale and silent after learning Farrow was dead," Higgins said, "but she was as mad as the devil when Mother and I took her out of the church. If she'd gotten to the cog just then, she might have poisoned it herself. But we put her right into the car and had the driver take us straight to Rowan Hall."

Pickering choked on his tea. "Henry, how can you imply she would poison the cog?"

"He's being sarcastic, Colonel. No one believes the Duchess murdered Ambrose Farrow. But if it wasn't his mistress who killed him, then someone else at the wedding had a deadly grievance against the bride and groom." Eliza became distracted by the tiered plate of iced scones Mrs. Pearce carried into the dining room. A maidservant followed with a platter of potatoes and kippers, a favorite of the Professor's.

Eliza loved mealtimes at Wimpole Street, especially breakfast. She woke each morning to the tantalizing smells of sausages, fresh bread, and coffee, along with whatever delectable pastry Cook decided to whip up at dawn. Until she became Professor Higgins's pupil last summer, Eliza's days had begun with a cup of boiled tea dust, an apple if she was lucky, and whatever slices remained of a loaf of stale bread bought at Covent Garden – which had to last a week, sometimes more. Not only had this past year under Higgins's and the Colonel's tutelage helped her to speak and act like a lady, she was also as well-fed as one, too.

Looking about the dining room with its mahogany paneling, ivory linen tablecloth, blue and white china, and carved wooden sideboard, Eliza didn't know if she could ever bring herself to leave Wimpole Street. It was the first place that felt like home, and she was fond of the four maids, Mrs. Lennox the cook, and the beloved Mrs. Pearce.

Colonel Pickering had become dearer to her than her own father. Certainly, the Colonel never treated her with the caustic neglect and contempt Alfred Doolittle often did. As for Professor Higgins, she thought he was probably the best friend she ever had, even if people mistook their frequent spats and teasing for something less harmonious. The more strait-laced sometimes questioned the propriety of a girl of twenty living with two older men who were not family members. But Mrs. Pearce served as stalwart chaperone of the household, not that Eliza needed protection from Higgins or Pickering. In fact, she worried she might never live in such a wonderful place again, even if she did marry Freddy.

To make it more ideal, she and Higgins gave elocution lessons in the house's laboratory and study. Of course, today's lessons had to be canceled. As Eliza learned these past few months, murder had a way of disrupting one's routine.

An unexpected ring at the front door caused everyone to look up from their eggs and bacon. "Who the devil is that?" Higgins growled. "If it's your young man come scrounging for another free meal—"

"Freddy's at his tailor's this morning," Eliza interrupted. "His suit for Clara's wedding needs altering."

"Perhaps one of your students forgot their lessons have been canceled," Pickering said, pouring himself another cup of tea.

But Mrs. Pearce ushered Eliza's cousin Jack Shaw and his fiancée Sybil Chase into the dining room. Happy to see the young couple, Eliza jumped up to hug them both. Pickering graciously got to his feet, but Higgins only speared a sausage.

"If either of you have come for the scones, sit down quick," he said. "Eliza's finished off two so far."

"I'm so sorry for interrupting your breakfast." Sybil handed Eliza a striped hat box. "But Selfridges mistakenly delivered your bridesmaid hat to my house."

Eliza peeked inside and smiled. "How loverly. I can't wait to wear it." After placing it on the sideboard, she turned to the housekeeper. "Mrs. Pearce, please bring more sausage and eggs."

"Oh, we've already eaten, but thank you," Sybil protested as Eliza led them to the table.

Jack brushed back his always unruly black hair. "I wouldn't mind a sausage or two, and maybe some of those potatoes and kippers."

Mrs. Pearce smiled. "I'll bring out a pot of coffee for you, Inspector. I know you like coffee with breakfast."

Higgins snorted. "That proves how many times I've fed you, Jack. I should bill you for groceries."

Despite Higgins's long suffering expression, Eliza knew he liked the Scotland Yard police detective. Rather surprising given the two men met under tense circumstances when Higgins was the prime suspect in a murder case.

Jack only laughed. "Don't worry. We're about to go to considerable expense feeding you and dozens of others at our wedding."

Sybil rolled her eyes. "Will you listen to him? Acting as if he, and not my father, is paying for everything."

"You can't blame me. We've talked about little else for months."

"He's exaggerating," Sybil said. "It's only these last few weeks that have been filled with bridal minutiae."

"The Egyptians spent less time preparing to build the pyramids than we have for this wedding. And we're not done yet." Jack took a large bite of his scone. "There are ten days left to obsess about flowers and the right shoes."

Sybil handed him a napkin. "Don't talk with your mouth

full. Really, all this fuss and complaining over a few wedding details." She unpinned her white straw hat and placed it on the empty chair beside her. "At least Jack should enjoy today's appointment. We're off to see the caterer on Sloane Street to decide between two different fruitcakes."

"One with sultanas, I hope," Eliza said eagerly. "Or you could do what Clara did. Break with tradition entirely and have a tiered buttercream cake instead."

"I've already broken with tradition by refusing to carry a bouquet of orange blossoms. But Mother insists we have the usual fruitcake." Sybil took a sip of tea. "And she's a bit nervous. All my friends are suffragettes, while most of Jack's friends are policemen. I suspect some of his friends have arrested a few of mine. Mother's worried a battle might break out in the church."

Higgins grinned. "Now here's a wedding I can look forward to."

"Speaking of weddings, what did you learn about Ambrose Farrow's death?" Eliza asked her cousin.

"Most of the details are in the morning papers. As expected, the cause of death was poison. The preliminary toxicology report points to cyanide, which kills quickly. Had you gone to the vestry five minutes earlier, Eliza, you would have found Farrow gasping for breath and in the throes of a seizure. Whoever poisoned the drink wanted no chance for their victims to survive long enough to get to hospital." Jack finished off his scone. "But have no doubt. There was a murderer at that wedding. A murderer who wanted death to be swift but painful."

The atmosphere in the dining room turned gloomy as everyone grew silent except for Eliza. "Where does one get cyanide?" she asked.

"It's a common substance. One finds it in everything from wallpaper to paint." Jack seemed to realize he had cast a pall over the breakfast. "There's no reason to dwell on the Farrow murder. The police in Kent are handling the case, so I won't hear much more. It is, after all, not my jurisdiction." He winked at Sybil. "And I have more than enough to do before the wedding."

Sybil nodded. "Yes. Jack still has to reserve a restaurant for the bachelor dinner. And purchase a gift for his best man and ushers."

Jack leaned over to kiss Sybil, which flooded her face with color. "True. I also have a triple homicide I'm overseeing, one involving a member of Parliament and an opera singer. Although I grant you, the murders aren't as urgent as choosing engraved cuff links."

Eliza smiled as she watched them. "Sybil, you truly are a blushing bride."

"Probably because I'm feeling overwhelmed. Like Jack, I had no idea how many details need to be kept track of. I didn't spend my girlhood paying attention to these things as I never had any desire to marry. All I cared about was fighting for the rights of women." She shot Jack an affectionate look. "Then I met this fellow."

Jack grinned. "I *am* irresistible."

"But it means so much to my parents that everything be done properly," Sybil continued. "I owe them that. Having a suffragette daughter has not been easy. They dread I'll be arrested during a demonstration."

Colonel Pickering looked surprised. "If you were, being married to a Scotland Yard detective inspector ought to assure them you wouldn't be held by the police long."

"She won't be held at all," Jack said. "I've made certain every police constable knows what Sybil looks like and that she is not to be touched. Even if she's slinging tomatoes at Lloyd George himself." He turned to her. "I hope you have no intention of doing such a thing."

"Of course not, dear. I would never take such a risk." Sybil and Eliza exchanged quick smiles. This past summer both of them barely escaped arrest at a Votes For Women rally. A rally Lloyd George drove right into the middle of, which prompted a few tomatoes hurled his way.

"Farrow's killer certainly took a risk, poisoning the cog at the church when anyone might have walked by and witnessed it." A thought suddenly struck Eliza. "And the cog must have been tampered with there. The best man told me it was made at the church by her butler."

"A Scotsman, of course," Higgins said. "Can't believe he'd want to poison anyone."

Jack sipped his coffee. "The sexton stood beside the butler while he made it. And he swears all the bottles were sealed before the butler began. The cog was poisoned afterward."

Eliza pushed her plate away. "I feel rather guilty about Mr. Farrow's death. After all, I asked if the groom could stay somewhere in the church until the guests had all left. How dreadful the vicar took him into the room where a poison drink lay waiting."

"You and the vicar couldn't have known that," Sybil assured her.

"This crime appears to have been planned well in advance," Jack said. "I daresay if this attempt had failed, another one would have followed."

"Who do the police suspect? We did tell them about Pearl Palmer arguing with Farrow before the wedding. And Mrs. Higgins informed them about the rumors they were lovers. It seems obvious Miss Palmer killed him out of jealousy."

"Eliza, you and I both know the obvious suspect is not always the one who did it." Higgins no doubt recalled his own unhappy time as chief suspect this past spring.

"True," Jack said, "but I agree with Eliza. Miss Palmer had motive and opportunity."

"While we were waiting for the police," Eliza said, "both the sexton and best man told me a young woman came looking for Farrow shortly after he arrived at the church. And that they went outside for a short time. Obviously it was Pearl Palmer."

"That confirms what you observed in the graveyard." Jack reached for another scone. "When the Kent police brought Miss Palmer in for questioning, the sexton identified her as the woman."

"But everyone at the wedding had the opportunity to poison the bridal cog." Eliza frowned. "It was on display in the church vestibule for over an hour while the guests arrived. We all walked past it."

"Well, I doubt everyone at the wedding had a reason to want Farrow and the Duchess dead," Jack said. "After all, both of them were supposed to drink it."

"The morning paper claims the police questioned the wedding guests." Higgins pointed at the folded paper beside his plate. "Including those two children who carried the cog to the altar."

"They questioned the chauffeurs, the organist, the best man, the sexton, even the piper. No one saw anything suspicious, nor did anyone seem to have a reason to want Farrow or Her Grace dead." Jack raised an eyebrow. "Except for Miss Palmer. Unless another wedding guest with a motive surfaces, Pearl Palmer remains the prime suspect. But the police must not have enough evidence. Otherwise they would have arrested her."

"Do you think she killed him, Jack?" Eliza asked.

"Probably. But I don't have enough information. If I were handling the case, I'd push her hard for the truth. She's only twenty-two and prone to hysterics, at least according to my friend with the Kent police. A little pressure at the right time and I suspect she'd confess."

Sybil frowned. "Seems a bit cold-blooded, sweetheart."

"Not as cold blooded as putting cyanide in the bride and groom's wedding drink. A good detective reserves his sympathy for the victim, not the killer. But I can understand why Miss Palmer might have done it. The man she loved was about to marry another woman. By the way, Miss Palmer's an American like Farrow. They came to England together. Only natural for her to feel abandoned and betrayed when he decided to marry the Duchess."

Eliza sighed. "I wish I'd seen her face. I have no idea what she looks like."

"Miss Palmer must be attractive," Sybil said. "She's a mannequin at Maison Lucile. I can't imagine Lady Duff-Gordon hires young women to model who aren't pretty. I hear her clothes are both fashionable and exorbitantly expensive."

Eliza sat back in surprise. When Mrs. Higgins told them Pearl was a mannequin, she hadn't mentioned the girl's employer was Lady Duff-Gordon. Freddy's sister had ordered her wedding gown from Maison Lucile, and Eliza accompanied Clara to her first fitting. While there, Eliza had paid attention to the gowns modeled by the mannequins, not the young women themselves. She wondered if she'd already seen Pearl Palmer. Clara wanted Eliza to go with her again this Friday for her next fitting. She preferred spending Fridays at the cinema, but now Eliza thought the dress fitting with Clara might prove more interesting. Especially if she could see – and perhaps speak with – Pearl Palmer.

Sybil looked around the table. "All three of you are looking rather formal for a Wednesday breakfast at home. Especially you, Professor."

Eliza, Pickering, and Higgins were decked out in their Sunday best, albeit in sober colors. Eliza was amused by Sybil's consternation at Higgins's presentable appearance. The Professor was notorious for taking his breakfast in a ratty bathrobe and carpet slippers. This morning he looked ready to attend a Cabinet meeting.

"She's right," Jack said. "You're all dressed up."

"Perhaps I should have worn a walking suit today like Eliza." Sybil looked down at her simple pink skirt and white blouse.

"Don't be silly," Eliza said. "You're off to order your wedding cake. You should look all summery and girlish. Whereas we must attend a memorial service for a man who was murdered. That requires dark colors and long faces."

"Is this service for Ambrose Farrow?" Jack asked.

Higgins pushed away his now empty plate. "The Duchess felt it was only proper to hold some sort of memorial for the chap, even if he did jilt her. It appears he has no family, at least not close enough to take care of funeral arrangements. My mother spoke with her yesterday. Her Grace has arranged for Farrow to be buried at Highgate, but there's to be no formal funeral. Just a memorial reception today at his art gallery in Mayfair." He gave a great sigh. "And I have not been able to come up with a good enough excuse to avoid it."

"Seems a bit odd, don't you think?" Sybil said.

"Not really," Higgins replied. "Minerva has her own way of doing things. And being a duchess, she usually meets little opposition."

"If you finish with the baker early, why not come to the gallery and meet us?" Eliza asked. "Jack might be able to learn something interesting about Mr. Farrow."

"Absolutely not." Sybil shook her head. "This morning is devoted to marriage, not murder."

Higgins laughed. "I think you may find there's no way to separate the two."

CHAPTER FOUR

Ⅶ

HOW STRANGE WHEN A MEMORIAL service for the
dead appeared more festive than a wedding. Oh, Higgins
had been to a rollicking Irish wake or two in his time. And
it didn't surprise him when people felt the need for frivolity
after a somber church service with its painful reminder of
death. But this reception seemed like the wake without the
funeral.

The Farrow Gallery bustled with fashionably dressed people, none of whom wore black. Paintings by popular Art
Nouveau artist Alphonse Mucha hung on the walls, their
bright colors and sensual charm unmarked by a single piece
of traditional crepe. A string quartet played a sprightly Viv-
aldi selection near the wide window overlooking Regent
Street; the music could barely be heard over the laughter and
conversation. Two waiters moved among the crowd with
trays of champagne flutes and glasses of sherry. Higgins was
most struck by a long linen-covered table which literally
groaned under the weight of silver platters heaped with food.

"The Duchess has a veritable banquet laid out," Higgins
remarked to Eliza and Pickering. "Smoked salmon, oatcakes,
game paté, lamb shanks, and shortbread with what looks to
be butterscotch sauce. What in the world is she thinking to

offer up such a feast?"

"It's Minerva's wedding menu." The three of them turned to face Higgins's mother. "In fact, it's the actual food which was to be served following the wedding. She had the servants store it in the larder. They brought it all to London this morning."

Higgins smiled. "I should have remembered those ancestors of hers."

"What do you mean?" Eliza asked.

"The Scots waste nothing. Although it may be approaching bad taste to also serve the wedding cake, which I believe is on that table as well."

"I'm afraid it is." Mrs. Higgins adjusted the collar on her dress. Higgins noticed that only she and Eliza wore suitable half-mourning ensembles: his mother in a dove gray gown, Eliza outfitted in a navy blue walking suit.

Pickering scanned the crowded gallery. "Where is the Duchess?"

"Minerva arrived an hour ago in the company of Mr. Thaddeus Smith. The two of them have been inseparable ever since." Mrs. Higgins motioned towards the quartet of musicians near the window where the Duchess stood pressed close to Smith.

The couple seemed to be enjoying the music, if their small smiles and whispered comments to each other were any indication. Higgins was surprised to see the Duchess in a claret red skirt and jacket, accompanied by a two-foot wide white hat crowned with velvet roses.

"I fear Her Grace may be giving the appearance of not grieving for Mr. Farrow."

"I think that's the point, Colonel," Eliza said. "She must feel humiliated after being jilted at the altar. When you add a murdered groom to it . . ."

Mrs. Higgins sighed. "With the papers now reporting Mr.

Farrow's death, all of London knows she was rejected by her groom. It's been difficult for her. Minerva is a proud woman."

"She may be relieved," Higgins said, "especially with Mr. Smith hovering about."

"But he's only a church organist. A duchess would never marry such a fellow."

"Why not?" Higgins said to Eliza. "She was willing to marry an art gallery owner."

Eliza regarded the tall, red-haired man with open curiosity. "He looks around the same age as Mr. Farrow."

"Not quite. Thaddeus Smith is more than ten years older than Farrow. Until the American appeared on the scene last year, he was Minerva's favorite. One of several male protégés she's championed over the years. The arrival of the dashing Ambrose Farrow pushed the organist into the wings." Mrs. Higgins shook her head. "And so it begins again. I can't imagine why Minerva wishes to marry for a third time. Once was quite enough for me."

Higgins laughed. "I'll remind you of that the next time you wonder why I've no wish to marry. I inherited it from you, Mother."

"My marriage was most congenial, even if it did result in a son as maddening as you. Although after a certain number of years, I do admit the wedded state can become tedious."

"Speaking of tedious, my niece is here, along with her repulsive fiancé." Higgins's mood plummeted when the couple walked in their direction.

"Don't be rude," Mrs. Higgins warned him. "We may not care for the gentleman, but Charles is relieved that Beatrice has finally made a match."

"My brother's a bigger fool than I thought. Winterbottom has all the charm of a hangman. And his pomposity is boundless. The fellow just works at the British Museum. To hear him talk, you'd think he was Heinrich Schliemann and discovered the ancient city of Troy."

"Winterbottom did help excavate that Hindu temple in India," Pickering said.

"Oh, I don't care a fig about him." Eliza smiled. "I'm excited to finally meet your niece, Professor. I see she has your coloring. And her outfit matches her hair."

Higgins bit back a caustic remark. No need to tell Eliza that his niece invariably wore drab colors, brown being a particular favorite. Today was no exception. Beatrice Higgins sported a nut-brown jacket and skirt that matched her hair, as did a small hat boasting but a single brown feather. Beatrice always brought to mind a rabbit, shy and easily frightened; her enormous eyes, tiny nose and protruding front teeth heightened this image. Since Winterbottom resembled a ferret, Higgins shuddered to imagine what their children would look like.

"Auntie Grace," Beatrice said when the couple reached them. She exchanged kisses with Mrs. Higgins. "Uncle Henry."

His mother introduced them to Eliza and Pickering.

"I believe I saw you at the Duchess of Carbrey's wedding," Winterbottom said to Eliza. "You have a talent for solving crime, at least according to the newspapers."

"She doesn't solve them alone." Damned if Higgins knew why everyone only remembered Eliza's part in catching killers. Probably because of her spectacular appearance on the stage of the Drury Lane Theater when she brought one of them down. But Higgins saved the day in front of thousands of people at the racetrack only last month. One would think he'd get a little credit for that.

"The Professor is right," Eliza said with an impish grin. "Once in a great while, he plays the heroic detective, too."

"Once in a great while? You impertinent little brat."

She ignored him. "I'd like to thank you for the wedding invitation, Miss Higgins."

Beatrice's glum expression didn't change. "It was only proper to do so. After all, you currently reside with my uncle, although it does seem an unusual living arrangement."

"Also a bit questionable," Winterbottom said. "You should take greater care with Miss Doolittle's reputation, Professor."

"I wasn't aware I had a reputation." Eliza smiled.

"You do, but it's one that claims you are a most clever girl." Higgins turned his attention back to Winterbottom. "Keep in mind Colonel Pickering also resides with me. And Eliza and I are fellow instructors of elocution, not clandestine lovers. As I'm sure you both know, passion and romance are not the concern of every couple."

"Henry, really." His mother shot him a warning look.

"Are you excited about the upcoming wedding, Miss Higgins?" Eliza asked quickly. "My cousin Jack is getting married, too. He and his fiancée were complaining about how much is still left to do. I don't think Sybil has even picked her bridesmaids' gifts yet, although it's sure to be jewelry. And my young man's sister is marrying the Baron of Ashmore next month. I'm to be a bridesmaid at both their weddings. May I ask what your bridesmaids' gifts will be?"

Beatrice eyed Eliza with alarm. "Prayer books, of course. Anything else would be unsuitable and frivolous. Marriage is a solemn occasion."

Eliza looked disappointed by her answer.

"Some weddings are more solemn than others, Eliza." Higgins nodded towards Winterbottom and Beatrice. "And far more dreary."

Mrs. Higgins took her great-niece by the arm. "Come with me, my dear. St. Cuthbert's vicar has entered the gallery. He is an old friend of your Uncle James and I know he wishes to extend his congratulations to you on your upcoming wedding."

After his fiancée left, Winterbottom seemed relieved. "You might think marriage is dreary, Professor, but I doubt there's anything more dreary than murder."

"Dreary?" Eliza asked. "Horrible, certainly. But how can you call murder dreary?"

He waved his hand at the assembled guests. "Look at us. Forced by convention to show up at a silly art gallery. And for what? To pretend to grieve for a man few of us really knew, and even fewer liked."

"I met Farrow this past summer and he seemed an engaging fellow," Higgins said. "Why would so few people like him?"

Winterbottom sneered. "He was an American. That's reason enough."

His remark annoyed Higgins. Since the beginning of his career, he had instructed a number of American heiresses on how to speak the King's English before marrying their affianced duke or earl. He found most of them pleasant and agreeable; indeed one young American heiress in particular captured his heart many years ago. But no one had to know that but him – and her. Winterbottom's contempt for Americans made him sink even lower in Higgins's estimation.

"I like Americans," Eliza said. "Every one I've met is so friendly and warm. They remind me of the Irish."

"Exactly." Winterbottom's laugh sounded nasty. "Yet another mongrel group of people whose accents set my teeth on edge. A pity every American and Irishman isn't struck dumb."

"Oh, I don't know. I certainly prefer their accents to listening to someone who hails from the Dorset region of England." Higgins paused. "Especially Lyme Regis."

Winterbottom flinched. Obviously he didn't know that Higgins was an expert linguist, able to place a person within a block of their birthplace just by listening to them speak a few words. And Higgins had correctly guessed Winterbottom hailed from Lyme Regis.

"Was that an insult, sir?"

Higgins gave a lazy grin. "I don't know. Was it?"

Pickering cleared his throat. "I heard Lady Winifred Ossler introduced you to Miss Higgins, and that she also introduced the Duchess to Mr. Farrow. Is that why you felt obligated to attend his wedding? Through your mutual association with Lady Winifred?"

Winterbottom shot Higgins a resentful look before turning to Pickering. "In part. But he and I had professional dealings. Farrow acquired *objets d'art* from around the world, some with questionable provenance. The museum was interested in items which came into his possession; in particular, the Indian antiquities. As an East Asian scholar, it fell to me to work with him."

"I believe you were one of the British Museum's staff sent to excavate the Temple of Parvati in southern India." Pickering looked over at Higgins and Eliza. "There was a bit of drama about the museum's acquisition of artwork from the temple, especially the contents of the treasure house. The native authorities protested their removal to England. Maharajah Sidhu is still working to get the treasure returned."

"For a soldier, you seem remarkably well versed in antiquity gossip," Winterbottom said. "I had no idea Army colonels were even aware India possessed precious artwork. The ones I met while I was there spent most of their time napping and getting drunk."

"Colonel Pickering is a famous scholar." Eliza's eyes flashed with anger. "And he's the author of *Spoken Sanskrit,* which every specialist in his field holds in great regard. He spent years in India studying the language and is as great a phonetics expert as the Professor. So I don't know why you're surprised that he knows such things. In fact, I wonder you have never heard of *him*. You can't be such a great scholar if you haven't."

Lady Ossler suddenly appeared in their midst. "I agree. Colonel Pickering is highly respected in England and India. An antiquarian such as yourself should know that, sir."

Like most of the women at the gallery, Winifred Ossler was dressed gaily for the occasion. Her two-piece suit, a rich golden color, matched a teardrop hat crowned by an enormous single quail feather. "I went to live in India over a dozen years ago when my husband was posted there. Even then the British colonies in Bombay and Calcutta talked about the strides Colonel Pickering had made in translating Sanskrit."

"My apologies, Colonel," Winterbottom said stiffly.

Ignoring him, Pickering introduced Lady Winifred to Eliza and Higgins.

She beamed at Higgins. "Ah, you are Grace Higgins's youngest son. I've heard a great deal about you and your brother Charles."

"I hope some of it was good."

"A pity your gown is pinned with a Florentine gold brooch today," Pickering said. "I spied you wearing an antique necklace at Her Grace's wedding. I regret I never got a chance to see it up close. The medallion looked to be of sapphire and maniratna, which means it must be part of your celebrated collection of Indian jewels."

"Sir Ian gave me the necklace for our twentieth wedding anniversary. In fact, my dear husband marks each of our anniversaries with an antique gemstone from wherever he is stationed. That particular necklace hails from the Mughal period, late seventeenth century."

"Ah, I was mistaken then. I thought it was fourteenth century."

Lady Winifred smiled. "You're partially correct, Colonel. The maniratna part of the medallion hails from a much earlier period when such serpent stones were worn as talismans. It's not my favorite piece. I'm much fonder of a gold Vanki armlet from south India. By the way, I was surprised to see you at the wedding. The papers announced you were to be a speaker at the Sanskrit conference in Bristol last weekend."

"Canceled. The conference host fell off his horse and fractured both arms. It will be rescheduled after his recovery."

Winterbottom sniffed. "I wonder the Indian locals didn't object to your taking the jewels out of the country, Lady Winifred. They're becoming insufferable about these things."

"How could they object? My husband paid princely sums for all the jewelry I own, as he has paid for every piece of art in our collection." She sighed. "Sadly, that collection has grown too large. It necessitated my return to England last year. With his duties as Lieutenant General of the Bombay regiment, Sir Ian could not come home to curate the artwork. That duty has fallen to me, and I hope to complete it soon. I can't abide another English winter."

"I don't know how you tolerate living in India," Winterbottom said with distaste.

Pickering and Lady Winifred looked offended. "But India is a glorious place," Pickering said. "I only left last summer because I was determined to meet Professor Higgins here in London. The one thing that outweighs my love for India is my love of language and phonetics."

"How can any civilized Englishman love India? Beastly heat, insects the size of your hand, monsoon rains that leave one drenched for weeks. And the atrocious odors."

"You seem rather delicate," Higgins observed. "I wonder you ever left the nursery."

"I doubt you've been to India, Professor," Winterbottom shot back. "If you had, I daresay you'd agree with me. As you would agree the Indians have no right to protest when museum scholars remove their antiquities. Without the British, how many ancient sites around the world would remain neglected? Or undiscovered?"

"But if it belongs to another country, we shouldn't take it for ourselves just because we want it," Eliza said. "If you did that in the East End, you'd get your head bashed in. And your legs broken for good measure."

Higgins nodded. "Or as the natives here call it, 'law and order in Whitechapel'."

"I don't know why I'm bothering to speak to you about this," Winterbottom said.

"Let me call over Mr. Misra and his wife. As a native of India, he'll be happy to debate the issue." Lady Winifred raised her hand and waved. "Taral and Basanti are a dear couple."

Higgins noticed for the first time that the Indian pair from the wedding were among the guests. Amazing he hadn't seem them before, given that the man wore a turban and his wife a glittering blue sari. Then again, about a hundred people had come to enjoy the free food and drink. He doubted even half of them had been invited.

Winterbottom looked distressed at the very suggestion. "I have no wish to speak with Taral again. Since arriving in England, he has repeatedly harassed me and the other museum administrators. Seems he is here as an envoy of that blasted maharajah. And he's mistaken if he thinks he'll convince us to return the temple antiquities."

Lady Winifred lifted an eyebrow. "I have been a guest of the Misra family during my visits to the Mysore province. Taral's father owns the largest iron and steel company on the subcontinent. You would do well not to insult him."

"I believe you are far too fond of these filthy Indians."

"And I believe you are a boor, Mr. Winterbottom," she

replied with venom. "On second thought, I suggest you leave before the Misras reach us. I have no wish to subject them to either your rudeness or your ignorance."

Winterbottom flushed crimson. He opened his mouth to speak, but stalked off instead.

"I owe your niece an apology, Professor," she said. "I regret introducing her to Mr. Winterbottom. But Beatrice and her father seemed quite taken with the suggestion."

"No need for apologies," Higgins said. "Both of them would have agreed to a marriage with Ebenezer Scrooge if he'd presented himself."

"At least Scrooge had a change of heart." Lady Winifred adjusted her hat. "I'm not certain Mr. Winterbottom even has a heart."

"Blimey," Eliza said. "Maybe your mother should convince Beatrice not to marry."

"Miss Doolittle, too many women view spinsterhood as far worse than an ill advised match. How else to explain the alarming number of dreadful marriages I have witnessed?"

"Madam, I salute you." Higgins bowed. He found Winifred an attractive woman, although her features and coloring were similar to those of Beatrice. Unlike his niece however, Lady Winifred possessed a vivacious nature, along with a high degree of intelligence. He had yet to discern either in Beatrice.

Eliza turned her attention to the Indian couple drawing near. "I wish I could wear a sari, although I couldn't hope to look as beautiful as she does."

Indeed, both husband and wife put the other guests to shame. They were slender, attractive, and splendidly attired. As he had at the wedding, the young man eschewed European dress and instead wore a white turban and high–collared jacket of dark blue silk which matched his pants. As for his wife, she drew all eyes with an azure blue sari, its flowing skirt and veil embellished with delicate gold stars. But Higgins suspected everyone's attention was caught by the gemstone-studded gold headband that held her veil in place.

Lady Winifred embraced the Indian couple when they joined them. "Miss Doolittle was commenting on how beautiful you look in your sari, Basanti."

The Indian woman met Eliza's smile with one of her own. "Thank you. I was not certain how one should dress for such an occasion."

"Looking around, I fear no one else did either," Higgins remarked.

After handling the introductions, Lady Winifred said, "I asked the Misras to stay with me at my London home, but I failed to convince them."

"We are honored by the kindness of Lady Winifred." Taral bowed his head in her direction. "But we are recently married and wish for privacy. I thought it best to take rooms at the Hotel Russell. It is my dear Basanti's first trip to England, and I do not wish her to feel out of place. That is why I brought along furnishings from our country."

"Incense, too," his wife said in a sweet voice. "Taral has turned our hotel suite into a most delightful abode. If I close my eyes, I can believe we are still in Mysore."

"Are you enjoying England?" Pickering asked her.

"Oh, yes. It is a land of much wonder and strangeness."

Taral allowed himself a smile, which he bestowed with open adoration upon his bride. "I am pleased my wife has enjoyed our stay here in London. I was not certain she would."

"When are you returning to India?" Eliza asked.

"When my business is complete," Taral said. "I am here to conduct negotiations for my father's company, and to ask the government and the British Museum to behave with honor."

"He's been sent as an envoy from Maharajah Sidhu in

Mysore," Lady Winifred explained. "In all my years in India I have yet to meet a man more worthy of being called a 'philosopher king.' Being so wise, the Maharajah understands that one cannot hope to be independent one day if a foreign government is allowed to steal his country's treasure."

Pickering looked uneasy by this turn in the conversation. "Talk of independence often leads to revolution or anarchy, Lady Winifred. Let us not forget the Mutiny in 1857."

"No one has forgotten the Mutiny, sir," Taral said. "Although given that you are a Colonel in the British Army, I do not expect you to understand what led to the violence."

An uncomfortable silence followed.

Eliza broke it by saying, "Colonel Pickering couldn't have fought in the 1857 Mutiny. He was born in 1848. The Colonel would have only been—" She paused to do the math.

"Nine years old," Higgins finished. "Therefore Pick had nothing to do with the events of 1857. I believe he was also absent at Waterloo."

Taral cast an unblinking gaze upon both Pickering and Higgins. "I never said he was involved with the Mutiny. But I agree with Lady Winifred. My countrymen cannot hope to build a future of our own if we allow others to steal our past. That is one reason I have come to England. India's past has been taken from us. I shall reclaim it – along with our honor."

Both Basanti and Eliza seemed unhappy with this new topic. As if a change of subject might relieve the tension, Eliza said, "I do love your blue sari."

Basanti impulsively took her hand. "You must visit our rooms at the hotel. I have a trunk filled with saris, one in every color. Perhaps you would like to try one on."

Eliza's smile grew wider. "I'd love to come. And when I visit, I won't wear anything gloomy. I only dressed this way today because it's a memorial service. Maybe I'll put on a hat with tall plumes. I have dozens of those. One of them has ostrich and peacock feathers."

"Eliza has singlehandedly kept the milliners of England in business this past year," Higgins said. "Heaven knows how many birds she has had stripped bare."

Eliza pulled out a calling card from her drawstring bag. "You can reach me here."

Basanti took it with a shy smile. It occurred to Higgins that both women were probably the same age. Sometimes he forgot how much time Eliza spent with older people like Pickering and himself.

"This will be a most delightful occasion," Basanti said. "We shall have tea, too. Taral has brought a chest of our favorite Darjeeling."

Before the two could move on to what sweets would accompany their tea, someone rapped loudly on a glass. Everyone turned to see the Duchess of Carbrey at a lectern set up on a small stage. Behind her stood Thaddeus Smith, a water glass and silver knife in his hands. Although the Duchess looked composed and calm, Higgins knew her too well. She would hate anyone to see how much being rejected by her deceased groom had rattled her. He wondered if she would even admit it to herself.

"Thank you all for coming here today," the Duchess began in a strong voice. "It is the second time this week I have asked friends to gather on my behalf. I regret that both occasions turned out unhappily. We do not yet know why Mr. Farrow was killed, or who would be evil enough to commit such a terrible act. I have no alternative, however, but to leave it in the capable hands of the police."

"Good luck with that," Higgins muttered.

"As everyone knows, Ambrose was an American who came to Mayfair last year to open this gallery. Most of you have been to exhibitions here or are artists yourselves. No matter your connection to Mr. Farrow, I'm confident you were impressed by his acumen, his artistic eye, and his charm." Her voice broke on that last word.

"Poor woman," Eliza whispered. "I feel terrible for her."

"As do I," said Lady Winifred.

A moment later, the Duchess continued. "Therefore let us celebrate our happy memories of Ambrose Farrow. We wish him eternal peace in a heaven that is filled with even more beauty than this wonderful gallery. Thank you all for coming."

The vicar from St. Cuthbert's moved behind the lectern and began to intone passages from Proverbs. For the first time all afternoon, the gathering felt like a memorial. The crowd silently parted as the Duchess and Mr. Smith made their way to the exit.

Higgins doffed his hat as she approached. "I am most sorry, Minerva."

Her face crumpled and she threw herself into Higgins's arms. Startled, he wrapped her in a tight embrace as she wept onto his shoulder.

Eliza was now crying, too. This was turning into a proper funeral after all.

Several minutes later, the Duchess pushed herself away and wiped her cheeks with a handkerchief Mr. Smith provided. "I shall be fine, Henry," she said in a low voice so as not to drown out the vicar. "But I won't rest until the murderer is caught."

"With luck, the police in Kent will make an arrest shortly," Higgins said.

"You can't imagine I will leave the murder of Mr. Farrow in the hands of those Kentish dolts. I plan to visit the commissioner at Scotland Yard today. I shall insist one of his detective inspectors take over the case." The Duchess looked at Eliza. "I want that cousin of yours to handle it,

Miss Doolittle. Detective Shaw proved himself quite capable when confronted with the trouble at the racetrack this summer. I'm confident he will find Ambrose's killer."

Eliza bit her lip. "You might have to settle for another detective, Your Grace. Jack's getting married soon, and he and his bride have their honeymoon all planned."

"Solving my fiancé's murder is far more important than some silly honeymoon." The Duchess suddenly gasped. "What is *she* doing here?"

A slender woman stood near the gallery entrance. No one could miss her; she was the only person at the service dressed entirely in black. Although the woman's face was hidden by a thin black veil, the Duchess cried, "How dare Pearl Palmer come to Ambrose's memorial."

Thaddeus Smith frowned. "Shall I ask her to leave?"

"No. She might cause a scene. I do not want you embroiled in any of her cheap histrionics, Thaddeus."

Higgins wondered if that was true. Miss Palmer stood apart from everyone else, her attention focused on the vicar's prayers. But he noticed the young woman's shoulders shook. She was weeping. "Minerva, she might leave once the prayers are over."

"Nonsense, Henry. She is incapable of leaving anything alone." Her grief now replaced by fury, the Duchess signaled to a nearby waiter. "Fetch my driver Luther. Look for a fellow with a broken nose and light brown hair. He's wearing a chauffeur uniform and standing next to a cream-colored motorcar trimmed in gold. And hurry."

"Your Grace, perhaps we should leave by a back door," Smith suggested.

"I refuse to skulk out of Ambrose's memorial because that tramp has decided to make a mockery of my grief."

Luckily, no one else in the gallery realized what was going on, although Higgins feared that would change. Too soon, the waiter came back with the Duchess's chauffeur. Higgins recognized the chap who had driven them from the train station to St. Cuthbert's church. He recalled the few words the driver spoke that day, marking him as someone raised in the notorious London slum known as Bluegate Fields. If anyone knew how to handle a situation that might get out of control, it would be him.

Luther marched over, his chauffeur hat tucked under one arm. "You called for me, Your Grace." His accent confirmed for Higgins that the fellow hailed from Bluegate.

She pointed at the weeping Pearl Palmer. "Get that woman out of here."

"You want me to drive her somewhere or just scare her away?"

"I don't care if you feed her to wolves."

He nodded and strode off.

"I hope he doesn't frighten her," Eliza said.

The Duchess shot her an indignant look.

"Who is this woman?" Basanti whispered, but everyone was too upset to reply.

"This is most unpleasant," Colonel Pickering murmured. "Most unpleasant."

Higgins held his breath as Luther approached Pearl Palmer. Before he got too close, she noticed him. "Get away! Don't come near me!"

Luther kept walking towards her. "Come on, miss. Let's go. You're not wanted here."

"Go away!"

At her outburst, the vicar stopped reading from Proverbs. Everyone in the gallery now turned their attention to Pearl Palmer and the chauffeur.

"Let's go quietly," Luther said in threatening tone. "Or I'll be forced to carry you out."

Pearl backed against the wall. The painting behind her

wobbled when she pressed against it. "I came to pay my respects to Ambrose. I have every right to be here." She began sobbing. "Why didn't everyone leave us alone? He'd be alive now. He'd be with me."

"Luther!" The Duchess's voice rang out in the now silent gallery.

The chauffeur grabbed the frightened girl by the arm. She recoiled at his touch. As he yanked her from the wall, she kicked his ankle. It took him off guard, and he released her.

"That's enough," Higgins called out. "Let the girl be. She's not causing any harm."

Luther looked at his employer for further orders.

"How can you say that, Henry?" the Duchess demanded.

"Because it's true." Higgins felt his own anger rise to the surface. "And you know it. This is just mean spirited and petty. Allow the girl to grieve and go on her way."

"He's right," Eliza said. "After all, she loved Mr. Farrow, too."

The Duchess grew pale. "Take me out of here, Thaddeus. There's a back room in the gallery. I shall stay there until that woman is gone." After throwing a reproving glance at them, he quickly led her away.

Pearl's sobs grew wrenching and loud. She gazed out at the sea of staring faces. "I know the police think I killed him, but I didn't. But one of you did. I know you did. You're a coward. You're all cowards!"

With a last frightened look at Luther, Pearl ran out of the gallery. After a shocked moment, everyone erupted in excited conversation.

"Is this what English funeral services are like?" Taral asked.

Lady Winifred shuddered. "Good heavens, no. Usually it's a long church service accompanied by a few discreet tears. Nothing as bombastic as this."

"Do you think she actually knows who the murderer is?"

Eliza glanced around at the crowd. "If so, how foolish of her to say such a thing. The killer will be after her next."

Pickering grimaced. "Grief makes a person desperate."

"So does murder," Higgins said. "And I have a feeling we're not done with either yet."

CHAPTER FIVE

SITTING BENEATH THE GLITTERING CHANDELIER
of the Maison Lucile, Eliza felt self-conscious. Why hadn't
Clara told her their shopping excursion to Lady Duff-Gordon's dress salon included an invitation only 'mannequin
parade'? If Eliza knew she'd be rubbing elbows with socialite
Linda Morritt and actress Kitty Gordon, she might have worn
something fancier than a pearl gray walking suit. Especially
since Clara was outfitted in a Paul Poiret summer dress of
yellow crepe de chine. It was an engagement gift from Clara's
only prosperous relative, Aunt Lavender, a Bohemian artist
with an eye for fashion. Eliza felt under-dressed beside Clara
– and in the Maison Lucile, of all places.

As soon as she saw the chauffeured motorcars lining the
street before No. 23 Hanover Square, Eliza knew it was
not business as usual at the salon. And she gasped when the
beautiful and renowned singer Lily Elsie entered the white
Georgian row house just ahead of them. Eliza grew even
more nervous at the sight of a willowy woman in rose chiffon, who stood guard just beyond the curved front doorway.

"She's taking cards from everyone," Eliza whispered.
"They must be tickets."

Clara pulled a small vellum envelope from her pocketbook. "They're invitations, and I have one. Don't look so worried. Mine includes a guest, and you're my guest, silly."

The woman in rose chiffon stopped them, but one glance at the card in Clara's gloved hand and they were waved through. "I thought we were only coming for the final fitting of your wedding gown," Eliza said. "And for last minute alterations to your trousseau."

"We are," Clara replied as they followed the other guests into the couture room where a string quartet played softly in the corner. Small tables set for two lined a long upraised walkway in the center. "And my wedding dress had best fit properly or I don't know what I shall do."

Eliza waved her arm at the tea tables now filling up with women dressed in the height of fashion. She gulped to see Lady Asquith sitting at a table next to them. "I recognize almost everyone here from the society columns."

"Naturally. This is one of Maison Lucile's famous mannequin parades. Lady Duff-Gordon hosts one every season. The models will soon come out and show us her latest dresses. And we get tea and cakes while they do so. Souvenirs, too." Clara pointed at the small gift wrapped boxes set beside everyone's teacups. "Isn't this fun? I'm so glad Tansy told me about it. A shame she's in Devon today and couldn't come."

Tansy was Lady Hortense Saxton, an old school mate of Clara's. Having met her this past summer at Ascot, Eliza thought the young viscountess was a proper snob. Still, Lady Tansy was the person who introduced Clara to her fiancé Lord Richard Ashmore. It was the reason Clara was about to become a baroness, earning her an invitation here today. Seeing how happy Freddy's sister was, Eliza felt grateful to Lady Tansy, who otherwise was insufferable.

Naturally, Freddy and his mother were just as excited over the upcoming wedding. They could hardly believe eighteen-year-old Clara was about to marry the most powerful baron in England. Eliza found it hard to believe herself. Not that Clara wasn't a pretty girl. But until now, her big blue eyes and curly blond hair had not been enough to attract a gentleman willing to rescue her from genteel poverty. Although Clara deserved to be happy, especially after being rejected this past spring by a banker's son, whose father squashed any hopes of marriage due to Clara's lack of dowry and family connections.

Unfortunately, Clara's engagement had inspired her brother to intensify his desire to marry Eliza. It did little good to protest they hadn't known each other long enough to become engaged. After all, Clara and Lord Ashmore's courtship had been so swift, Higgins dubbed it 'cyclonic' rather than 'whirlwind'. From the moment Lady Tansy introduced the baron to Clara, the girl set her cap on him. Clara had even hinted to Eliza that she was willing to use all her wiles to obtain a proposal and brief engagement. Since their wedding would take place a mere seven weeks after their first meeting, Eliza feared there might be another reason – aside from romantic fervor – for such a quick courtship. However she hadn't been able to work up the nerve to ask Clara if the cries of an infant would be heard eight months from now.

She preferred to worry over whether Lady Duff-Gordon would meet the challenge of fashioning Clara's wedding dress and trousseau in such a short time. Eliza was surprised the Ashmore family didn't object to the quick wedding. Of course, it was quite possible they did. Clara rarely mentioned Lord Ashmore's mother and sisters, which wasn't a good sign.

"After the mannequin parade, I'll be taken away for my fitting." Clara smiled in anticipation as waiters in black jackets began serving tea. "While I'm doing that, you should go to the Rose Room and have them show you Maison Lucile's lingerie." She leaned closer to Eliza. "I bought scads of it for our honeymoon. Richard will be thrilled."

"You've bought a trunk-load of clothes this past month." Eliza looked on approvingly as the waiter placed a tiered plate of finger sandwiches and iced cakes on the table. "Lord Ashmore is a wealthy man, but twelve thousand pounds a year only stretches so far."

"Don't be a goose. Twelve thousand is only what Richard gets from his barony. But he's heir to three more titles; that means even more money and land. And he's got investments in lots of companies and businesses. I could buy Lady Duff-Gordon's entire fall line, and Richard wouldn't blink an eye." She giggled. "I'm going to be even richer than Tansy. Isn't that fun."

Eliza sat back in astonishment. How in the world did Clara manage to land such a catch? Richard Ashmore was attractive, wealthy, and only twenty-eight years old. Why hadn't a dozen other debutantes with titles already snapped him up? Could he really have fallen so madly in love with Freddy's sister? Or was he marrying her to save Clara from being disgraced if she was indeed with child?

"I'm surprised you wanted to marry in such a rush." Eliza gave her a shrewd look. "You could have postponed until later in the year. Think how lovely a Christmas wedding would be."

Clara avoided her gaze. "Oh, Richard wouldn't agree. He's as eager to marry as I am." The gilded crystal chandelier overhead dimmed, while two spotlights appeared on the white curtain. "Oh look. Lady Duff-Gordon is about to begin the show." She nodded towards the older woman who walked out from behind the curtain at the back of the stage.

Eliza had briefly glimpsed the famous designer the last time she was here. Born Lucy Sutherland, the fifty-year-old matron reputedly learned to be a fashion designer by making clothes for her dolls when she was a child. Since then, she had married twice and built a fashion empire which now included salons in London, Paris and New York. Eliza adored her clothes which favored draping, ease of movement, and handmade details that were perfection.

Despite her success, Lady Duff-Gordon ran into a rough patch last year when she and her husband sailed on the Titanic. It was rumored she bribed the sailors on her half-empty lifeboat not to return to the ship where they could have rescued their fellow passengers. Scandal surrounded her salon after a court inquiry brought the Duff-Gordons in for questioning. Found innocent of any wrong doing, the indomitable designer quickly won back her influential clients. Eliza suspected most women were willing to overlook character flaws in their dressmaker as long as her creations were as heavenly as those found at Maison Lucile.

Lady Duff-Gordon looked out over the gathering as if she were an empress surveying her court. She wore one of her "personality dresses" celebrated for their slit skirts and low necklines.

"I welcome all of you to Maison Lucile's mannequin parade," she said. "What I shall present to you today comprises my newest designs for the autumn line. Each of these ensembles marks yet another chapter in my dream to create the most modern and carefree fashion for the twentieth century woman. Enjoy."

The white curtain opened and the first of Maison Lucile's mannequins stepped onto the long, narrow walkway. A striking redhead, the young woman wore a draped, cream-colored evening gown with a wide black bodice and bow. Eliza thought it a darling dress, and one which would be most comfortable to wear. As the mannequin glided down the walkway, Lady Duff-Gordon said, "Miss Osgood is wearing a gown I call 'Evening in Athens' due to its draping inspired by the columns of the ancient Parthenon."

If Lady Duff-Gordon introduced her models as they came out, this would make it easier for Eliza to find Pearl Palmer afterwards. But Eliza soon became so riveted by the fashions, she forgot about Miss Palmer, at least until the end of the show when a shapely brunette appeared.

Lady Duff-Gordon announced, "For those chilly autumn days when one wishes to do little else but take tea at Claridge's, Miss Palmer wears the ideal outfit to do so. The white chiffon blouse has bell sleeves and a wide flowing collar, while the slim black skirt boasts a bolero sash; a splash of color is provided by the green soutache of metallic thread along one side. Please note the shorter hemline. I call this creation 'October Sonata'."

Eliza wasn't certain what was more entrancing: the flattering skirt and blouse or the dark-haired mannequin who paraded past her. Once again, Eliza felt sorry for the Duchess. She could never have held Ambrose Farrow's attention with such a young, desirable woman vying for it.

Clara whispered, "I see that one has caught your eye. Tansy told me that if you like any of the dresses shown during the mannequin parade, you can ask to see it in a private dressing room afterward."

Eliza watched Pearl Palmer glide to the end of the walkway, pose briefly, then walk back. "I may do just that."

And if she could afford it, she'd blooming well buy that outfit, too.

Afterwards, Eliza followed Clara through white French doors into the area of the salon where clients were shown Lucile creations in the privacy of sumptuous dressing rooms. Eliza admired the pale gray carpet, wallpaper, and silk upholstered furnishings. Sheer draperies had been tied back with cords of tiny pink silk rosebuds, the only hint of color. Such a pale palette was designed to allow the clothing to be seen to best advantage.

Clara did not seem overwhelmed by her grand surroundings. In fact, she gave the impression of a young girl about to play dress up with her mother's clothes. It occurred to Eliza that the enormity of the change about to take place in her life had not fully dawned on Clara.

The tall, slender woman in rose chiffon who had greeted them at the front entrance now swept Clara away for her fitting. Another woman, just as willowy and intimidating, came to take Eliza to her private viewing room. "I am Miss Estelle. Please follow me."

Ushered into a room lined with mirrors and filled with what Colonel Pickering had taught her was called French provincial furniture, Eliza turned to the woman before she left. "You will send Miss Palmer in, won't you? The 'October Sonata' outfit looked especially fine on her."

Miss Estelle nodded. "But of course."

Somehow Eliza had to learn as much as she could about Pearl's relationship with Ambrose Farrow, and whether or not she had a hand in changing her lover's mind about marrying the Duchess of Carbrey. After all, an hour after meeting Pearl in the church graveyard, Farrow jilted his bride. What if Pearl had slipped into the church vestibule before she met him? Had she intended to poison the Duchess, guessing the bride would drink first? Farrow would have then inherited everything from his recently deceased wife. Only he couldn't have known about the poison, or else he'd never have drunk the lethal brew.

Sitting on a tufted velvet chair – more comfortable than it looked – Eliza listened to the murmur of voices. Several guests had followed Eliza's example and were now ensconced in various parts of Maison Lucile for their own private showings. She took a deep breath. The salon smelled as if the carpeting were made of crushed gardenia. Looking at her expensive surroundings, Eliza feared she would not be able to afford anything at Maison Lucile. At least not until her racehorse had a few more victories under his belt.

"Here is the 'October Sonata', Miss Doolittle." Miss Estelle waved in the raven-haired mannequin. "If you have any questions, or wish to try on the outfit yourself, Miss Palmer will assist you." She left without a backward glance, leaving Eliza alone with Pearl Palmer.

While Eliza felt suddenly awkward, the same could not be said for Pearl. The young woman proceeded to walk about the small room, hands on hips, head held high. She was quite beautiful. Enormous dark eyes, complexion as smooth as alabaster, and lips so full and lush, Eliza hardly believed they were real. A stylish coiffure made her dark hair appear like a soft cloud pinned about her face. Higgins would have called her profile Grecian, which Eliza took to mean perfect. Except now that she saw Pearl up close, Eliza glimpsed sadness in those large eyes, along with an air of melancholy that surrounded her just as much as her jasmine perfume. Despite her elegant hauteur, it was clear Pearl Palmer was grieving.

"This design will see you through the autumn season," Pearl said in what Eliza recognized as an American accent. "The skirt is wool, but the decorative green braid is made with metallic thread. And the blouse is silk and chiffon. Would you care to try this on, Miss..."

"Eliza Doolittle of 27-A Wimpole Street. To be honest, I'm not certain the outfit's in my price range. I simply found it so lovely when I saw you model it that I wanted another look." She leaned forward as if to take Pearl into her confidence. "I'm only here to keep a friend company while she has her fittings."

For the first time, Pearl smiled. It made her even lovelier. "I understand. As a mannequin, I can't afford even a pair of Lucile gloves. But at least I get to wear her dresses every day."

"All the ladies at the salon seem to be a socialite or a famous actress or singer."

"Ballerinas, too," Pearl added. "Lydia Kyasht of the Ballets Russes is here."

"I don't know how I dare show my face. At least my friend is about to marry a baron. However I did become part owner of a racehorse this summer. His winnings have allowed me to expand my wardrobe. Maybe by winter, I'll be able to afford that darling skirt you're wearing."

"If he's as good a horse as that, you're sure to make money on stud fees." She paused. "I know something of horses."

"Please sit down, Miss Palmer. You must be dying to get off your feet for a moment."

She looked longingly at the tufted chair beside Eliza.

"Go on. I won't tell anyone." Eliza almost laughed when Pearl dropped onto the chair with an audible sigh. "It must be difficult, parading back and forth all day."

"Oh, it's an easy job. Most of the time I enjoy it, but these shoes are a bit tight."

"Excuse me, but you look familiar. Have we met before?"

"Don't think so. I'm American, and I've only been in England for a year." She lowered her voice. "I'm awful homesick. I miss Oklahoma. That's where I'm from. And it sure doesn't look anything like this." Pearl waved a hand at the elegant décor. "Or London either for that matter. It's rough country – prairies and mesas – but I'd trade all of Hanover Square for one more glimpse of the Ouachita Mountains."

"It sounds wonderful. I've never seen a prairie or mesa. Or a mountain."

"I didn't used to think it was wonderful when I was a child. Times were hard, and I had to help my family make ends meet."

"So did I. Lady Duff-Gordon might be shocked if she knew that only last year I was selling flowers out of a Covent Garden barrow."

Pearl seemed surprised. "And yet here you are."

"Yes. Professor Henry Higgins taught me to speak like a lady. And Colonel Pickering taught me how to act like one. But it took a lot of hard work, believe me." Eliza cocked her head at her. "How did you happen to come to London?"

She clasped her hands. "I met an art gallery owner in New York while on tour with a Wild West show. We fell in love right away. I could hardly believe my luck. He decided to come to England to open a gallery here, and he asked me to come with him. How could I refuse?"

"Sounds very romantic."

"It was."

"Was?"

"He died." Her large hazel eyes filled with a sheen of tears.

"I'm sorry. If you only came to England last year with him, he must have died recently."

She nodded. A long pause followed as Pearl fought back tears.

Eliza felt uncomfortable and wanted to prevent her from completely breaking down. "You said you were in a Wild West show. That sounds exciting. What did you do in the show?"

"I was a sharpshooter. A good one, too." She shot Eliza a watery smile. "I grew up dirt poor in Oklahoma. My brothers and me had to help feed our family. That's how I learned to shoot. People were amazed a young girl could shoot and ride as well as I did. But don't let my looks fool you. I was a better trapper than my brothers, too."

"I bet you blooming were."

"A scout from a Wild West show happened to be in Tulsa when I was competing in a Fourth of July shooting match.

He offered me a job right on the spot. Since I was only fifteen, he needed my parents' permission." She laughed. "They nearly pushed me out the door. We Millers were poor, and one less mouth to feed came as a relief to Ma and Pa." Pearl leaned closer to Eliza. "My real name's Gertie Miller. Pearl Palmer's a stage name."

"I don't know much about Wild West shows. Were you famous?"

She shrugged. "Not as famous as Annie Oakley. But I made a good living for five years. By then, I had moved up to the Kit Carson Buffalo Ranch Wild West show, the best there was. We played all the big cities, even Madison Square Garden in New York. That's where I met my gentleman. He was such a cultured, handsome fellow. So different from the hayseeds and con artists in the shows. He read me poetry, and taught me about fine wine and things like opera. I loved him so much, and he loved me. I was also bone weary of living out of a trunk. When he asked me to stay in New York with him, I left the show. We were happy until we came here."

"Too bad you couldn't convince him to go back America."

"He had big plans in London. I couldn't ask him to leave." A longing look crossed her face. "And I would never leave a man as wonderful as Ambrose Farrow."

Eliza feigned surprise. "Ambrose Farrow? Is he the same man who was supposed to wed the Duchess of Carbrey? My goodness, I attended the wedding. Her Grace and I are fellow horseracing owners. I'm so sorry. That was such a tragedy, him being poisoned."

Pearl shuddered. "Tragedy? It was evil. The work of a monster! I didn't even know Ambrose had been killed until the police showed up on my doorstep. Can you imagine how awful that was? I'd just been told the man I loved had been murdered, and those heartless police treated me like *I* was the killer! The devil take them all."

"How horrid to find out about his death that way."

"I still can't believe he's dead. I can't. It must be a sick joke. Or a mistake." Pearl brushed a tear from her cheek. "I don't know how I'll be able to live without him."

"Yet he was about to marry another woman. That must have been painful to you as well."

"Painful, but not surprising. The Duchess is rich and important. And Ambrose was a handsome young man. Of course, she wanted to marry him. He would have been a right fool not to marry her."

"But he jilted her at the altar. I was there. Everyone in the church was shocked."

Pearl hesitated. "I wasn't shocked. Ambrose told me he couldn't go through with it. What did shock me is that some filthy scoundrel planned to poison him."

"The Duchess, too. The bride and groom were both meant to drink the poisoned cog."

"That's what I don't understand. Why kill both of them at the wedding?" She shivered. "The murderer was at the church. He had to have been. Probably wanted to enjoy watching Ambrose and his bride die in front of him. The cold hearted bastard." Pearl shot Eliza a defiant look. "And I won't apologize for my language. Back in Oklahoma, we'd call him a lot worse."

"Back in the East End, we would, too." Eliza wondered how far she dare push Pearl for answers. "I'm not surprised the police are interested in you. After all, you moved clear across the ocean to be with Mr. Farrow. Now he was marrying another woman. Who else had a better reason to want both the bride and groom dead?"

"If you knew me, you'd realize how downright loco that sounds. What did I care if he married another woman for her money? I had his heart. Yes, and his soul, too. Have you ever been in love, Miss Doolittle? Have you ever loved another man so much that your every waking moment is about making him happy? Even your dreams at night are filled with the sound of his voice, his scent, his touch. Do you know what that's like?"

"No, I don't." Although she cared for Freddy, Eliza knew her feelings for him did not resemble what Pearl felt for Ambrose.

"I don't know whether to pity you or envy you." Pearl choked back a sob. "No one here guesses that I was Ambrose's lover. We had to keep our romance secret from the Duchess. Now I have to walk about, modeling clothes, making small talk, pretending my world hasn't broken in half and I'm screaming inside. I couldn't even grieve at his memorial. They chased me out like I was a mongrel dog!" She clutched Eliza's hands. "What am I supposed to do? How do I keep from going crazy with grief?" She bent over and began to sob.

Eliza knelt down and took Pearl in her arms. "Shush, you just cry it out. That's what you need to do. Let it all go." She wasn't certain how long she knelt there, holding Pearl Palmer. When Pearl finally straightened, Eliza smoothed back her hair, then handed the stricken woman a handkerchief.

Pearl blew her nose. "If anyone from the salon walked in right now, I'd be fired."

"I'll say I made you cry with a sad tale of my own. I do have a few, which I'm sure you'd understand. After all, we both grew up poor."

"I shouldn't be telling a client my problems. And you're too young to hear any of this."

"I'm hardly a child. I'm twenty."

Pearl gave a rueful laugh. "I'm twenty-two, but I feel years older."

"Maybe you should take a few days off from work and stay home. You need to recover from your loss." She patted Pearl on the shoulder. "And to grieve properly. Parading about here won't help you do that."

She wiped her eyes with Eliza's handkerchief. "You're very kind, Miss Doolittle. But there's no peace for me at my apartment. The police are hounding me. And now Scotland Yard is involved. Some dreadful detective called Jack Shaw had me brought in yesterday. He treated me as if I was a hatchet murderess like Lizzie Borden."

Eliza feared Jack was being overzealous. "He's just doing his job."

"No, he's determined to get me to confess. Never stopped asking me the same questions, no matter how many times I answered. He kept me in his office for hours. Telling me how jealous I must have been over Ambrose marrying another woman. How I wanted to see Ambrose and the Duchess dead. Over and over and over. I swear, if I had my rifle with me, I might have shot him dead just to shut him up."

"I don't blame you." Eliza frowned. "Men can be stubborn fools."

"He's the worst I've seen in a long time."

"Oh, Eliza!" Clara burst into the drawing room. "There you are."

Eliza and Pearl quickly got to their feet.

Clara wore a travel suit of sapphire blue moiré silk, with wide lapels and black frog closures at the waist. Lace fell from the sleeves and the back collar. The suit made her look less like a girl and more like a woman. After surveying her broad-brimmed feathered hat in the tall gilt mirror, she turned to Eliza with a look of concern.

"This is the dress I plan to wear when we take the train to Dover to start our honeymoon. What do you think? Will Richard approve? It's not too dark a color. Is it?"

"Not at all," Eliza said. "The dress seems perfect for a September trip."

Pearl Palmer took a step forward. "And that's a lovely color on you, too, miss."

"Thank you." Clara admired herself in the mirror. "But I won't model my wedding dress for you, Eliza. I want it to be a surprise. I only hope those other weddings you're going to this month aren't too fancy. I'd hate for you to be disappointed when you come to mine. Although I can't imagine the wedding gown of that suffragette your cousin Jack is marrying will be the height of fashion."

"Sybil will look beautiful in anything she wears." She hoped Clara didn't mention Jack again.

Clara gave a derisive laugh. "Whatever she wears, I'm sure she'll be more stylish than her groom. Then again, what can you expect from a Scotland Yard detective."

Pearl turned an anxious face to Eliza. "Your cousin is a detective?"

"Of course, he is," Clara answered for her. "A bit famous, too, thanks to Eliza's exploits this past summer. You've probably read his name in the paper. Detective Inspector Jack Shaw."

"Detective Shaw is your cousin?" Pearl went deathly pale.

"Yes, he is. But—"

Before Eliza could say anything else, Pearl ran out of the room.

"What was that all about?" Clara asked, fussing with her hat.

"Murder," Eliza said glumly.

"Oh, you and murder. I swear, you should join Scotland Yard yourself. At least you'd get a salary for playing detective." She examined the buttons on her dress. "I wonder if I should ask Lady Duff-Gordon to change these black frog enclosures to pearls."

Eliza walked over to Clara and stared at the girl's reflection in the mirror. "Leave the enclosures. It makes the dress more sophisticated."

"Yes, sophisticated. That's exactly what I look like in my new clothes. Sophisticated and modern." Her grin turned catlike. "Except for my lingerie. I look like a proper hussy in those. Or rather, an improper hussy." Clara giggled, and Eliza couldn't help but join in.

Why in the world was she getting involved with Mr. Farrow's murder? She barely knew the man. His death had nothing to do with her or any of her friends, except for the Duchess of Carbrey. And judging from her appearance at the memorial service with Mr. Thaddeus Smith, she seemed to be recovering nicely. Besides, the Duchess would have succumbed to the poisoned drink herself if Ambrose had not rejected her. In a way, he'd saved her life.

Eliza vowed to focus on nothing but weddings for the rest of the summer, especially since it was Jack and Sybil's wedding next week. She refused to allow anything to spoil it.

And while she felt sorry for Pearl Palmer, it was Jack's responsibility to figure out who killed the art gallery owner and why. Unfortunately, the Duchess had convinced Commissioner Dunningsworth to assign Jack to the Farrow case, the last thing he needed right before his wedding. Pearl's description of his harsh treatment towards her proved he was determined to make an arrest before his honeymoon. But Eliza didn't believe Pearl killed Ambrose Farrow, even if they had quarreled the day of his wedding. Her grief over his death seemed far too genuine and deep.

"Did you decide to buy the outfit your mannequin was wearing?"

Eliza shook her head. "I didn't ask the price, but I'm sure it's too dear."

"You may have to ditch my brother for someone with a

title. I'm sure Richard has lots of bachelor friends who'd find you quite sweet. And it would serve Freddy right for not pursuing a profession. The lazy fool." This sent Clara into giggles once more.

Eliza suspected Clara was not entirely joking. Yes, she probably could attract a baronet or knight if she put her mind to it. Then again, look how far she had come on her own, with a little help from Higgins and Colonel Pickering.

Taking in the posh surroundings of the famous Maison Lucile, Eliza felt a stirring of pride. To think she'd once walked the streets of the East End in a patched coat and a squashed hat she pulled out of a dustbin. Now she was an invited guest at one of Lady Duff-Gordon's prized fashion shows. And if she counted her guineas and took on a few more students, she might be able to afford a Lucile creation by the end of the year.

Best of all, she wouldn't have to marry anyone to do so.

CHAPTER SIX

SCREAMS OF LAUGHTER FROM THE bedroom sent
Sybil's father running out of the house. Eliza and her fellow bridesmaids were supposed to be helping the bride get
dressed. Instead, they were swapping stories of misadventures
shared by the suffragettes. Even Sybil's older sister Susan –
a conservative married woman with two young children
– regaled them with an amusing anecdote about trying to
stop Sybil from painting VOTES FOR WOMEN on the Free
Trade Hall. Susan wound up being chased for blocks by the
bobbies, while Sybil remained undetected behind the shrubbery.

Eliza had spent time with Sybil's fellow suffragettes before.
Only last month, the two women attended a big rally in
London and ended up running from the police. They'd even
been given a lesson in ju-jitsu by Edith and William Garrud,
who trained the female bodyguards entrusted with the protection of suffragette leaders. Eliza believed in the suffrage
cause and was impressed by their courage and dedication.
Today, however, she was seeing a more lighthearted side of
these women. Sybil's bridesmaids were all young and eager
to have bit of fun. Indeed, they'd been having fun at the top
of their lungs since everyone arrived this morning.

Because the ceremony was to take place at St. Marylebone Parish Church, it seemed practical for Sybil to dress for the wedding at her sister's home, which was less than a quarter of a mile from the church. Susan was married to prominent architect Kenneth Henchard, a man able to afford a spacious Georgian house with an upper floor bedroom suite that easily held six bridesmaids. The extra space was necessary since Sybil wanted them to get ready together.

"Will your mother be upset at the bridesmaid dresses you've chosen?" Eliza clasped the groom's gift about Sybil's neck. The delicate silver necklace dotted with amethysts must have cost Jack several month's salary.

Sybil turned her head from side to side, examining herself in the dressing table mirror. She gave one last pat to her hair, now pinned high atop her head. "Mother knows the dresses are lilac, but she isn't aware of the green trim. I'm hoping she'll be so overcome with joy to see me walk down the aisle, she won't realize my bridesmaids are wearing the colors of the suffrage movement."

"Oh, she'll realize what you've done. Only she won't be able to do anything about it." Her sister handed her a delicate blue garter trimmed in lace. "Here's your 'something blue'. You should at least be traditional enough to follow the old English rhyme: 'Something old, something new, something borrowed, something blue'."

"Don't forget 'And a sixpence in your shoe'." A curly-haired bridesmaid called Emma tossed a sixpence to Sybil.

Emma's twin sister Amanda handed the bride a small satin box. "After Jack gave you an amethyst necklace at the rehearsal dinner, Emma and I knew this would be perfect as your 'something borrowed'."

Sybil opened the box, which held a pair of peridot teardrop earrings. "How lovely."

"Now you'll be wearing green and purple jewels as well,"

Amanda said.

"Don't lose them," her twin warned. "They've been in our family for years."

Sybil laughed. "I promise to have Jack's best man watch my ears all day to make certain they never fall off."

Eliza pointed to Sybil's necklace. "Here's your 'something new'."

"And I'm carrying Great-Grandmama's handkerchief in my bag, which qualifies for 'something old'," Sybil said. "So no one can accuse me of completely ignoring tradition."

"You look like a most traditional bride to me," Eliza said.

In fact, Sybil had chosen a bridal gown not even Queen Victoria could find fault with. Made of embroidered net lace, the white dress boasted a square neckline and billowing ruffled sleeves that ended at her elbows. The gown also had a small train, and would be accompanied by a tulle veil held in place by a circlet of flowers. Sybil planned to wear gloves, preventing even the most straitlaced from being alarmed by her bare forearms.

Of course the politically astute would recognize that her circlet – composed of purple and white flowers intertwined with green ivy leaves – were the colors of the suffrage movement. As was her bouquet of purple and white sweet peas nestled in ivy. Her allegiance was also evident by a small Women's Social and Political Union brooch pinned to the bridal gown's velvet waistband. This was Sybil's way of waving the suffragette flag as demurely as possible.

However she made no such compromises for her attendants. In a break with tradition, Sybil wanted her bridesmaids to wear the same dress, something most unusual. Aware of the different financial situations of her friends, Sybil chose affordable tea dresses from Selfridge's department store: pale lilac batiste embellished with green embroidery trimmed in Cluny lace. As the matron of honor, Sybil's sister wore a slightly different dress, although it too was lilac with a hint of green. The entire bridal party would be wearing the colors of the WSPU.

"Eliza, is that Freddy down there with Sybil's father?" Jennie Prespare Thompson, another bridesmaid, stood looking out the bedroom window. "It certainly looks like the young man who accompanied you to the rehearsal dinner last night."

She went over to the window. Yes, the man in a morning coat and top hat standing on the pavement below was indeed Freddy. Eliza didn't know whether to laugh or groan.

"Freddy, you should be at the church," she called out the open window. "The Professor and the Colonel are sure to be there by now."

Freddy looked up at her, his face breaking out in a wide smile. "My darling girl, I thought I would come and drive with you to the church."

"I told you. The bridesmaids are riding together." She pointed at the line of motorcars parked in front of the house.

"Mr. Chase said only two bridesmaids will be assigned to each car. That leaves room enough for me." He swept off his top hat, revealing his golden blond hair. "And I'm mad with desire to see you, darling. It's the wedding. It reminds me of how much I want to marry you."

Eliza noted with embarrassment that Sybil's father was listening to their conversation. "You're not spoiling Sybil's plans, Freddy. Now take a taxi to the church. I'll meet you there."

As she turned away, Freddy yelled, "But I never have any luck hailing a taxi!"

Jennie picked up her bridesmaid's bouquet. "He seems quite taken with you. I'm sure the reverend wouldn't mind if another couple joined Sybil and Jack at the altar today."

Everyone laughed, except for Sybil. Eliza knew Sybil did

not approve of Freddy's wish to marry her. She thought him too young and far too idle.

"Sybil is the only bride today." Eliza walked over to the bed where the tulle veil was laid out, along with the circlet. "Now let's get her ready for her grand entrance." The silver clock on the wall chimed the half hour. "We only have thirty minutes before the ceremony."

Hats were re-pinned, dresses smoothed down, and rouge and powder re-applied. The suite exploded with fragrance as each bridesmaid gave a last spray from several different perfume atomizers. Eliza had no idea why men accused suffragettes of being unfeminine. They liked to look attractive, as any other female did. But they also cared about justice for women, which obviously frightened many men. Eliza suspected it frightened some women, too.

Susan's rambunctious daughters, Alice and Constance, suddenly ran into the room. As their aunt's flower girls, the children were outfitted in lilac dresses trimmed in green, but with multiple tiers of flounces. Four-year-old Alice got so caught up in the excitement, she began scattering the white rose petals in her flower basket.

"Oh dear, we must get them to the church. Otherwise there won't be a flower petal left to toss." Susan snatched the basket from her daughter, who burst into tears. She also removed the flower basket from her six-year-old, who had already strewn flowers about the carpet, but much more surreptitiously.

Emma and Amanda each took one of the flower girls by the hand. "We'll bring them outside," Amanda said. "They can pick flowers out there."

"We'll let the girls start on your hollyhocks." Emma laughed.

Susan sighed as the four of them left the room. "Sybil, we cannot be late."

"I'm not quite ready," murmured Sybil as Eliza placed the circlet of flowers over her veil.

Susan kissed her sister on the forehead. "You look far lovelier than I did at my own wedding." She gave a sly grin. "Although at twenty-six, you are rather a doddering old bride."

"Doddering but determined." Sybil smiled back at her. "I shall be downstairs as soon as Eliza finishes with my veil."

Eliza muttered under her breath, not certain she could get this blooming circlet to stay properly attached to the tulle. Susan and the other bridesmaids filed out of the bedroom, leaving Eliza and Sybil alone.

"There, I think I have it." Eliza patted the circlet, now securely fastened. "Unless you do a ju-jitsu move and throw Jack over your shoulder, I think it will stay in place."

Both women looked in the mirror. Sybil was an attractive woman, but not a great beauty. Today however, Eliza thought no one could compare to her. Sybil's roses and cream complexion seemed especially enchanting this morning, and her blue gray eyes appeared to sparkle.

"I'm over the moon to be marrying your cousin, Eliza. I never thought to meet a man I could ever imagine as my husband. But I do love him so."

Eliza squeezed her shoulder. "And you must know how happy I am that you and I will be family. You're like the sister I never had."

"Well, you're the suffragette sister I never had."

Both of them laughed, then hugged each other. "Jack is very lucky to have met you."

"He certainly is." Sybil broke their embrace to dab at her eyes with a handkerchief.

A knock on the bedroom door stopped any further endearments. "Sybil, we must leave soon." It was her father. "Or else your groom may end up marrying one of the wedding guests."

"I'll be down in a moment," she called back.

Eliza hurried to retrieve Sybil's gloves from another box lying open on the bed. "You and Jack probably can't wait until you leave for the Cotswolds. The past month has been so hectic with wedding plans."

"It's been even worse since the Duchess of Carbrey complained to Commissioner Dunningsworth. Jack is not happy he's been forced to investigate the Farrow murder. Added to all the other cases he's handling, the poor man has barely slept." She slipped on her white gloves. "I fear he will sleep through our entire honeymoon."

"Oh, I rather doubt that," Eliza said with a laugh.

Sybil blushed. "Perhaps I will be able to keep him awake. But it's so unfair."

"At least the Duchess can't stop you two from leaving. After all, you'll only be gone a week."

"Jack's going on this honeymoon even if he has to murder the Duchess. And I'm only half joking. In fact, I feel rather sorry for Pearl Palmer. Jack's had her in for questioning every day. If she's not the murderer, he's treated an innocent woman most unfairly."

"Sybil!" Her father shouted from downstairs.

Grabbing their respective bouquets, they hurried out the door. As soon as they joined the bridal party outside, Freddy raced over with a worshipful expression.

"You look radiant, Eliza. And you quite outshine the bride," he whispered.

Eliza gave him a gentle shove. "Garn, the only thing that could outshine the bride today is that beautiful August sun." They looked upward, basking in the cloudless blue sky.

Mr. Chase cleared his throat to get the party's attention. "Everyone into your cars. Two bridesmaids for every vehicle, except for the second car. The flower girls need their mother." Like Freddy, Mr. Chase wore a formal morning coat, striped trousers, waistcoat, and top hat. "The bride shall ride with me in the first car. Sybil, step along, my dear. We are running a bit behind. Your mother will never forgive me if we arrive late."

The bridesmaids headed for the black shiny cars, all hired especially for the occasion. Jennie pointed at the last car. "We can ride together, Eliza."

"I shall come, too." Freddy followed them.

"No, Freddy. It's not right. Only the bridal party is supposed to ride in the cars."

"Nonsense. The chauffeurs are in the cars. They're not part of the bridal party."

"You're being too literal," Eliza complained as he helped her into the vehicle. "And far too forward."

Jennie sat in the backseat, her bouquet on her lap. "Oh, let Freddy ride with us. No one will pay any mind to him anyway. It's the bride everyone's come to see."

With a resigned sigh, Eliza scooted next to Jennie. Being a small car, they found themselves pressed together when Freddy joined them on the back seat.

"Mind the flowers." Eliza held her bouquet aloft. Unlike the bride's bouquet of sweet peas, the bridesmaids carried purple Michaelmas daisies. "I don't want to lose any blooms."

The car's revving engine halted conversation for a moment. As they pulled away from the curb, Freddy announced, "I think our bridesmaids should wear white dresses. And carry tulips or iris."

Eliza threw him an amused look. "I gather you'd like a spring wedding then."

"Oh, you're right. That won't do at all. I'm hoping to marry you much sooner than that. Winter perhaps." Despite the cramped space, Freddy managed to wrap his arm around her shoulders. "Or maybe autumn. You could carry chrysanthemums."

Eliza squealed with laughter as Freddy nuzzled her on the neck. "Stop, Freddy! We aren't alone."

"Don't mind me," Jennie sang out. "I'm to marry next month, and my young man has no sense of decorum either." She elbowed Eliza. "The cheeky darlings."

That only encouraged Freddy, who had the audacity to pull Eliza onto his lap. "I'm mad with love for you. We've been keeping company for months. Months! You must realize we're destined for each other. I knew I loved you as soon as I met you at that tea at Mrs. Higgins."

"Except you actually met me the previous summer near Covent Garden. Only I was a poor Cockney flower girl back then. You fell in love with the young woman Professor Higgins and Colonel Pickering taught to speak and act like a lady. I doubt you'd be throwing yourself at me if I was still selling violets to the toffs."

Her answer only made him kiss her again. "I honestly don't remember meeting you last summer, Eliza. But I do recall being struck with love at that tea. Struck clear through the heart!"

"Freddy, if you don't leave off, my dress will be wrinkled when we get to the church." She put her hand on his chest and kept him from another ardent embrace. "And I swear if a single daisy falls off this bouquet, I shall kick you out of this car – while it's moving!"

"Don't do that, Eliza. You might rip a stocking." Jennie tapped the driver on the shoulder. "Would you be willing to eject Mr. Eynsford Hill if it becomes necessary?"

The man nodded. "If that's what you want, miss. But we're almost at the church."

They had already passed Paddington Square Gardens, along with most of the imposing cream colored buildings that lined the streets leading to St. Marylebone Parish

Church. The same moment she heard the pealing bells, Eliza also caught sight of the church's arched windows and towering steeple. When they drew closer, sunlight glinted off the eight gold statues that graced the second story, as if giving their blessing to the wedding.

Once the bridal cars pulled up to the curb, Eliza slid off Freddy's lap. "Is my hat on straight?"

Jennie nodded. "How about mine?"

Before she had time to smooth her dress, the driver opened the back door. Freddy jumped out. Eliza took his hand and exited the car. Several guests smiled at their first sight of the bride and her attendants. They didn't have long to admire them before Sybil and her father swept quickly through the church entrance. The bridesmaids and flower girls followed close behind. Jennie broke into a near run to catch up with them. Organ music could be heard from within.

"Freddy, you must go inside and sit down." Eliza tried to prevent him from embracing her once more. But Freddy was too quick and managed to snatch one last kiss. Eliza breathed a sigh of relief when he finally bounded up the steps and disappeared inside.

"What in the world was Freddy doing in the car with you?" Higgins appeared from behind one of the columns on the church's portico.

"Making a nuisance of himself. I'm afraid this wedding is giving him ideas. He's pushing me to set a date again."

A young man came out from behind the column as well, followed by the Colonel. "I didn't realize you and Mr. Eynsford Hill were engaged, Miss Doolittle."

Colin Ramsey, a newly promoted detective at Scotland Yard, sounded amused. Jack thought highly of him. So highly that he was actually one of Jack's ushers. Eliza met him at the rehearsal dinner last night and found him both intriguing and irritating. At times he seemed almost as sarcastic as the Professor. However he was not unattractive, if one cared for short, muscular men with wavy brown hair and dark, probing eyes.

"We are not engaged, Mr. Ramsey. Although that doesn't stop Freddy from asking me to marry him every week."

"I see that you and your fellow bridesmaids are dressed in green and purple. Seems a radical choice for a wedding. Will you all be carrying political banners down the aisle?"

She made a face at him. "Aren't you supposed to be escorting guests to their pews?"

"Aren't you supposed to be attending to the bride's every need?"

"People are still arriving, so I can't imagine why you're loitering out here with the Colonel and the Professor." She threw Higgins and Pickering a reproving look. "Who should be inside themselves."

Ramsey chuckled. "Loitering's more respectable than being kissed by an amorous young man on the church steps." He paused. "Unless the couple are the bride and groom."

"Heaven forbid she marry Freddy. That is a wedding I have no wish to attend." Higgins shuddered.

"You are all being quite rude. And I should find Sybil."

Ramsey pulled on his cuffs. "Actually I do need to get back inside. I don't know when I've seen so many suffragettes and policemen in the same place outside of a demonstration in Trafalgar Square. I hope you don't plan to pull a rotten vegetable out of your bouquet and start hurling them at the ushers, Miss Doolittle."

"Don't be silly," Eliza said. "I wouldn't think to disturb the wedding ceremony. I'd wait until the couple were pronounced man and wife first. But your fellow officers might want to duck afterwards." She pointed her bouquet at him. "Especially you, Detective."

With a laugh, Ramsey hurried off.

"You should join the bride," Pickering said. "It's almost time for the ceremony." The pealing bells in the steeple died away. "See, they've stopped the bells until after the vows."

"Crikey, you're right." Eliza accompanied Higgins and Pickering to the church entrance. "Is Dad here?"

"Rose, too. It's one of the reasons Pick and I came outside. We needed a reprieve from meeting all the Doolittle and Shaw relatives. Most of whom don't appear to get along."

As soon as they walked inside, Eliza saw the long carpeted aisle down which ushers still escorted guests to the proper pew. At the end of the aisle lay the altar beneath an impressive decorated dome. The pews seemed filled to bursting. Even some of the seats in the balconies were taken, a testament to how well liked Sybil and Jack were.

"Eliza, over here."

She turned to see Jennie gesturing from a side vestibule. Behind her clustered the other bridesmaids, with Sybil standing in their midst.

Eliza smiled at Higgins and Pickering. "This is going to be such fun."

"I hope the wedding turns out happier than the last one," the Colonel said.

"Jack's wedding is going to be perfect. Besides, who would want to harm anyone here?" She shook her head. "No, today is a day for celebration and love and joy. And if anyone tries to spoil it, they'll have to deal with me."

Higgins held up his hands. "Calm down, Eliza. No one will ruin this wedding."

"They'd better not." The thought of anything awful happening here like at the Duchess's wedding sent a jolt of fear through her. "And tell my father and Rose that if they talk during the vows, I'll box them both about the ears. I swear I will."

Eliza went to join the bridesmaids. She'd had more than

enough of murder and danger these past few months. Jack and Sybil's wedding had to go off without a hitch. If it didn't, Eliza would make sure there would be the devil to pay.

Eliza's prediction came true. Higgins thought it was a perfect wedding, perhaps due to his genuine fondness for the bride and groom. He did notice Sybil's mother seemed distressed at the sight of six bridesmaids marching down the aisle in green and purple. Her disapproving expression changed to happiness, however, when she caught sight of her daughter. And Sybil did look a proper and demure bride, although his eyes were sharp enough to spot the WSPU brooch pinned to her waist. He wanted to laugh at Eliza when she walked down the aisle. Oh, she looked elegant and pretty, but she kept scanning the pews as if she were a police constable herself. Ready to take action if anyone so much as sneezed.

Waiting at the altar, Jack seemed uncomfortable in his formal morning suit. But as soon as he saw Sybil arm in arm with her father, his expression changed to one of bliss. For a moment, Higgins envied him. Jack had found a woman who was his ideal match. There was a time when Higgins believed he had done likewise, but the obstacles to his happiness were insurmountable. Higgins counted himself lucky to have experienced those feelings at all. But it had made him wary of marriage, and determined to build a full and satisfying life without it. He doubted most Englishmen enjoyed their lives half as much as he did, especially the married ones.

After Jack and Sybil were pronounced man and wife, Mendelssohn's *Wedding March* sounded from the great organ on the balcony. Everyone got to their feet as the newlyweds walked back up the aisle, their smiles so wide, one could not help but smile in return.

"Ain't they a loverly sight to see." Alfred Doolittle smacked Higgins on the back. "Always knew Jack would make something of himself. Although I tell you, it still makes me nervous he's a copper. Where I come from, you spend your time dodging the police, not becoming the fellow what tracks people down."

"Don't be telling the Professor that." Rose fanned her flushed, perspiring face with a coral-colored fan that matched her lace dress. "He'll be thinking you was a criminal instead of an honest dustman."

Alfred leaned closer to Higgins. "I've had my moments. But she don't need to know."

"Neither do I," replied Higgins.

"Hey, there's my Lizzie!" Alfred waved to Eliza as she walked past with one of the ushers. Obviously relieved that everything went well, she waved back.

"She's next. I'm telling you, Rose, Lizzie will be the next bride walking down the aisle with that Freddy."

Rose snorted. "You better get ready to pay for a fancy wedding then. Your daughter has gotten awful high and mighty since living with the Professor. She'll be wanting her wedding in Westminster Abbey. And the reception at Buckenham Palace, see if she don't."

"If she does, I ain't gonna pay for it. She's an independent woman who makes her own living. Why should I be paying for flowers and a silly white dress? It ain't fair. All these middle class rules for a blooming wedding. You agree with me, don't you, Professor?"

"Eliza is not getting married anytime soon, however your nephew just did. Why don't we concentrate on that wedding right now." Relieved that the bridal party had walked past, Higgins nudged Pickering and both men stepped into the aisle.

"Walk faster, Pick," he murmured as they joined the crowd

of wedding guests streaming out of the church. "Having to sit with Alfred and Rose, without Eliza serving as a buffer, is more than any man should bear."

Pickering turned to him. "Why he is carrying on about paying for Eliza's wedding? Mr. Doolittle has done nothing for his daughter her whole life but complain she's a burden. He and his exasperating wife tossed the poor girl out on the street with little more than a half penny in her bag. I should go back and tell him that I will pay for Eliza's wedding."

Higgins shook his head. "The blasted girl isn't even engaged. Can we please go outside and give our best wishes to the couple? The sooner we do that, the sooner we can leave for the Criterion and the wedding breakfast."

This was easier said than done. Somewhere beneath the covered portico of St. Marylebone Church were the bride and groom. But Higgins and Pickering would have to wade through a mass of wedding guests, each one engaged in lively conversation. Not surprisingly, the conversations of the Doolittles and Shaws were louder than those of the Chase family and guests. Although, to be fair, the pealing church bells forced everyone to raise their voices.

"The bridal party is supposed to have their photograph taken on the church steps. I don't know how that will be possible with this mob of people. Oh, look, there's Eliza." Pickering took off his top hat and waved.

Whipping out his notebook and pen, Higgins began scribbling a phrase he'd just heard.

"I say, old man. This is not the proper time to be engaged in phonetics research."

Higgins finished writing. "It's always time for phonetics research. This is a fascinating group, linguistically speaking. The immediate Chase family hails from Kingston-on-Thames, but a few relatives' speech mark them as Cornishmen." He tucked his notebook and pen away with regret. "As for the Doolittles and Shaws, their dialects range from Swansea and the west Irish coast to Spitalfields and Whitechapel. Just now I overheard a colorful turn of phrase from a guest who grew up in Bluegate Fields, like that driver of the Duchess."

Pickering groaned. "Let us hear no more of the Duchess today. Or her driver."

"Agreed. Here comes Eliza. The girl is rather adept at pushing her way through a crowd. Unfortunately, she's also clearing a path for Freddy."

"What are you two doing over here?" Eliza asked when she reached them. Freddy stood behind her. "The ushers are trying to get everyone off this porch and into their cars."

"That might take a long time."

"The ushers are policemen, Colonel. They know how to hurry people along."

Proving Eliza right, within minutes the ushers had cleared off most of the wide stone portico.

"Professor, why didn't you sit with me in the church?" Freddy asked. "I saved a seat for you and the Colonel."

"Eliza's father insisted we sit with him and Rose." Higgins wondered if it would have been preferable to sit with Freddy. The Doolittles had exhausted him today.

"Did you hear what Annie Kenney has done?" Eliza leaned forward with a delighted smile. "She put a VOTES FOR WOMEN sign on the side of the wedding car. And Mrs. Garrud is doing the same with the cars for the brides-maids."

Freddy didn't look as pleased as Eliza. "If this keeps up, there will be a skirmish with the police. Can't these women put politics aside for one day?"

Eliza straightened Freddy's hat. "Oh, it's all in fun. Sybil would have done it herself if she didn't fear upsetting her mother. Besides, there will be no skirmish unless the police start it. After all, everyone was quite friendly in the church."

"Eliza!" Sybil's sister called

"Susan wants me to join the bridal party. Time for photographs. Follow me."

"I am not posing with the bridal party." Higgins hung back.

"Who asked you to? But you and the Colonel should come with me to give best wishes to Sybil and Jack." She took Pickering by the arm. "Then all three of you can drive over to the Criterion while the photographs are taken. Dad and Rose have already left."

Higgins's stomach growled. That seemed like an excellent idea. Especially since the Criterion was his favorite restaurant in London.

By the time they reached the bridal party, the ushers had shooed all the wedding guests off the steps and towards their cars. The photographer, a lanky fellow with a birthmark on his cheek, busied himself with moving the attendants into the best position on the top step. Jack and Sybil stood right below them, whispering to each other. Higgins noticed the photographer kept stopping to rearrange Sybil's veil and the angle of Jack's head. But all this careful posing went out the window when the couple caught sight of Higgins.

"About time you showed up, Professor!" Jack called out. To the photographer's dismay, Jack and Sybil left their assigned spot on the steps and walked over to them.

"Best wishes to you both," Freddy said.

"Indeed, all the best." The Colonel took Sybil's hand and bowed over it with a kiss. "The wedding ceremony was extremely well done."

"Why so formal, Pick? They're like family." Higgins gave Sybil, then Jack, a quick hug. "To be honest, I like them a damned sight better than most of my family."

Eliza looked over at him with happy approval.

"It was a beautiful wedding, wasn't it?" Sybil asked, beaming.

Jack put his arm around her. "And not a single tomato thrown by a suffragette."

She winked at Eliza. "Only because I told them not to."

Freddy looked up at the steeple. "Those bells make it hard to hear oneself think."

Higgins agreed. They were nearly shouting at each other. "We'll let the photographer do his work. Like the Colonel said, it was a wedding well done. Now let's see if you've picked wisely for the Criterion wedding breakfast."

"What?" Jack leaned forward.

Those bloody bells. Was the bell ringer drunk? "I said I hope you've chosen my favorite items at the Criterion!" Higgins shouted. "Especially their blancmange."

Sybil looked puzzled. "Did you say blancmange?"

He shook his head. "Conversation is pointless while those bells are ringing."

Jack stepped away to say a few words to Detective Ramsey. Pickering looked around with an alarmed expression.

"What's wrong, Colonel?" Eliza asked.

"Did you hear that?" Pickering raised a hand and scanned the passing traffic on Marylebone Road. "There it is again."

Baffled, Higgins looked around him.

"Is that gunfire?" Jack turned in the direction of the Royal Academy of Music.

"Get down!" Pickering shoved Jack to the ground, but he was too late. A trickle of blood ran down Jack's neck. With a speed belying his years, Pickering shielded Jack with his body.

Sybil cried out. It all happened so fast. No more than a second. Long enough for Higgins to realize Jack wasn't the only one who had been shot. Colonel Pickering now lay motionless over Jack's body. Higgins froze in horror when he saw the crimson stain of blood streaming down the Colonel's back. He couldn't be seeing this. It wasn't happening. It could *not* be happening.

The sound of the church bells faded away. Now all he heard was Eliza screaming.

CHAPTER SEVEN

ONCE AGAIN ELIZA FOUND HERSELF in a hospital ward, breathing in the sharp tar-like smell of carbolic. Not even the starch from freshly laundered sheets and bedside vases of flowers could mask the unpleasant odor. She wasn't certain if it was the odor making her ill or sheer terror. But she was grateful St. Mary's Hospital was just north of Regents Park in Paddington, much closer to the church than any other.

Within minutes of Jack and Colonel Pickering being shot, the police transported both of them here. Although she wouldn't have been surprised if the wounded men, along with family and friends, had been taken instead to the nearest lunatic asylum. It felt like the world had gone mad. As soon as the shots were fired, pandemonium broke out on the church steps. Some of the bridal party followed the photographer, who ran for cover in the church. Everyone else gathered about the bleeding men. Eliza had never been so scared and confused. What had just happened?

Things didn't get any calmer at the hospital. Jack refused care until Pickering was taken into surgery. Even after the unconscious Colonel was wheeled away, Jack insisted on staying with Eliza and Higgins in the nearby waiting room for the next hour, rather than going off to have his neck wound looked at. It took another hour of tearful coaxing by Sybil and Eliza before Jack agreed to accompany them to an adjacent ward for treatment.

Once there, Eliza gave thanks the ward was only half full; she welcomed the privacy and quiet. Jack sat on the bed while a doctor in a white coat worked on him. A nurse hovered nearby, holding a basin. Sybil stood beside her new husband, clasping his hand.

"Please sit still, Detective Shaw," the doctor said.

"Doctor, I need to return to the surgical area to wait for word on Colonel Pickering. Besides, my wound is only minor. His condition seems much more serious."

"There's nothing you can do. He's still in surgery. But Dr. Souter is a fine surgeon."

Jack's skeptical expression showed he was not reassured. Eliza didn't blame him. She was sick with worry. The horror she felt at seeing Jack and Pickering bleeding on the steps of the church had been so great, she didn't even remember how she got to the hospital. Eliza assumed Higgins brought her, but it was a marvel she hadn't passed out. Maybe she had. Now she was overcome with dread. What if her dear Colonel didn't survive the operation?

As she began to pace, she sidestepped the furious strides of Professor Higgins. Neither of them had been able to remain still since the shooting.

"How could something like this happen?" Higgins asked. "Those shots couldn't have come from a passing vehicle on Marylebone Road. The gunman probably fired from a rooftop."

"Or a window. Most likely the Royal Academy of Music. It's less than three hundred feet from the church. Detective Ramsey learned an orchestra rehearsal was scheduled there this morning. The building was unlocked during the time of the shooting." Jack winced. "Ow!"

"Sorry." The young doctor soaked another cloth and continued swabbing the dried blood.

"One of my men also found cartridge shells on the ground outside the Academy," Jack continued. "Point 303 caliber. The weapon was probably a Lee-Enfield repeating rifle which is common in the British Army. And easy to use." He paused. "Even for a woman."

"Darling, of course a woman would be able to shoot you." Sybil kissed the top of Jack's head. "After all, their reflexes are as good as any man's."

Despite her worry, Eliza bit back a smile. Sybil was a devout believer in the rights of women, even gun toting ones. But the fact that Jack had been shot from a distance with a rifle made Eliza's blood run cold. Since arriving at the hospital, Eliza's thoughts were focused on praying for the recovery of Colonel Pickering. Now that things had calmed down, she finally turned her attention to the crime itself. Who had the skill and motive to do such a thing?

Pearl Palmer seemed the only possible suspect. Such a realization was upsetting. Eliza had liked the girl when they chatted at the dress salon.

"Do you think the same person is responsible for Farrow's death?" Eliza asked.

"You're the second groom to be targeted at a wedding in the past two weeks," Higgins said. "First, Ambrose Farrow. And now you. Coincidence? I doubt it."

"Hold still, please." The doctor examined the wound he had cleaned.

"Jack, please try to relax." Sybil brushed the usual stray lock of hair out of his eyes.

"Relax? You were on those church steps, too, Sybil. You could have been shot!" Jack's fury was clear. "And I won't be able to live with the guilt if Colonel Pickering dies from trying to defend me."

Eliza knew he was right. If not for Colonel Pickering, who'd first heard the shots and thrown himself on top of Jack, her cousin would be in the morgue.

"If you don't stop moving, Detective, I'll never be able to close your wound properly."

"Does it need stitches? I thought I'd only been grazed."

"It's deep enough to require a few." He dropped the blood-stained cloths into the basin the nurse held. Another nurse arrived with a silver tray.

Eliza turned away, unable to watch as the doctor prepared a threaded needle. Jack's shirt was stiff with dried blood; Sybil's lovely wedding dress showed brown splotches as well. Would Pearl try to kill a bridegroom as he stood on the church steps with his blissful bride? If so, she was a fiend. As awful as it was to discover Ambrose Farrow poisoned at his own wedding, this had proved to be far worse. Farrow was little more than a stranger to her. Jack and the Colonel were family. To have both of them endangered was too much to bear.

"Will the Colonel be all right?" she asked Higgins for the tenth time.

"He'd better be."

His terse reply hadn't changed since they arrived, but he sounded less sure. She suddenly recalled the Professor's words last month after the events at the Eclipse Stakes. Both she and Higgins had almost been killed while trying to catch a murderer at the racetrack. Afterward, the Colonel felt terrible that he had not been there to help. As a joke, Higgins told him, *"The next murder case Eliza and I stumble across, we'll let you be the one who nearly gets killed."*

And now it had come true.

What if Colonel Pickering died during surgery? If only Higgins hadn't spoken those terrible words aloud! Eliza circled the ward, glancing at the other patients. One held an older woman's hand, most likely his mother. Eliza bumped into Higgins.

"Sorry," Higgins said. That wasn't like him. He always grumbled whenever she blocked his way. Perhaps he also recalled his prediction and felt overwhelmed by guilt.

"How much longer will he be in surgery?" Higgins's agitation increased with every step. "It's been almost two hours. We told the medical staff where to find us when it was over."

"Given the injury, it's not surprising," the attending doctor said. "Also the patient had to be prepped and given anesthetic, which takes time."

"You ought to be done stitching me up," Jack said and then yelped.

"Sorry, that's sure to be the worst of it. I'm nearly finished. Here's Dr. Souter now."

Higgins and Eliza looked up when an older doctor entered the ward, his white gown stained with blood. The man stripped it off and handed it to a passing nurse, who nodded her veiled head at his whispered command. She hurried out, and soon returned with a fresh white coat. After Dr. Souter watched his colleague tie off the last stitch on Jack's wound, he cleared his throat. Everyone, including Jack, Sybil and the younger doctor, gave him their full attention.

"Have you come to tell us about Colonel Pickering?" Eliza's voice shook.

"Are you family or friends of the Colonel?"

"The latter," Higgins said. "I'm not certain if he has any family left in England."

"He mumbled something about Edmund several times. And also asked for Jasmine."

"Damn all that! Did he survive the surgery?" Higgins asked.

"Yes, he did. We were careful with the ether, of course, given his advanced age—"

"How badly was he wounded?" Eliza interrupted.

"The Colonel is very lucky. Thanks to his long military service in India, he is quite fit for his age. It will take time for him to recover, however."

She breathed a sigh of relief. "How long?"

"Five or six weeks, if he is tended to properly." Dr. Souter smiled. "He went through far worse on the subcontinent, given the X-ray we needed to take. There's scar tissue on his lower back and more on his upper arm. It appears he was wounded years ago."

"And where did the bullet hit him today?" Eliza asked.

"Shoulder muscle, just missed his brachial plexus. We were able to remove the bullet. Having served as a medic in the Second Boer War, I knew the bullet came from a far range Lee Enfield rifle. Like I said, he was lucky. I tested the sensation in his hand, fingers, and thumb. The median, radial, and ulnar nerves are all fine. After we extracted the bullet from the trapezius…"

While Higgins followed with rapt attention, Eliza stopped listening to all the confusing terms the surgeon tossed about. Instead she clasped her hands in a silent prayer of thanks. Although relieved the Colonel would recover, she felt terrible that she had never thought to ask him about old injuries. He never complained about physical ailments, unlike Higgins, who moaned for an hour if he stubbed his toe. Now she knew Colonel Pickering had once been a brave soldier in battle. Look how courageously he behaved today, throwing himself in front of Jack with no regard for his own safety. There was no finer gentleman in England. But it seemed they knew little about him beyond his reputation as a renowned Sanskrit scholar. Did he have siblings? Was Edmund a relative or a friend? Who were his parents? Why had he remained a bachelor? The name Jasmine sounded rather exotic. Had she been a sweetheart in India?

After knowing Colonel Pickering for over a year – and benefiting from his kind generosity – she ought to have asked him more about his past. "When can we see him, Dr. Souter?"

"He'll be groggy for a bit, so I'd wait an hour or two."

Jack and Sybil joined them in the center of the ward. After Sybil carefully helped him with his coat, she took the blood-stained celluloid collar from him. "Let's leave this here."

"How do you feel, Jack?" Higgins asked.

"I'll survive. It was little more than a flesh wound. I'm just relieved the Colonel's safely out of surgery."

"Well, I owe Colonel Pickering a huge debt of gratitude," Sybil said. "If not for him, I might be a widow now."

"We are all grateful to Pick," Higgins added. "Damned heroic fellow that he is."

Sybil clutched her husband's hand. "We plan to stay here until the Colonel wakes up," she said. "It's important we thank him in person for saving Jack's life."

"It's your wedding day," Eliza protested. "You mustn't stay."

"Sybil, your guests are waiting at the wedding reception. They'll be disappointed if you don't join them," Higgins said. "I'm sure they're worried sick."

"Half of them are policemen." Jack shrugged. "They'll understand."

"But what about your family, Sybil?" Eliza asked.

"Soon after we got to hospital, I sent my parents to the Criterion to let everyone know what had happened. They were to insist all the guests be served breakfast."

"You and Jack ought to be enjoying that breakfast, too. This way you can report the good news about Colonel Pickering. We'll come as soon as we can. I promise." Eliza touched Jack's blood stained shirt. "Although you may want to send someone to get a fresh shirt for you." Indeed, Eliza's dress and Higgins's morning coat were also spotted with blood.

"Just be careful," Higgins cautioned. "The shooter may still be out there waiting."

"Not if Detective Ramscy does his job," Jack said. "I had the good sense to send him off before they brought us here."

"Sounds as if you might have an idea who the culprit is," Higgins said.

"I have a good guess, and it fits with who might have killed Ambrose Farrow." Jack began to sway and grabbed Sybil by the waist. "Oh. Maybe I ought to sit."

"You've lost more blood than you realize." Supporting him on the other side, Eliza led the way back to the bed.

Once he sank down on the thin mattress, Jack announced, "I sent Detective Ramsey to arrest Pearl Palmer."

Although Eliza wasn't surprised, Higgins looked startled. "You said there wasn't enough evidence to arrest her for Farrow's murder."

"We discovered her former profession." Jack thanked the nurse who brought him a glass of water. "Someone recognized her from a playbill posted in New York. Pearl Palmer is a name she adopted since coming here. She was born Gertrude Miller in Oklahoma, but left home as a young girl to be a sharpshooter in a Wild West show."

Eliza said nothing. She had learned Pearl's background that day she visited Maison Lucille. Jack would only be upset if he knew she'd kept the information from him. She hadn't even told Higgins about her conversation with Pearl. It didn't seem important or relevant – until now. Eliza still didn't understand why Pearl Palmer – or Gertie Miller – would want to kill Jack. Yes, she complained about his hounding her, but to go so far as to shoot him? With dozens of policemen watching? What a senseless act. Pearl must know she would find herself dragged into Scotland Yard again. And

Eliza knew she wanted to avoid that.

Then with chilling clarity, she remembered what Pearl told Eliza after complaining about Jack's treatment of her. *I swear, if I had my rifle with me, I might have shot him dead. . .* Pearl had to have been the person who shot Jack, and nearly killed the dear Colonel. Eliza felt equal parts rage and dismay wash over her.

"I understand why Pearl would kill her lover," Higgins said. "But why you?"

"I've been pretty tough on her since I've taken over the Farrow case. She may have wanted to get me out of the picture before I had enough evidence to lock her up. I'll find that out when I question her again. And I heard about her appearance at Farrow's memorial service."

"But she seemed so frightened at the memorial," Eliza said. "And truly grief stricken."

"Maybe it was all an act," Higgins said. "Or maybe she was genuinely sorry for having killed the man she loved. After all, she did have the best reason to poison the bride and groom. Now we learn she had the skill to shoot from a distance with a rifle."

"Ramsey should be bringing her to the Yard as we speak." Jack stood up and smiled at his wife. "Are you ready, sweetheart?"

She nodded. "The sooner we get some of that expensive breakfast my father paid for into you, the better. You look far too pale."

He kissed her. "Despite your stained gown and lost veil, you're the most ravishing bride I've ever seen, Mrs. Jack Shaw. A pity our honeymoon will have to wait."

"Oh, no! You can't postpone your honeymoon. Even the Duchess agreed you should be allowed a week away. Bad enough your wedding was spoiled."

"It wasn't spoiled, Eliza. The church ceremony was perfect, and I'm now married to the man I love, who has nicely recovered from being shot. But I know he won't rest until he finds the person responsible."

"Do you see why I married this magnificent woman?" Jack hugged her close.

Eliza planted a kiss on her cousin's cheek. "Take care of him, Sybil."

"Please come with us," Sybil said. "You can't do anything until the Colonel wakes."

Higgins and Eliza looked at each other. "Breakfast sounds lovely," she said, "but neither of us would be able to enjoy a bite until the Colonel wakes up and we can speak with him."

Jack glanced up. "There's Ramsey now. I hope he has good news."

The young detective strode purposefully towards them. "I sent men to Miss Palmer's apartment, like you asked, sir," he began. "Their search turned up several rifles in her closet: a Marlin, a Winchester, and a Remington. Then thirty minutes ago I found a Lee-Enfield rifle stuffed in a storage room on the top floor of the Royal Academy of Music. The weapon had been fired recently. We'll check for prints, but I bet it's been dusted clean. I also bet the rifle was smuggled into the building inside an instrument case."

Jack gave his detective a sharp look. "I assume you've taken Miss Palmer into custody."

Ramsey frowned. "I'm afraid not, sir. We've checked her lodgings, the art gallery, and that exclusive dress shop she works at. She hasn't been seen for hours."

"Damn it," Jack muttered.

"She can't have vanished into thin air," Higgins said. "You're sure to find her soon."

But Eliza knew that Pearl Palmer had no intention of being found.

CHAPTER EIGHT

⚓

I T RAINED ALL NIGHT AND into the morning. Out-
side, the shifting skies were gray, giving the streets a dismal
autumnal cast. But as gloomy as it was outside 27-A Wimpole
Street, the atmosphere was far gloomier within.

Eliza had just finished her Monday morning lesson with
Miss Agnes Dudley. Unlike most of her pupils, Miss Dudley
was not anxious to lose an embarrassing accent. Instead, Miss
Dudley was raised in a respectable middle class household in
Essex. An intelligent woman of twenty-three, she spoke in
a cultured manner that Eliza's other students hoped to emu-
late. What frustrated her was a stutter that had plagued Miss
Dudley since childhood.

Fortunately, this impediment did not prevent her from
working as a type writer for a biscuit manufacturer. Miss
Dudley's typing skills enabled her to earn a nice living since
her parents died five years ago. But she suffered from crush-
ing shyness whenever she wasn't sitting before her machine.
Embarrassed by a tendency to stammer whenever she was
nervous, Miss Dudley avoided any woman who wished to
befriend her, and any gentleman who showed an interest.
That changed three months ago when a new clerk joined
the firm.

The young man seemed quite taken with her. Rather than risk losing him, she had come to Eliza for instruction. Miss Dudley was the first pupil who needed a stutter corrected, and Eliza had been doubtful at first. But after four weeks, she showed great progress. So much so that Miss Dudley had agreed to attend a concert with her new suitor.

Eliza walked Miss Dudley to the front door. "You're doing splendidly. I don't expect you to have any problems during your outing with the gentleman."

She tugged at her gloves. "Thank you, Miss Doolittle. I feel almost as confident in my abilities as you do."

"You need only relax. Do not rush while speaking. And we have discussed those words that give you particular trouble. You have a large vocabulary. Simply choose an easier word." Eliza handed the woman her umbrella. The day was much too stormy for a mere parasol.

Miss Dudley took it with a grateful smile. "Until next Monday."

With a heavy heart, Eliza closed the door behind her and walked to Higgins's lab. Time for elevenses, and she wagered he needed tea as much as she did. Higgins sat slumped in his favorite chair by the Victrola.

She flung herself down on the leather sofa. "Your lesson ended early."

"My pupil needed to leave at half past the hour. It appears he had a previous appointment with his wife. Or as he put it, 'Sozz, Professor, but I needs to take the auld baig to doctor cause she's sick. Even though it's likely she's blaggin' me 'ead. An arl arse life it is.'" Higgins shrugged. "There was more, but I don't think you need to hear it."

Eliza couldn't help but smile. "I wish I had a few Scousers. I like a good Liverpool accent."

"You would. They speak almost as atrociously as you Cockneys."

"Not this Cockney, at least not any more."

She gazed about the drawing room, which Higgins had long ago turned into his speech laboratory. When she came to the Professor for instruction a year ago, it was in this very room that he agreed to take her on as his pupil. She never guessed she would spend every waking hour here for the next six months. It seemed tortuous at the time. But she'd grown fond of the tall, book-lined shelves, comfortable leather furniture, and writing desk heaped with papers. She was less enamored of the lamp chimneys, laryngoscope, and life-size model of a human head, all of which reminded her of how difficult her linguistic journey had been.

Her eyes fell on the dessert bowl atop the piano. She jumped up to retrieve a chocolate cream. Sighing with pleasure at her first bite, Eliza reached for another. Her sweet tooth was insatiable. In fact, Higgins had used sweets as a reward when he was struggling to teach Eliza not to drop her aitches. The smell of pipe tobacco wafted over her, and she looked down to see Colonel Pickering's pipe and tobacco pouch sitting on a side table. Her already low spirits plummeted even more.

"The house doesn't feel right without the Colonel here." She sat down again on the couch with a handful of chocolates.

"No, it doesn't. And I'd hold off on the chocolates. Mrs. Pearce should be bringing in tea any moment."

"I've never seen her so upset. I've reassured her a hundred times that he'll be fine, but she doesn't believe me." Eliza popped another candy in her mouth.

"I'm not certain I believe you either. Yes, I know the doctors say Pick is recovering nicely after the surgery removed the bullet. But the fellow is sixty-five years old. It's much harder to rally when you're up in years. One tiny setback could be disastrous."

Eliza flung a chocolate cream at him. It hit Higgins squarely on the forehead. "Don't you dare say that! The Colonel will be fine. The doctors said so, and they know more than you. You just teach people to speak proper. What do you know about bullets and surgery and such? The Colonel is getting better each day."

Higgins looked as miserable as she felt. "It's only been two days since he was shot."

"But he seemed better when we saw him early this morning."

"True. I should not have said anything. My apologies."

This made Eliza feel worse. Higgins never apologized. He must be as terrified as she was over Pickering. Clasping her hands, she leaned forward. Eliza was torn between uttering a prayer for the Colonel's speedy recovery and having a good long cry. She was prevented from either when Mrs. Pearce entered the room with a tray.

"Here's your tea. Sorry there was no breakfast today, Professor, but Cook and me wanted to visit the Colonel before we started work." Mrs. Pearce set the tray down. "That poor man. It broke my heart to see him sitting in hospital, looking so weak and pale. I'll not take an easy breath until that dear man is back in Wimpole Street."

"The doctors say he might be home in a week," Eliza said.

"A week? Lots can happen in a week. People die in hospitals all the time." With a muffled sob, the housekeeper rushed from the room.

Eliza and Higgins looked at each other. "I have a feeling we shouldn't expect luncheon or dinner today either," he said.

She walked over to the tray with its teapot and plate of biscuits. Quickly pouring out two cups, Eliza handed one to Higgins. "It doesn't matter. I'm not hungry."

Higgins smile was rueful. "Nor I. Although I predict that bowl of candy will be empty within the hour."

"You have another pupil at half past twelve, if I remember. And my next pupil arrives at one. I think we should cancel them, along with the others scheduled today."

"I assume you want to spend the day at hospital." Higgins took a sip of tea. "I won't argue about it. But we spent all of Saturday and Sunday with him. You even slept beside his bed the first night, and we visited him shortly after dawn today. He may want a break from our company. Giving lessons could be a nice distraction for us both."

"I agree. We don't need to spend every waking minute at the Colonel's bedside. But there are more useful things we can do than remain here correcting someone's fractured vowels."

"You mean chasing the murderer? Eliza, let's leave this in the hands of the police."

"Don't you have a high opinion of the police all of a sudden." She set aside her tea without tasting it. "Whoever shot Jack nearly killed the Colonel. And a misfired shot might have killed Sybil, too."

"Or you and me."

"These past few months have proven we can take care of ourselves. And we know how to get answers out of people who have too many secrets. I suggest we start doing that as soon as possible. The killer must be aware Jack survived. What if another attempt is made on his life? Could you live with yourself if something happened to Jack and we did nothing to stop it?"

"I'm certain I couldn't live with you after that."

She got to her feet. "I hate to say it, but the most obvious suspect is Pearl Palmer. Grief must have driven the woman mad. We'll start with her."

"I do believe she disappeared on the day of Jack's wedding." Higgins gave her a jaundiced look. "Although I suppose we could purchase a bloodhound and try to catch her scent on the London streets."

"Don't be smart. We'll start with people who might know something about Miss Palmer. And I bet the Duchess knows more than she's telling."

"Are we supposed to simply barge in on her unannounced?"

"Of course not. We're not cave people. Call her London house and say we'd like to stop by for a visit. She likes you."

"After what happened at the gallery reception, I'm not sure that's true."

"Jack's life is at stake." She stared hard at him.

With a great sigh, Higgins got to his feet and went to the phone on the desk. She waited impatiently while he placed the call and spoke to Her Grace's butler.

After he hung up, she walked over to him. "Well?"

"Minerva is attending a musical rehearsal at St Martin-in-the-Fields with Mr. Smith. Where I assume you're about to drag me." He sat with a grunt. "Can I finish my tea first?"

"Yes, you may. I'm going upstairs to change. The weather has turned quite chilly."

"That's right. We mustn't catch cold," he muttered after she walked out.

Eliza immediately reappeared at the open door. "No, we can't afford to get sick, Professor. Not when we have to catch a killer." She pointed at his teacup. "Now drink fast."

Higgins couldn't remember when he'd been inside so many churches in such a short period of time. If he visited several more, people might think he was considering ordination. At least St Martin-in-the-Fields had admirable acoustics, along with ravishing architecture. Located amid the hustle of Trafalgar Square, the elegant church resembled a neo-classical temple with its wide portico and Corinthian columns. The exterior of the building held no religious symbols; even the church's looming steeple was crowned by a weather-vane, not a cross. But despite the surrounding traffic in the square, a feeling of peace and serenity surrounded visitors as soon as they climbed the front steps and walked inside. It didn't surprise Higgins that the Royal Family chose St Martin-in-the-Fields as their parish church.

As they walked through the doors, Eliza and Higgins heard music within. Soon enough they spied a quintet of musicians at the nave's far end. Higgins didn't recognize the piece they played; it sounded a bit like Delius with a little Ralph Vaughn Williams thrown in. Thaddeus Smith stood before the musicians, his arms moving. Was Smith a conductor now?

"Looks like it's official. The Duchess is once again the patroness of Thaddeus Smith. He'd never be conducting at St. Martin without her imprimatur."

"I don't know what 'imprimatur' means, but I assume it's good news for Mr. Smith." Eliza sighed. "Although given what happened to the last man she championed, I might be a little nervous if I were him."

"Minerva must be here." Higgins's gaze swept over the church sanctuary, organ case, stained glass windows, oak pulpit, and the Royal Arms over the chancel arch. A dozen people sat in the pews up front, but otherwise the galleries were empty.

Eliza pointed to the paneled nave ceiling. "That's beautiful, it is."

He agreed. In the eighteenth century, architect James Gibbs did an admirable job designing this latest incarnation of St Martin-in-the-Fields. "A pity it's raining today. In bright sunlight you can see all those cherubs, clouds, and scrollwork." At least the domes and statuary could be appreciated, even in the afternoon gloom.

"Henry," a voice echoed. "What are you and Miss Doo-

little doing here?" The Duchess of Carbrey sat on one of
several wooden benches placed flush against the wall. Whoever sat there faced the opposite wall, not the altar.

No wonder Higgins hadn't spied her upon entering. Unlike
her colorful ensemble at the memorial service, today the
Duchess wore a coffee brown dress which blended into the
dark oak of the bench. Even the ostrich plumes on her wide
touring hat were a muted brown. In her green walking suit
and white blouse, Eliza seemed positively festive compared
to the older woman. Perhaps the Duchess was mourning
Farrow after all.

The older woman waited until Higgins and Eliza sat on
either side of her. "May I ask what prompted the pair of you
to visit St Martin-in-the-Fields on a rainy Monday afternoon?"

Higgins evaded the question. "I assume you're here to give
support to Mr. Smith. Given that he's rehearsing a chamber
music piece, I also assume it will be in the upcoming concert
program to celebrate the archbishop's retirement."

"Just so, Henry. You do have your ear out for more than
speech patterns." She shot him an approving look. "Yes, a
concert of new music written in his honor has been planned
next month. One of the composers – a German fellow from
Leipzig – had the bad taste to be arrested for public drunken-
ness last week. They needed another new piece quickly, and
from a composer less inclined to losing control. Of course I
suggested Mr. Smith. You may not know this, but Thaddeus
is as accomplished a composer as he is an organist."

Higgins cocked his head and listened for a moment. "The
piece sounds pleasant."

"Faint praise indeed." She gave him a playful tap on the
shoulder. "Then again, we all know your musical tastes run
to Gilbert and Sullivan."

"And your musical tastes run to the shocking, like Mr.

Stravinsky."

"I do like a good scandalous performance almost as much as I like horse racing."

In fact, the Duchess spent most of her free time at the racecourse or her stables. Only a new attractive paramour would tempt her into spending a day listening to church music rather than meeting with trainers and jockeys.

She turned to Eliza. "And you, Miss Doolittle. What sort of music do you prefer?"

Eliza smiled. "The tinkling of the piano when I'm at the cinema. I know when I hear that sound, it's time for the film to start." She grew serious once more. "Speaking of the scandalous, we're still recovering from the horrible attack at my cousin's wedding."

"How is dear Colonel Pickering? I couldn't believe it when I read the papers."

"He's better," Higgins replied. "But he did lose a lot of blood. At his age, such assaults are not simple to recover from."

"Yes, sixty-five can be a perilous age." The Duchess sighed.

Higgins didn't remind her she was only five years younger. Yet he had to admit she possessed the energy and appetite of a thirty-year-old. Perhaps that was why she preferred much younger men. They were the only ones who could keep up with her.

"Colonel Pickering showed himself to be quite the brave soldier," the Duchess went on. "Throwing himself on top of Inspector Shaw to shield him. Not many are willing to sacrifice their own lives in such a way."

"He's a wonderful man, the finest man I ever knew." Eliza's eyes welled with tears and Higgins feared she would cry. She'd been doing that quite a lot since Saturday.

"Which brings us to the reason we're here," Higgins said quickly. "The person who shot Jack and the Colonel may also have killed Mr. Farrow."

The Duchess sat back. He had taken her by surprise, and the worldly Minerva was not easily surprised. "But there's no connection between Ambrose and Detective Shaw."

"Pearl Palmer is the connection."

"We're not certain," Eliza added. "But things aren't looking good for her."

Higgins leaned forward. "Miss Palmer had a strong reason to poison the cog at your wedding. After all, the man she loved was marrying another woman. Then you asked Commissioner Dunningsworth to put Jack on the Farrow case. Since then, he's brought her to the Yard every day, pressuring her to confess. She might have felt persecuted."

"Infernal woman." The Duchess's eyes narrowed with anger. "Yes, it makes sense such a conniving creature would try to get rid of a Scotland Yard detective, too. She should have been hauled off to jail the day Ambrose was killed."

"Not without proof, Minerva. That's what they need for an arrest. They still do, but Miss Palmer has now made herself look even guiltier by disappearing the day of Jack's wedding."

She stamped the tip of her parasol on the oak floor. "Will this business never end? How can it be so difficult to put that woman in handcuffs! She never seemed all that clever to me."

"You actually met Pearl Palmer?" Eliza asked.

"Once. When Ambrose opened his Mayfair gallery, he held a champagne reception. Lady Winifred told me that he had an astute eye for artwork, and I decided to attend with her."

Higgins also thought she must have heard Farrow was a handsome young man. "How do you know Lady Winifred? Hasn't she lived in Africa and India most of her adult life?"

"Winifred is the wife of a soldier, not an inmate in a penal colony," she answered. "The wife of a high ranking officer, too, which means she returns to Britain whenever she has a taste for Yorkshire pudding and a week or two of shopping on Oxford Street. I met her a few months after the siege of Mafeking was lifted. She and Sir Ian were in England for a well deserved furlough. Given what they had been through in South Africa, all of London society clamored to play host to the brave pair. My late husband and I were among them."

"Why was Lady Winifred at Mafeking?" Eliza looked puzzled. "I was only seven years old when the siege was lifted, but I do remember all the celebrations in the street when it happened. How did a woman end up at a military siege?"

"The Osslers have no children, therefore Lady Winifred has accompanied Sir Ian wherever he is posted. They were already living at the garrison there when rumors of an attack surfaced. Most women in the town fled; others chose to remain with their men. Those that stayed found themselves trapped the entire time the Dutch Boers laid siege." She grimaced. "Two hundred and seventeen days. Can you imagine? That brave group of people surrounded on all sides by an army four times their size."

"Lady Winifred must have incredible stories to tell," Eliza said. "I'd love to hear them."

"Indeed." Higgins would like to hear those stories as well, but at the moment, tales of the siege were not why he was here. "Since you've known Lady Winifred for years, I understand why you attended Mr. Farrow's gallery opening with her. I assume Miss Palmer was also at the champagne reception."

"Oh, Pearl was there, swanning about as if she was the hostess. But Ambrose assured me she was only some woman he'd known in America. They had a dalliance back in New York, but he broke it off when he came to England. The trollop had the nerve to follow him here."

Eliza and Higgins exchanged dubious glances. It appeared the Duchess preferred her own version of the story.

"What did you know of Miss Palmer's background?" Higgins asked.

"Do you mean her life in America? I heard she was some sort of cowgirl. Probably rode a pony or two, in between spreading her legs for any cowboy who asked." She looked at Eliza. "Forgive me. But that woman brings out the cruder aspects of my nature."

"I spoke with her last week when I visited Maison Lucile. She told me she spent five years touring with a Wild West show."

"Why in the world did you keep this from me, Eliza?" Higgins felt offended she hadn't shared this information with him.

Eliza waved a dismissive hand. "At the time, I wanted to concentrate on Jack and Sybil's wedding. It only seemed important after the attack at the church. And the police learned about her past almost immediately. There was no need to irritate Jack by admitting I'd gone off to question Pearl Palmer without his knowledge. Anyway, Pearl told me she was once a sharpshooter. Like Annie Oakley."

The older woman looked up at the echo of approaching footsteps on the stone floor. "Thaddeus, I've learned something most enlightening about that awful Pearl Palmer."

Thaddeus Smith stood before them, looking more self-assured than he had at the memorial reception. He was as tall as Higgins, giving him an imposing air. His auburn beard and mustache were trimmed neatly, and Higgins caught a whiff of lavender, bergamot and verbena, which meant the organist had begun wearing the Guerlain men's cologne *Mouchoir de Monsieur*. He was also dressed in a charcoal gray broadcloth suit that likely came from Savile Row. In two weeks, he had turned into quite the dandy.

"What's this about Miss Palmer?" Smith asked in an officious tone. Higgins suspected Thaddeus Smith would turn into a proper snob with just a few more favors granted by Her Grace.

"Not only did she kill Ambrose, but it appears she may be responsible for the shooting at the church on Saturday. Pearl was in a Wild West show in America, which means she is a skilled markswoman." The Duchess shuddered. "What a horrid creature."

Thaddeus raised an eyebrow. "She may be the only woman in London with the ability to do such a thing."

"I doubt there are many men who could hit their target from that distance."

"I disagree, Professor. Most men in society spend their autumns shooting grouse. Even among the lower classes, there are countless chaps who learn to shoot in the military."

"Exactly," the Duchess said. "Oh, not that I think anyone but Pearl shot at Jack and the Colonel. But my first husband was a crack shot. My second husband, too. I daresay Colonel Pickering learned to be quite the marksman in the army as well." She gave Thaddeus an indulgent look. "You, my dear, are too much the sensitive artist. No one expects a musician and composer to wield a gun with any accuracy."

Higgins narrowed his eyes at Smith. "No military experience, then? I hear a trace of Afrikaans in your speech. Were you in South Africa during either of the Boer wars?"

"You guessed correctly, Professor. I'm from the Transvaal."

"It wasn't a guess. I can hear the intonations of a person raised in the Transvaal. Also a word or two that indicates you spent several years at Cambridge." He paused. "And Surrey."

The Duchess laughed. "I told you Henry was a linguistic wizard."

Thaddeus's brief smile lacked warmth. "Impressive."

"Was he also correct in thinking you fought in one of the

Boer Wars?" Eliza said.

"I was never a soldier. My father had a homestead in South Africa when the Dutch began raiding British farms. Like every boy in the Transvaal, my brother and I were taught to shoot from an early age so we could hunt game and kill boomslangs. They terrified Mother."

"What in the world is a boomslang?" the Duchess asked.

"A poisonous snake with large fangs and slow-acting venom. They love to hide in the shrubbery and trees. We always had a gun at the ready if one suddenly appeared."

"Then you only used the gun for hunting game and killing snakes," Higgins said.

"Until the Dutch started to cause trouble. After that, we were expected to help protect our land. And that involved guns, knives, axes. Even an occasional stick of dynamite." His face darkened, as if this had evoked unhappy memories.

The Duchess regarded the church organist with renewed admiration. "Thaddeus, I had no idea you had a thrilling boyhood."

"Unfortunately, fighting in the war ended my boyhood. No one remains a boy after such things. When we moved back to England in '82, Mother was relieved. But my brother and I loved living in Africa. I even miss the boomslangs."

"Then you learned how to be a good marksman." Higgins was determined to confirm that.

He looked confused. "Yes, but I left when I was fourteen. I haven't picked up a rifle in thirty years. What are you imply-ing? That I shot Inspector Shaw?"

The Duchess seemed amused. "Why would Thaddeus want to kill Shaw or Ambrose?"

"You were engaged to Mr. Farrow. And before you met Farrow, I have been told Mr. Smith was your protégé. He might have wanted to rid himself of a rival."

The Duchess and Thaddeus laughed. "I may be the first

church organist to be accused of such a colorful secret life. I'd also be curious as to why I'd wish to kill Inspector Shaw."

"Yes, please tell us, Henry." The Duchess wore a challenging grin.

Higgins glanced at Eliza, who shrugged. "I have no idea. Which leaves us with the elusive Miss Palmer."

"You said you met her at the art gallery, Your Grace," Eliza said. "Was that the only time you and she were in the same place?"

She nodded. "Until the memorial service. After Ambrose and I began to keep company, I made it clear I did not wish to be embarrassed by any adventures he might have with other women. But I'm not a fool. I know gentlemen enjoy a dalliance or two on the side, and I saw no reason to force the issue. Time enough to rein him in after we were wed. I certainly knew he visited the shameless hussy at her apartment now and then."

"How do you know?" Higgins asked.

"More than one friend informed me they'd seen Ambrose's yellow Pierce-Arrow parked outside Pearl's apartment." She rolled her eyes. "If Ambrose planned to cheat on me, you'd think he would have asked me to buy him a less ostentatious motorcar."

"I assume you will be selling it," Higgins said.

Thaddeus looked as if this was a foregone conclusion. "Of course. In fact, her Grace found a buyer three days ago. She will never have to look at that garish machine again."

Higgins wondered when the Duchess would buy Mr. Smith his own motorcar. Soon, he suspected.

"Exactly," she added. "I also dismissed that brute of a driver. I only hired him because Ambrose insisted, though I never understood why. Luther North was an insolent fellow. And sounded like he came from the slums." She turned to Higgins. "You'd probably be able to tell exactly where."

"Bluegate Fields."

Her face registered distaste. "As I thought There's not a filthier slum outside Whitechapel. No doubt that's where he returned now that I've let him go."

Eliza didn't look pleased at this description of Whitechapel. Many of her relatives still lived there. "I don't know if it's as filthy as all that," she muttered.

"When did you dismiss him?" Higgins asked.

"The same day I sold the motorcar. Good riddance to both."

Nothing more could be learned from the Duchess or Thaddeus Smith. If anyone had information about Pearl Palmer, it would be the man who drove Ambrose Farrow to his secret assignations with her. That meant their next stop was Bluegate Fields.

The prospect gave Higgins pause. Bluegate Fields might not be the filthiest slum in London. But it was the most dangerous.

CHAPTER NINE

E LIZA STARED AT THE WHITE Hart pub entrance, barely visible in the haze of tobacco smoke. "Dad, are you certain Billy said he'd meet us?" she asked. "It's half past four."

Alfred Doolittle gulped deep from his glass of ale, then swiped his mouth on his sleeve. "If Billy says he'll be here, he will. I trust him." He belched loudly.

"Why would you trust a yob? At least I think that's what I've heard you call him." Higgins sipped his dark brown ale and winced. Definitely not the best quality. Then again, what did he expect in a seedy Whitechapel pub. "Doesn't that mean he's a thief?"

"Not any longer, he ain't. You met him at Ascot. Billy Grainger's one of the best bookmakers in London, he is. And what does being a thief got to do with it?" Alfred downed the rest of his drink. "Who's to say you're innocent as a babe in his mother's arms, Professor? 'Specially after your shenanigans with my daughter this past summer."

"What does that mean?" Eliza turned her attention back to the table where she sat with Higgins and Alfred.

"It means the pair of you are wily rascals at heart. How else could you have tracked down those killers?" He scooped up a few peanuts from a chipped dish, and chucked them into his mouth. Alfred's cheeks were flushed, and his nose even redder. Clearly he'd come early to the pub and downed his fair share of pints. "If you two put your crafty minds together, you might be damned fine criminals. Something to consider if those elocution lessons don't pay enough."

Eliza's response was to throw a peanut at her dad. Higgins sat back, irritated beyond measure that this blasted relative of Eliza's had kept them waiting so long. He couldn't even spend the time in linguistic research since there were no more than ten other patrons in the pub and saloon. And he recorded their speech patterns in his notebook two hours ago.

Being mid-afternoon, the White Hart hadn't yet filled with workers from the docks and clay pipe factories in the East End. The rainy afternoon didn't help, although he doubted if much light ever penetrated the grimy windows. He squinted at the narrow wood-paneled interior and the bar's scarred counter with pumps jutting upward. A jumbled array of bottles sat crammed onto shelves behind it. While Higgins often encountered unwashed bodies on his linguistic jaunts throughout London, the odors in the small, airless pub were impressive. Especially the sickening smell of damp, sweat-soaked wool combined with alcohol. He felt like he'd been trapped in a pen of drunken, wet sheep.

From the table behind them, Higgins heard one man telling a tale. "You was there for the crossing near Tiger Bay, between that chee-chee and some josser who couldn't see straight."

"Right-o! He must've been off his chump."

Out of habit, he reached for his notebook, only to drop his pencil under the table. Higgins dared not reach a hand down to locate it, given the state of the sticky tables and buzzing flies. And he'd glimpsed mice scurrying among the sawdust sprinkled over the floor.

A couple shoved past Higgins to clap Doolittle on the back. The man wore an eyepatch and the woman sported a dirty crocheted shawl over her faded dress. Atop her untidy dark hair sat a straw hat tied with a frayed strip of ribbon. Her cheeks were streaked with equal parts grime and rouge. And the cheap lilac water she doused herself with made his head swim. Higgins slid his chair sideways to put distance between himself and the couple.

"Bring us a glass, darlin'," the man called to the barmaid. He sported a tattered coat and patched pinstripe trousers, with several days growth of beard. "Good t'see you agin, Alfie. Yer lookin' fine today, all gussied up like a guv'nor! Can you spare a couple quid?"

"I gave you a fiver two weeks ago!" Doolittle pushed him away.

"Aw, come on. You can spare it. And me dollymop needs a new dress."

"Then you shoulda used that fiver I gave you instead of pissin' it away."

The man now looked at Higgins. "This gent here must be a friend, ain't he? I bet he can afford to give me even more than you can."

His dollymop flashed Higgins a gap-toothed smile. "What you say, guv? Like to buy me a pint or two?" She leaned closer, "I'll sit on yer lap, if you like."

"As delightful as that sounds, I must refuse," Higgins said.

She draped herself over his shoulder. "Are ya sure, lovie? I can be awful fun, I can."

Higgins had no idea how to politely extricate himself, especially with everyone in the bar watching them. Given how finely he and Eliza were dressed, he'd suspected they might have trouble in Whitechapel. Only he hoped Alfred would serve as their bodyguard. And Doolittle might have... about four pints ago.

Eliza pointed at her. "Move away from the Professor before he catches your fleas."

The woman stiffened. "You filthy cow. I should kick yer teeth in."

"I'd like to see you try." Eliza half rose from her chair.

The fellow with the eye patch yanked the woman away from Higgins. "Let's go. These people got no heart. Fortune smiles on 'em, so they look down on us. Bloody snobs."

As the pair stalked away, cursing under their breath, Higgins shook his head. It was one thing to wander about the East End taking notes, quite another to sit for hours in a dim pub surrounded by suspicious denizens. Truth be told, he felt trapped. If trouble broke out, he needed to ascertain how to get Eliza and himself safely away. Although in all likelihood, it would be Eliza who would help him escape.

"It seems a bit odd, don't you think?" Eliza turned to Higgins with a pensive expression. "Both Lady Winifred and Mr. Smith were involved in the Boer War."

"What's so odd about it? You do realize there were two Boer Wars. Smith fought in the first one back in '80 and '81, but the siege at Mafeking occurred in the Second Boer War in '99. Their 'involvement', as you term it, took place years apart. Smith simply had the bad luck to be a British farmer's son in the Transvaal when the raids began. And Lady Winifred is married to an Army officer. It's only natural she might occasionally find herself in the middle of a military skirmish." He paused. "Or even a siege."

"Thought about being a soldier meself," Doolittle piped up. "But I had to take care of little Lizzie here, 'specially since her mum died. That's what being a father means. Caring for some bawling brat even when you'd rather be killing people for King and country."

"I recall you going missing a time or two when I was a child. Once you disappeared for five months." Eliza's quiet voice rang with bitterness. "I ended up being sent to the workhouse."

"Hey, it weren't no workhouse. It was a school. Why do you think it was called the Central London District School for Paupers?"

Eliza glared at her father. "The only thing I learned there was how to scrub floors. And how to avoid being sent to the punishment room for a flogging."

"That's appalling. How old were you?" Just when Higgins thought he had heard all the sordid tales of Eliza's wretched childhood, another dark incident cropped up.

"Nine," Eliza said.

Higgins shot Alfred Doolittle a disapproving look. "Did you really abandon your child to the workhouse?"

"Abandon? She makes it sound like she weren't getting two meals a day and a roof over her head in the workhouse. Besides, I had business in Swansea that needed my attention."

"Business meetings? I thought you made your living as a dustman."

"For a time, Dad set up cock fights," Eliza explained. "That year, he was holding matches in Wales. He finally came home when he lost all his money. And all his fighting birds."

"Now there's no need to be walking down memory lane, Lizzie girl. It's water under Tower Bridge, as far as I'm concerned. And I did right by you. Otherwise how would you be sitting here in your fancy clothes and talking like you was the Duchess of Marlborough." He looked around for the barmaid. "You think I'd get a little thanks for that."

"Should she also thank you for throwing her out on the street when you met your present wife?" Higgins's voice dripped with sarcasm. "After all, if she hadn't been a half-starved flower seller when I met her, I might never have taken her on as my pupil."

"Exactly," Alfred said with a wide grin. "Being my daughter helped toughen her up."

Eliza held up her hand. "Let's get back to Mr. Smith and Lady Winifred."

"What's so interesting about that pair?" Higgins asked, confused.

"Maybe Pearl didn't shoot Jack. After all, Smith fought beside his father in the First Boer War. And Lady Winifred must know something about guns if she spent her entire marriage living in garrisons and military outposts."

"Do you suspect that either of them shot Jack?" Higgins glanced down at the glass of ale in front of Eliza. It looked untouched, which meant she was perfectly sober. "They don't have a reason to want Jack dead. Pearl Palmer does."

"But Smith does have a motive for wanting Mr. Farrow out of the way," she persisted.

"And what about Lady Winifred? Why would she want to kill Farrow? Eliza, I know you feel sorry for Pearl, but from where I sit, she's the only possible murderer."

"I know. Except she seemed so lonely and homesick when I spoke with her. And so sad." Eliza got to her feet and waved at a man entering the White Hart. "He's here!"

The cheerful fellow doffed his derby in response. Even through the haze of tobacco smoke, Higgins recognized him as Billy Grainger, whom he'd met in June at Royal Ascot. An inch or two taller than Eliza, Billy was stocky and compact with a wiry mass of red hair.

Although Eliza stood waiting, Grainger stopped to greet about seven friends along the way. His hearty belly laugh echoed off the walls. Like all Doolittle friends and family, he was twice as loud as he needed to be.

"Where's me racing money, Grainger?" a drunken man bellowed from the bar.

"Ah, you're a whiskey soaked fool, you are," Billy replied. "I already paid yer winnings for that run of good luck. Be ready for St. Leger's, though."

"Hey, Billy, what odds will ya give me for the cockfight in Limehouse this Friday?" It appeared the barkeep was also a betting man. At this rate, the bookmaker wouldn't reach their table for another hour.

"Billy, you're late!" Eliza shouted. "So get your blooming arse over here!"

Higgins chuckled when the other bar patrons looked stunned. In her Mayfair walking suit, feathered hat, and elegant coiffure, Eliza resembled a debutante. Little did they know.

The bookmaker spread his arms wide as he walked towards her. "Darlin' Lizzie, heard you got in a spot of trouble at the Eclipse Stakes! Glad to see you lookin' so fine and fancy."

Higgins admired the natural rhythms of the man's speech, similar to that of Alfred Doolittle. Billy Grainger must be doing well in his new line of trade. Unlike the other men in the pub, his brown and yellow checked suit looked clean and well pressed — with a silk waistcoat and fancy watch chain besides. And he wore his bowler at a rakish angle.

After giving Eliza a bear hug, Billy gripped Higgins's hand firmly. "Bet this is your first visit to the White Hart, Professor."

"Indeed it is."

Alfred kicked the chair next to him. "Sit yerself down, Billy. I'll get us a fresh round." He waved at the barmaid as Billy sat between Eliza and Alfred.

"The Professor doesn't care much for ale," Eliza said. "Sherry is more to his taste."

"Bein' a professor, I bet he likes history though. And the White Hart's got plenty of it. Bloody history it is, too. A man once worked as a barber in this very building. A man who might've been using his razor as old Jack." He leaned over the table. "The Ripper himself."

Alfred sighed. "Too bad there wasn't enough proof to hang him."

"I never heard any of the suspects in the Ripper murders was a barber," Higgins said.

Eliza shivered. "Billy scared me silly with tales of Bloody Jack when I was growing up."

"Right you are, Lizzie. Taught you to keep yer wits and eyes about you when walkin' about the neighborhood." Billy winked at Higgins. "Jack the Ripper's neighborhood."

He had no interest in the Ripper murders, though. That was over twenty years ago. He was here to ask the book-maker about Bluegate Fields so a new killer could be tracked down. But Billy had now settled back with a pint of ale and a wide smile.

"The White Hart's famous for Jack working 'ere," he began. "Old George ran a barber shop near St George-in-the-East. And they say Georgie worked magic with his razor."

"Magic, indeed," Alfred grumbled. "Bloody Jack, he knew how to cut a tart from stem to stern, didn't he now. Taking a few kidneys and other parts."

Eliza put her fingers in her ears. "Can't we talk about something else?"

"Mr. Grainger, we had Alfred contact you today for a rea-son," Higgins broke in. "Eliza and I need you to track down someone for us in Bluegate Fields. I hear you grew up there, which means you are no doubt well acquainted with the residents, including those along the docks."

"That I am." Grainger drained his glass and set it on the table with a thud. "I was born and raised in Bluegate. Me mum still keeps lodgings there. Who is it yer lookin' for?"

"A man called Luther North," Eliza said. "He recently worked as a chauffeur in London. But we have reason to believe he's from Bluegate."

For the first time, the bookmaker's ever present smile vanished. "Yeah, the Norths are from Bluegate. I've known the family since I was a boy, but most of the Norths have died or moved away. Luther's father was a sailor in the British Royal Navy, and he followed in his dad's footsteps. Wanted to see the world, Luther said. Especially since his parents died young. Enlisted as a bluejacket before he was sixteen. Not surprising for a fellow raised on the docks." His eyes narrowed. "Why do you want to know about Luther?"

"He may have information about a young woman we're interested in," Eliza said.

"Nothing dangerous, I hope. We're not talking information about a crime, are we?"

"Why do you say that?" Higgins asked. "You just told us Luther was a sailor. What makes you suspect he might be involved in anything shady?"

"Professor, if you're a boy from Bluegate, you got two choices: the seafaring life or the criminal life. And sometimes you choose both. Unlike me, Luther chose the sea, and I ain't heard nothing to ever say he changed his mind. He's a fine seaman, too. Got his training at Shotley where he learned to be a gunner and an engineer. Luther spent about eighteen years in the Royal Navy, too. He came back home now and then, and we shared a pint whenever he did. When his contract was up, he decided not to re-enlist. But me mum learned from a friend that Luther went back to bein' a sailor again." He shrugged. "Trouble is, once you hear the call of the sea, nothing else can compare. Or so they tell me. I get seasick meself."

"Then he rejoined the Royal Navy?" Eliza asked.

"Nah. This time he chose the Merchant Navy. An engineer from all accounts, which means he's a good mechanic. Not surprised he's driving cars now. He could probably find himself work in a garage if he wanted."

"If you find him, would you please call on me?" Higgins drew a card from his outer jacket pocket. "We need to ask him a few questions. It's quite important."

Eliza cleared her throat. "Of course, we'll make it worth your while."

Billy's wide grin reappeared. "Well, if that's the case, there's no need to delay. Come with me now to Bluegate and you can ask your own questions. I'll introduce you to people who might have heard if he's about. If Luther's working as a chauffeur, he needs money. That means he's probably taken a room in the old neighborhood."

"I'm not certain this is wise." Higgins didn't like the sound of this plan. "It's getting late. I never intended to visit Bluegate after dark. Especially with Eliza."

"Ain't it better and quicker to come with me while I'm doin' it? And now is as good a time as any. We've wet our whistles. Might do us some good to pad the hoof for a bit."

"All right, then." Eliza straightened her hat. "You coming, Dad?"

"Nah. You go on, Lizzie." Alfred rubbed his face. "Rose wants new curtains in the house, and she has some fancy draper coming over to bring samples. If I'm not there, she'll order the most expensive thing he's got, and I'll be crushed by the weight of those bills for months."

At the moment, Higgins would have preferred to spend the rest of the day with Rose Doolittle choosing draperies. He was not looking forward to their trip to Bluegate Fields. Whitechapel was dicey enough.

Eliza didn't seem to share his apprehension and pulled Higgins toward the pub's entrance. Billy Grainger followed but only after stopping to speak to a group of new arrivals. While Higgins and Eliza waited on the wet pavement outside, he looked longingly at the East Aldgate tube station across the street. If only he dare make a dash for the next train. He'd love nothing better than to be heading home to his warm fire and slippers at Wimpole Street.

A gusty cold breeze blew down on them, and Higgins turned up his collar. It had rained on and off all day. The overcast sky gave no indication of the hour, but it seemed as gloomy as twilight. Higgins glanced at the sooty and ramshackle buildings lining Whitechapel Road. He'd heard nothing good about the area between Limehouse and St. Katherine's Docks, otherwise known as Bluegate Fields or Tiger Bay.

"Are you certain we ought to be searching this late?"

"We'll be fine, Professor." Eliza patted his arm. "And I'd hate to lose this chance. We can turn back if things get a bit too rough, never fear."

But Higgins was afraid. Despite Eliza's confidence – and the spirited Billy Grainger as their guide – he expected trouble.

Maybe the Professor was right. Eliza kept a firm grip on Higgins's arm as they followed Billy along the narrow street. Too many unsavory looks were cast their way. Slack-jawed women eyed her up and down, as if wondering what they could get for hawking her clothes, while rough men licked their lips. She'd seen plenty of that when she sold flowers on the street. Eliza had fought off more than a few unwelcome advances, but her Covent Garden mates had watched her back. The three of them were outnumbered here, however.

This area looked far worse than Lisson Grove where she'd been raised. Even her piggery in Angel Court was a palace compared to the weather-beaten and sagging buildings on Cannon Street. Ragged urchins cowered under rickety stairs, and an occasional strange grunt sounded from the shadows. She fought the urge to run back to the pub in Whitechapel. And the farther they walked, the more Eliza's instincts flared. Someone was following them. But whenever she glanced over her shoulder, she saw only the sullen glances of people watching from a dark doorway.

Billy stopped to speak to two men wrapped in layers of mismatched clothing. One worked his toothless jaw in silence as he squinted at Higgins.

"I think I seen Luther at the rooming house owned by Mick Whistler. If I was you, I'd head over there," the other fellow said.

"We're sure to find Luther now," Billy said as he hurried across Commercial Street.

In an effort to keep up with Billy, Higgins pulled Eliza at such a fast pace, she nearly fell. She knew Higgins was nervous. And that made her nervous.

A minute later, Billy greeted a burly man who staggered out of the darkness into the dim light of a nearby gas lamp. "'Ello, Mick. I ain't seen you in a month of Sundays. 'Ow are things with you and yer trouble and strife?"

"No worse than usual," he said, staggering a little.

By Mick's slurred speech, Eliza marveled the man could stand upright. While he and Billy caught up on old times, she kept looking over her shoulder. A mist had fallen in the past hour, shrouding the wooden houses leaning against each other. And the slow dripping from the eaves was maddening. Eliza had foolishly left behind her umbrella at the pub. A pity she'd chosen a summer walking suit this morning. The weather had turned wet and cold the past two days, and Eliza would give ten pounds to be wearing thick woolens and a mackintosh.

"Try the dock-shes." Mick slurred his words. "Luther always goesh after sundown. Wans t' see if any choice bits, a crate of 'baccy or so, gets tossed off a ship. Accidental, a'course."

Billy slipped Mick a coin. "Thanks, mate. You take care not to slip on the docks yerself."

The man stumbled up Grove toward Commercial Street, before vanishing into an alley. Meanwhile a knot of young men, no doubt sailors by their tattoos and striped shirts, whistled at Eliza. Fear pooled in her heart.

After a few threatening jeers and a rude gesture or two, Higgins caught Billy's arm.

"I sorely regret bringing Eliza," he said. "This isn't safe."

"Aye, guv, you're right about that. 'Oo knows how long it'll take to root out the likes of Luther? We should leave Lizzie with me mum a few streets over, on Back Church Lane. No need to worry. Mum will watch out for Lizzie."

"I am rather cold," Eliza said. "So I wouldn't mind sitting with your mother awhile. And I've known Bessie Grainger since I was a child, Professor. It will be fine."

"Thank God for Bessie." Higgins drew Eliza between them, one arm around her waist.

Billy led them down to the corner and then south before turning west in the maze of short streets; the houses and buildings all looked the same dingy gray, with few lanterns to illuminate the night. Billy ducked between two brick walls with an open arch and then inserted a key; he twisted it and pushed the wooden door aside. Relieved, Eliza stumbled into an open room that looked surprisingly normal.

A plump older woman looked up from the stove, a shiny kettle in her hand. "Now, Billy. You should've warned me you was bringin' company. I would have changed me dress."

"'S'alright, Mum. This is Alfie Doolittle's daughter. You remember Lizzie. Brew a fresh cuppa for her while Professor Higgins and I take care of some business."

"Lizzie girl, I ain't seen you for nearly five years." Bessie swept Eliza up in a bear hug. "What brings you to my home after all this time?"

The woman had such a kind face and welcoming smile, Eliza didn't have the heart to confess that fear had brought her to Bessie's doorstep.

CHAPTER TEN

❦

ALTHOUGH HIGGINS SPENT NUMEROUS AFTER-NOONS jotting down speech patterns in the East End, he rarely visited after nightfall. And he had never stepped foot in the notorious dockside slum known as Bluegate Fields. He'd been a fool to come tonight. But since he was already here, he might as well make the best of it. Thank heaven Eliza was taking tea with Bessie.

The weather wasn't helping. The whole day had been chilly and damp. When the rain stopped an hour ago, it left behind a summer fog which only added to the ominous atmosphere. But even if this were a sunny morning, Higgins knew he'd still feel uneasy.

The shadowy streets and alleys were filled with people muttering or throwing suspicious glances his way. An occasional surly man stepped in front of them and demanded to know what they wanted. Billy invariably recognized the fellow, averting danger once again. Higgins regretted coming to the East End dressed so clean and respectable. It would be a miracle if he got out of here with his wallet and pocket watch – or even his life. Billy seemed unconcerned, acting as if he were taking a stroll down Oxford Street, doffing his derby and calling out greetings. If anything happened to Billy, Higgins would have a devil of a time finding his way out of this confusing warren of suspicious men and dark streets.

"Step lively, Professor," Billy chided. "I know a lot of people 'ereabouts, and I can keep most of 'em from strippin' you clean. But with a few of 'em, there may be angry feelings."

"Which means?"

"In me former profession, we sometimes disagreed when it came time to divvy up the spoils from a job. Got knifed a few times for my trouble. Knifed a few in my turn, too. Rather not run into any of those dodgers again, if you get my meaning."

Billy grabbed Higgins by the elbow and pulled him away before he accidentally stepped on a pile of rags in the street. Only then did Higgins realize a person was huddled somewhere beneath those rags; whether male or female or even alive or dead, he had no idea.

Through the fog, Higgins spied a brightly lit house and felt a moment's relief. But as they approached, his heart sank. It was a brothel. Sailors unsteady on their feet made their way to the open doorway where a half-dressed woman stood waiting. Shouts drew his attention to a nearby gin shop where three men took turns kicking another fellow, who lay moaning on the wet street.

"Billy, I think we've been here long enough."

The devil take Luther North. Tracking down Pearl Palmer was Scotland Yard's responsibility, not his. And it certainly wasn't Eliza's. The poor girl had already survived twenty years in an East End slum. There was no reason for her to ever return to such misery.

"Now don't go all dainty on me, Professor." Billy again took Higgins by the elbow, this time propelling him away from the brothel and towards the Thames. The smell of river mud and dead fish grew overwhelming. "We need to get closer to the docks and wharves, we do. That's where Luther's likely to be. Lots of cargo goes missin' after dark."

Higgins leaned closer to Billy, who was a good seven inches shorter. "Smugglers?"

"Whatcha whisperin' for?" Billy laughed. "Ain't no one along the wharves right now 'cept for whores, smugglers, and jossers."

"And us too, unfortunately," he muttered.

"Wait 'ere." Before Higgins could protest, Billy sprinted off to have a few words with two men who stood smoking near the wooden pilings.

"We've had some luck," Billy said when he returned. "One of those blokes says they saw Luther along these docks no more than ten minutes ago. We need to walk up and down the river looking for him."

"You don't think this might get our throats cut?"

Billy shrugged. "That's a chance you take anytime you come to the East End. But I been 'ere me whole life without a cut throat. I'm not expectin' it tonight either. Besides, lots of blokes around 'ere are interested in that, not us." He pointed to a wooden building up ahead, a single lamppost illuminating its shabby exterior.

"And that might be?"

"A joss house, what you would call an opium den. Most popular one around, owned by a Chinaman called Gan Heng. Every Lascar from East India who docks 'ere pays a visit. Lots of British seamen got a taste for the joss stick, too. And some sailors be cartin' bundles of opium off their ships to sell. Don't you toffs know nothing about the East End 'cept for Jack the Ripper? Bluegate was famous for opium since afore I was born."

As Billy and Higgins walked along the docks, Higgins could now hear the lapping of the river against the shore and wood pilings. But the growing dusk and fog made it impossible to see the water itself. He felt safer away from the alleys and narrow streets, although heaven only knew what hid in the mist and the shadows.

"Will Luther North be looking for opium?"

"Maybe. Ain't seen the rascal in years. Don't know what Luther's developed a taste for. "

A tall shadow emerged from the fog to their left. They stopped in alarm, and even Billy let out a strangled cry.

"Why is my name bein' tossed about by you two bastards?" the stranger asked.

Billy slapped his leg. "Luther, you sneaky dodger. I been lookin' for you."

"Billy Grainger?" Luther shook his head. "What are you doing on Tiger Bay's docks? I heard you was a bleeding bookmaker now. Did you come back here to nick a few pieces from the ships?"

"Nah, I lost me taste for jail time and running from the peelers. I'm only 'ere as a favor to a friend of a friend." He clapped Higgins on the shoulder. "This 'ere is Professor 'enry 'iggins. A famous gent who teaches idjits to speak proper. The Professor's a friend of Alfie Doolittle from Wapping. Anyways, the Professor and Doolittle's girl Eliza are lookin' for ya. They got questions about some bint called Pearl Palmer."

"Pearl? What do you want with her?" Luther moved closer and struck a match.

Higgins instantly recognized the craggy features and broken nose of the Duchess of Carbrey's former chauffeur.

"I know you," Luther said, tossing the match to the ground. "I drove you and your friends to Ambrose Farrow's wedding."

Higgins nodded. "That you did."

Luther no longer wore his braided driver's uniform, which had given him a rather jaunty air. In his rumpled jacket and cap pulled low over his face, Luther now looked like every other sailor wandering about the docks.

Luther chuckled. "The wedding didn't end well, did it?"

"No. And the wedding of another friend almost ended in disaster, too. You probably read about it in the papers. Someone tried to shoot Detective Inspector Shaw on the steps of St. Marylebone Church. It was sheer luck no one died. But we don't want to take the chance the killer will strike again. That's why I need to ask you about Miss Palmer."

"If you think Pearl's the murderer, you're cracked. The girl wouldn't hurt a fly."

"She was a sharpshooter in a Wild West show back in America," Higgins replied. "That means she had the skill to do it. And the motive. Inspector Shaw's been hounding her since Farrow's death, trying to get a confession. He might well have driven her to a desperate act."

"Bleeding police are dumber than these wood planks. I seen Farrow and Pearl together lots of times. If he told Pearl to throw herself in front of a train, she'd be lying on the tracks before you could say, 'Watch your step.' No way she killed him. Nor shot anyone neither."

"Seeing him marry another woman could have pushed her over the edge."

"Nah. Farrow and Pearl had their eye on the Duchess of Carbrey's money."

"You're saying Pearl had no problem with Farrow marrying the Duchess?"

"Yeah, that's what I'm saying. I heard them talking in the backseat of that fancy car. They looked on the marriage as their safety net."

"Safety net?" Billy asked before Higgins could. "So they had money from another source."

"Damn right they did. And some of that money belongs to me."

Higgins's eyes had adjusted to the gathering dusk, and he could see Luther's angry expression. "Money from the Farrow Gallery?" Higgins asked. "From what I've learned, the gallery profits were modest. The fellow never had the time to make it truly lucrative."

Luther turned to Billy. "See why it's so easy to rob these gents blind? They only notice what's right in front of their faces."

"What I see in front of me is a man who's being evasive and frustrating." Higgins's customary impatience pushed aside his fear. "Are you implying Farrow dealt in something illegal? Given you're a sailor, I assume you mean smuggling. Was he in the London opium trade?"

Both Billy and Luther laughed. "You ain't seen the men what deal in opium," Billy said.

"That's right," Luther added. "If you had, you'd know Farrow wouldn't last more than a day in that line of work. Pretty Princeton boy from America like him. He only had that London gallery 'cause his father died and left him some money. But not as much as he needed. That's why he took up with the Duchess. The old lady thought him a tasty piece, she did. And she wanted him in her bed so bad, she was willing to marry him."

"Then whatever he was smuggling couldn't have been all that profitable."

"Oh, he made himself a nice sum once in awhile, even back when he had his New York gallery. I was in the Merchant Navy when I first heard about Farrow. As chief engineer, I had the run of the ship, especially the cargo hold. Spent years docking in places like Singapore and Bombay. I knew the names of every harbor official who could be bought off, which made it easy to turn my head to smuggling." He shrugged. "But only when the profits seemed worth it."

Higgins cursed himself for not figuring it out sooner. "Farrow was smuggling artwork."

"That he was. Me and a few mates knew lots of art dealers and collectors round the world willing to pay for antique jade, gold necklaces from royal tombs, goblets studded with gems. But I never took enough to draw attention to myself. Until I heard about this Hindu temple in India. A temple with a treasure house filled with bloody riches."

"So you and Farrow arranged to smuggle as much as you could out of the country."

"We weren't the only ones. With a treasure like that, everyone wants their share. Some of the people what do are legit: rich families, museums, government ministries. You mess with them, you're likely to meet the hangman. I only took what Farrow said he could hide away until it could be fenced proper."

"Did you bring it to England?"

"I kept up my end of the bargain, like I always do. Delivered it to a Thames warehouse all boxed up. Farrow took it away for safekeeping. Only I don't know where. Fool that I was to never force the answer out of him. That's why I quit the Merchant Navy. I weren't about to leave London until the bastard sold the treasure and gave me what I was owed."

"Is that why you became his chauffeur?"

Luther nodded. "I made him hire me as soon as the old lady bought him that Pierce Arrow. What better way to keep an eye on him? I drove Farrow everywhere. Now that he's gone, I need to find Pearl."

"Why do you want to find Pearl Palmer?" Higgins now feared for the young woman. He doubted Pearl wished to stumble across Luther North on a foggy London night.

"Because Farrow told her everything. The fool did love her, I'll give him that. If anyone knows where the temple treasure's being kept, it's her."

This was turning into a blasted mess. "What's the name of

this temple in India the treasure came from?" Higgins asked.

"I already told you more than you need to know. And that might have been a mistake."

Billy cleared his throat. "Don't you be worryin' about the Professor. He won't be tellin' tales to the peelers."

"He better not. Otherwise the next time he goes wandering in the East End, he might wind up in the river."

Higgins's temper flared. "Keep talking like that and you might end up in Wandsworth Prison."

After an uneasy pause, Luther laughed. "You've got brass for a gent, I'll give you that. Then again, Ambrose Farrow had brass, too. And look what happened to him."

"I'm more concerned about what may have happened to Miss Palmer. Especially if she knows anything about the latest attack at the wedding."

"She ain't the sort who'd normally come to Bluegate. But if she thinks the police are after her, she might be desperate enough to hide out here." Luther pointed his finger at Higgins. "Now seeing how we both want to find Pearl, I say we look for her together."

"I don't see any purpose in looking for the girl now." Higgins cursed himself again for coming to such a dangerous neighborhood after dark. He also didn't like leaving Eliza alone with Billy's mother. "I propose we meet up tomorrow morning and begin our search then."

Luther took a step closer to Higgins. "And I propose we start searching for that blasted girl now! Before I lose my temper."

This last proposal sounded like a threat.

Eliza didn't regret leaving Higgins and Billy to their search of Bluegate Fields. Bessie Grainger was lively company, and she served a nice pot of tea. Fine tea too, not brewed with cheap tea dust like most East Enders drank. Looking around Bessie's first floor lodgings, Eliza could tell Billy took good care of his mum. Yes, the furniture was mismatched, as was the china, but Eliza suspected it all came from Billy's career as a former thief. Back in the day, he was a great one for breaking into the well heeled households of Kensington. And despite the three different china patterns, and chairs and sofa upholstered in a bewildering array of colors, Bessie Grainger's home was clean, neat, and smelled of fresh baked soda bread. A vase of daisies even sat between them on the wooden table.

Bessie herself did not resemble a Kensington matron. In her bright yellow dress with a red plaid shawl thrown about her shoulders, she seemed to possess the alarming fashion sense of Rose Doolittle. At least she didn't dye her hair as Rose did; instead Bessie boasted a mass of gray hair barely contained by pins and a large amber clip. Eliza's attention was drawn to one of the rings Bessie wore: a ruby as large as a raspberry. She hoped the elderly woman never ventured out of doors wearing it.

"This is wonderful tea," Eliza said as she finished her first cup.

"My Billy gets it straight from the Tetley merchant ships when they dock." Bessie poured another cup for them both. "Fine stuff from Ceylon, it is. And he brings me rock sugar from Germany. Combine the two and you get a lovely cuppa."

Eliza took a sip while gazing about the room. "You've done up the place quite nice. But did you never think of moving to another neighborhood? One a bit safer. Dad lives in Pimlico now."

"Oh, I'd never leave Backchurch Street. Raised all nine of me kids 'ere. Back then this downstairs was a chandler's shop, and we was all squeezed into the two rooms upstairs.

Now I got lodgers up there paying me rent. And I got the whole downstairs to meself."

"It is cozy. I was so wet and chilly walking about, I'm glad to visit." Eliza hesitated. "I had the funniest feeling of being followed. I didn't say anything to Billy or the Professor. They'd just think I was nervous being in such a dodgy neighborhood, but I was raised in streets like these. I know the difference between a man looking to grab my purse, and a person watching me from the shadows." She sighed. "You probably think I'm silly."

"Now why would I be thinkin' that?" Bessie cut another slice of soda bread and pushed the plate toward her, along with a pot of jam. "If you says someone was following you, then it must be true. You might have a little of the second sight. Just like your mum."

"You remember my mother?" Eliza's always voracious appetite vanished. "I didn't realize you knew my family that long ago."

"Whatcha talkin' about, girl? We're related, leastways on your da's side. Third cousins or the like. I even remember when you was born. Your mum was pretty, she was. In fact, you've the look of her. Big brown eyes, shiny brown hair. And a sweet little nose. Where did you think you got yer looks from? Cor, Alfred's nose is bigger than the loaf of this 'ere bread. And to tell the truth, 'e is a bit of an ugly blighter." She winked at Eliza. "But you're easy on the eyes, like your mum. Alfie was bloomin' lucky she ever paid him any mind."

"What do you remember about my mother?" Try as she might, Eliza couldn't dredge up a single memory of her. Then again, she was only two years old when her mum died.

"Sarah? Like I said, she was pretty, but with a fiery nature. Doted on you, she did. Don't think she ever let your da pick you up, not that Alfie was ever around much. Sarah loved music. Being Irish that's no surprise. And I never saw your mum take a drop of liquor. She was right sharp, too. A woman that clever, she weren't happy strippin' tobacco or being a laundress." Bessie sighed. "And it weren't easy livin' with a dustman. Specially one as lazy as Alfie."

Her tale saddened Eliza. What a shame her mother didn't have the opportunity to be schooled by Professor Higgins as she had been. And how awful for both of them that she died so young, leaving Eliza motherless and unloved.

"Do you remember what she died of? Dad says it was some kind of fever."

"Don't know for sure. Alfie and Sarah moved away about six months before. You know your dad. Always one step ahead of the landlord and the bill collectors. I was right sad to learn she passed. Only a girl, she was. No more than five and twenty. Too young for Alfie. But little Sarah Fennimore was right off the boat from Ireland when they met. And your dad's got a gift of gab that makes a person forget they shouldn't be listenin'."

"One day I'd like to go to Donegal and see if I can find her people."

"Blimey, I wonder if some of 'em even know poor Sarah died." She shook her head. "To think after all the women Alfie's played 'ouse with, that foul tempered Rose Cleary is the only one who gets to be Mrs. Doolittle before the law. Don't seem right."

Eliza sat up with a start. "What do you mean? My mother was Mrs. Doolittle, too."

Bessie gave her a pitying look. "Ah no, dearie. Didn't you father tell you? Alfie never married your mum. Not many of us in the East End do get round to makin' it legal. Me and Billy's dad never did, but I'm Mrs. Grainger all the same. And after bearin' the fool nine children, I earned the bloomin' right to be looked on as his wife!"

This was too much to take in. What else was Dad keeping from her? Eliza was about to pepper Bessie with more questions when a quiet knock sounded at the front door.

"Now why would Billy be knockin'? The boy's got a key." Bessie stood and turned to the wooden hutch behind her. She pulled a knife out of one of the drawers. Eliza's eyes widened at the sight of its large, sharp blade. "If it ain't Billy at the door, best be prepared for whoever's on the other side. In Backchurch Lane, we don't go callin' after dark."

Eliza followed close behind the older woman. Most buildings in the East End had a back door that led to an alley. If trouble had come knocking, she planned to use that as her escape. She hoped Bessie could run fast.

"Who's there?" Bessie growled. "Speak up!"

A soft voice responded, too quiet to be intelligible. Bessie frowned. "Stand back, Lizzie. If I thinks there's danger, I'll be swingin' wide with this." She held up the kitchen knife.

Eliza took a few steps back, wishing she had her own knife to wield.

Bessie creaked open the door and stuck her head out. "And who might you be?" she asked. Again the reply was too quiet for Eliza to hear.

As Bessie swung the door open, Eliza held her breath, preparing to run if need be. Instead she was stunned to realize that she knew the person who stood in the doorway.

"Miss Doolittle!" The uninvited guest rushed over and threw her arms about Eliza.

Bessie shut the door with a perplexed expression. "You know this girl, Lizzie?"

"Yes." Eliza didn't know what else to do but pat the shivering young woman on the back. "Her name is Pearl Palmer."

CHAPTER ELEVEN

ONCE BESSIE JUDGED THE GIRL to be harmless, she began clucking over Pearl like a mother hen. A fresh pot of tea was brewed, and Bessie added plates of cold herring and several hard boiled eggs to the table. Pearl wolfed down two thick slices of soda bread in quick succession, and now spread jam on her third. Eliza eyed Pearl's damp clothes. Her pink walking suit was liberally spattered with mud. Pearl must have been outside most of the rainy day, giving her the bedraggled appearance of a half drowned kitten. And it took thirty minutes before a blazing coal fire until her shivering ceased. Watching her, Eliza wondered if it was only the cold that set her shaking. Perhaps it was fear as well.

When Pearl's appetite seemed satisfied, Eliza cleared her throat. It was time for a few questions. "Miss Palmer, why did you come to Mrs. Grainger's house? She's never met you before. And I doubt you know her son Billy."

Pearl put her half-eaten slice of bread back on the plate. "I came here because I needed to speak with you. I've been following you all day. I followed you here."

"Whatever for?"

"You may be the only one I can trust. Certainly you're the only person who's been nice to me since Ambrose was killed."

At their last encounter at the Maison Lucile, Eliza was struck by Pearl's air of innocence. She found it hard to imagine this feminine and beautiful young woman firing shotguns and riding Indian ponies in a Wild West show. Yet Pearl had done so, which meant she could have been the person who shot Jack and Colonel Pickering.

"My cousin was shot on Saturday," Eliza said, noting how Pearl flinched at the coldness in her voice. "He might have been killed except for the bravery of my dear friend, Colonel Pickering. Not only were you a sharpshooter, but the police found three rifles in your apartment. And someone hid a gun at the site where the shots were fired. Do you expect me to believe you're not the person who did this terrible thing?"

"But I didn't do it. I swear!" Pearl's eyes filled with tears. "It wasn't me. Those rifles in the apartment were from my Wild West days. I brought them with me in case I fell on hard times and needed to make a living as a sharpshooter again."

"You told me at the dress salon that my cousin Jack was trying to get you to confess to Mr. Farrow's murder. Maybe you thought killing him was the only way to be left alone."

"I would never kill anyone. Besides, the police are the least of my troubles."

"What troubles, dearie?" Bessie sat back in her chair, arms folded across her bosom.

"I've never been so unhappy and lonely. I don't belong here. Now that Ambrose is gone, everyone I care about is far away. All I want is to go back to America. I want to go home!"

"Is loneliness the only thing troubling you, child?" Bessie asked. From her gentle tone, Eliza guessed Bessie must be a loving mother. She envied Billy Grainger and his eight siblings.

"No. I'm afraid. I've been afraid for too long. Even before Ambrose was killed."

"What are you afraid of?" Eliza asked, trying to curb her impatience.

"Ambrose was a decent and kind man. And he loved me. But he had grand dreams, too grand. He took risks that got him killed. Now I'll be killed over them."

"I saw you arguing with him the day of the Duchess's wedding," Eliza said. "You struck him in the face. If he was such a decent, kind man, why were you so angry?"

"Because he wanted to back out of marrying the Duchess. Ambrose and I agreed months ago it was the best thing for us. The Mayfair gallery expenses had put us in debt. And he spent all his father's money moving us to London, plus maintaining my apartment and his rooms at the Savoy. I don't earn enough as a mannequin to be of much help. We thought it was a stroke of luck when the Duchess took a fancy to him."

"Ambrose was marrying the Duchess for her fortune." Eliza didn't hide her disapproval.

"I know it sounds cold and greedy. But we were sinking into debt. We hoped one of Ambrose's art sales would bail us out, only things didn't go as planned. Marrying the Duchess guaranteed our financial future." For the first time Pearl looked ashamed. "After all, she's so much older than Ambrose. How much longer could she live? A few more years at most."

Bessie gave a snort. "We old birds can live a long time, dearie. You'd be surprised how tough we are. Unless you planned on doin' away with the Duchess."

"Why does everyone think I'm a heartless killer? I had no reason to wish her harm. After his marriage, Ambrose was going to buy me a lovely house near Kensington Park and visit me whenever he could. I wouldn't have to work anymore either. It seemed such a nice life. I would have Ambrose *and* financial security."

"But Mr. Farrow changed his mind," Eliza said.

"Yes. The week before the wedding, he thought he'd found buyers for some art pieces he'd been trying to sell. He'd be a rich man without having to marry the Duchess. But he'd come close to selling before, and the deal fell through. I was afraid it might happen again and we'd be left with only the bill collectors breathing down our necks. That's why we argued at the church. He decided to call off the wedding, but I said he had to marry her. I wish now I'd made him leave with me. He'd still be alive."

Against all reason, Eliza believed Pearl. Higgins would think her mad, but he didn't understand what poverty and debt could drive a person to do. He'd been a damned fortunate man his whole life. "Then why was Ambrose Farrow killed?"

Pearl looked over her shoulder as if someone lurked in the corner. "Because of the art pieces he was trying to sell," she said in a low voice.

"Someone murdered him over a few paintings?" Eliza had been to the National Gallery once; a pleasant visit, but she couldn't imagine why anyone would turn murderer for the sake of canvases splashed with paint.

"Oh no. It's a treasure. Gold coins, rings, necklaces, jeweled crowns, emerald armbands, swords studded with rubies. It lay hidden in a jungle for centuries until some man discovered it in an ancient temple. A treasure fit for a queen. Ambrose said they call them maharanis in India."

"India?" Eliza suddenly thought of the Indian couple who were at the wedding and memorial. "Is this temple connected to Taral Misra?"

Pearl appeared confused. "I don't know what that is."

Eliza glanced at Bessie. She knew they were both thinking

the same thing. "If your Mr. Farrow had such a treasure at his disposal, he was already a rich man. Richer than most."

"But he couldn't let anyone know he had it. Not officially. The only people who knew were those who had a hand in stealing it. And they kept fighting among themselves."

"It's not good when thieves turn on each other," Bessie muttered.

"Things were getting dangerous," Pearl continued, "If the government found out Ambrose had it, he'd be arrested. And there were rich people in England who bought the right to take the treasure from India. They would have gone after Ambrose, too. I regret the day the treasure ever arrived in London. Ambrose took me to the warehouse that night and opened the crates. It made me dizzy to see so much gold and jewels. I knew then we were in trouble." A tear slowly ran down her cheek. "I knew we would be killed over it."

"Is the treasure still in the warehouse?" Eliza asked.

"Ambrose moved it to a secret location. So secret he wouldn't even tell me. He thought this would protect me. The sad joke is that everyone believes I do know where the treasure is. But all I know is it's hidden away somewhere in London until the right buyer comes along."

Bessie whistled. "Let me tell you, if Billy were still in the game, he'd sniff out that treasure in less than a day. That boy has a gift for what don't belong to him, he does."

"But why you were following me today?" Eliza asked.

Pearl got to her feet and paced about the table. "After your detective cousin began to harass me, I decided to go back to America. Only I didn't have enough for the passage home. I needed another two months wages to earn the full price of a ticket."

Eliza still didn't understand, but she didn't rush Pearl, who wrung her hands now in obvious distress.

"Last Saturday I went to the salon even though it was my

day off. I hoped Lady Duff-Gordon would let me work anyway, seeing how I needed the money. But she had enough mannequins and sent me home. Only when I got close to my apartment, I saw Scotland Yard out front, and detectives going in and out of the entrance. I knew they were looking for me. And I was terrified I'd be arrested for Ambrose's murder. So I ran away."

"They were there because of the shooting at the church," Eliza explained. "Not Farrow's murder."

"I know that now. I learned about the shooting a few hours later when the newsboys hawked the evening papers. But the shooting meant I was in even worse trouble. The police blamed me." She gave a mirthless laugh. "And why not? I would have been able to shoot the hat off your cousin's head from a hundred yards away and not even mussed his hair. Only Annie Oakley could have done it better."

"Annie who?" Bessie asked.

"You probably felt trapped." Eliza pitied the young woman.

"On all sides. By the person who killed Ambrose for the treasure, and now by the police." Pearl turned to Eliza. "You were the only one I could think to ask for help. I didn't dare go to any of the women who work at the salon. I was afraid the police had already been to see them, filling their minds with terrible stories of me being a murderer."

"I don't understand why you think I can help you."

Pearl sat down again. "I need to get into my apartment. All the money I saved up so far for my ticket home is hidden away in a box in my bedroom. Only I can't go back, not with the police watching the building. But they wouldn't stop you from going in. Please retrieve my money. Otherwise, I don't know what will happen to me." Before Eliza could reply, Pearl fished out a key from the pocket of her skirt and held it out. "Please."

Eliza stared at the key, then looked over at Bessie who

shrugged. "I don't even know if the police will let me through, Miss Palmer."

"Other young women live in the building. The police will think you're one of them."

With a sigh, Eliza took the key. Things were getting far too murky. Her instincts told her Pearl could be trusted, yet the facts screamed that this sharpshooting woman was a possible murderess. "I'll do what I can."

Pearl grabbed Eliza's hand and gave it a kiss. Embarrassed, Eliza pulled away.

"You don't know how much this means to me, Miss Doolittle. I've barely a shilling left. On Saturday morning when I went to the salon, I only had a pound note in my purse." She held up the drawstring bag. "I never thought I wouldn't be able to return to my apartment. All I've had to eat these past two days is a biscuit and a pear from a street vendor." She turned to Bessie. "And I thank you greatly for the meal, ma'am."

"My pleasure, dearie. Many's the time I had to live on less meself."

"Where have you been staying since Saturday?" Eliza asked.

"I used the last of my money to rent a cheap room last night. On Saturday night I slept on a back stairway along Wimpole Street."

"Why in the world did you do that?"

"When we spoke at the salon, you mentioned where you lived on Wimpole Street. I waited outside your house for hours, only you never showed up. I fell asleep on the stairs leading to the servants' entrance."

"I was at the hospital all Saturday night and most of Sunday. So was the Professor. We were worried about the Colonel." Eliza frowned. "We still are."

"I wasn't sure how bad your cousin had been hurt. I

couldn't bear another night sleeping outside, though, especially when it rained on Sunday. That's why I rented a room. I got up at dawn today and returned to Wimpole Street. You finally appeared, but with that professor. I didn't want to talk with him so I followed you, hoping to catch you alone. You led me on a merry chase. Trafalgar Square, Whitechapel. Then this awful neighborhood." She looked down at her damp suit. "It was more bad luck that it rained all day."

No wonder Pearl's hair was coming loose from its pins, and her skirt and jacket were wrinkled and stained. Even the rose-colored plume on her hat drooped from the rain.

"You could have approached me and Professor Higgins at any time," Eliza said.

"But I'm afraid of him. You've no reason to fear him because he's keeping you."

Eliza held up her hand. "The Professor is not keeping me. We're colleagues."

Bessie laughed at that, while Pearl shot her a disbelieving look.

"I'm telling the truth. He's an elocution teacher and last year he taught me the proper way to speak. Now we both give language instruction at Wimpole Street."

"I understand. Ambrose taught me many things, too. Including how to talk like a lady. We're more alike than I thought. People are unkind to women like us."

Eliza wanted to protest, but why bother? After all, these two women had lived with men for years without a marriage license. Crikey, she just learned her own parents had done the same.

"I was relieved when I saw those two men bring you here today. Only I needed to make sure they weren't coming back. So I waited." Pearl shivered. "I've never been so nervous in my life. Bluegate Fields is filled with nasty people."

Bessie shrugged. "You get used it."

"Whoever killed Ambrose must have wanted the treasure. Which means I'll be next because they think I know where it is." She hid her face in her hands. "I was happy in America, especially after I met Ambrose. I wish we'd stayed in New York. Now Ambrose is dead." She shuddered. "And I will be, too, soon enough."

Bessie rose to her feet with a grunt. "You're much too young to be talkin' like that, dearie. Why, your whole life is ahead of you. Mustn't let a setback or two keep you down. And if dangerous people are lookin' to do you harm, then you got to become dangerous yerself."

She rummaged about in the drawers of the wooden hutch again. This time she produced a knife nestled in a leather holder.

Bessie drew out the knife. The gaslight jets made the thin wicked blade and scrolled handle gleam. "This 'ere is an Eye-talian dagger called a stiletto. And this fancy leather thing is a scabbard. Billy came across it years ago and never got round to sellin' it. Sharp as a needle it is, but a sight more deadly. Keep this in your pocket or handbag." She replaced it in the scabbard and held it out to Pearl. "Anyone tries to hurt you, pull that out and give 'im what for."

Pearl took the stiletto with a grateful expression.

"I don't think this is a good idea, Bessie. After all, Miss Palmer doesn't even know how to use a knife."

"But I do." Pearl stood and slid the knife into the side pocket of her skirt. "Half the men in the Wild West show owned Bowie knives. I learned how to throw one."

Eliza marveled that Pearl feared anything, given how adept she was with weapons. Handing a stiletto to a desperate woman could only lead to trouble, however. Bessie's sitting room suddenly seemed too small – and hazardous as well. Pearl Palmer was little more than a stranger. What if she had killed Ambrose and tried to murder Jack? Eliza felt trapped. Higgins was off who knows where, while a suspicious woman had just been gifted with a dagger. She ought to leave. The streets of Bluegate Fields suddenly seemed safer than Bessie Grainger's kitchen.

"Thank you for the tea, Bessie," Eliza said. "But I should be going."

"Billy told me I was to keep you 'ere till 'im and the Professor returned."

Pearl grew alarmed once more. "But I can't be here when your professor arrives."

"Why are you afraid of the Professor?"

"His niece is going to marry Clyde Winterbottom," she said in obvious exasperation. "And Ambrose told me to never trust that man."

"Wait. Is Winterbottom a thief, too?" Eliza wished Higgins were present to hear this.

"I don't know what he is. But Ambrose said to never turn my back on the fellow."

They all froze at the sound of loud voices outside. When Eliza heard Billy talking with Higgins, she wanted to weep with relief. But Pearl looked like a fox who had just heard the pursuing hounds.

Eliza grabbed her arm. "Pearl, please tell Higgins what you've told me."

She shook her head. "No, no. You don't realize how dangerous all this is."

Then they heard a third person speaking in a Cockney accent that seemed vaguely familiar to Eliza. Pearl's expression turned to horror.

"No, not Luther! Why would Luther North come here?" Pearl pushed Eliza aside. "I can't let him find me."

Bessie gestured with her head to the back room. "Slip out the rear bedroom door, dearie. There's an alley will take you out to a cross street."

"Don't tell her that." Eliza reached for Pearl again, but the sound of the door opening gave the girl renewed strength. Shoving past Eliza, Pearl fled to the back bedroom. At that moment, Higgins, Billy, and a man she recognized as Luther North entered the room.

"Who was that?" Higgins asked. He had arrived in time to see a fleeing figure.

"Pearl Palmer. You frightened her off."

"You let Pearl go? Bloody hell!" Luther raced towards the back room.

"We have to go after them." Eliza tugged on Higgins's jacket lapels. "Pearl's scared out of her mind. In her state, she might harm herself. And I don't know what Luther may do to her."

Higgins must have seen the frantic concern in her eyes. "Right, Eliza. Let's go."

They bolted for the back of the house as Billy yelled, "I'll go out the front and see if I can get to the cross street afore they do. Meet ya there."

"Look for a brunette woman dressed in pink," Eliza called after Billy as she raced for the door to the alley.

But when she opened the back door, she hesitated. Night had fallen, and the alley was black as pitch. It would no doubt be years before the streets of Bluegate were supplied with electric lighting.

Taking a deep breath, Eliza hiked up her skirts. "We'd best run."

She hurried down the dark alley, dimly hearing Higgins order her to slow down. At the alley's end, she stopped. Which way? Higgins bumped into her as he skidded to a halt.

"Follow me," Eliza said.

Fear for Pearl's safety made her so quick, not even Higgins's long legs could match her pace. "Where are you going?" he yelled after her.

But she had no idea where she was. Backchurch Lane? Cannon Street? Or was she running down Commercial or Cable Street? People shouted at her to stop. Some tried to grab her. But she knew how to use her elbows to knock aside anyone who dared get too close. With Luther chasing after Pearl, Eliza feared for the girl's safety.

She finally stopped for breath, allowing Higgins to catch up to her. "Damnation, Eliza! You must have the wings of Mercury on your feet. What do you think you're doing?"

"Trying to find Pearl before Luther does."

"The two of us running pell-mell along every street in Bluegate isn't doing much except driving me to exhaustion. You actually leaped over a barrow. If you'd taken flight like Peter Pan, I wouldn't have been surprised."

A wave of sadness swept over Eliza. "I have a bad feeling."

"As do I," Higgins said.

"And where is Billy?"

In answer to her question, the bookmaker's voice called to them from down the street. "Professor! Eliza! Over here!"

Together they set off down the fog shrouded street, only this time Higgins kept a firm grip on Eliza's arm. Billy had apparently run to meet them, and the three almost collided.

"I been lookin' for you two these past fifteen minutes. I thought maybe you both hightailed it back to Wimpole Street."

Higgins sighed. "We've covered enough ground to reach it."

"This fog makes it hard to see anything." Eliza turned in a circle, peering in all directions. "Where did Pearl go? She couldn't just disappear!"

"Follow me." Billy left them little choice but to hurry after him.

Eliza now realized their chase had taken them to the river.

Two men stood on the dock, both holding kerosene lamps high.

Billy turned to her. "You said Pearl Palmer was wearing a pink dress?"

Eliza nodded, her heart in her throat.

"Then I think we found the girl." Pushing Higgins aside, Billy took Eliza's arm and led her to the water's edge.

For a moment, she wanted to run again, only this time far away from the sinister streets and bone chilling fog of Bluegate Fields. Billy walked around the sailors holding the lamps. Both men glanced her way, but quickly returned their attention to the river. With a muffled cry, Eliza looked at the dark water below, now illuminated by the lanterns.

Pearl Palmer floated face down in the Thames. Sticking out of her back was the knife Bessie Grainger had given her.

CHAPTER TWELVE

ONCE AGAIN, ELIZA AND HIGGINS found themselves at Scotland Yard. She dreaded each time they were required to make an appearance at the Metropolitan Police headquarters. The only reason for a visit was because someone she knew had been murdered This time it was Pearl Palmer. And she could not get the girl's forlorn corpse out of her mind – along with the Italian dagger planted in her back. Eliza had tossed and turned all night, haunted by that image.

"You're dragging your feet," Higgins said when they arrived at Derby Gate, the south entrance to the Yard.

"It's the weather," she lied.

The chilly air brought on by the recent storms had moved on. Today was once again uncommonly warm and humid. The steamy heat had already wilted the tulle-trimmed collar of her silk blouse. Even her buff linen skirt felt too heavy.

"I'm also dragging my feet because they hurt," Eliza added. No surprise there, given how extensively she and Higgins explored Bluegate Fields last night.

He shot her a rueful smile. "Mine, too. A pity I couldn't have stayed in bed."

Higgins seemed just as troubled by last night's events. What a terrible week, with the attack at the church, worrying over Colonel Pickering, and now the brutal murder of Pearl Palmer. How did everything turn so ugly and frightening? This month was supposed to be a giddy round of weddings, and Eliza had looked forward to weeks of celebrating, dressing up, and eating cake. Instead, they had to give police statements and visit hospital wards.

Higgins pointed at the red brick building up ahead. "Do you know the prisoners at Dartmoor quarried some of that granite? I feel like a damned prisoner, too, every time Jack summons us here."

"With this heat, it will feel like a prison cell today. I wish Jack ranked farther down the chain of command. His office would be on an upper floor if he was."

When New Scotland Yard opened its doors in 1890, the lower floors were reserved for top brass only. Indeed, the commissioner oversaw his police force from a turreted office on the second floor. Jack's promotion last year earned him a spot on the floor just above, which meant his office was sure to feel as fiery as a smithy. Although Scotland Yard employees farther down the pecking order had to climb extra flights of stairs to their offices, they were rewarded with refreshing river breezes wafting through upper floor windows.

The familiar sight of men in navy suits and stiff collars hurrying through the halls greeted Eliza and Higgins as soon as they entered. Long lines of visitors snaked in two directions: one leading to the department handling traffic complaints, the other to the Lost Property Office. Jack once told her that over fourteen thousand umbrellas were stored there. She wondered if the umbrella she left behind at the White Hart would join them one day. Then again, it may have been sold to pay for another round of drinks or a bed for the night.

Higgins nodded to the sergeant presiding behind his tall desk, who waved them along. A woman in a black straw hat and shabby paisley dress held a summons in hand and visibly quaked in fear. Eliza had seen her here twice before, each time in the same anxious condition. Three constables walked past. One of them doffed his blue helmet and called out, "Miss Doolittle. Professor Higgins."

"We're getting too well known around here," Higgins said as he and Eliza made their way to the stairs. "Your cousin ought to issue us uniforms. Or at least give us a consulting fee."

Two detectives clattered down the steps towards them. Eliza recognized the taller fellow as one of the policemen at the docks last night in Bluegate. "Excuse me, Detective. Professor Higgins and I spoke with you after we found Miss Palmer's body. Can you tell us if Luther North is still being questioned?"

"Or has he been charged already?" Higgins added.

Both detectives looked at each other. "May as well tell them," the other murmured.

"Sorry, miss, but North was released over an hour ago," the man said. "We didn't have enough evidence to hold him."

"That can't be true!"

Higgins looked furious. "Damn and blast, man."

He frowned. "Sorry. We had no choice. If you'll excuse us, we have an appointment." They both hurried through the crowd and out the door.

Eliza felt like she'd been kicked in the stomach. "This is terrible. Pearl wasn't stabbed by a stranger lurking in the shadows. It had to be Luther North. Why didn't they arrest him?"

"There's only one way to find out. Let's talk to your cousin."

By the time they climbed to the third floor, Eliza and Higgins were drenched in sweat.

"Why is there no bloody ventilation in this building?" Higgins wiped his sleeve across his damp forehead.

Eliza regarded her stained blouse. "We'll have to go home and change before visiting Colonel Pickering. Otherwise he'll think we ran all the way to the hospital."

"I wouldn't mind running after Luther North. I'd force a confession out of him."

Eliza and Higgins walked to Jack's office, both of them wincing with each painful step. "I can't believe Jack thinks Luther is innocent," she said. "We told the detectives what happened when they arrived at the docks."

Higgins halted, one hand on the door knob. "I'm not happy we always appear to be two steps ahead of the police. It's a disgrace they released Miss Palmer's obvious killer. Small wonder the editors of *Punch* dubbed Scotland Yard 'the Defective Police Force.'"

But when they entered Jack's office, her cousin's bad mood seemed to match their own. Well, the devil take Jack. Eliza owed something to Pearl. After all, the poor girl had come to her for help.

"We heard Luther North was released an hour ago. Jack, how could you?"

"Sit down, Lizzie, and be quiet. Both of you." Anger was evident in his voice.

After signing a set of papers, he handed them to the waiting constable. Jack watched until the man closed the door before facing them. Eliza perched on the chair's edge, but Higgins remained standing. The two men eyed each other like boxers in the ring at Wonderland in Whitechapel. She half expected them to raise their fists and begin sparring.

"What in hell were the two of you doing in Bluegate Fields?" His left eye twitched madly. "Those docks have the worst reputation in London. You could have been killed."

"Did you call us down here for yet another lecture?" Eliza said. "You did that yesterday."

In truth, there hadn't been time for Jack to do much more

than scowl at her and Higgins last night, what with finding the dead body and trying to round up witnesses. After
his detectives took their statements, Higgins and Eliza were
allowed to go home with instructions to be at the Yard the
following day. She should have known Jack wasn't done
haranguing them.

"I've got more to say. You've both risked your lives more
than once chasing down murderers. Only that's our job.
We're the police. Remember? I've told you a hundred times
about the dangers. Now for the love of God, stay out of this
investigation."

"By Jupiter, we understand perfectly well how dangerous
this is. You were shot right in front of us three days ago."
Higgins folded his arms across his chest. "And so was my
friend Pickering. While trying to protect *you*, I might add."

Jack glared at him.

"We agreed with you about Pearl," Eliza said. "She
seemed the most likely person to have shot you. Especially
when she went missing after your wedding. So the Professor
and I decided to track her down. We figured the only link
to Pearl was Luther North, and all we knew about him is
that he was from Bluegate Fields. Well, so is Billy Grainger.
It made sense to ask Billy to help us find him. But Luther
didn't know where Pearl was either. Jack, we only wanted
to find her before she could hurt you again. We're worried
about your safety, too."

"I understood the risks from the first day I took this job.
Neither of you do."

"If you continue to patronize us, I swear we will come to
blows," Higgins said.

"Why don't you admit that you need our help?" Eliza said,
unwilling to turn this into a brawl. "Otherwise, how could
you let Luther go?"

Higgins spoke up before Jack could reply. "Luther North

was an engineer in the Merchant Navy. Last night he admitted to me that he helped smuggle a treasure from some Indian temple off his ship. Billy was with me when Luther said it. He also told us part of the treasure fell into Ambrose Farrow's hands when it reached England."

"And Pearl warned me not to trust Clyde Winterbottom," Eliza said. "It's possible he was also involved with stealing this treasure."

Jack slumped down on his chair. "After reading your statements, we spent the entire morning checking out Mr. Winterbottom. He seems to be just what he appears: a dull but respected employee of the British Museum."

"He's also an ambitious, calculating creature," Higgins added.

"Many people are. That doesn't make them criminals."

"Pearl was in fear for her life. And she was right, wasn't she? Someone stabbed her in the back." Eliza jumped to her feet, too agitated to stay seated. "Both times I spoke to her, I thought she was being honest with me."

"You spoke to Pearl twice?" Jack barked. "When was the previous time?"

Eliza hesitated before answering, "Two weeks ago at Maison Lucile."

"You didn't report that to me? Why are both of you impeding a police investigation?"

"Impeding it?" Higgins's exasperation matched Eliza's. "We're furthering it, and you bloody well know it! We've interviewed suspects, uncovered motives, accessed evidence—"

Jack cut him off. "Hold on. What evidence?"

Eliza cleared her throat. "Pearl was desperate to go home to America, but she didn't have enough money. Last night she gave me a key to a box in her apartment where she keeps her savings. She was too frightened to go back to her lodgings, so she asked me to do it."

Jack held out a hand. "Give it over." He waited while she groped inside her small pocketbook. Once she surrendered it, he quickly sealed the key in an envelope. "Detective Ramsey should be back soon. He's gone to search her apartment, plus follow a few other leads. We couldn't hold Luther North, however. Even though we questioned him for hours."

"But Pearl was terrified of Luther. As soon as she heard his voice at Bessie Grainger's door, she ran away. And he took off right after her."

"North claims he never saw Miss Palmer last night until she was fished out of the river."

"What? She was with me when Luther arrived with the Professor and Billy. Just hearing him at the door put the fear of God in her."

"Luther says otherwise."

Higgins looked at Jack in disgust. "You value the word of Luther North over the veracity of Eliza and me?"

"Don't be ridiculous. I never said that."

"If you don't believe us, ask Billy's mum," Eliza said. "She was a witness to my entire conversation with Pearl. She heard all about the stolen treasure and Winterbottom and how someone thought Pearl knew where the treasure was hidden. That's why her life was in danger." She waved her hands in the air. "My God, Bessie believed Pearl's story so much, she gave her a stiletto for protection. The same one found in Pearl's back. Talk to Bessie Grainger."

"Don't you think I sent my men to ask her for corroboration? She swears Pearl Palmer was only there a few moments. And that the girl took off through the back door when the men arrived. Bessie claims Pearl never mentioned anything about a treasure. Or said a word about Luther North." He looked grim. "And she says Pearl must have stolen her knife."

Eliza and Higgins exchanged stunned looks. "Damnation," Higgins muttered.

"Lizzie, you've been out of the slums only a year. You can't have forgotten how East Enders feel about the police," Jack said in a pitying tone. "They don't trust us, they never have. Sometimes with good reason. It's why I joined the force, to try and make a difference. I'm never surprised when they lie, especially if telling the truth gets them in worse trouble."

Because she knew he was right, Eliza grew more frustrated. "What about Billy then? He was there when Luther went chasing after Pearl. Crikey, we all went looking for her, including Billy. Luther found her before anyone else, overpowered her, and then used Bessie's knife to stab her."

"Luther must have thought Pearl knew where the temple treasure was hidden," Higgins said. "The man's a scoundrel, Jack. Hell, he even threatened me, saying I'd end up in the river. Billy heard Luther say that, too. How much proof do you need?"

"It's your word against theirs." Jack ran a hand through his tangled hair. "Billy swears he and his friends were with Luther the whole time you were searching for Miss Palmer."

Eliza's mouth fell open. "That's a bold-faced lie!"

"It's the truth, it is." Grainger stood at the doorway. Billy wore the same plaid suit as yesterday, and twirled his bowler hat with one hand. But his easy smile was gone. Eliza wondered when Billy opened the door. She, Jack, and Higgins had been so intent on their conversation, they hadn't noticed.

"You know blooming well you were helping us find Pearl and Luther."

"Sorry, Lizzie. I ain't changin' me story no matter what Detective Shaw's boys do to persuade me." He looked over at Jack. "They said I could go. Is that right?"

"Yes, but we may ask you to return." Jack waved at Eliza to prevent any interruption. "And we'll be keeping a close eye on you, Billy. I've told my men that if they see you even spit on the pavement, they'll haul your dodgy ass in again."

Billy nodded. "So that's the way you're gonna play it. Keep forgettin' you're a copper now."

"That's right. I'm a copper. And I don't like people who lie to the police."

He shriveled under Jack's furious gaze. "Sorry 'bout that Miss Palmer. But I got nothin' to do with it. She probably ran across someone who fancied her purse or wanted a tumble. A pretty thing like her got no chance against the rum lot in Bluegate. Pity she wandered by the wrong bloke. A rascal who was carryin' a knife."

"That filthy rascal was Luther North," Eliza said, "and you know it."

"Fog last night was thick as treacle. Who knows 'ow Miss Palmer ended up in the river."

Jack looked exhausted, even though it was only noon. "We questioned everyone in the area, Eliza, down to the drunks and opium eaters. No one saw or heard anything unusual."

"But we ran all over Bluegate looking for Pearl," Higgins protested. "And we shouted her name the whole time. We saw dozens of people, and damn near pushed a couple to the ground."

He shook his head. "It's like you were never there, Professor. Several men we questioned along the dock claimed Luther was with them the whole night. Says he was never out of their sight. I'm sorry, but we don't have any reason to hold Luther North or Billy. Not yet."

Eliza shot a disgusted look at the bookmaker. "They're all lying. And I wouldn't be surprised if Billy had something to with the smuggling of this Indian treasure. After all, he's spent most of his life breaking into people's houses and picking pockets on Oxford Street."

"Bollocks! I been clean for years, and you know it. I won't stay and be insulted." Billy sniffed. "A shame too, seein' how the Doolittles and Graingers are distant cousins."

"That's probably a lie, too." Eliza now stood toe to toe with him.

Billy gave her a wary glance. "If there's nothin' else you need from me, Jack, I'll be off now. And I'd steer clear of any place near me dear mum's lodgings, Lizzie. No tellin' what may come of another visit to the old neighborhood. Day or night."

Higgins took a step towards Billy, while Jack growled, "Are you threatening her?"

"No, just giving Lizzie a friendly piece of advice."

Clapping his bowler atop his head, he turned to go. However he didn't get more than two steps before Eliza planted a swift kick on his behind. When Billy stumbled to the floor, Higgins and Jack hooted with laughter. Scrambling to his feet, Billy spun around to face Eliza, but she slammed the office door in his face.

"If I ever see that lying thief again, I'll run him down with Dad's roadster."

"Just make certain to do it when no constables are around," Jack warned.

Eliza sank in the chair by his desk. On the wall hung a large map of London dotted with colored pins. A red pin indicated a murder had occurred at that location. Eliza stared at the red pin now marking the Thames where Pearl's body had been tossed off the docks.

"Pearl didn't try to kill you or her lover," Eliza said with a defeated sigh. "She wanted Farrow to marry the Duchess of Carbrey. Her money would have helped pay off their debts. Farrow only changed his mind when he found a buyer for this stolen treasure. Now Luther North wants his share, and he's willing to kill for it."

"I did submit the stiletto for fingerprints," Jack said, "but sometimes all we get are smudges. We won't know until the results come back."

Grabbing a folder from the desk, Higgins fanned his damp face. "It's like a furnace in here. You might want to invest in an electric fan." He glanced over at the open window where bright August sunshine flooded in, but not a trace of a breeze.

A knock sounded on the frosted glass of Jack's door. Detective Colin Ramsey peeked his head inside. "Sorry, sir. But there's no one at the desk out here to serve as go-between."

Jack waved his hand. "I sent Charlie off to the morgue."

Ramsey nodded towards Eliza and Higgins. "Should I return at a better time, sir?"

"No, come in. We all want to hear your report."

Eliza smoothed down her hair. Ramsey unsettled her for some reason, especially when he caught her eye and winked – as if he found her presence both challenging and delightful. He'd never actually flirted with her, but more than once she glimpsed the same admiring expression that Freddy always wore. Of course, Ramsey was nothing like sweet, handsome Freddy. Yet there was something intriguing about the young detective. Eliza tried to dismiss it. Besides, she had her hands full with her present suitor. And Eliza suspected Ramsey would be far harder to control than Freddy Eynsford Hill.

Luckily, Colin Ramsey seemed all business while he reported what he found in Pearl Palmer's apartment. None of the information proved enlightening or pertinent to the case.

"But I have two men on Mr. North's trail," he finished.

"So you're keeping an eye on Luther North?" Eliza asked.

"Of course," Jack said. "The next chance you get, Ramsey, see if you can find out if Clyde Winterbottom has ever met with him."

"Yes, sir." He paused. "I did find something interesting. That organist fellow, Thaddeus Smith, warrants looking into. Seems he attended Cambridge, then the Royal College of Music. Both on scholarship."

Eliza sat up in alarm. "If Smith went to the Royal College of Music, it means he knew how to get into that building on Saturday and take a shot at Jack. You did say your men found cartridge shells outside the College."

"The shots came from the Royal Academy of Music, Lizzie," Jack explained. "The Royal College of Music is in South Kensington, about three miles away. Although it's easy to get the two confused."

She shook her head. "Too many buildings in this city are called 'royal.'"

"Miss Doolittle is right to wonder about Mr. Smith, sir," Ramsey said to his boss. "He may not have attended the Royal Academy, but he has performed there five times; the most recent concert was only last month. He certainly would know the layout of the building."

"If he's been there as often as that," Higgins suggested, "he must be a familiar face to the staff and students. Maybe someone recognized him the morning of the wedding."

Ramsey nodded. "I've sent Detective Jeremy to question Mr. Smith about his whereabouts last Saturday. But I've learned something else about him. Although Thaddeus Smith appears to have led an exemplary life, the same can't be said for his younger brother. Philip Smith worked as a bookkeeper for a bank in The City. Convicted of embezzlement nine years ago. Perhaps you remember the case, Inspector?"

"A bookkeeper by the name of Philip Smith?" Jack settled back in his chair, deep in thought. "Back in 1904? That was one of my earliest cases."

"Yes, sir. The brothers were quite close. Philip was killed two years into his prison sentence by one of the other inmates. It's possible this organist blames you. He may have been the one who fired those shots on Saturday."

"Mr. Smith lived in the Transvaal," Higgins said. "He admitted he and his brother learned to shoot as boys. They helped protect the family farm from the Boers. Like Miss Palmer, he has the skill to shoot someone from a great distance. *And* he has a reason to want Jack dead."

"This muddies up things even more." Eliza thought a moment. "Smith may or may not have held a grudge against Jack. He may or may not have shot Jack. Luther North may or may not have killed Pearl Palmer, although I bet he did."

"Neither of which answers the question as to who poisoned the bridal cog that killed Farrow," Ramsey added.

Eliza frowned. "Except Thaddeus Smith did have a reason to kill Farrow. He was the Duchess of Carbrey's favorite before she met Ambrose. Being cast aside no doubt angered him. Now that Farrow's dead, the organist is her little pet once more."

"Is there any way to link Smith with Miss Palmer's murder?" Higgins asked.

Jack turned to Ramsey. "Find out if he ever knew Pearl Palmer."

"Yes, sir." The young detective pulled out his notebook. "Should I bring him in if he does confirm knowledge?"

"Yes." Jack tapped his pencil on the desk. "And send word if Luther North shows up at the British Museum."

"It's high time we visited the Colonel in hospital." Higgins glanced at Eliza. "He might know more about this Indian temple treasure."

"Good idea. Give him my regards. If you do learn anything more, come to me with the information." Jack flashed Eliza a warning look. "Immediately."

"Try to avoid another lark into the East End, Miss Doolittle," Ramsey added. "It's no place for amateurs."

Eliza raised an eyebrow at him. "Given your lack of success so far, Detective Ramsey, it appears it's no place for the police either."

Instead of being irritated, Colin shot her a devilish grin. Damn the fellow. She couldn't predict what he would say or do. In fact, if they'd been alone, she feared he may even have stolen a kiss.

What disturbed her even more is that she might have kissed him back.

"How glorious to see both of you," Colonel Pickering said in his usual cheery tone. "But forgive my appearance. I'm in desperate need of a shave. I look like a castaway."

Eliza thought he looked splendid. She had squealed in delight when they entered the hospital ward and realized how much he'd improved. Wearing his favorite blue plaid dressing gown, Pickering leaned against a barrage of pillows, his right arm encased in a cotton sling.

Higgins caught himself from clapping Pickering on the back in joy. "You seem most presentable to me. But if you like, I'll send round a barber. Should have thought of it myself."

"Can you manage eating this lovely custard?" Eliza uncovered the china bowl on a tray and set it on his lap. "Cook made it just for you. She said it should boost your spirits."

"I say, I shall do my best." He tucked into the rich vanilla pudding sprinkled with nutmeg. The afternoon sunshine brightened his face, which was a relief. For several days after the shooting, Pickering had looked haggard and gray.

Eliza related the story of Pearl Palmer while Pickering ate. He listened intently, except for an occasional comment about food. "This custard is quite excellent. A nice change from what they consider edible here in hospital. I actually dreamed last night about shepherd's pie."

"If you're done scraping the custard bowl, let's have a jaw about this Indian temple business." Higgins pulled up a chair while Eliza sat on the end of the bed. "You mentioned some temple at Farrow's memorial service. I remember Winterbottom, Lady Winifred, and that Indian fellow all weighing in with an opinion. How was this temple discovered? And why was the treasure still there? Seems like thieves would have made off with it long ago."

Pickering dabbed his mouth with the napkin Eliza handed him. "I was visiting friends in the region when the site was discovered. An employee of the Misra Mining Company stumbled across an abandoned Hindu temple while searching for iron fields. Must have given him quite a shock to glimpse the statue of a goddess hidden by all the jungle overgrowth. This fellow had no idea what he'd found, so the local authorities asked me to examine the site and assess its importance." He shrugged. "Even though I'm a Sanskrit scholar, not an archaeologist, I was the closest thing to an expert in the area. I realized immediately it was an intact Hindu temple."

"How old was it?" Eliza asked.

"I was able to date the temple to the mid-fourteenth century. At that time a cholera epidemic wiped out most of the local population, along with the royal family. After that, no one wanted to go near the place and the jungle reclaimed it."

Higgins had a vague memory of reading about the discovery of a Hindu temple in the newspapers a couple of years ago. But if it didn't involve linguistics, Higgins often lost interest. "Where exactly is this temple?"

"Southwest India. Very remote part of the country, primarily used to hunt tigers by the Maharajah and his friends." Pickering had a faraway look in his eyes. "Extraordinarily beautiful, too. Hard to imagine it was once the site of a dreadful plague. After I climbed to the temple's highest level, I saw tigers sunning themselves on a rocky outcrop. Simply marvelous."

"Did you see the treasure?" Eliza asked.

"Part of it. I know something about the layout of Hindu temples, and many have a *toshakhana*, which translates to 'treasure house.' Given the age of the site, it meant that a treasury was likely. Inscriptions on the stones proved that the temple had been dedicated to the goddess Parvati, and we subsequently learned the entire complex was built in honor of a queen, Maharani Lakshmi." Pickering dabbed at his forehead with his napkin. Even in the hospital ward, the day's heat seemed tropical. "I don't know much more about its archaeological significance. Winterbottom is the East Asian expert. Ask him."

Higgins had a list of things he planned to discuss with Winterbottom. "How about Lady Winifred? She's lived in India for thirteen years. Could she give us more information about this temple and the treasury?"

"Perhaps. She and her husband spend outrageous sums on art, jewelry, and antiquities. But Winifred cares less about the history of a piece than she does its aesthetic value."

"You still haven't told us about the treasure," Eliza said.

"I hired local villagers to help me search the site. After three days, we found the entrance to the treasure house. Took us a week to finally make our way inside. When we did, the chamber was nearly impassable, what with the fallen stonework and vegetation. But I was able to see enough to know I had stumbled upon a literal treasure trove."

"How exciting," Eliza said, awestruck. "Was the treasure as magnificent as Pearl Palmer described? Golden crowns, ruby swords, emerald armbands."

"What treasure I did uncover was quite spectacular. After all, the entrance had remained sealed since the cholera epidemic. That made the temple infinitely valuable. And vulnerable. While the jungle had done a splendid job hiding the temple, it wouldn't take long for looters to hear of the discovery. I had to act fast."

"What do you mean?" Higgins asked.

"There are few ancient tombs or temples that have not been robbed over the millennia. This was a rare find, potentially worth a fortune. I wanted the art, treasure, and its historical importance to be preserved. I immediately contacted wealthy investors in Europe, men with a love of antiquities. Baron Ashmore was the first to respond. He bought the rights to recover the treasure, then conferred with the British Museum. They sent Winterbottom to oversee the excavation and cataloguing, which allowed the museum to claim a share."

"That explains how Winterbottom became involved," Higgins mused.

The Colonel nodded. "Both Ashmore and Winterbottom were keen to save the collection from further decay. Several statues had lost their gold leaf patina, and some jewels had come loose from the eye sockets. They had to work fast."

"I'd love to see such a treasure." Eliza's eyes sparkled with excitement.

"Why not ask Clara for a tour of Banfield Manor?" Pickering suggested. "The Ashmore Collection on the estate has the lion's share from the temple. The British Museum kept most of the large architectural pieces and an assortment of jewelry. But the Ashmores have the rest."

"Not quite," Higgins reminded him.

"Ah, you're right. I'd forgotten. The ship transporting the treasure from India to England encountered bad weather off the coast of Ceylon and ran aground. I heard one of the crates holding the temple treasure ended up in the Bay of Bengal."

"I doubt any of it remains underwater," Higgins said.

"That crate was smuggled off the ship with Luther North's help. He was chief engineer. And he brought it to England where he handed it over to Ambrose Farrow. Now the treasure's hidden somewhere in England."

"Waiting for the right buyer," Eliza added. "Or the cleverest thief."

Pickering seemed amazed. "This might explain why Mr. Farrow was poisoned. After all, few motives are more powerful than greed. And men have killed for treasure since the pharaohs built the pyramids."

"Probably why the pharaohs laid a curse on anyone who dared to rob their tombs," Higgins said with a rueful smile. "A shame there wasn't a curse laid on this Indian temple."

"But there is. The Curse of the Cobra. It derives from a legend passed down from the few survivors who fled during the cholera scourge. When the Maharani Lakshmi was on her deathbed, she asked the god Vishnu to curse anyone who stole from the goddess's temple."

"I thought the temple was devoted to Parvati, not Vishnu," Higgins said.

"A number of deities share the sacred space with her. Vishnu is regarded as a great protector. A blue-skinned god, he is often portrayed with the five-headed snake Sheshnag, known as king of the snakes. Many Hindu temples, including this one, are covered with images of them. The cobra is said to bring death upon those who violate the Parvati temple."

"Considering all that's happened since the treasure was discovered," Higgins said, "even someone as civilized as I am might give credence to such a curse."

"If there is, that means Lord Ashmore is in danger." Eliza bit her lip. "Clara, too."

Pickering shifted on the bed, glancing around at the other patients who dozed in the hot room. "It was no curse that killed Richard's brothers. Baron Ashmore's oldest son died in a car accident. He'd been drinking and ended up driving his car into the river. His premature death came as no surprise. The gentleman had a reputation for dissipation."

"What happened to the second Ashmore son?" Eliza asked.

"I heard he died from complications due to syphilis," Higgins said, "which seems like the biggest curse of all."

Pickering sent Higgins a disapproving look. "Don't listen to him, Eliza. The fellow died of scarlet fever."

"Let's not protect Eliza's delicate sensibilities at the expense of the truth."

"Oh, hang my sensibilities, Professor. Where I come from, we all knew some unfortunate who suffered from syphilis." She leaned forward. "I'm more interested in the unexpected deaths of the Ashmores. What did Richard's father die from?"

"Consumption. He'd been ill for years. All the Ashmore deaths are easily explained. The two eldest Ashmore sons made poor choices through the years, and they paid the price. I am glad the present young baron was born much later than his brothers. They had little contact or influence over him while he was growing up." Pickering lay back on his pillows. "I've heard only good things about the young gentleman. Clara's made a fine choice for her husband."

"Lord Ashmore does seem like a wonderful person, which is why I'm worried. If someone is willing to kill over this temple treasure, why wouldn't he be the next victim?" Eliza looked over at Higgins. "Although Smith may have poisoned Farrow out of jealousy, it's also possible he was killed due to the treasure. Certainly Pearl was murdered because of it."

Higgins grew grim. "I wouldn't be surprised if Winterbottom is neck deep in this mess. The problem is how to convince my bull-headed brother and niece to call off the wedding."

"What if Lady Winifred is involved? Colonel, you told us how much she spends on antique jewelry. She might love to get her hands on some of those temple gemstones."

Pickering smiled at her. "Winifred is a notorious spendthrift. Buying her jewels from smugglers would probably cost her far less money. But she's also a superstitious woman. She won't even attend a dinner party if it falls on what the stars decree as an unlucky day. The years she's lived in Africa and India have only increased her respect for omens and portents. Shortly after I was called in to assess the Temple of Parvati, I published a monograph on the site. Of course I included the history surrounding the Curse of the Cobra. Lady Winifred took it most seriously." He chuckled. "Or as she likes to tell me, 'There are more things in Heaven and Earth, Horatio, than are dreamt of in your philosophy.'"

Eliza sat up straight. "Hamlet, Act One, Scene Five." This past spring, a guest at Wimpole Street gave Eliza a copy of *Hamlet* to prepare her for an upcoming performance she was to attend. Enthralled with the story of the Danish prince, she'd memorized every line.

Higgins rolled his eyes. "I shall never hear the end of this play."

"Well, it certainly seems as if this temple treasure is cursed," Eliza said. "Everyone involved in any way with it is now dead. Yes, the old Baron was sick, but he didn't die until after he bought the rights to the Indian temple."

"I suppose," Pickering said. "Although the second son died a month before the Baron did. I believe his death hastened that of his father. The other son died less than a year ago."

"Exactly. The three Ashmore men died only after the temple treasure was bought by the family." Eliza held up her fingers and counted them off. "Then someone poisoned Ambrose Farrow, and Pearl was stabbed. That makes five deaths since the temple was discovered."

Higgins cleared his throat. "Except the next murder attempt was directed at Jack. Unless he's moonlighting as a smuggler, I believe Jack has nothing to do with the temple."

"Quite true," Pickering agreed. "In fact, I was the only one at Jack's wedding who had any connection to the treasure."

Higgins turned to Eliza. "Good grief! How did we not see this?"

"See what? Pickering asked.

"My dear Colonel, the gunman might not have been shooting at Jack." Eliza went cold with fear. "He could have been trying to kill you!"

CHAPTER THIRTEEN

⚬

SHOPPING AND TAKING TEA WERE two of Eliza's favorite activities. After yesterday's exhausting visit to Scotland Yard, they seemed more enticing than ever. Especially if she could combine them with sleuthing.

After their visit with Pickering, Eliza and Higgins discussed how best to continue their investigation into the murders and the temple treasure. Jack may not like them playing detective, but they loathed the idea of Luther North roaming free.

The Professor planned to drop in unannounced on Clyde Winterbottom at the British Museum. Given Higgins's open dislike of the man, Eliza would have enjoyed witnessing that encounter. Instead, she made a telephone call to Taral Misra's wife at the Hotel Russell in Bloomsbury. She'd been intending to stop by for the tea that Mrs. Misra suggested at the memorial reception for Ambrose Farrow. The shootings at the church had pushed the pleasurable outing aside. Except there was a more important reason for the visit now that she'd learned an employee of Taral's company in India had discovered the temple.

Because Colonel Pickering's life might be in danger, Eliza was determined to learn what she could. She felt sick at the memory of Pearl sitting at Bessie's table, weeping about home like a lost little girl. It pained her even more that, like Ambrose Farrow, no one in England mourned her passing. Except for Eliza. But she needed to do more than shed a few tears for Pearl Palmer. Eliza vowed to track down the monster who brutally murdered the girl and tossed her body into the Thames like so much garbage. With luck, taking tea with Taral Misra and his wife later today might provide a few missing pieces of the puzzle.

Until then, Eliza could divert herself with Clara's wedding preparations, starting with a visit this morning to Cartier. She was looking forward to it, and not only due to the Ashmore family's link to the Indian temple. Too much of the past four days had been spent in a hospital, Scotland Yard, and the dangerous streets of the East End.

She and Freddy now waited with anticipation outside Cartier on New Bond Street. Eliza gazed in delight at the glittering jewelry display in the store windows.

"I rather fancy that pocket watch." Freddy pointed to an engraved silver timepiece, its face circled by diamonds. "If I had Lord Ashmore's income, I'd walk out with that tucked in my vest pocket. Although the platinum ruby ring is splendid, too."

"And I believe the diamond and amethyst dragonfly brooch would suit my outfit." The sparkling pin did seem ideal for Eliza's violet fitted jacket and skirt. Sadly she didn't have the funds for such an extravagant purchase, despite her racetrack winnings. However she could probably afford the delicate gold neck chain with a pearl encrusted heart pendant. It would look charming nestled against the white lace of her blouse.

"Whoever imagined Clara would one day shop at Cartier?" Eliza marveled.

Freddy squeezed her hand. "I can hardly believe that little

brat will be a baroness next week. And I'm afraid she'll insist we call her Lady Clara."

"I wouldn't be surprised if she expects us to curtsy."

They smiled at each other. Eliza was pleased for his sister. The Eynsford Hills were a family whose income barely permitted them to keep up the appearance of gentility. Now through a matchmaking miracle, Clara would soon become the 5th Baroness of Ashmore. Eliza suspected marriage into the titled class was sure to make her completely insufferable. Money and position changed people. And if one was as young and foolish as Clara, it shouldn't come as a surprise if sudden good fortune unbalanced her.

A moment later, Eliza was almost knocked off balance as Clara flung her arms about her. "I'm so happy you came. I heard you found another dead body on Monday." Clara stepped back with an amused pout. "I was afraid you'd prefer chasing after murderers again."

Lord Ashmore took Eliza's hand and bowed over it. "I told Clara she was silly to worry. No woman can resist an invitation to Cartier."

Eliza smiled at the young man, who seemed especially sporty this morning in a navy blazer and white summer trousers. "Absolutely. Although after the bridesmaids' gifts are chosen, I'm off to play Sherlock once more."

They all laughed, although Eliza was quite serious. But sleuthing was forgotten once she and Freddy followed Clara and her fiancé into the Cartier store where a tall man in a bespoke black suit waited for them. After introducing himself as Artemis Kressley, he swiftly ushered them past glass display cases filled with jewels. Bright sunlight streamed through the windows, setting the gemstones on fire. Men stood behind each case, speaking in muted tones to clients dressed even finer than they were.

"I wish I was a baron," Freddy whispered to Eliza.

"Oh, I don't know. I prefer this lovely blond fellow on the London Rowing Club. He has the bluest eyes and sweetest smile."

"How I do adore you." Freddy nuzzled her neck, making Eliza giggle.

Clara looked over her shoulder. "We're in Cartier. Behave yourselves."

Properly chastened, Eliza and Freddy followed them into an elegant room with a chandelier sparkling overhead. On a polished ebony table sat two expensive leather cases. Once they were seated, a young man brought a tray of crystal champagne flutes. Eliza relished the idea of drinking champagne at eleven in the morning. Or as her dad would call it, "a glass of fizz".

"Lord Ashmore, Miss Eynsford Hill. Cartier was notified of your wish to select gifts for the bridal party." Kressley said. "I've collected a number of pieces. If these do not meet with your approval, I'll be happy to show you as many others as you desire."

Ashmore grinned. "I daresay I won't be hard to please. Most of my ushers are fellow soldiers in the British Army. They won't expect anything too fancy."

Eliza bit back a grin at the disappointment on Freddy's face.

"Allow me to show you what I've selected for your best man and ushers. Because of your preference for gold rather than silver, all of these pieces are eighteen karat." Kressley opened one of the long leather cases. Atop the velvet lining sat an array of gold signet rings, stickpins, pocket watches, and cuff links. Many pieces included diamonds, pearls, or sapphires. One signet ring boasted a large ruby she was sure had caught Freddy's eye.

"They all appear splendid. I have no idea which one I should select as their gift. What do you think, dear?" Ashmore looked bemused.

Clara cocked her head at the display. "Why not let Freddy choose? After all, he's one of your ushers. If he likes it, I'm sure it will please the others."

"Freddy it is." He pointed at the jewelry case. "Go on, old chap. Choose your favorite."

As Eliza expected, Freddy slipped the ruby signet ring on his finger and watched it glitter beneath the chandelier's light. "This is a ripping fine piece. Simply ripping."

"I told you I wouldn't need much time to choose gifts," Ashmore said with a shrug.

Eliza liked the young baron. An attractive fellow, he boasted few airs and seemed remarkably down to earth for someone who'd just acquired a title and the Ashmore estate. Perhaps being the youngest of three sons, he never dreamed to inherit the barony. Instead Richard Ashmore had joined the Army and lived a less privileged life than his two brothers.

"If you like, we can engrave the gentlemen's initials on the rings, Baron Ashmore." Mr. Kressley closed the leather jewel case. "Would you prefer the best man's ring to be different?"

"Yes, engrave them all. And my best man's ring shall have a diamond rather than a ruby. That was easy." Lord Ashmore lifted his champagne flute with a mischievous smile. "We can sit back and drink while Clara spends the rest of the day making her decision."

"Oh, I may surprise you," Clara said. "After all, girls begin planning their wedding while we're still in the pram. I know exactly what I shall give my bridesmaids."

Eliza raised an eyebrow at that statement. The idea of Clara not wanting to spend endless amounts of time shopping for expensive jewelry seemed unthinkable. "I expected to be here for hours, looking at every earring and necklace in Cartier."

"I would if I were buying the jewelry for myself." She smoothed down her white taffeta dress. "But there's no reason to waste the whole day on my bridesmaids' gifts."

"What a relief." The love-struck baron winked at Clara. "We spent four hours in this very store choosing her engagement and wedding rings."

"Well worth the time." She whipped off the glove from her left hand. "I've never seen a more delightful setting." Clara held out her hand to show them.

Kressley nodded with approval. "A 2.5 carat diamond set in platinum, surrounded by three dozen European-cut diamonds. One of our more modern designs."

"Of course. I'm a modern woman." She gazed at her ring with pride.

"And what have you chosen for your modern bridesmaids?" Eliza asked.

"Something much better than the dreary gift Sybil gave her bridesmaids." Clara threw a scornful look at the cameo pin gracing the lace collar of Eliza's blouse.

"Cameo brooches are lovely gifts," Eliza said. "I was happy to receive it."

"One gives cameo pins to a maiden aunt, not bridesmaids. Unless they're as old as my mother." She gestured at the remaining leather case. "Please open it, Mr. Kressley."

Eliza caught her breath at the dozen gold bracelets on black velvet. Some were gleaming wide bangles, others delicate bands boasting intricate scrollwork. All sparkled with gemstones in varying shades of green, red, and blue.

"It's quite the rage to give bridesmaids a piece of jewelry made in their birthstone. How lucky to have a May birthday, Eliza, since your birthstone is emerald." Clara picked up a gold bracelet dotted with three gemstones. "Poor Lady Tansy. Her birthday falls in January, so I must give her a garnet. Cousin Joanna was born in August and shall receive a peridot bracelet."

"You *have* thought this out." Lord Ashmore beamed at her.

"Of course." She sighed. "Although I regret having to give Gwendolyn Stafford a sapphire bracelet. If only she'd been born in October. She deserves no more than an opal."

Eliza admired the emerald bracelet. "This seems too expensive for a bridesmaid gift."

"Don't be silly. Richard can afford it." She gave him her most adorable smile.

"Whatever my Clara wants." He took her hand and kissed it. "And she has another surprise gift awaiting her at the wedding reception."

Clara looked like a kitten with a nice bowl of cream. "I can't wait."

Eliza and Freddy exchanged curious glances. "What is it?" he asked his sister.

"It's a surprise, silly. Not even I know what Richard plans to give me. But I suspect the gift includes a lovely gemstone or two."

Her fiancé laughed. "She's right. It's an Ashmore tradition. Every baron takes his bride out to the folly in our garden maze and presents her with a family heirloom."

"What's a folly?" Eliza felt confused.

"An ornamental building found in parks and gardens," he replied. "Ours is in the shape of a Hindu temple. My great grandfather had it built when he returned from India."

"Just before I throw the bouquet, Richard will escort me to the folly." She giggled.

"I never realized so much jewelry was handed out at weddings." Eliza gestured at the bracelets on the table. "Those alone must cost a small fortune."

"Don't complain. This will be the first piece of emerald jewelry you've ever had. And if my brother doesn't find a way to become rich, it may be your last."

"I say, Clara. Really." Freddy scowled at her.

"All I need do is select which bracelets I prefer." She laid them on the table in a row. Clara swiftly chose one design for the bridesmaids, and another for Eliza and Tansy, her respective maid and matron of honor. "These bracelets have more gold than the others."

"Thank you, Clara. And Baron Ashmore. But it does seem extravagant."

"Please call me Richard. Freddy is soon to be my brother-in-law, and you are one of Clara's closest friends." He threw Freddy a sly glance. "And may soon be related by marriage. We're almost family, so let us drop the formalities. Are we agreed, Eliza?"

"If you say so, Richard."

Kressley finished replacing the bracelets in the case. "I saw how you were looking at the bracelet," Clara said. "Well, you can't have it until next week's rehearsal dinner. Cartier is going to box it up splendidly, isn't that right?"

"Of course, Miss Eynsford Hill."

Eliza decided this was a good time to bring up the cursed temple jewels. "It's hard to believe some beautiful jewels are said to be cursed."

"Don't be silly." Clara gave Eliza a playful shove. "What nonsense."

Kressley cleared his throat. "Your friend is correct, Miss Eynsford Hill. In fact, one of the most famous cursed jewels was acquired by Pierre Cartier only a few years ago."

"He's speaking about the Hope Diamond." The baron took a sip of champagne.

"Is the Hope Diamond in the store right now?" Clara looked worried.

"No need for concern." Kressley locked the leather case. "Mr. Cartier sold the diamond two years ago to Mrs. Eva-lyn Walsh McLean, a rich American client. Mrs. McLean believes unlucky objects turn lucky for her. If so, she shall be fortunate indeed."

"He's exaggerating," Ashmore said. "Three generations of the Hope family suffered no ill fortune at all while they possessed the diamond."

Artemis Kressley pursed his lips. "I believe Francis Hope was forced to sell the diamond twelve years ago because he faced financial ruin."

"Due to Hope's penchant for gambling," Richard said. "And I doubt there's a family in Britain who doesn't have at least one inveterate gambler in their family tree."

"It also spelled misfortune for the French royal family, sir. The Capets owned the diamond for a number of years."

"I rather blame the political missteps of Louis XVI and Marie Antoinette for that."

Both men laughed. "You are correct, sir. However I've been in the jewelry business a long time, and the Hope Diamond is not the first cursed gemstone I've come across. Although none were as spectacular." Kressley looked at the women who hung on his every word. "It is an immense blue diamond, over forty-five carats. Roughly the size of a walnut or pigeon's egg."

"Cor, it must be worth a fortune." Eliza couldn't imagine a diamond of that size.

"Where did it come from?" Freddy asked.

"India," Ashmore replied. "There's a lurid story about a Frenchman who plucked the diamond from a temple statue in the seventeenth century. Supposedly the diamond was an eye on a statue of the Hindu goddess Sita. The stolen jewel is said to bring bad luck to whoever owns it. Some people claim the Frenchman was torn apart by wild dogs when he later visited Russia." He laughed. "Although I suspect the fellow died in his bed of old age."

Kressley stood. "I shall take these cases to my office and

make arrangements for their dispersal as wedding gifts. If you'll be patient a few minutes longer, I will return with the sapphire ring the Dowager Baroness asked us to remount. Excuse me."

After he left, Clara shivered. "That cursed diamond sounds positively wretched. Thank goodness your family only collects paintings, Richard."

Eliza turned to Ashmore. "But I heard the Ashmores collect all sorts of art and antiquities. Many of them from India."

"True. My family is rather enamored of East Asian art. Four generations of Ashmores served with the British Army in India, starting with my great grandfather in 1782. My great grandfather brought the first pieces of Indian artwork back to England. And my grandfather and father carried on the tradition. Our collection is so extensive, an entire wing at the family estate is devoted to it. If you're interested, I'll show you and Freddy when you come to Banfield Hall next week for the wedding." He chuckled. "I'll even point out the cursed pieces."

Clara turned in horror to her fiancé. "You own cursed objects? How dreadful."

"I'm teasing, my sweet. There are no such things. Although some say a curse is why the firstborn Ashmore son either never becomes the baron, or only lives a short time after acquiring the title. How else to explain such dismal luck." When Clara let out an alarmed cry, Ashmore quickly took her hand. "My darling, remember I was not the firstborn Ashmore son."

"But what if we have a son?" Clara wailed. "The curse will claim him!"

"Hush, sweetheart. I'm beastly sorry. I don't believe in curses."

"You ought to, Richard! Just ask Eliza."

"Me?" She stared at them both. "I don't know anything

about—"

"You've been to two weddings this past month, both ending in violence," Clara said. "The couples *must* have been cursed. How else to explain it?"

Eliza felt compelled to warn the baron. "Richard, there may be a grain of truth to this curse. I spoke to Pearl Palmer before her death, and she said Ambrose Farrow was poisoned due to his connection with the Temple of Parvati. Pearl was convinced she was in danger, too. The Colonel told me yesterday that while the British Museum took some jewelry and statues, your family owns most of what was found at the temple. He also mentioned the Curse of the Cobra."

"A cobra!" Clara grabbed Richard's hands. "You must get rid of whatever your family took from the temple. If you don't, something terrible will happen at our wedding. What if someone is killed by a cobra? They're poisonous."

"Darling, there are no cobras slithering about England. Besides, no one knows why Mr. Farrow and Miss Palmer were killed. And why did someone shoot Detective Inspector Shaw at his wedding? Shaw has no connection to the temple." He looked at Eliza. "Correct?"

"We have reason to believe Colonel Pickering may have been the real target. After all, he was the one who first informed your father about the temple treasure." She paused. "Although someone may have wanted to kill Jack, too."

"Exactly. As far as I'm concerned, Shaw is the obvious target. He's a policeman. More than one criminal in London must hold a grudge against him."

"It makes sense to me," Freddy piped up, "but Eliza does love a mystery."

"Not if it involves the murder of innocent people. That's why I'm calling on Mr. and Mrs. Misra today. An employee from his family's company discovered the temple. I'm hoping to learn more about the treasure, and who might be involved with it."

"I can tell you about Misra's involvement," Ashmore said. "He's acting on behalf of some Maharajah. They want everything from the Temple of Parvati returned to India." His voice hardened. "I was kind enough to show him the collection, but it only strengthened his resolve. Now Lady Winifred plans to bring him to the wedding, where I am sure he will be a nuisance."

"This Indian man cannot be allowed to ruin our wedding." Clara shot to her feet. "I won't have it. You must call him right this minute and tell him to stay away."

He tugged her back down. "Lady Winifred is an old family friend, and she's been shepherding the Misras through London society during their visit. Mother would be outraged if we insulted her by excluding them."

"What shall I do, Eliza?" Frantic, Clara turned to her. "I'll be frightened out of my mind someone will try to poison Richard or shoot at me. I'll never be able to enjoy my wedding."

"I never meant to frighten you, Clara." Eliza regretted not discussing this with Lord Ashmore in private. "And while I don't believe in curses, someone may be killing people over this treasure. You must both be careful."

Clara didn't look convinced. "There is a wedding curse. Eliza, you must put the fear of God into this Indian man at tea today. I know you can do it. I've seen you frighten Professor Higgins sometimes. But be careful. He could be the murderer."

Eliza sighed. She'd hoped for no more than a nice cup of tea, a discussion about the temple, and a glimpse at Mrs. Misra's saris. She did not fancy browbeating anyone.

"Don't worry, Clara. I'll have your big brother along for protection."

"I'm going to tea with you?" Freddy asked. "I thought you

planned to ask Sybil."

She straightened the collar of his beige linen jacket. "I've changed my mind. I may require the impressive muscles you've acquired from being a member of the rowing club."

"True." Freddy looked quite pleased. "There's no such thing as a physically weak oarsman. I'm strong enough to protect you from any man."

Eliza hoped so. Especially if Taral Misra was the killer.

CHAPTER FOURTEEN

⚘

THE EMERALD EYES OF A tiger stared down at her from the mantel.

Eliza gazed back in fascination. In fact, she could hardly keep her attention on her hosts. Taral and Basanti Misra had transformed their suite at the Hotel Russell into an enchanting wonderland. The ivory enameled statue of the tiger was just one of many exotic objects decorating their rooms. Colorful rugs in dazzling patterns blanketed the floor, azure blue and purple pillows nestled atop low-lying divans and chairs, gold figurines sat on side tables, and peacock feathers graced enormous brass vases in every corner. A carved silver elephant stood guard by the bedroom door, while a garland of pink and orange flowers decorated the mantel beneath the green-eyed tiger.

The suite was also as fragrant as Covent Garden's flower market, although she couldn't identify the scents. Even their manservant was colorful. He wore a simpler version of the Indian clothing Taral Misra sported: a high-necked long jacket and turban. Except Taral's jacket was made of fine green silk, and his turban was jeweled.

But Basanti was truly eye-catching. Today the lovely young woman wore a turquoise sari and veil heavily embroidered in gold. The bold colors beautifully accented her brown skin and large dark eyes, as did the intricate gold headpiece strung across her forehead. Eliza was especially fascinated by two gleaming gold bracelets in the shape of a snake which wound about her wrists and forearms. She wondered if they were cobras.

Eliza held out her teacup for a refill. Unlike those she was used to, this teacup had no handle. Even the orange teapot, painted with swirling designs, did not resemble those seen in English homes. Everything about this tea was different, including the fact that she was drinking something called chai. The spicy hot beverage was so marvelously sweet, Eliza feared she might drink the entire pot by herself.

"What is that wonderful scent? I thought I knew the fragrance of every flower."

"But it is not a flower, Miss Doolittle. It is incense of sandalwood." Basanti nodded toward a gold dish placed at the foot of a brass statue. Eliza noticed a tiny stream of smoke wafting above it. "Sandalwood is said to calm the mind and spirit."

Freddy held up his cup. "I say, this is quite good. What's in this chai?"

Taral took a sip before answering. "Masala chai is Indian black tea brewed with milk and sugar. We add spices such as ginger, cardamom, nutmeg, cloves, and cinnamon."

"Do not forget the pepper," his wife said. "Pepper is what makes the tea so – how do you say? – pungent."

Taral nodded. "It is our custom to serve chai to guests. Although we also drink it many times throughout the day. I am glad you enjoy it."

"Ripping." Freddy took another sip. "Eliza has a sweet tooth. I wouldn't be surprised if you have to brew another pot."

"But you must have as much tea as you wish." Taral clapped

his hands. "More chai."

When his manservant hurried off, Eliza didn't protest. The Misra couple had been most gracious from the moment Eliza and Freddy arrived, ushering them to carved wooden benches that circled a low round table. Trays filled with sweets of sugar, milk, coconut, and various nuts had been brought out immediately.

"This is all quite wonderful," Eliza said. "I don't even feel as if I'm in England."

Basanti smiled. "My devoted groom packed up much of our house in Bombay. It is my first trip away from India. Taral was afraid I might suffer from what you call home-sickness."

"I know how strange one can feel in a foreign land," he added. "And I care only for her happiness. Bringing our things with us seemed the best choice. And I, too, am grateful we are surrounded with our possessions from home. I find myself missing India more every day."

"Will you be leaving soon?" Eliza asked.

"My business is not yet completed." Taral sighed. "That is most vexing. It is my dearest wish to be back in Mysore after the rainy season ends."

"In October, the maharajah holds his first tiger hunt of autumn," Basanti said.

"I say, you hunt tigers?" Freddy's eyes grew wide with excitement. "What a thrilling sport. Have you actually killed one?"

"Oh yes. In fact, I have had the pleasure of shooting three tigers." Taral's voice held a hint of pride. "A most dangerous business, and not one any man should take lightly. Being a good marksmen is mandatory. Otherwise it is the tiger who takes the hunter down."

Was Taral expert enough with a gun to have shot at Jack and the Colonel? "Are you ever frightened hunting tigers?"

Eliza asked.

"Yes. But to shoot such a magnificent beast as it charges straight towards you is an experience like none other. Last year, I also bagged a panther."

"Dash it all. I would love to go to India and hunt tigers."

Eliza raised an eyebrow. "I didn't even know you hunted, Freddy."

"I don't. Although I did go to Cubby Parkinson's shooting party last year. Good old Cubby, he hosts the best weekends."

"What did you shoot?" Taral regarded him with renewed interest.

Freddy seemed ashamed to answer. "Grouse."

The Misras were too polite to show their amusement or contempt. Just then the manservant carried in a fresh pot of chai, and Eliza breathed in the heady scent.

"Are you attending the wedding of Mr. Winterbottom this Friday?" Basanti asked. "I am most looking forward to it. Lady Winifred said it will be a traditional English wedding, and I wish to observe your customs. It seems the Duchess of Carbrey's wedding was not traditional."

"That's true. Few weddings end with a murder." With a contented sigh, Eliza sipped her chai. She wondered if she could figure out how to brew this herself back at Wimpole Street.

Taral cocked his head at her. "I have heard your cousin is a police inspector, Miss Doolittle. Has Scotland Yard learned anything that may lead them to the killer?"

Pleased he'd presented her with the opportunity to discuss the murders, Eliza nodded. "Professor Higgins and I were at Scotland Yard yesterday. The only connection between the murders of Mr. Farrow and Miss Palmer may be artwork stolen from a temple in India." She put her teacup back on the table. "The Temple of Parvati."

Startled, Basanti turned to her husband and murmured something to him in Hindi. He whispered something back.

"I am surprised to hear Scotland Yard has been apprised of the Temple of Parvati," Taral said. "Of course, my people are aware of how it has been looted by your countrymen."

"I hope you don't blame me. I had nothing to do with it," Eliza said quickly.

"Oh, we would never assign blame to someone such as yourself." Basanti patted Eliza's hand. "You are a fine lady, Miss Doolittle. But those who should have known better treated this temple with much irreverence. That weighs heavy upon all of us, but especially my husband."

His face now set in a somber scowl, Taral looked like a displeased Indian king in his tall jeweled turban. "The theft of the temple is a stain upon my honor."

Eliza was puzzled by his comment. "Colonel Pickering said the temple was discovered by an employee who works for your family's company."

"It is I who discovered the temple, Miss Doolittle," Taral said.

Now it was Eliza's turn to be surprised. "I had no idea."

"My father is Vijay Misra, the owner and founder of Misra Iron and Steel. All of his sons are therefore his employees. And my three sisters have married men who work for the company."

Basanti took her husband's hand. "It is one of the most important steel companies in the world. To be a Misra is to take pride in such a legacy."

"Even as a boy, I knew I wanted to work for my father and the company he built." Taral straightened. "The best way to serve him was to become a scientist. I attended St. Xavier's College in Bombay and the Indian Institute of Science in Bangalore. For years I thought of nothing but my studies, and I was proud the day I became a mineralogist. My first job for the company was to discover new iron fields, and I was successful at it. But during one of my expeditions in southern India, I came upon a hidden temple. One that had lain untouched for centuries."

"So you called in Colonel Pickering to confirm the discovery?"

"I did no such thing, Miss Doolittle. I went to the local authorities. It was their responsibility to contact the proper people. I assumed these would be fellow Indians who were scholars and archaeologists. But I did not have time to sit around while the village elders decided who to send for in Bombay. I returned to searching for iron. Not for many months did I learn that a retired British colonel had been brought in to see the temple. And that through him, a rich family in England had taken over the temple and all its treasure." His voice trembled with anger.

"Colonel Pickering only did what was asked of him," Eliza said. "He meant no harm."

"But he did a great deal of harm! It was to the British in Bombay and Calcutta that your colonel gave the news of the discovery. And then he informed his rich colleagues in Europe, to see which of them was willing to fund the looting of the temple."

"Colonel Pickering feared thieves would find the temple and take whatever they liked."

He gave a bitter laugh. "Instead the English did exactly that."

The atmosphere in the hotel suite had turned tense and unpleasant. Eliza suspected it might be time to take their leave, which she regretted. She hoped to have a look at Basanti's saris first. When she nudged Freddy with her foot, he quickly put his own teacup down on the table.

"Do you know who is more to blame than Colonel Pickering or the British?" Taral continued. "Myself. I should not have left the temple without exploring it first. All I saw were stone buildings and a few statues buried in jungle vegetation. How was I to know the goddess's gold and jewels lay beneath my feet?" He bowed his head. "I should have protected it from the thieving hands of outsiders. Instead I abandoned it to greedy liars. I have shamed myself and my family. And I must find a way to make amends."

Basanti turned to them. "He will have no rest until the holy treasure is returned to India."

"Is that why you came to England?" Eliza asked.

He raised his head and gave her a mournful look. "I have spent many hours at the British Museum and with Lord Ashmore, explaining why the treasure should be returned. My efforts have not borne fruit, but I refuse to leave until honor has been served."

Eliza felt uneasy. Was murder one way to avenge Taral Misra's honor?

Even Freddy seemed uncomfortable. "Perhaps you're unaware of this, but Lord Ashmore is to marry my sister. I must say, he appears to be a most decent chap."

"Then he should act like it," Taral snapped.

"What I think Freddy means is that you might be able to convince Lord Ashmore to give part of the treasure back," Eliza added.

"I did not come here to only retrieve part of the treasure." He scowled at her.

"Isn't that better than nothing? Is there anything in the treasure more sacred to the Indian people? If so, that's what I would ask for."

"The temple was built centuries ago by the king in honor of his beloved wife and queen, Maharani Lakshmi," Basanti said. "The goddess Parvati was her protectress and six statues of Parvati were taken from the temple. Two were made of gold, two of ivory, and two of stone. It is a great sacrilege to steal statues of the goddess. They should be returned."

Eliza smiled. An idea was beginning to form. "Anything else?"

"A life-size gold statue of the queen which Taral says is most glorious. A large ruby is set in her forehead, while the eyes are blue diamonds."

"Like the Hope Diamond?"

Taral appeared startled that she'd heard of it. "Yes, but not as large."

"The Hope Diamond is said to be cursed. Colonel Pickering mentioned a curse connected to the temple as well."

"Sacred temples and tombs are protected by such things, Miss Doolittle," he said. "Many ancient writings warn that to steal from the gods will bring down the sufferings of a curse. But the temple has been untouched for six centuries. It is too soon to know if there is a curse attached to its desecration."

"Some people might disagree. The Colonel says the Temple of Parvati was protected by the Curse of the Cobra." Eliza pointed at Basanti's gold bracelets. "I see you're wearing snake jewelry. I was wondering if those are supposed to be cobras."

Basanti crossed her arms, hiding the bracelets from view. "Images of serpents are held in high esteem in my country."

"Hindu temples are the palaces of our gods and goddesses, Miss Doolittle." Taral's expression grew more severe. "They are protected by numerous images of animals. The cobra is one of many. But I will concede the five-headed Sheshnag is a powerful ally of Vishnu and should not be taken lightly."

A long silence followed as the Misras stared at Eliza and Freddy.

The friendly atmosphere had turned chilly. "I don't hold with curses myself," Eliza said, "but I wouldn't blame people for thinking a curse was connected to the Temple of Parvati.

Look at what happened to Ambrose Farrow. And we learned he was involved in stealing part of the temple treasure when it was being delivered to England."

Basanti said something in Hindi, but Taral hushed her.

"The Duchess of Carbrey's driver served on that ship. He helped smuggle the stolen treasure to England," Eliza continued. "He swears it's hidden away somewhere in London."

Taral and Basanti exchanged glances. "This is troubling," he said.

"So are the murders of Ambrose Farrow and his mistress." Eliza took a deep breath. "And it's possible the shooting at my cousin Jack's wedding had nothing to do with him. The person may have been aiming at Colonel Pickering. After all, the Colonel is involved with the temple, too. The killer could be taking revenge on anyone responsible for the treasure leaving India."

"I hope you are not implying I had anything to do with these acts of violence." Taral's anger had returned.

Eliza wasn't certain what Taral Misra's role was in the deaths and shootings, but she wasn't foolish enough to say such a thing right now. "People might look at these deaths and suspect the Temple of Parvati is the reason behind it. Others may believe the temple treasure is cursed."

Freddy exchanged a knowing glance with Eliza before saying, "My sister would gladly get rid of anything connected to the temple."

"Exactly," Eliza added. "Why don't you make a list of what you want returned from the Ashmore Collection? And mention there is a curse attached to the stolen treasure."

Taral sighed. "Lord Ashmore does not believe in curses."

"It's not Lord Ashmore who needs convincing," Eliza replied. "But if his bride Clara thinks the temple treasure is cursed, she'll be throwing it out the day after the wedding."

Basanti leaned close to Taral. "My dear husband, we may

be able to retrieve the most sacred pieces."

"But there is still the British Museum," he said grimly. "And now I learn about this additional treasure smuggled off the ship."

"One step at a time, Mr. Misra. Work on Lord Ashmore first. Perhaps Colonel Pickering or Lady Winifred can use their connections to influence the British Museum. As for the smuggled treasure. . ." Eliza shrugged. "That's best left in Scotland Yard's hands."

"Perhaps you are right, Miss Doolittle," Taral said with a sigh. "If I must resort to a deceptive tale of temple curses, then I shall do so."

"You're a brilliant girl," Freddy whispered in her ear.

Basanti seemed as relieved as Eliza. "Would you like more chai, Miss Doolittle? Or perhaps another tray of sweets?"

"Even I have had enough sugar for the moment. What I would like is to see your wardrobe of saris."

"Of course." The young woman gracefully rose to her feet. Eliza gazed in admiration once more at her flowing skirt of turquoise and gold, cropped blouse, and long sash draped over one shoulder. Eliza's purple outfit and white feathered straw hat seemed dull by comparison.

"And you must choose your favorite. It will be my gift to you for helping my husband."

This prospect so excited Eliza, she nearly ran ahead of Basanti on the way to her bedroom. All this talk of temple treasure, tigers, and blue diamonds held little meaning to Eliza. The prospect of having her own sari seemed far more wondrous. And if anyone tried to steal that sari, she'd blooming well put a curse on them.

CHAPTER FIFTEEN

❦

BEFORE HIGGINS QUESTIONED CLYDE WINTER-
BOTTOM at the British Museum, he thought it wise
to first inform his mother. Especially since he now suspected
the museum curator of being involved with smuggling. And
possibly murder. He knew his niece and brother would turn
a deaf ear to anything Higgins told them. But his mother –
being a Higgins by marriage only – was a sensible woman.
She might regard the suspicions swirling around Winterbottom as reason to delay the wedding. And her opinion carried
far more weight in the family than his.

But when he arrived at her flat on the Chelsea Embank-
ment, the maid looked at him as if he were a marauding
Viking.

"Madame is occupied with her committee, Mr. Higgins,"
Daisy said. "She does not wish to be disturbed."

Damn. He'd forgotten his mother hosted her weekly
meetings on Wednesdays. An august group of ten ladies
with a fondness for opera and fund raising, the Royal Opera
Matrons were responsible for holding endless luncheons,
benefits, and balls to help fill the coffers of Covent Garden's opera company. Apparently staging new productions
of *La Traviata* and replacing the costumes for *Don Giovanni*

required ridiculous sums of money that only respected society matrons could wring out of London's titled and wealthy opera lovers.

Standing in the foyer, he heard the chatter of women accompanied by the clink of spoons against teacups. He almost turned tail and ran, but the image of Winterbottom at the altar beside his niece gave him courage. "I wouldn't interrupt her meeting without cause."

Daisy looked as though she didn't believe that for a second.

"If you don't tell her I'm here, I'll burst in unannounced." He wagged his finger at the diminutive servant. "And don't think to stop me. I'm a foot taller than you, and heavier by five stone. You wouldn't stand a chance."

Since the maid had worked for his mother for over a decade, Daisy knew him far too well. "What should I say is the reason for your visit, Professor?"

"Her niece Beatrice's wedding. I have urgent news about the groom."

She went off with a long suffering expression. Higgins felt pleased with himself, until his mother marched down the entry hall towards him. She looked as forbidding as the sternest headmistress, albeit one who was outfitted in mauve silk and French lace.

"Mother, I didn't expect you to come to me," he said. "I thought we would speak privately in your sitting room."

Her gaze was positively withering. "I have no intention of allowing our conversation to last longer than a minute. And since you have the bad manners to disrupt my committee meeting, you deserve to remain in the foyer like a delivery boy."

"I forgot about the opera committee. I would never have come if I remembered."

"Hah!"

"But this is important. I've learned something disquieting

about Clyde Winterbottom."

"Unless you are here to tell me Mr. Winterbottom has run off with the Queen, I can think of no reason which justifies disrupting my business with the Royal Opera Matrons."

"I have reason to suspect Winterbottom of being involved with the theft of a temple treasure from India."

Her face remained impassive. "I'm waiting to hear something shocking."

"How can you not find that shocking? The fellow may have helped smuggle artwork out of the subcontinent."

"Good grief, Henry. Much of the artwork in museums and great households was probably acquired in ways best left unexamined. Your own father purchased a painting reputedly stolen from a King of Navarre. It currently hangs in Charles's study."

"If simple theft seems excusable, how about murder?" he asked in a stage whisper.

She lifted an eyebrow. "Mr. Winterbottom is now murdering people, is he? I do find that shocking. I would have thought he had little energy left after all his preening and posturing."

"You're not taking me seriously. If you won't believe me, perhaps you should know that before Miss Palmer was killed, she warned Eliza not to trust Winterbottom."

This got a reaction from his mother, but not what he desired. "As if I would trust anything that wayward woman said." Her quiet voice now held an edge. He may have gone too far. "I read about Miss Palmer's demise in the papers, so I shall not speak ill of the dead. But do not ask me to lend credence to the statements of such a person."

"What if Winterbottom is involved in her murder? Or Mr. Farrow's."

"What if he's Father Christmas? You have as much proof of that as the others."

"I may not have proof, but there is suspicion surrounding him. I don't want to wait until after he's married Beatrice before any scandalous truths emerge. Mother, you should talk to Charles about postponing the wedding. He won't pay me any mind, but he'll listen to you."

"Have you lost your reason along with what's left of your manners? I shall do no such thing." She reached up and straightened his tie. "And unless you have evidence that Mr. Winterbottom is guilty of any wrongdoing, I expect you to play the dutiful uncle tomorrow at Chelsea Old Church. Charles and Frances will have your head stuck on Tower Bridge if you misbehave at their daughter's wedding. And I shall assist them."

His frustration grew by the minute. If he didn't find out anything incriminating during his talk with Winterbottom today, it seemed the unsavory chap would indeed become part of the family. "I have grave misgivings about Winter-bottom. Beatrice could not have chosen worse."

For the first time since he arrived, his mother's expression softened. "I, too, hoped she would have settled on a more agreeable gentleman. However, Beatrice has made her choice and nothing you nor I could say will dissuade her." She patted his arm. "Despite your appalling manners, I am happy to see you are such a concerned uncle."

This didn't make him feel better. "Thank heaven I've only two more weddings to attend this summer. All this exposure to brides and grooms have put me in a foul mood. And who-ever is behind these murders seems as elusive as Professor Moriarty. I feel quite off balance."

"Henry, leave the crime solving to Detective Shaw." She turned to go, then paused. "You will be attending Lord Ashmore's wedding next week at his estate. When you're at Banfield Manor, please stay away from the garden maze. It is said to be filled with all manner of twists and turns. And you, my boy, already seem hopelessly lost."

After his futile visit with his mother, Higgins was relieved to pass the ironwork gates where he stopped to admire the British Museum's iconic Greek columns and frieze. London's thick fogs had left their mark. The mid-afternoon sun showed every bit of grime clinging to their curves and lines. The museum held fond memories for him, especially the endless hours spent researching in the Round Reading Room. And he never tired of strolling through the Graeco-Roman, Egyptian, and Assyrian galleries. Since he was a phoneticist, the cuneiform tablets and Rosetta Stone received particular attention. But there was no time for such pleasures today.

Instead, he needed to focus on this temple treasure business. He had the foresight to send a note to the Asian department, requesting Winterbottom meet him at the grand staircase at two o'clock. Pickering informed him that Winterbottom was hired by the museum shortly after he graduated from Cambridge. This meant Winterbottom had enjoyed a respectable – though not exceptional – career. Upon acceptance into the Royal Asiatic Society, he was named curator, with special interests in Tibetan and religious history in India. And he'd written a book, *History of Sculpture in Southeast India*, which had been fairly well received. Still, more than one younger colleague at the museum had received greater respect and attention than he had.

The museum was crowded and Higgins rushed to make his appointment. He was surprised to see Clyde Winterbottom already pacing near the huge ceremonial urn in the entrance hall. He had expected Winterbottom to keep him waiting. The fellow threw him a forced smile, which exaggerated the lines around his mouth and eyes. At forty-five, he was simply too old for Higgins's niece. With his pomaded mass of graying hair, high creased forehead, and slight paunch, Winterbottom seemed Alfred Doolittle's senior.

He was also a bit of a popinjay. Higgins noted that Winterbottom's ash gray suit was clearly bespoke. And his vest looked to be made of Belden satin; the silver chain of a full hunter looped from one of its pockets. Winterbottom's boots were polished to a high sheen, reflecting the light from the entrance hall's windows. No doubt he would soon give his bride grief about a servant's lack of studious care for those boots.

"Professor, how good to see you." Winterbottom shook his hand with a firm grip, almost too firm. "Didn't expect to see any of Beatrice's family today. After all, the wedding ceremony is tomorrow."

"Yes, the momentous event is almost upon us. As a long time bachelor, I wondered if you were getting cold feet." Higgins paused. "You still have a chance to back out of the wedding."

"Why should I back out? I leave that sort of disgraceful behavior to men such as Ambrose Farrow."

He shrugged. "If one has second thoughts, best act on them before the ceremony."

"But I am not having second thoughts, although I suspect you would like me to." Winterbottom's expression turned wary. "Have you come here to convince me to jilt your niece? If so, I must disappoint you."

"Deeply in love, are you?"

"Don't be ridiculous. But I would never humiliate Beatrice so publicly. It would put me in quite a bad light. And unlike you, Professor, I have long wished to marry. I only required the appropriate young woman." He smiled. "And the appropriate family."

"Ah, yes. My brother does seem to have a bright political future ahead of him."

"Sir Charles may reside at No. 10 Downing Street one day soon."

"If so, he will be in a position to wield his influence." Higgins wanted to smack the smug grin off Winterbottom's face. "I wouldn't be surprised if his future son-in-law benefits greatly from such influence. But I hope you're not marrying my niece only for the favors her father might throw your way."

"I have no interest in your hopes, Professor Higgins." He narrowed his eyes. "Beatrice tells me her family barely tolerates your eccentricities. I see now what they mean. But not even I imagined you thought a man in my position marries only for love."

"Oh, I never took you for a man in love."

Winterbottom nodded at the museum visitors streaming about them. "I suggest we continue our conversation somewhere less congested, especially if we're going to discuss romantic love. I have a reputation to maintain, and would rather not be overheard discussing a topic this absurd."

"I've as little interest in romance as you," Higgins replied as both men began to walk through the crowd. "But I am interested in my niece's welfare."

"As am I. And Beatrice is just as devoted to my welfare."

Higgins remained silent. His mother was correct. Nothing would prevent this blasted marriage. Charles seemed relieved his oldest daughter would at last be married off, although Higgins suspected his sister-in-law Frances was less enthusiastic about the match. Then again, Beatrice was neither a beauty nor a wit. And her Uncle James had fostered a religious fervor in the young woman that sometimes made her company insufferable. If Winterbottom hadn't been introduced to Beatrice, he would have been replaced by a man just as callow and ambitious. Or more likely, there would have been no further candidates for her hand.

"If talk of romance hasn't brought you here today, what has? Would you like a private tour of Baron de Rothschild's Waddesdon Bequest Room? Or perhaps Lawrence's Carchemish artifacts."

"I'm far more curious about the Temple of Parvati you helped excavate in Mysore."

"There's not much I can show you at this time. The Parvati exhibit will not be available for public viewing until November. At the moment, museum staff are still engaged in cleaning and restoring the pieces, especially those covered in gilt." Winterbottom waved at a museum guard. "If you're too impatient to wait until November, I advise asking the Baron of Ashmore for a tour of his collection. He made off with most of what was excavated in Mysore."

"That's not what I heard. Apparently some of the treasure was lost in a shipwreck in the Bay of Bengal."

Winterbottom sniffed. "I didn't realize archaeology was a passion of yours."

"I have a passion for many subjects. Archaeology, language, music." Higgins glanced over at him. "Murder."

His smile vanished. "I fear I can only enlighten you about archaeology. I'll leave language, music, and murder to you." Winterbottom's pace increased. Higgins guessed the man wanted to find a way to get him out of his hair as soon as possible.

"It appears you've led me to the world of the Greeks," Higgins declared as they entered a gallery filled with marble statues and a great frieze. "The world of Phidias, to be more exact."

"A genius sculptor, one of the great artists of the ancient world." For the first time, Winterbottom appeared humbled, or as humble as he would allow himself to be. "As I'm sure you're aware, these are the Elgin Marbles. So named because the 7th Earl of Elgin spent eleven years having the statuary, panels, and frieze carefully removed from the Parthenon, Propylaea, and Erechtheum. After shipping them to England at great cost, he sold the marbles to the government for far less than he had expended on them. All because he wanted the government to pass the marbles on to the British Museum, which they did. They've been safe here for nearly a century."

"A great deal of controversy has swirled around the Elgin Marbles," Higgins said, admiring yet again a glorious sculpture of a horse's head. "Many people believe Lord Elgin had no right to strip the Parthenon of its artwork and have it carted off to England."

"Would you rather they have remained in Greece?" Winterbottom asked with obvious disgust. "The Turks were running things then, you know. The Ottoman fools used the Parthenon as a military fort. Idiotic bastards accidentally set off dynamite within the temple itself. That's why it is now partially in ruins. Before the bloody Turks, Athena's temple stood intact!"

Several museum visitors broke off their admiration of the frieze on the wall to cast worried glances at Winterbottom. He moved closer to Higgins. "And if any statuary fell off the walls of the Parthenon, do you know what the Turks did? They burned the marble for lime. So don't tell me again how Lord Elgin had no right to bring the marbles to England. He saved the marbles. If not for him, who knows how much of all this would have survived." He swept an arm to encompass the entire gallery.

"My good man, I only mentioned the controversy surrounding Lord Elgin and the marbles, which you can't deny. And I wouldn't be surprised if the museum faces another public outcry when the Parvati temple objects are put on display."

"Art belongs to those who recognize its worth and know

how to preserve it. Like Lord Elgin did. And Lord Ashmore."

"You discussed the temple at Mr. Farrow's memorial," Higgins said. "Lady Winifred claimed there are powerful people in India who want the artifacts and temple treasure back."

"Hang that fool Maharajah she's so fond of. A considerable amount of money went into this project, along with our efforts. And we obtained permission from the local authorities. Why should we send anything back? Without us, the temple would have rotted in the jungle. It was a miracle we stumbled upon it in the first place."

"We? I thought an employee of the Misra Mining company found it."

"A happy accident." Winterbottom steered Higgins towards a bench where no one would overhear. "They didn't know a thing about how to prevent thieves from looting. There were occasions when we had to fight off thugs while we worked."

"Such a find must have given quite a boost to your career." Higgins watched for the man's reaction and was rewarded with a shrewd look.

"Yes. And I'm not going to waste this chance." He sat on the bench, hands clasped in front of him. "I should be farther along in my career. But I don't possess a toadying nature or blue blooded connections. If I did, I'd be running this museum, and have a knighthood besides."

Higgins took a seat beside him. "That could soon change. When the Parvati exhibit opens, you may become as celebrated as Charles Dawson and his Piltdown Man discovery."

"I'd be far more celebrated if the exhibit included the temple treasure that Baron Ashmore has. All the museum owns are columns, several statues, a few jewels. Ashmore has statues of gold, not gilt. Along with ivory figurines, jewels, scimitars and swords."

"A pity part of the treasure was lost in the shipwreck."

"Yes, a great pity," Winterbottom said with a strange smile.

"Perhaps you'll be able to convince Lord Ashmore to donate part of his collection to the museum," Higgins suggested.

"I've asked him many times. He's always refused. But he may be more amenable if Sir Charles makes the request. As a member of Parliament, my future father-in-law is associated with men of great power and influence. That makes him powerful and influential as well. I have a feeling Lord Ashmore might reconsider once I marry Sir Charles's daughter."

Higgins felt even more dispirited. "I assume that's one of the reasons you're marrying Beatrice. To use her father's influence to advance your career."

He shook his head. "You're wrong. It's not one of the reasons. It's the only reason."

The two men looked at each other. Higgins didn't bother to hide his disgust. "I didn't think you'd admit it. I expected at least a pretense that you had some regard for the girl."

"Come now, Professor. Beatrice is not a beauty. And her conversation is as scintillating as cold oatmeal. But her father is an important man, and she lives in fear of being a spinster. Especially since her younger sister seems likely to be engaged by the end of the year. Beatrice would marry a Welsh coal miner if it meant putting a 'Mrs.' before her name. And I am a far better catch than a coal miner."

"It rather depends on the coal miner," Higgins replied. "Does Beatrice know you don't love her?" He tried to control his anger. "Is she aware you don't even like her?"

Winterbottom shrugged. "I have no idea what Beatrice is aware of, aside from her prayer books and fondness for collecting butterflies. Fortunately, she is an amenable creature. Once we're married, I'm certain she will do exactly as she is told."

"This seems destined to be a most disagreeable marriage."

"Is there any other kind?" He got to his feet. "If you'll excuse me, Professor. My wedding is tomorrow, with a honeymoon to follow. Since I don't expect to enjoy either, I hope to at least enjoy my work until then. Good day." He left the gallery without a backward glance.

As soon as the curator was gone, Higgins headed for the exit. The more distance he put between himself and Winterbottom the better. But before he could enjoy the fresh air and sun, someone called his name. Detective Colin Ramsey stood just outside the museum entrance.

"Your housekeeper told me you'd come to the museum, Professor."

Higgins panicked. "Did Colonel Pickering take a turn for the worse?"

"No, it's about the dagger that killed Miss Palmer. Or more correctly, the stiletto. As you know, the handle was dusted for fingerprints."

"The Yard found a match so soon?"

"There was one legible mark, more than half a thumb print, with a distinct whorl. Luckily, we printed Mr. Grainger and the other men we questioned that night along the docks."

"That means you know who killed Pearl Palmer."

Ramsey nodded. "Yes, we do. All we have to do is find him."

"Well, who was it, man? Tell me."

"The scoundrel we suspected all along," Ramsey said. "Luther North."

CHAPTER SIXTEEN

❦

ONLY A MURDER COULD LIVEN up this wedding. Eliza felt ashamed for thinking such a terrible thing, even in jest. But the morning had been duller than warm milk. She gazed about Chelsea Old Church, each pew filled to bursting. Over half the wedding guests were friends and members of the Higgins's family, each attired in expensive ensembles meant to exhibit their refined good taste. If only they didn't act so proper. How in the world did someone as lively as Professor Higgins come from such a stiff-necked family? She suspected he had his delightful mother to thank for that.

And she never realized how important Higgins's oldest brother was. Apparently being an MP from Hereford meant people spoke in hushed voices around you. The groom's guests consisted of a handful of museum associates and nervous relatives. Eliza actually observed Winterbottom's aunt drop a curtsey when introduced to Sir Charles Higgins on the church steps. This sent the Professor into such gales of laughter, his top hat fell off. Now he sat beside Eliza, engaged in a running commentary about the wedding guests. Mrs. Higgins sat on his other side pretending to be exasperated with her son. But she smiled too often for that to be true.

Freddy fidgeted on Eliza's left, looking like the most dashing man here in his crisp morning coat, striped trousers, and waistcoat. Eliza was just as pleased with her outfit: a peach silk charmeuse gown draped in lace with a line of pearls running down either side of the slim skirt. A Tam o'Shanter crown dress hat covered in peach taffeta silk – embellished with three white aigrette feathers – perched atop her head. Once again, Eliza wore the cameo brooch given to her by Sybil, which perfectly matched her ensemble.

Looking about the crowded church, Eliza thought only Basanti Misra wore a more becoming outfit this morning. Basanti's sari of saffron yellow was so beautiful, it took one's breath away. Eliza smiled to think of the sari which Basanti had given her two days earlier. She wished she had been daring enough to wear it to the wedding.

"Winterbottom's finally emerged," Higgins announced when the groom and best man walked out from the vestry, followed by the Reverend James Higgins. "He looks even more like a pinch-faced ferret than usual. What an atrocious fellow."

A woman in the pew directly in front of them turned around. "I say, Henry, you must keep your voice down. His relatives are certain to hear you."

"I'm sure they're already aware he looks like a ferret. He behaves like one too, although I'm insulting ferrets by saying that."

The woman, introduced earlier as Higgins's sister, sighed. Eliza thought the slender brunette looked nothing like Higgins or his brothers. Instead, she seemed a younger version of Mrs. Higgins. "Mother, can't you control him? He will embarrass us all."

She gave a tiny shrug. "Does your brother ever do anything else? Now hush, Victoria."

"Henry Arthur Higgins, you are an uncivilized beast,"

Victoria hissed.

"Coming from you, I take that as high praise."

She shook her head so vehemently, several beads on her Merry Widow hat flew off and bounced on the floor. Victoria scowled even more before facing front again.

"Few things are more fun than teasing Vicky, unless it's teasing James." Higgins nodded towards the altar with a chuckle. "Look at my sainted brother up there in his starched white surplice and church robes. I've seen statues of saints that appear less self-righteous. No doubt he wishes he could call down a lightning bolt to get rid of me."

Reverend Higgins bore a striking resemblance to the Professor; both men were taller than average, clean shaven, and with straight brown hair. Only James wore spectacles and was much thinner than his younger brother, almost gaunt.

"Is your brother ill?" Eliza asked.

"Good grief, no. The fellow is always fasting. Sometimes James forgets that he's not Roman Catholic. Such a pity. I'm sure he would love to be Pope."

Mrs. Higgins turned to them. "James has decided he will not eat any food unless it is mentioned in the Bible. His cook has had difficulty providing three scriptural meals every day."

Higgins snorted. "Let's hope Charles serves a fatted calf at the wedding breakfast."

"I pray this latest dietary regimen does not last long," his mother added. "He's grown much too thin and it's bound to affect his health."

"I agree. He looks like a scarecrow. Then again, my brother does have straw for brains."

Victoria glanced over her shoulder. "If you don't keep your voice down, I will smack you with my fan."

"I'd like to see you try."

"Henry, Victoria. That is quite enough," Mrs. Higgins

said. "The two of you haven't behaved this badly since the nursery, when you tormented Nanny Fletcher. Stop such ridiculous behavior. Neither of you are to spoil Beatrice's wedding."

Victoria was about to protest, but the look on her mother's face obviously changed her mind. Higgins sat back with a wide grin.

The organ music changed to a more stately hymn. Eliza craned her neck to glimpse Thaddeus Smith seated at the church organ. While a perfectly fine musician, she had no idea why every well-born bride and groom insisted on hiring him as organist. Did they wish to gain the Duchess of Carbrey's approval? If so, the effort was wasted today. Both the Duchess and Eliza's father were at the Windsor stables where their racehorse was being readied for an upcoming race. Since she was part owner, Eliza should have been with them. But the prospect of a Higgins wedding was too good to miss. A shame it had turned out to be a tedious affair so far.

Having forgotten her fan, Eliza waved the wedding program to cool her face. Since it was the end of August, the weather had turned warm – and wet – again. Rain streamed down the church's stained glass windows. The earlier fine mist had become a steady downpour. Eliza felt sorry for the bride, who no doubt feared her gown would become wet and muddy. At least the church looked festive: garlands of white flowers hung along the pews, ropes of foliage were wrapped about the columns, and a bridal arch, studded with white lilies, stood before the altar. Clyde Winterbottom waited beneath it.

"I detest that man," Higgins muttered. "He is sure to make her extraordinarily unhappy."

"Maybe you should have tried to talk her out of it," Eliza said.

"Impossible. The foolish girl cannot be reasoned with. And Charles is desperate to marry her off." He lowered his voice again. When Higgins wanted to be discreet, he was fully capable of doing so. "If his children make respectable marriages, it benefits his political career. This snake of a museum curator apparently qualifies as a son-in-law, although the idea of being linked to him by marriage is a horror."

Eliza sat back, now uneasy. Higgins was genuinely worried for his niece. She observed the unsmiling groom at the altar. Winterbottom's thin prominent nose and suspicious gaze did call to mind a ferret. And Pearl had sworn he was not to be trusted. She felt the urge to stand up and protest the entire wedding. But at that moment, Thaddeus Smith unleashed the first notes of the wedding march. Everyone noisily rose to their feet.

Eager to see the bridal party dresses, Eliza was disappointed when the first bridesmaid appeared. Having met Beatrice at Ambrose Farrow's memorial reception, she knew her to be a somber young woman. Not surprisingly, her five bridesmaids all wore slightly different ivory chiffon dresses with high collars and pleated skirts. Instead of hats, short tulle veils flowed about their shoulders. Each carried a single white calla lily and a small white prayer book, which Eliza knew to be their gifts from the bride. Of course, she hadn't expected anything as daring as Sybil's suffragette themed wedding. But given the money and prestigious career of Sir Charles Higgins, more fashionable gowns might have been in order.

The music swelled, and excitement rippled through the church at the bride's first appearance. Freddy was taller than Eliza and could easily see over the heads of the standing guests. "What does her gown look like?" she whispered.

"It's white," Freddy replied.

Higgins laughed. "Did you expect her to wear red?"

When Beatrice walked past arm in arm with Sir Charles, Eliza saw the wedding dress was indeed white. It was also the height of fashion – if the year had been 1890. Like her bridesmaids, Beatrice's tightly corseted gown displayed a high neckline and bloused sleeves. In fact, had the sleeves been a tad fuller, they would have resembled the leg o' muttons popular in an earlier generation. Despite its old-fashioned appearance, the gown was made of expensive Liberty satin and mousseline lace. The pleated dress also boasted a train that streamed at least fifteen feet behind her. And Eliza could find no fault with the voluminous tulle veil or the orange blossom diadem that crowned it. The diadem matched the bride's orange blossom bouquet.

Eliza was relieved to see Beatrice smiling, something the groom had yet to do. She prayed there wouldn't be another last minute decision to ditch the bride at the altar. Higgins would be pleased, but Eliza dreaded witnessing yet another hopeful woman having her heart broken and her pride dashed to pieces.

Mrs. Higgins leaned over to whisper. "Beatrice is wearing her mother's wedding gown. Frances had it altered to make it more fashionable."

Having recently learned her parents never married, Eliza felt sad that she would not be able to wear her own mother's wedding gown.

When the bride reached the altar, Winterbottom stepped forward to greet her. For the first time, a smile lit up his face. But it did not seem motivated by love, joy, or gratitude. Instead it seemed like the smile of a wily gambler who had just had his winnings handed to him. She didn't blame Higgins for his low opinion of the man.

As everyone sat down once more, Eliza threw a quick glance behind her. She was startled to see Jack and Colin Ramsey standing at the back of the church.

She tugged Higgins's sleeve. "Why are Jack and Detective Ramsey here?"

He glanced over his shoulder. "Damned if I know. But I can hazard a guess. They're probably expecting disaster to strike once more."

A wave of fear ran through Eliza. "That's dreadful. Do you think so as well?"

"As far as I'm concerned, this wedding is the worst possible disaster. That social climbing prig is about to become family. I'd prefer a good honest murder to that."

Despite Higgins's misgivings, the ceremony and photographs occurred without mishap. Due to the heavy rain, the bridal party posed for photographs inside the church; afterward, everyone made it safely to the elegant Hotel Café Royal on Regent Street via chauffeured cars. A dining room had been reserved for the Higgins-Winterbottom wedding breakfast. Seeing that conniving rascal's name attached to his own set Higgins's teeth on edge. He doubted he would enjoy a morsel of the costly meal his brother and sister-in-law had arranged. Higgins just hoped he could restrain himself from poisoning the groom's wedding punch.

Eliza and Freddy seemed to be enjoying themselves. Apparently they'd made friends with the Indian couple, Taral and Basanti Misra. The four of them had chatted nonstop since their arrival at the restaurant. Indeed, the Misras were stealing attention away from the bride and groom. Beatrice's wedding gown couldn't possibly compete with Basanti Misra's diaphanous yellow sari, which wafted behind her like the plumage of an exotic bird. She was also draped in more gold and gemstones than he had seen outside the windows of Cartier or Tiffany. As for Winterbottom, he looked like a bank clerk when compared to Taral Misra in his turban, gold brocade jacket, and white silk pants. A shame Higgins couldn't have attended the Misra wedding in India. It must have been a spectacular occasion.

"Enough with your brooding." His mother tapped him on the shoulder with her fan. "There's nothing to be done now except enjoy the breakfast."

"How can I? It will be like eating at a wake."

"Stop carrying on." Victoria joined them. "You act as if Beatrice was your daughter."

"She's *our* niece. And your grand-niece, Mother. The girl deserves better."

The two women exchanged long suffering glances – yet another time when his sister and mother joined forces against him. Certainly they looked remarkably alike this morning; Vicky's goldenrod lace gown complemented his mother's paler silk taffeta. As the Misras also wore gold and yellow today, Higgins wondered if a secret missive had gone out telling guests to wear the same colors.

"She may be our niece," Vicky said, "but let's not pretend the girl has ever been our favorite."

Mrs. Higgins sighed. "I fear poor Beatrice has never been anyone's favorite."

"Only because she makes no effort. Beatrice has no clever talk, and cares little for fashion or music. Nor is she a blue-stocking. I have never heard her utter a word about politics." Vicky gave a careless shrug. "If she's made a dreary marriage, she has only herself to blame."

"I blame Charles," Higgins said. "If he wasn't so bent on becoming prime minister, he'd think twice about handing his daughter over to that cold-blooded cretin."

He frowned at Winterbottom, who now escorted Beatrice to the center table reserved for the bridal party. Ropes of white roses and orange blossoms draped the chandelier over-head, matching the table's centerpiece. Higgins noted the place cards, shaped like wedding slippers, were also trimmed with orange blossom rosettes.

"If Charles's instincts are this terrible when it comes to choosing a spouse for his children," Higgins continued, "he'll be an atrocious prime minister."

"I pray the breakfast lightens your mood," Mrs. Higgins said. "Come along, it's time we all sat down."

"I'm not sitting with the family. Bad enough I showed up for this debacle. I won't give the marriage further sanction by sitting too close to Winterbottom the Weasel."

"And here I thought he was a ferret," Vicky said as she and their mother went off arm in arm.

As he scanned the crowded dining room, Higgins spied Thaddeus Smith conducting a small chamber group in the corner. In addition to his duties as church organist, Mr. Smith was also providing music for the wedding breakfast. Unfortunately, there were so many guests chattering in the dining room, the violins and flute could scarcely be heard.

"Why are you hovering by the door? Do you plan to skulk out before we've even toasted the bride and groom?"

Higgins turned at the sound of Charles's voice. It didn't raise his spirits to see his brother James standing there, too. "I only wish Beatrice had skulked out of the church." Higgins paused. "*Before* she said her vows."

"Droll as always." Sir Charles chuckled. "And rude. But I expect nothing less from you."

His oldest brother possessed an alarming measure of self-confidence. Higgins wasn't certain why. Charles Higgins was not especially intelligent; his academic career at Cambridge had been lackluster, and he boasted few athletic skills. But he did possess a razor sharp memory which rivaled Eliza's. Charles never forgot a face, a name, or a single detail he'd ever witnessed or overheard. Higgins suspected his brother had risen so far in the political world due to that skill of 'remembering' embarrassing things about his colleagues. A distinct advantage, indeed.

"You are the only person here who is not happy Beatrice is at last married." Charles sniffed the white rosebud pinned to the lapel of his morning coat. "If you had children, you'd understand how important it is to secure their future with a good marriage."

"I agree. What a pity Beatrice doesn't find herself in one."

His brother James shook his head. "Why do you persist on being so insulting?"

"I prefer to think of it as being honest."

"James, don't let him trap you into defending yourself. Henry's expertise is language, and he will use your own words against you. Best to simply pray for his exasperating soul."

James shot Higgins a most un-Christian glare.

Higgins was once more struck by how different his brothers were from each other. Unlike James, Charles was a physically robust man. Although shorter than his younger brothers, Charles had a commanding presence that easily intimidated. His bushy mustache and sideburns had turned dark gray, and he had been balding for years. But like Alfred Doolittle, the fifty-year-old politician seemed to possess the energy of a man half his age. Charles was also a difficult man to upset. Even Higgins had to admit there was something to admire about his eldest brother's cool composure. When they were growing up, Charles was the only one in the family resistant to Higgins's teasing. Of course, Charles had the advantage of being ten years older.

"Aren't wedding breakfasts limited to just close friends and family?" Higgins asked.

"As if you have much experience of weddings." Charles laughed.

"Our brother is an important man," James said. "His circle

of friends and his sphere of influence is much wider than ours. It is only fitting he honor these connections."

"Don't you sound like a proper toady. Soon you'll be bowing to him."

James flushed. "If you ever behaved like a decent gentleman, I would be struck dumb."

"Perhaps I should attempt to do so, if only to shut you up."

"You are a shameful boor, Henry. I won't submit myself to this any longer." James marched off to the table where his wife waited with obvious resignation.

"James gets rattled too easily. I blame his eating habits." Charles turned to Higgins. "Do you know he's confining himself to biblical meals now?"

"He's far too sanctimonious. And his self regard is so inflated, I wonder he doesn't take flight like a balloon."

"To be fair, I daresay all three of us think highly of ourselves." Charles lifted an eyebrow. "Some of us with more reason than others."

"Speaking of a high self-regard. . ."

Both men laughed.

"I may not know much about weddings, Charles, but more people are attending this breakfast than the first session of Parliament. Including the church organist."

"Frances insisted Mr. Smith play at the wedding. Seems the fellow is quite in fashion this season, like wristlet gloves and French waistcoats. I figured I'd get my money's worth by having him conduct the music at the breakfast, too." He lowered his voice. "Also Smith is once more the favorite of the Duchess of Carbrey. Remaining on Minerva's good side is always wise."

"He's to be the organist at the Ashmore wedding," Higgins said.

"Hardly surprising. As I said, he's the latest fashion. I also heard Smith's parents were once in service at Banfield

Manor. I believe the father was a groundskeeper."

"Mr. Smith told me his father farmed in the Transvaal during the first Boer War."

"That may be true," Charles said. "The Smiths were servants of the Ashmores, not their serfs. They probably took advantage of the opportunity to homestead in South Africa. No doubt the war convinced them to return to England. I do know Thaddeus Smith attended Cambridge. He was one of several young men whose education was financed by Lord Ashmore, the elder. I hope the new baron is as generous as his father."

"I wasn't aware you knew the old baron."

"I didn't. As an alumnus of Cambridge, I make it my business to be kept apprised of important people with ties to the university. If the most powerful baron in England shows an interest in certain individuals, I take note. The Ashmore family must think well of this musician. I suspect it will benefit my career if I do likewise."

"You could have given lessons to Machiavelli." Higgins gestured at the table where Eliza, Lady Winifred, and the Misras sat. "I understand including guests who might further your political career, but what possible use are Taral Misra and Lady Winifred?"

"Lady Winifred introduced Winterbottom to Beatrice last year at a charity function. I wanted her here because of her husband, Sir Ian Ossler. When Lord Curzon was Viceroy of India, Sir Ian was Curzon's favorite on his staff. Curzon's political star is rising, and he may sit on the Cabinet soon. When he does, it could help my cause to have Lady Winifred or her husband put in a good word for me." Charles shrugged. "Assuming Sir Ian ever leaves India. I've heard he and Lady Winifred are having financial difficulties. He's probably not avoiding England so much as he's avoiding his English creditors."

"And Taral Misra?"

"Misra Steel is expanding its marketing headquarters around the world. Misra Steel means jobs. Jobs help get men elected to Parliament. I would trade thirty of our relatives to have Taral Misra as my guest. Lucky for me, Lady Winifred is acting as the couple's chaperone while they're in London."

Leave it to Charles to find a use for even those guests he'd never met before. Still, Higgins couldn't get rid of a nagging concern over his niece. "Let's be frank. You must know Clyde Winterbottom is filled with little more than ambition and envy."

"How does that make him different from every other man here?"

"Hang your cynicism. Winterbottom not only doesn't love Beatrice, I think he actually dislikes her. That cannot be acceptable to you or Frances. If it is, both you and your wife make me ashamed to know you."

"Calm down, Henry. We are well aware he's not marrying for love. Neither is Beatrice. My daughter wants the status and respect being a married woman will give her. This dour chap will serve as well as any other." Charles's expression turned icy. "But if Winterbottom ever humiliates my daughter or causes her grief, I will destroy his career. And then I shall destroy him. Now excuse me, I have to propose a wedding toast."

It seemed Charles was more formidable than even Higgins had guessed. His brother might make a fine prime minister after all.

Although he swore he couldn't choke down any breakfast, Higgins found himself eating with as much gusto as Eliza. The breakfast began with chilled sherbet glasses filled with fresh melons, peaches, and pomegranates, all dipped in sugar. This was followed by clams on ice, sweetbreads, mushrooms on toast, a green salad, and broiled squab. The breakfast concluded with coffee, accompanied by frozen custard with blueberry compote. Each table also held silver dishes of bonbons circling a large centerpiece of delicate white freesia and maidenhair fern. And of course, endless glasses of punch and champagne were available for the wedding toasts.

Higgins couldn't find fault with any of it. Then again, the Café Royal was famous for its kitchen. He also caught sight of a table filled with boxed and beribboned slices of wedding cake for guests to bring home. He'd best keep an eye on Eliza when they left; she was sure to take more than her assigned slice.

"This custard is heavenly," Eliza said as she spooned the last of her dessert.

Higgins had snagged a seat at her table, sparing further conversation with his relatives. While Taral Misra discussed politics with Higgins and Lady Winifred, Eliza answered Basanti's numerous questions about English wedding traditions. Freddy paid little attention to anything but the food until he began entertaining Taral with the finer points of rowing.

"I do not understand why English brides carry only orange blossoms," Basanti mused. "Your country grows many delightful flowers. In India, we adorn our wedding ceremonies with water lilies, orchids, marigolds, lotus, lady's slipper, and jasmine."

Eliza reached for a bonbon. "Orange blossoms represent good fortune."

"Something this marriage will need in abundance," Higgins muttered.

Beside him, Lady Winifred chuckled. "If you continue in this vein, Professor, I shall feel quite guilty about introducing Beatrice to her new husband."

"You should."

She glanced at Winterbottom holding court at the bridal table. "I heard he distinguished himself at both Eton and Cambridge and no doubt expected his career to grow with each passing year. Except the chap has abominable social skills."

"Frankenstein's monster was probably a warmer fellow."

"Exactly. One must know how to make the right personal connections, and to understand when to be ingratiating or clever or pleasant when it's called for. Winterbottom has no aptitude for that. And he's highly disliked by fellow members in several professional societies."

While not surprised, the information frustrated him. "I fail to understand why any of you thought Winterbottom was an acceptable husband for my niece."

"I hate to be blunt, but Beatrice was well on her way to spinsterhood, which would have made her as bitter as Winterbottom. Perhaps marriage will make the girl less tense and guarded. Certainly Clyde's new status as Sir Charles's son-in-law should lessen his envy." Lady Winifred gently elbowed Higgins. "And if there are children, it may be the best thing for them both."

Higgins groaned at the prospect of offspring. But at that moment the bride and groom rose to their feet, distracting him.

"I believe they're about to head to a hotel suite upstairs and change into travel attire," she said. "The couple is driving to Broxbourne for their wedding night. I've been told a family member has lent them their country home."

"My aunt and uncle," Higgins said glumly.

"Do you know the groom has bought himself a shiny new car? I caught a glimpse of it outside, a white two-seater with black leather seats and brass trimmings. Quite expensive."

"No doubt purchased with Beatrice's dowry."

"You can't blame him for showing off. His father-in-law is

an important man.”

“Are we expected to cheer when that wretch drives off into the sunset with my niece?”

“Oh, it’s far too early for sunset, although this wedding seems like it’s lasted for hours.” Lady Winifred adjusted her emerald pin which was fashioned in the shape of an elephant. “Thank goodness we can leave once they’ve had a proper send off. A pity the rain hasn’t let up.”

The Café Royal’s tall windows revealed a gloomy sky and pouring rain. “The weather seems perfect for the occasion,” Higgins grumbled.

“If this silk gets wet, my outfit will be ruined.” She looked down at her green fitted gown festooned with small bows. “I hope Luther is able to bring my car to the front entrance.”

Higgins sat up in alarm. “Did you say a man named Luther is your driver?”

Distracted by pulling on her gloves, Lady Winifred waited a moment to reply. “Yes. Luther North.”

“Why in blazes is he your chauffeur?”

She looked puzzled. “Why not? My former driver left recently. I was forced to place an advertisement to fill the position, and Luther was the first to apply. I don’t see why I shouldn’t have hired him. After all, he worked for your friend, the Duchess.”

Higgins felt his frustration grow. “Actually he worked for Ambrose Farrow.”

“Except Her Grace bought that lovely car Luther drove Mr. Farrow about in. I did ring her up before I hired the fellow. She said he might be rather sullen but had no problems with his driving. I’ve had no issues either. Then again, he’s only been in my employ three days.”

“I must find Jack.” Higgins stood.

Eliza stopped mid-sentence in her conversation with Basanti. “What’s wrong?”

"Luther North is here."

"What!" She scrambled to her feet quicker than he had. "We must find Jack."

"I believe I just said that."

To the clear consternation of everyone else at the table, Higgins and Eliza left without a word of explanation. "When is the last time you saw Jack or Detective Ramsey?" she asked.

Higgins had trouble leading the way around waiters, tables, and milling guests. "I haven't seen them since we arrived."

"I noticed them by the kitchen door when I sat down. After that, I was too busy eating to pay attention. What the devil is Luther North doing here anyway?"

"He is now Lady Winifred's chauffeur."

"Are you joking?" Eliza shouted so loud, a dozen people turned in her direction. "Doesn't she know he killed Pearl Palmer?"

"How would she know that? We haven't spoken to her since the murder. And the police only learned yesterday that Luther's prints matched those found on the stiletto."

She scanned the noisy crowd. "It shouldn't be difficult to find two policemen. Except for the waiters, they're the only men here not decked out like trick ponies."

"Maybe they're outside. It's almost time for the bride and groom to leave."

"Oh, hang good manners." Eliza pushed through a knot of people until she stood by one of the windows. "Jack Shaw! Jack, it's Eliza! I need to talk to you! Jack!"

Guests threw offended looks at her. But Higgins wanted to hug Eliza in gratitude when Jack and Detective Ramsey wove their way around the guests to join them.

"What happened? What's wrong?" Jack took her arm. "Are you all right?"

Colin Ramsey stood in front of them, as if he feared an

imminent attack.

"Luther North is here," she said.

"How do you know that?" Jack asked.

Higgins repeated what Lady Winifred had told him. Both detectives looked troubled. "If he's outside with the other cars and drivers, he won't be hard to miss," Jack said. "But we need a good description of Lady Winifred's car."

"I agree." Ramsey frowned. "At least three dozen are lined up along Regent Street, and even more are parked around the corner."

Higgins and Eliza led them back to their table where Freddy, Taral, Basanti, and Lady Winifred were still sitting. All four of them looked worried.

Freddy took Eliza by the hand. "What's wrong? Why were you shouting for Jack?"

Lady Winifred bit her lip. "I hope this has nothing to do with my driver. Professor Higgins appeared rather upset that I'd hired Mr. North."

"Please describe your car," Jack said.

"A red Renault with brass fittings."

"Should be easy to spot," Ramsey said to his boss.

"Is your driver wearing a uniform, Lady Winifred?" Jack asked.

"Dark navy with silver buttons."

Jack smoothed back his hair in a nervous gesture. "Right. Everyone stay here."

Just then, Sir Charles tapped his punch glass with a knife to gain the guests' attention. His wife sat beside him, looking exhausted. "Frances and I wish to thank you all for coming to our daughter's wedding," he said once everyone quieted down. "The happy couple are about to depart. Sadly, the weather is not cooperating, but if we gather by the Café Royal entrance, we should be able to bid them a proper farewell."

"Now we'll have to fight through this mob," Jack muttered.

He and Ramsey rushed for the front entrance. Eliza and Higgins followed, but a group of excited young women at the foot of the hotel stairway blocked their way. On one of the steps stood Beatrice, who now wore a cinnamon brown walking suit and small matching toque. With a shy smile, she waved her orange blossom bouquet. This elicited a fit of giggles from the young women below, especially the bridesmaids.

"Blimey, she's about to toss the bouquet," Eliza said. "If we don't hurry, we'll never get past the ladies once they start fighting over it."

Given her brilliance at pushing through crowds, Higgins allowed Eliza to lead the way. This time Freddy hampered her efforts by hanging onto her arm like a sea urchin. Without warning, a collective scream went up and a startled Higgins found himself rocked from side to side. All around him, young women reached for the orange blossoms headed straight for them. He nearly lost his footing in the resulting melee. When the commotion subsided, Higgins was shocked to discover he had somehow caught the bridal bouquet!

Eliza howled with laugher as a bridesmaid snatched the flowers from him with an unladylike curse. Embarrassed, he shoved Freddy towards Eliza who continued to laugh all the way to the front entrance. When they got there, Jack and Ramsey were nowhere to be found. He assumed they were outside hunting for Luther. But wedding guests now crowded about the door, chatting and making certain they had their umbrellas. Higgins could barcly move.

"Let the groom through, please!"

Like the sea parting for Moses, everyone stepped to either side of the foyer as Clyde Winterbottom strode past. A gray raincoat concealed most of his suit, but he was obviously outfitted for motoring. After adjusting the goggles perched on his hat, Winterbottom tugged on a pair of kid leather driving gloves. Higgins wagered they cost at least three quid.

Higgins stepped into the groom's path. "See here, old chap. You'll have to wait before you depart. The police are out there looking for someone."

Winterbottom sneered at him. "You and your Scotland Yard friends can play detective tomorrow. This is my wedding day, and I'm the only one who gives the orders."

"Orders?" Eliza asked. "It's a wedding, not a war."

"Well, it's *my* wedding, and I shall do as I please."

"And you've married *my* niece, so I suggest you treat her well," Higgins shot back.

Winterbottom moved closer, his voice menacing. "I shall treat Mrs. Winterbottom any way I wish. And if you persist on irritating me, I may treat her roughly tonight. I don't think you want that on your conscience, *Uncle* Henry."

Eliza gasped. "You're a right bastard, you are."

"Get out of my way, Miss Doolittle. You too, Professor."

Furious, Higgins itched to boot him in the arse, but stepped aside.

"I must retrieve my roadster," Winterbottom announced to the guests in the foyer. "To prevent my dear wife from getting drenched, I intend to drive it to the front entrance. But someone's black Daimler is taking the reserved space for my vehicle. See that it's removed by the time I return." He nodded to the doorman, who opened the glass entrance door.

Winterbottom exited, opening his large umbrella as soon as he was outside.

"Despicable man."

"I'm sorry, Professor." Eliza patted his shoulder. "I hear they're honeymooning by the sea. Maybe he'll drown."

"That's rather harsh, darling," Freddy chided.

She looked at him in disbelief. "If you were that awful, I'd drown you myself."

The minute the doorman closed the door, Detective Ramsey flung it open again. He didn't look happy.

"I take it you didn't find Luther," Higgins said with a sinking heart.

"There must be fifty motorcars and drivers out there. Jack sent me inside to call the Yard for more men." The detective ran in the direction of the lobby.

Before Eliza and Higgins could follow him, the bride and her attendants surged into the foyer. Beatrice caught sight of Higgins. "Thank you for coming, Uncle Henry."

"Be careful, Beatrice." He stepped in front of her. "And if Winterbottom doesn't treat you right, you must leave him straightaway."

"But he has always treated me with perfect manners." The young woman appeared weary. "You worry as much as my mother. I don't understand why." She looked over his shoulder. "Oh, there's Clyde now."

A two-seater white motorcar pulled up to the curb, and Beatrice hurried out the door. Higgins and Eliza trailed after her. They huddled beneath the Café Royal's green canopy, the rain now coming down harder than ever.

Higgins grabbed Beatrice by the arm. "I want to warn you that your new husband may not remain so well mannered. He may have pretended to act decently while he was courting you. Now that you're married, things may change."

"*He* may change," Eliza added.

"This has grown tiresome," Beatrice said. "I'm about to leave on my wedding trip, and you're both delaying me. Now let me go to my husband. I don't want to keep him waiting."

Suddenly, a deafening explosion filled the air. Pieces of metal rained down, and a thick plume of smoke billowed and steamed. Eliza and Beatrice screamed and threw their hands over their heads. Higgins was knocked to his feet. Shocked and in pain, he looked over at the curb.

The roadster – and its new owner – had been blown to bits.

CHAPTER SEVENTEEN

Ⅱ

THE MOURNFUL TOLLING OF THE bells above St Martin-in-the-Fields seemed to mock Higgins. He wasn't sorrowful at all, nor was he alone in his lack of grief. Among the gathering of mourners in the church, no one wept except for his niece. And he wasn't certain if it was a tear Beatrice dabbed at with her handkerchief, or a bit of face powder fallen into her eye. Winterbottom's relatives seemed unmoved, while Higgins's family looked more mortified than anything else. It was bad taste to have the bridegroom blown up at the wedding.

With a groan, Higgins scratched the sticking plaster on his jawline. It itched abominably. A shard of glass from the automobile's explosion had left a jagged wound, the worst of his injuries. The doctor didn't believe it would scar, although Higgins doubted that.

They'd been damnably lucky though. The Café Royal's canopy shielded them from the larger pieces of flying metal thrown by the explosion. Eliza suffered a few cuts and scratches, but was otherwise unhurt. It was Higgins and Beatrice who took the brunt of the scattered debris. His niece suffered a deep gash on her left arm, requiring stiches and a cotton sling. And none of them could hear properly until the following day. Higgins still felt stiff and sore from the nasty tumble he took when the explosion knocked him down. Who knew when his lower back would stop sending jolts of pain up his spine whenever he bent over?

The last four days had been hell. Everyone, including his family, were stunned by Winterbottom's murder. How could such a thing happen in the heart of London? Piccadilly Circus, no less. And yet it had. Watching the car explode was a shocking sight, especially because it killed a man about to leave on his honeymoon. Higgins despised Winterbottom, but not enough to wish such a death on him. On the other hand, Higgins believed the tragedy saved Beatrice from a worse fate. She was far better off as the widow of Clyde Winterbottom, rather than his wife.

After the service, Higgins and Eliza filed out of the church. Motorcars, trucks, and buses filled Trafalgar Square, their engines so noisy he couldn't hear himself think. No surprise since his hearing was not fully restored. Being midday, the sun beat down without mercy, and several women snapped open black parasols. He tore off his black armband and stuffed it into his pocket.

"How horrible for your niece," Eliza said as members of his family, dressed in mourning, headed for waiting motorcars.

"At least Beatrice can now say she was officially married. When the shock has worn off, she may be grateful it was only for a few hours." Higgins watched the black Rolls Royce carrying his niece drive away. "As a widow, she'll have far more freedom than she would if her husband had lived. He would have made her life a misery."

"Who knows how much more misery Luther North will cause before he's caught?"

Higgins shared Eliza's concern. The explosion had resulted in complete chaos. Guests ran out of the Café Royal screaming. As the only police detectives there, Jack and Colin had their hands full trying to restore order. Small wonder Luther escaped in the ensuing furor. At least the papers had alerted the public about the manhunt for Luther North. Higgins had no time to do anything about it. He had spent the past four days convalescing, while Eliza divided her time between him and Pickering. Neither had the chance to meet with Jack, although they'd glimpsed the detective this past hour in a back pew of the church.

"Luther must have planted the bomb while everyone was at the wedding breakfast," Higgins said. "He had more than enough opportunity, especially since Winterbottom's car was parked around the corner. And the weather helped. Passersby were only concerned about getting out of the rain. In his uniform, people would have assumed Luther was the Winterbottom chauffeur."

"But how would he know how to make a bomb?" Eliza asked.

"As a naval engineer, Luther no doubt had experience transporting gunpowder and cordite. The Royal Navy has suffered several explosive mishaps during the shipment of such material."

"It reminds me of the assassination attempt on the Viceroy last December." Lady Winifred Ossler joined them. Her navy suit matched a wide-brimmed straw hat topped with a huge ecru lace bow. A diamond heart pendant on a silver chain hung from her neck. "Lord Hardinge suffered serious injuries, although his wife and Lord Curzon were unharmed."

"Was it a motorcar explosion like this one?" Eliza asked.

"Oh, no. Something far more exotic. They were riding an elephant in New Delhi. Someone threw a bomb into the howdah, which is the saddle. I witnessed what happened along with my husband. It was appalling. His servant was killed outright."

"Why would someone want to kill Lord Hardinge?" Higgins wondered.

"The natives disagreed with Hardinge's decision to transfer the capital from Calcutta to New Delhi. They still haven't found the man who threw the bomb. Sadly, it's rather easy to concoct one. I watched the soldiers garrisoned at Mafeking put together explosive devices."

Higgins exchanged pointed glances with Eliza. He knew both of them were thinking the same thing: Did Lady Winifred have the expertise to make a bomb?

As if confirming their suspicions, Winifred continued, "One could probably make a bomb at home if the materials were available. I'm sure that's how the suffragettes acquire their bombs, or so my husband believes."

"The suffragettes I know would never do such a thing!"

"There are extreme factions within every political movement, Miss Doolittle. When political feelings run high, violence is often the response."

"Politics isn't the only thing that leads to violence," Higgins remarked. "The murders of Farrow, Winterbottom, and Miss Palmer had nothing to do with politics."

"Don't forget that Beatrice would have been killed had the car exploded two minutes later." Eliza shuddered. "At least Winterbottom didn't suffer."

"Poor man. And poor Beatrice, having her wedding day end so disastrously. I'm grateful now she wasn't in love with Winterbottom. She would be far more upset if she had been." Lady Winifred opened her parasol. "I need some fresh air. Shall we take a turn about the square?"

"Excellent idea." Higgins took Eliza's elbow, then held out his other arm to Lady Winifred. "I'm wondering about my niece's financial situation. My mother said Winterbottom recently bought a house for them in Notting Hill."

Lady Winifred nodded. "Oh yes, Clyde negotiated an

impressive marriage settlement when he became engaged to Beatrice. So impressive that he was able to afford the Notting Hill house, the roadster, and a number of costly furnishings. All of which your niece will now enjoy, along with his nest egg from the museum and the monies from his various insurance policies. Winterbottom was a man who liked to plan ahead."

"I hate to seem coldblooded," Higgins said, "but Beatrice is now able to run her own household and enjoy more independence that she ever has before."

"Absolutely. Don't be surprised if a more lively Beatrice emerges from that prim chrysalis she's been hiding herself in all these years." Lady Winifred's eyes sparkled. "I know of a gentleman who might suit your niece perfectly. He teaches entomology at Durham University and is no more than thirty-one. Much closer to Beatrice in age. And he's a widower, which gives them something in common."

"I don't think this is the right time to talk about Beatrice's next marriage." Eliza didn't hide her disapproval. "Her husband was just blown to bits. It doesn't seem proper."

"Never fear. I shall begin my matchmaking at the appropriate moment."

Higgins guided them towards the splashing fountains in the square. "I'm less interested in Beatrice's future suitor than why someone planted a bomb in Winterbottom's roadster."

"I'm grateful the bomb wasn't placed in my car as well," Lady Winifred said. "After all, it was my depraved chauffeur who was the murderer."

"It seems obvious the murders are connected to the Temple of Parvati," Eliza said. "Luther killed Pearl because he thought she knew where the temple treasure was hidden. And I bet Winterbottom knew where it was as well. That's why Pearl said not to trust him."

Lady Winifred arched an eyebrow. "If the pieces are as

splendid as those in Ashmore's collection, the person who finds it will be a rich man. Providing they know who to sell it to."

"A pity you can't act as the agent." Higgins winked at her.

"I'd be happy to. Although I don't know when I'd find the time. Since arriving in England last year, I've been curating our own art collection. To be honest, Sir Ian and I have been overzealous in our acquisitions. It's been a financial strain, and rather embarrassing."

Higgins noticed the slight flush to her cheeks. "No need to feel embarrassed. I know of a duke currently selling off whole chunks of his estate, including the family silver."

"Oh, I've no reason to complain. We've merely sold some figurines and a few statues. No precious gems or jewelry. I couldn't bear to part with my jewels." She stroked her diamond heart pendant. "Although I did sell the British Museum a gold diadem that Sir Ian acquired ten years ago from a maharaja in the Vale of Kashmir."

"Good afternoon, everyone." Jack Shaw tipped his hat as he approached.

"I noticed you speaking with Sir Charles right after the funeral," Eliza said when he joined them. "Glad I was to see you, too. You've made yourself scarce since the wedding."

"I've been swamped with work. But I had questions for several funeral guests and thought it easier to come to the service." He nodded at Lady Winifred. "I hope you don't mind, ma'am, but I have questions for you, too."

"Ask away, Inspector."

"Do you recall anything Luther North may have said or did while he was in your employ that would suggest he harbored a grudge against Clyde Winterbottom?"

Lady Winifred let out an exasperated sigh. "You asked me that right after the explosion. And a detective was sent to my home the following day with the same question. I must give the same answer. He never said a word about Winterbottom. I didn't have the slightest idea he even knew him. Please remember the man worked for me less than a week."

"But you did know Clyde Winterbottom?"

"As I told the police, I met him last year while negotiating to sell artwork to the British Museum. I also introduced him to Professor Higgins's niece."

Higgins thought Jack looked far too unhappy. "Why all the questions about Luther? You have proof he murdered Pearl Palmer. And I don't think anyone but Luther rigged that bomb. You should be running the brute to ground, not interrogating funeral guests."

"I've done the next best thing. I hauled in Billy and his cronies from the docks. Now that Luther's prints on the stiletto prove he killed Pearl, they're changing their stories. Most of them confessed they hadn't been anywhere near him. But Billy says he did see Luther running away from the spot where Pearl's body was found."

"Coward," Eliza spat. "He's almost as bad as Luther, protecting him like that."

"Don't be too hard on Billy. Luther threatened to hurt his mum. And one of the other dockworkers actually saw what happened. This eyewitness swears Luther chased Pearl down in the fog. The girl tried to keep him away with that knife Bessie Grainger gave her. But Luther ended up stabbing her, then tossed her body into the Thames."

"He's a monster, he is. Too bad he wasn't blown up like Mr. Winterbottom."

"Don't worry, we'll catch him," Jack reassured her. "And it's almost certain he'll hang for Miss Palmer's murder. Not to mention the bombing of Winterbottom's car." He adjusted his hat to keep the sun out of his eyes. "It appears Luther is killing people to get his share of that stolen treasure Ambrose Farrow hid away. With Pearl dead, the only other person with any connection to the Indian treasure was Winterbottom." He paused. "Except Lord Ashmore."

"Wait a moment!" Lady Winifred snapped her fingers. "There was something suspicious, now that I recall. Luther drove me to Claridge's on two occasions. Both times he passed by the British Museum, which is not on the way at all. He must have been hoping to catch sight of Winterbottom. I don't know why he simply didn't walk into the museum."

"Maybe Luther wanted to confront him when no one was around," Eliza suggested.

"But if he hadn't confronted him yet, it makes no sense to blow the fellow up." Higgins thought a moment. "If Luther didn't kill Farrow and Winterbottom, who did?"

Jack shrugged. "I'll make sure to ask him when we bring him to the Yard in handcuffs. But Luther looks like our man. We know he killed Pearl, and he was at Farrow's wedding. Eliza told me that he came into the church to give her the fan she'd forgotten in the car. It would have been simple for him to poison the bridal cog sitting out in the church vestibule. He walked right by it. And he certainly had the knowledge to rig a bomb. That still leaves us with the person who shot me and Pickering." He looked over at Eliza. "Sorry, Lizzie, but I have a bad feeling the next murder attempt will take place at the Ashmore wedding. If this is about the temple treasure, Clara's groom will be the biggest target. After all, the baron owns most of the treasure."

"I can't bear to think what might happen at Clara's wedding. What if she or Richard are killed? Or Freddy?" She put her hand over her mouth in horror at the thought.

"No one is going to die at the wedding," Higgins said. "We'll make certain of that."

"It's the Curse of the Cobra," Eliza declared. "It's all coming true. Everyone connected to the temple treasure is being killed."

"In Bengal and Mysore the natives put great store in that curse." Lady Winifred's smile turned sheepish. "I'm superstitious myself. Whenever I need good fortune to smile on an endeavor, I take care to wear jewelry in the shape of images said to bring protection."

Jack seemed exasperated. "We're dealing with a murderer, not some silly curse."

"None of us believe there's an actual curse," Higgins said. "But someone could be using this curse to frighten those who do believe in it. The killer may want to scare them enough to give up the treasure, or keep them away from it."

"Aside from Luther, who wants the treasure that much?" Winifred asked.

"Taral Misra, for one. In fact, he gave me a list of the things from Lord Ashmore's collection that he most wants returned to his people. I have the list in my pocketbook." Eliza looked down at her empty hands. "Crikey, I left my pocketbook at the church. I hope someone hasn't nicked it. I'll be right back."

After Eliza left, Lady Winifred added her own colorful details about the Curse of the Cobra which she picked up during her many years in India. Bloody hell, but Higgins was tired of weddings, murders, and Indian treasures. In fact, he was beginning to think there was a curse. Only in this one, the victim died from frustration.

The heels of Eliza's calfskin pumps clacked so loudly on the tiled floor of the church, she slowed down in hopes of making less noise. Several people sat in the pews near the altar. One fellow sat closer to the exit, his head bowed. She didn't need to see his red hair and beard to recognize Thaddeus Smith. He obviously hadn't left the church since he finished playing a mournful dirge after the reverend's eulogy.

He seemed to be praying and Eliza didn't want to disturb him. She tried to tiptoe, but the *click-clack-clickety-clack* of her shoes echoed towards the rounded arches above her head. Eliza halted and scanned the empty pews around her. Where had she and Higgins sat? After a moment, she spotted her small black pocketbook on the very pew where Thaddeus Smith sat.

Eliza cleared her throat. The organist looked up at her, startled. "I'm sorry to disturb you, but I left my pocketbook." She pointed at the black leather purse half hidden by a hymn book.

He walked to the middle of the pew, picked it up, and handed it to her. "I saw it when I sat down. I assumed someone would return for it."

"Thank you." She hesitated. "Is something wrong, Mr. Smith? You seem troubled."

"My troubles are minor compared to Mr. Winterbottom's widow."

Eliza impulsively sat down in the pew. Smith did likewise. "I hope everything is well between you and Her Grace."

"Our friendship is as harmonious as ever. She has worked prodigiously this past month on my behalf. My debut here at St Martin-in-the-Fields last week went quite well, but I hoped to gain further recognition at the two society weddings I played at. A number of influential people were in attendance." He looked over at her. "As you know, both functions ended tragically."

"You'll have other opportunities. I've been told you're to be the organist at the Baron of Ashmore's wedding. I'm a friend of the bride, so I'll be there. I bet lots more lords and ladies turn up for that wedding than they did for Mr. Winterbottom's."

He leaned back against the wooden pew, his gaze on the altar. "It's not merely aristocrats whose attention I seek. Are you aware the music critic from the *Times* was at Her Grace's wedding? I was supposed to play at her home following the wedding breakfast."

"I thought you played wonderfully during the ceremony. I'm sure he remembers."

His laugh sounded hollow. "I doubt he remembers anything other than Farrow jilting his bride. Followed by the groom being poisoned to death."

Eliza thought he was being rather selfish. Who worried about such things when people were being murdered? "I also enjoyed your music at the Café Royal. Professor Higgins learned the music played by the quintet was a composition of yours. Truly lovely, it was."

"Thank you. You're probably the only wedding guest who remembers that. A pity because the conductor of the London Symphony Orchestra was there. And I am quite certain the only thing he spoke about the next day was the car explosion." He shook his head. "And I so wanted him to listen – and remember! – the piece of music I composed for the wedding quintet."

"Don't give up hope. After people stop gossiping about the murders, they're sure to mention the music at some point. Along with the name 'Thaddeus Smith.' You mustn't become discouraged."

"I've worked so hard to succeed," he said sadly. "You wouldn't understand."

"Oh, yes I would. I used to sell flowers in the street. If not for Professor Higgins, I'd still be there. Poor as a church mouse, and twice as hungry."

"Then it's true what I heard about you being a Cockney barrow girl."

"And I've heard your family was once in service to the Ashmores. You've risen far, too. Although I imagine you had to fight every step of the way to become a society organist."

He nodded. "I'll be returning to Banfield Manor for that wedding you mentioned. Been years since I've seen the place. My grandparents and great-grandparents worked on the Ashmore estates in Kent and Surrey. And my parents worked at Banfield. It wasn't enough for my father, though. He dreamed of owning his own farm."

"Is that why your family moved to South Africa?"

"Yes, but we lost the farm after the war with the Boers. My dad felt like a failure. He was lucky the Ashmores hired him again, this time as groundskeeper. But he was never the same. Sometimes I think he died of regret, not a heart attack."

"Then you lived at Banfield Manor when you returned from Africa?"

He made a face. "Certainly not. Those in service are not permitted to have their children running underfoot. My brother Philip was sent to live with an aunt and uncle in Yorkshire."

"And you? Where were you sent?"

"I would have gone with Philip, except I had an aptitude for music. We had an old piano in Africa, left from some previous tenant of our farm. I taught myself how to play. My proud mother bragged about me to the Ashmores, and I performed for them one afternoon. The old baron seemed especially impressed. Next thing I knew I was being packed off to boarding school and given a first-rate musical education."

"How generous of the baron. He must have been quite the music lover."

"Indeed. He paid for my schooling. Although I did earn a scholarship to the Royal College of Music after Cambridge. Since then, I've found steady work as a church organist. Of course, I compose music, too. For string and flute, an occasional brass piece, piano concerti."

"Did Lord Ashmore pay for your brother's education, too?"

A shadow fell across Smith's face. "Philip had no talent for music, nor much for academics either. He was good with numbers, which landed him a position as a clerk."

Although she knew his brother died in prison, Eliza wondered if Smith would admit it. "Where is your brother now?"

"He's dead," Smith replied after a long pause. "Philip took a different path than I did. It was a blessing our parents had already passed on."

She should take her leave. Higgins was probably wondering what had happened to her. Eliza also feared she'd made Thaddeus Smith sadder than he was when she entered the church.

"I must go," she said, taking a firm grip on her pocketbook. "But we shall see each other next week at the Ashmore wedding." A thought struck her. "My friend is marrying the new baron, and he seems most kind and generous. I realize now that he has inherited such generosity from his father. Is his son like the old baron?"

"Not really. His father had reddish hair, and the new baron is blond like his mother."

"But are their personalities alike?"

Smith turned his full attention on her. "Why in the world are you so interested in the Ashmores?"

"I told you. My friend Clara is to marry Lord Ashmore. She hasn't known him long at all, and I hate to think he has a dark side that Clara hasn't glimpsed yet."

"No need to worry on that account. The new baron seems as affable and generous as his father. But he may be like his father in other ways." His expression turned hard. "The old baron had a eye for the ladies. Few females escaped his wandering eye, especially if they were pretty."

Eliza didn't like the sound of this. "Have you heard any

rumors about the present Baron Ashmore? Does he have a taste for showgirls? Is he keeping a mistress?"

"I haven't the faintest idea about his romantic history. To be honest, I know very little about him. He's much younger than his two brothers. If you had asked me about them, I could tell you a story or two. I was only a year older than Edward, the heir. And three years older than the second son, Robert. For a time, we all were at Cambridge together."

"Were they like their father?"

He smirked. "They were like the rest of their kind: arrogant, uncaring, cruel. Neither of them possessed a drop of intelligence or talent. Typical sons of a rich and powerful man. They enjoyed a life of tremendous privilege, but had done nothing to deserve it. Which didn't stop them from treating students of lower status like dirt."

"Is that how they treated you?"

"Oh, yes. And not just me. I wasn't the only young man the old baron sponsored. If Lord Ashmore learned of a bright, enterprising boy born in unfortunate circumstances, he often arranged for proper schooling or an apprenticeship. I think his sons were rather jealous of all of us." A mirthless smile appeared on his face. "They weren't the only ones. Mr. Winterbottom and I were students at Cambridge together as well. His attitude towards me was just as insufferable."

This made Eliza sit up. "I had no idea you knew Clyde Winterbottom."

"We're the same age. Both of us were at Magdalene College at Cambridge. It's only natural our paths would have crossed."

"Apparently they crossed enough to make you dislike him."

"Winterbottom resented that my musical abilities garnered so much praise and attention. Since he couldn't compete in that field, he did what snakes like him do: cheat and lie.

There was a musical competition held that year, and Winterbottom stole my composition."

She gasped. "The lying dodger. Did he try to pass it off as his own?"

"Not even he was that arrogant. But he knew how much the Ashmore sons resented me, so he gave it to the oldest boy. It was Edward who claimed it as his own. The fool dabbled in music off and on, so it wasn't a total shock when he entered it that year. Not surprisingly, he won." Smith sounded bitter. "I went to the fellow in charge of the competition and told him the truth. He believed me. But the university had no wish to accuse the Baron of Ashmore's son of cheating. Not when the baron gave lavish donations each year. And how could I bring such a scandalous charge myself? Lord Ashmore had paid for my entire education."

"Then Edward Ashmore won the competition with music stolen from you." Eliza touched his shoulder. "That must have been hard."

"It was my final year at Cambridge. Winning the music prize would have been quite a feather in my cap." He took a deep breath. "I was pleased when I heard Edward died in a car accident years later. And just as happy when his brother passed away."

Eliza got to her feet. "No doubt Mr. Winterbottom's death did not grieve you either."

Smith laughed. "Don't look so worried. I had nothing to do with any of their deaths. But I'm happy they're all in the grave. A pity they lived as long as they did."

At that moment, she was grateful they weren't alone in the church. The organist had a reason to want Clyde Winterbottom dead. And he bore a grudge against the Ashmore family. Even worse, he might blame Jack for sending his brother to prison.

"I must leave, Mr. Smith. The Professor is waiting for me."

After nodding a farewell, she hurried up the church aisle. About to step outside, Eliza realized she'd left one of her gloves behind in the pew.

This time she wasn't going back for it.

CHAPTER EIGHTEEN

ELIZA WAS THOROUGHLY SICK OF weddings. Not even the prospect of dressing up in a new gown and eating more cake made her look forward to Clara and Lord Ashmore's nuptials. Yet, she could hardly bow out. After all, she was the maid of honor, even if she did have to share duties with the matron of honor. She wasn't looking forward to that either. The young Viscountess of Saxton, known to her friends as Lady Tansy, was far too full of herself. And her husband, Lord Saxton, was certain to get drunk as soon as the vows were said. The fellow was probably downing brandy in the study right now, while his wife viewed the wedding gifts. If only Clara wasn't so impressed by people who had a title. Most of them seemed either balmy on the crumpet, or as disagreeable as a bowl of haggis.

At the moment, Lady Tansy was being disagreeable. "I can't believe the flotsam some people send as gifts." She held up a green and yellow porcelain vase decorated with cherubs. "Who in the world sent this?"

Clara barely glanced at the vase. "Cousins of the Dowager Baroness."

"Which means they're related to me as well." Lady Tansy put the vase back onto the table with a shudder. "I've seen better pieces sold from a barrow at Covent Garden."

Clara didn't appear to have heard her. Eliza expected the young woman to be nervous about tomorrow's wedding, but Clara seemed positively agitated. The eighteen-year-old should have been excited to show off her wedding gifts. Because of the importance of the Ashmore family, the gifts had been sent to Banfield Manor rather than the modest family home of the Eynsford Hills in Earls Court. For the past month, an elegant drawing room at the Ashmore mansion had been steadily filling up with items, each expertly displayed on tables draped with white linen. A dozen people also sent paintings, which now hung on the wainscoted walls.

Both the mansion and the presentation of the gifts made quite an impression on Eliza. In fact, when she, Higgins, and Freddy arrived at Banfield Manor this morning, she was literally struck dumb. The estate was so much larger and grander than she had imagined. Even Higgins seemed taken aback by the sheer size of the rose-red brick manor house. Just how wealthy and important were the Ashmores? A lot more wealthy than she ever could have guessed. And although a few of the wedding gifts were unappealing objects like the cherub vase, most of what was on display appeared exceptional and costly. Yet Clara barely looked at the gleaming silver, cut-glass crystal, elegant bibelots, and endless array of porcelain.

"You must write a thank you note to everyone who sent a gift," Lady Tansy called out. "Even if they've sent something dreadfully ugly. You'll never be forgiven if you don't. I hope Richard reminded you to record the information from the gift cards in a special book."

"Of course I shall thank everyone. I'm not a fool." Clara fussed with the velvet belt tied about her red and white striped dress.

"And will you look at how many clocks you've been sent."
Lady Tansy laughed. "People must think you and Richard
have no sense of time at all. That, or they lack imagination
when it comes to choosing a proper wedding gift."

It was all Eliza could do to not kick the viscountess in
her arse. One of those clocks was Eliza's gift to the couple.
She sidled up to Tansy. "You may want to keep your voice
down. We aren't the only ones in here." Six other people
were admiring the wedding presents in the spacious drawing
room.

"If they've chosen unwisely, they deserve to be called
out." Her scornful expression suddenly changed to one of
approval. "Although this ivory set is rather nice."

Eliza agreed. Both extraordinary and exotic, the set consisted of a letter opener, magnifying glass, ladies' hand mirror,
three hat pins in varying sizes, and a man's stickpin. The
handles on the letter opener, mirror, and magnifying glass
were made of intricately carved ivory; the pins were topped
by the delicate ivory head of an elephant. Eliza thought the
workmanship was impressive, particularly the details on the
carved heads and handles.

"Lady Winifred sent them. She said carved Indian ivory
seemed appropriate, given how much Indian art the Ashmores have collected over the years." Clara frowned.
"Richard told me elephants are good luck. He plans to wear
the stickpin tomorrow with his boutonniere."

"I thought you'd be relieved to surround yourself with
good luck symbols," Eliza said.

"Not Indian symbols. Those terrible things are bad luck.
If Richard would let me, I'd have the gardener bury the
whole lot out by the orangery." Clara pointed at a tall copper pitcher inlaid with gemstones. "Along with that strange
pitcher which Richard says is called an aftaba. The couple
from India gave it to us, so you know for certain it's cursed."

"Don't be silly. You can't believe everything from India is cursed."

"How can you say that, Eliza? You've been to three weddings this past month, and a murder or attempted murder has occurred at all of them. Something horrible will happen at mine, too. I know it. And all because of this Indian curse about the cobra."

Lady Tansy waved a hand. "I blame it on poor planning. Someone was included on the guest list who shouldn't have been."

"Except whoever shot at Jack's wedding party couldn't have been a guest," Eliza said.

"Who knows if these murder victims are even connected to each other? Maybe the killer is like Jack the Ripper, only with a hatred of bridegrooms, not scarlet women." Tansy shrugged. "I, for one, have no intention of standing too close to Richard tomorrow."

With a muffled cry, Clara went to stand by the window.

"You're a blooming idiot," Eliza said to Tansy, then hurried over to Clara. "Don't pay any attention to her. She's got less sense than one of those pigeons out there on the lawn. But I'm worried about you. Are you all right?"

"I wish it were over," she whispered. "The wedding, I mean. I won't enjoy any of it."

"It's wedding nerves, perfectly natural. Especially after the awful things that have happened this month. But Jack and a dozen of his men will be here tomorrow. You won't be able to cut the cake or toss your bouquet without a detective standing two feet away."

"I'm sick with worry, and so tired." Clara sighed. "I could sleep for days."

"I don't wonder you're exhausted. You've planned this wedding in such a short amount of time. But there's only the church rehearsal and dinner tonight. Tomorrow all you have to do is put on your gown, say your vows, and look like the prettiest bride anyone has ever seen." She hugged her. "You'll be a baroness, too. Think about that."

Clara's blue eyes filled with tears. "But they don't want me to be a baroness."

"Who doesn't?"

"Richard's mother and sisters. They treat me like I'm the nanny or the lady's maid. And they've been so rude to Mother, she's hiding in her room upstairs. I can't imagine how the Dowager and her daughters will behave towards the rest of my family when they arrive."

"Tell them to sod off," Eliza said. "The only person who matters is Richard. He's the Baron of Ashmore and he wants you to be his baroness. Who cares what anyone else thinks?"

"What in heaven's name is that ghastly thing?" Lady Tansy asked in an offended voice.

Eliza and Clara looked over to see the Viscountess shaking her head at an oil painting.

"Aunt Lavender sent it, and it's not ghastly," Clara shot back. "It's a portrait of Richard and me at a picnic. She's an artist and painted it for us. I certainly like it more than the useless silver ladle you and your husband sent."

"The impudent nerve of that girl," Lady Tansy huffed as Clara ran out of the room.

"Stop acting like you're the Queen Mum," Eliza said in exasperation. "You're the same age I am. And a blooming sight ruder."

Before Tansy could come up with a reply, Eliza went after Clara. She found the weeping girl huddled on the steps of the grand stairway. Fortunately, not a servant or wedding guest was in sight. The bridesmaids and ushers had already arrived. Most of them would be spending the night at the manor, along with Eliza, Freddy, and Higgins. Additional Ashmore relatives traveling from more than six hours away would be arriving soon and they, too, would be spending the night. This brief moment of privacy wouldn't last long.

Eliza sat next to Clara on the polished wooden steps and handed her a handkerchief. Best let her friend cry it out. The cavernous entrance hall echoed with Clara's sobs, along with the sound of bells ringing from below stairs, and the murmur of voices from the drawing room. She also caught the sound of a car engine outside. Higgins, Freddy, and Richard's best man were being shown the groom's motorcar. Eliza shook her head. Show men a car or one of those new aeroplanes and they fell into an enchanted trance. Of course, she was fond of motorcars too. But after watching Mr. Winterbottom be blown to bits, Eliza found it hard to even sit in the hired car during the ride to Kent. Foolish or not, she worried the whole way about an explosion.

A gold-framed oil portrait high on the wall caught Eliza's eye. A strapping, auburn-haired man dressed in tall boots and tweeds held a hunting rifle. It had to be Richard's father, the old baron, or perhaps one of the Ashmore brothers. He reminded her of someone. That red hair. Tall, too. A thread of music drifted through her mind. . .

Eliza was startled by the click of heels coming from the front parlor. Clara jumped to her feet, so she did also. They watched silently as the Dowager Baroness swept past them. The older woman didn't acknowledge their presence by so much as a nod. The sunny entrance hall seemed to grow chilly after she made her way into the drawing room where the gifts were on display.

Clara shook her head. "She hates me."

"What did you expect? Your courtship with her son was shockingly fast. Richard's mother barely knows you."

"But Richard and I fell in love from the moment we met."

"I know. I was there when Tansy introduced her cousin to you at Selfridges. And that first meeting occurred less than eight weeks ago. Eight weeks! Three weeks later, you were engaged. Then you set the wedding date for the first week of September. Blimey, you barely left enough time for the banns to be read three times."

The girl had the sense to look embarrassed. "We had to arrange a wedding date as soon as possible. It would have been unwise to put it off."

Eliza sometimes felt she was twenty years older than Clara, rather than just two. Within days of meeting the young baron, Clara announced her intention of becoming his wife. And she had thoroughly dismayed Eliza by confiding her plans to seduce Lord Ashmore, if need be. Foolish girl. She was fortunate the baron was a true gentleman who insisted on marrying Clara once they became lovers. The speedy wedding was insurance against an unexpected pregnancy.

"His mother probably believes Richard is marrying you because you've trapped him. To be honest, I'm afraid everyone believes that. After all, no one gets married this quickly unless the groom is going off to war, or there's a child on the way."

"Everyone believes we're marrying *only* because I'm with child? That's dreadful."

"It would be a lot worse if Richard weren't marrying you." Eliza took Clara by the shoulders. "Are you going to have a baby? Tell me the truth."

This brought on a fresh wave of tears. "No. No, I'm not. I thought perhaps I was, but this morning I learned I'm not with child."

Eliza wasn't certain whether to be happy or alarmed by this news. "Does Richard know?"

"I haven't had time to tell him. And I'm a bit afraid to say anything. What if the only reason he asked me to marry him was to avoid the scandal of a baby?"

Even without the threat of another murder, this wedding

promised to be difficult and uncertain. Maybe Higgins was right. Perhaps marriage only led to deceit and unhappiness. Her sympathy for the Ashmore family grew. The Dowager Baroness had already lost her first two sons. Now her remaining son – and the heir to the title – was about to marry a girl who possessed neither money nor a distinguished lineage. She didn't seem to possess an ounce of sense either. With such a dismal beginning, Eliza feared Clara might never win over her in-laws.

"Richard is a decent chap who adores you. You need to be honest with him."

"Before the wedding?" Clara asked. "What if he calls it off?"

"Then it's best you know what his true feelings are before the two of you are joined for life. The last thing you want is to begin your marriage with a lie."

Clara began to weep again, which coincided with Richard and his best man Julian Dain coming through the front door.

Richard rushed over to Clara. "What is it, darling? Why are you crying? It's not wedding nerves again, is it? It will all be over tomorrow, and we'll soon be on our way to the Continent."

A sobbing Clara clung to him. Eliza hoped Richard did indeed care for Clara as much as he seemed to. If he called off the wedding now, the girl might never recover.

Feeling a bit awkward, Eliza looked toward the open front door. It showed a wide expanse of manicured lawn and a shiny red motorcar tooling along the gravel paths in the distance. "Where are Freddy and Professor Higgins?" she asked.

"Both fellows were quite taken with my new Stutz Bearcat," Richard said as he stroked Clara's hair. "After I gave the chaps a few driving lessons, everyone insisted on having a turn behind the wheel. Freddy is driving the Professor around the gardens. Only it's a bit hazardous. We've arranged for a flock of peacocks to decorate the wedding reception, and they've sent the swans into a fury. The birds are chasing each other all over the estate."

"I hope Freddy doesn't run over the birds."

Julian's brown mustache twitched with amusement. "Your young man is a natural born driver, Miss Doolittle. I think he'd enjoy competing in a few races."

"I'm sure of that. Freddy already loves boat racing. Motorcars seem the next step for him." Assuming Eliza was the one to purchase the motorcar. "How much longer are the two of them going to be larking about out there?"

"They'll be in shortly. We only have three hours before the rehearsal. I promised Higgins I'd show both of you the Ashmore Collection, especially the pieces from the Indian temple."

Clara grabbed Richard by his jacket lapels. "Not the Indian temple collection! Anything but that. It's cursed. You and I must stay far away from all of it until the wedding is over."

"Sweetheart, it's not cursed."

"Yes, it is. And I think it's already cursed our marriage!" Pushing herself away from Richard, Clara raced up the long, sweeping stairway.

Richard appeared baffled. "Excuse me while I see what this is all about."

Eliza and Julian watched as Richard followed his fiancée.

"Is the bride getting cold feet?" Julian closed the front door. "I certainly hope not. Richard is quite besotted."

"I'm relieved to hear that. They seem to be in love, but everything's happened so fast."

He brushed dirt from his dark blue blazer. While not especially attractive, he was a genial fellow. And he appeared to be not only Richard's best man, but his best friend. "Don't worry. Richard will make certain this engagement ends in marriage. Unlike his first."

"His first?"

"Richard was engaged nine years ago. He was hardly older than Clara is now when he fell in love with Miss Baxter. Emilia was the daughter of a classics professor at Durham. I was at university with Richard at the time, and can attest that their courtship was whirlwind. The two of them became engaged, and a wedding was planned for the following year."

"What happened?"

"Richard's parents were opposed to the match. Emilia came from a respectable family, but not a titled one. Nor was she an heiress. Lord and Lady Ashmore worked to undermine it. Richard's mother has family members on the board at Durham University. She saw to it that Emilia's father was dismissed from his position."

Eliza's opinion of the Dowager Baroness plummeted. "What did Richard do?"

"He told his parents to go to the devil. As a third son, he'd always been ignored by the Ashmores. And he stood to inherit nothing, which was why he went into the Army. They had no leverage with him. But Emilia broke off the engagement and moved with her family to Canada. Her father rightfully guessed Lord Ashmore would ruin his career if he and his daughter remained in England."

"Richard must have been upset."

"Don't know when I've seen a man so enraged – or heartbroken. He never forgave his family." Julian ambled over to Eliza. "I know Richard. He loves Clara. But I think he also enjoys the fact that she is viewed by his mother as even more unsuitable than Emilia. It must be frustrating to the old woman that she can't stop the marriage."

Eliza smiled. "Once she gets over her nerves, Clara's behavior will prove maddening to her mother-in-law. The girl is a force to be reckoned with."

"Then she isn't going to cancel the wedding?"

"Oh, no. But after their conversation upstairs, Richard might."

"Nonsense. Why would you think that?" A knowing look crossed his features. "Ah. Clara has learned there won't be the patter of little feet eight months from now."

Eliza stared back at him with raised eyebrows.

He leaned closer to her. "Richard would have asked Clara to be his wife even if they hadn't become indiscreet so quickly. This just hurried things along. However, I'm glad they'll have time to become better acquainted before they fill the nursery." Julian chuckled. "Richard must be enjoying how mortified his mother is by this hasty wedding. It will be even sweeter when the Dowager Baroness realizes they didn't marry because of a baby."

"As long as love outweighs revenge in this marriage," Eliza added.

"It does. Richard loves Clara. She reminds me a bit of Emilia, too. Young, impulsive, unpredictable." He rolled his eyes. "And drenched in romantic fervor. Rather like the character of Marianne in Miss Austen's *Sense and Sensibility.*"

Eliza hadn't read any of Jane Austen's novels yet, although she recently bought *Emma.* Perhaps she should acquire a copy of *Sense and Sensibility* as well. Sometimes Clara was damnably difficult to figure out. At least, there was one less thing to fret about tomorrow. The marriage was going to proceed as planned.

Now all they had to worry about was another murder.

While he was passionately interested in languages, Higgins was less thrilled by Indian columns, pilasters, and temple shrines. Lord Ashmore kept his promise and was now giving Eliza and Higgins a tour of the long gallery which held the Ashmore Collection. But after ten minutes, Higgins felt his mind wander.

Looking at statues seemed quite dull after an afternoon spent racing about the estate in Ashmore's two-seater motor-car. At times it seemed like an obstacle course, what with the bewildering number of peacocks and swans they'd almost run over a dozen times. Despite that, Higgins enjoyed being behind the wheel for the first time in his life. No wonder Eliza sometimes spoke about buying her own car, something she could afford now that she was part owner of a winning racehorse. Although at the moment, she was showing so much interest in the Ashmore Collection, he wondered if she was about to collect art herself.

She stood before the sinuous stone curves of a Hindu goddess. "Is this Parvati?"

"Yes, it is. Of course Parvati appears numerous times in the temple. As the consort of Shiva, she takes many forms. Mother goddess, goddess of spring and fertility." He laughed. "Listen to me. I sound like my father. To be honest, I don't care much for all this." Ashmore gestured at the gallery which took up an entire wing of Banfield Manor.

The skylight and floor to ceiling windows made the space so bright, Eliza's blue tea dress appeared almost luminescent.

"Why not donate it to a museum?" Higgins asked. "Or sell it?"

"I bet Taral Misra would buy everything from the Temple of Parvati," Eliza added.

The young man stiffened. "I don't like his attitude. He acts as if my father stole these objects." His gaze swept over the stone pediments, statues, and glass display cases of swords and gold jewelry. "Father paid a great deal of money to fund the excavation."

"Taral feels guilty," she explained. "After all, he was the one who discovered the temple. It never occurred to him that the British would come in and carry everything away."

"Why should my family be blamed for recognizing the value of the temple and taking steps to protect it?" Ashmore said tersely. "I've grown tired of Mr. Misra's arrogant demands. He's been to Banfield Manor several times, and grown more insolent with each visit. If it weren't for Lady Winifred, I would disinvite him from the wedding."

"Has he really been that rude?" Higgins asked.

"Yes, and my patience is at an end." As friendly and approachable as the young baron was, it appeared there were limits to his bonhomie. "To make matters worse, this Indian temple has upset Clara. She's convinced the whole thing is cursed."

Higgins snorted. "After what's happened at the last few weddings, I'm not surprised."

"Please don't tell me you believe in curses, too?"

"Don't be absurd." Higgins slowly circled a gold statue of Parvati. The goddess sat cross-legged on a gleaming base, arms upraised, crowned head tilted at an angle. "What I do believe is that a murderer is wreaking havoc at these weddings. The obvious link is the temple."

"The most obvious link isn't always the correct one." He frowned.

"True. But we'd be fools to ignore such a strong motive. Especially when so much gold and jewels are involved." Higgins gestured to the glittering temple objects scattered about them.

Lord Ashmore walked over to the windows which looked out at the vast gardens on the estate. A former captain in the King's Hussars, he had resigned his commission to take up the barony. Higgins wondered if the chap was still adjusting to his new title and position. Banfield Manor was an exceedingly impressive Jacobean mansion, and its vast grounds and gardens rivaled those at Hampton Court. Now the title and estate belonged to the young man, along with the privileges and responsibilities that came with it. He seemed an intelligent, attractive fellow and he should do well, even if he was foolish enough to marry Clara Eynsford Hill. Higgins only hoped tomorrow's wedding held no unpleasant surprises for the young baron.

"Do you not care about collecting art at all?" Eliza strolled over to stand beside the baron. The sunlight pouring through the windows cast a dazzling aura over their figures.

"I don't care about ancient art," Ashmore said. "Where's the sense of discovery in Egyptian and Graeco-Roman antiquities? No, I have a taste for the modern. Two weeks ago I bought a painting by a fascinating French artist by the name of Duchamp."

"Clara will certainly prefer modern art to this." Eliza waved her hand at the statues.

"Maybe I should sell the collection and start my own. Clara could help me. She'd like that. Trips to Paris to shop for clothes *and* art."

"I wish you were there now," Higgins said. "You'd be a damn sight safer."

"Do you believe there will be an attempt on my life tomorrow?"

"Judging from the presence of Scotland Yard, I'm not the only one. Be careful, Lord Ashmore. And take care of Clara. Because of this temple, she's in as much danger as you are."

The baron flinched, then turned on his heel and stalked off. Once his footsteps on the marble floor faded away, Higgins and Eliza slowly followed after him.

"The police weren't able to prevent Mr. Winterbottom's death." Eliza's grim expression mirrored his own. "They might not be able to protect Richard either."

"Agreed," Higgins said. "It may fall to us to keep disaster from striking again."

CHAPTER NINETEEN

T HE PEACOCKS SEEMED DETERMINED TO eat the wedding cake. For the third time in an hour, the colorful birds launched an assault on the linen draped table, only to have the servants chase them away. Eliza didn't blame the peacocks. Clara had rebuffed the traditional fruitcake, choosing instead an elegant tiered cake decorated with pink rosebuds and covered in fluffy swirls of white icing. She couldn't wait to sample it. The birds agreed, since they once more circled the table. Luckily, two footmen now stood guard.

The bride may have gone a bit overboard with her wedding decorations. Clara requested a variety of birds be let loose on the lush manicured lawns of Banfield Manor. Eliza counted at least a dozen peacocks strutting among the guests, along with just as many swans. And she couldn't tell which ones were more ill-tempered. Certainly the two dozen white doves proved the messiest. The best man's jacket had already been stained with bird droppings. Eliza ducked every time she heard the sound of wings.

Aside from the birds, things were going well. Best man Julian Dain and his wife sat with the bride and groom at a long table overhung with a trellis of pink roses. Both widowed mothers and the Saxtons joined them. On the opposite side of the terrace, Eliza, Freddy, Higgins, bridesmaid Alice, and two groomsmen sat together. The remaining attendants gathered at an adjacent table. The other guests enjoyed the wedding breakfast at smaller tables dotting the lawn.

Eliza popped a rose-shaped chocolate cream bonbon into her mouth. She loved every course: chilled white grapes and sugared violets, clam bouillon, salmon croquettes, green peas with Hollandaise, broiled squab with tiny creamed potatoes, and filet mignons in a mushroom and sherry sauce. A large crystal bowl of fruit sat on each table, luscious bonbons surrounding it.

"What a marvelous breakfast." Thoroughly stuffed, Eliza finally pushed away her plate.

"I agree." Freddy spooned up raspberries, unmindful of the peacock behind them.

"And such a beautiful sunny day," Alice said. "How fortunate for the bride and groom."

Eliza tossed a raspberry at the peacock who perched on the grass behind her. Two swans hurried over in hopes of stealing it, but the peacock let out a shriek which frightened them away. "Freddy, look how pretty they are. I do love birds. I had a canary once named Petey. But the little thing died one winter when I couldn't afford any coal for the grate."

He snorted. "Pretty? I think they're a nuisance. What was my sister thinking, having so many silly birds at her wedding? I certainly don't intend to have a single dove at our wedding. Assuming you ever agree to be my wife." Freddy drained his glass of champagne. "And that seems more unlikely by the day. I've proposed and been rejected by you dozens of times over the past few months. If this continues, I may leave off asking you altogether, Eliza."

"Thank God," Higgins said loudly. "Can we have that in writing?"

Eliza sighed. Freddy had been short with her all day. More

than once he mentioned how she'd refused his proposals of marriage. He'd become tedious. And rather drunk. Seeing his younger sister marry after knowing her groom only a few weeks had put him a foul mood. Freddy must be upset with her indeed. She'd never even seen him tipsy. If he kept this up, Eliza would spend the rest of the reception seeking out more congenial male company. She glanced over at the bridal table where Detective Colin Ramsey was posted. All the Yard detectives policing the reception wore formal dress in order to not make their presence obvious. Ramsey appeared quite dashing in his black suit and Ascot tie. When he caught her looking at him, he winked. She turned away. Best not give Freddy any reason to be jealous. This was one wedding she was determined should end smoothly.

So far everything had gone as planned, except for the birds running amuck. And the gardens of Banfield Manor were the perfect setting for an early September wedding. Large urns filled with pink gladiolus, camellias, white orchids, and lilies of pink and white had been placed here and there on the lawn. A tall arch of pink and white flowers graced the end of the terrace. Pink satin ribbons streamed from white tents where maids offered guests small iced fairy cakes, trifles, raspberry and blackberry fools, and custard cream. Other tents held chilled champagne, wines, coffee and tea, which waiters brought to the guests' tables.

"How is the port?" Eliza asked Higgins.

He nodded appreciatively. "Lord Ashmore's spared no expense. A superb tawny vintage from the house of Burmester. 1890, I believe. Pick will regret missing this."

"Haven't you had enough champagne?" a groomsman at their table asked a bridesmaid.

"But it's so deliciously bubbly." Joanna giggled. She was even more tipsy than Freddy, evidenced by the alcohol stains on her pink silk bridesmaid's dress.

Eliza raised her champagne flute. "It tickles my nose."

Alice brushed food crumbs from her own bridesmaid gown, which was a muted shade of rose. "I heard the Prince of Wales used to bathe in a red copper tub filled with champagne."

"I'll have to try that." Freddy lifted his arm. "Hallo, waiter! Come bring another round."

"No, thank you." Eliza shook her head when the young man approached their table, his gloved hands holding the napkin-wrapped bottle. "We've had plenty here."

Freddy next hailed a passing guest. "Aunt Lavender! Come join us." He rose to his feet along with the other gentleman at their table. "This is my mother's younger sister, Mrs. Lavender Stratton. We call her Aunt Lavender, of course. She's a most successful painter, even more famous than her late husband. And she's a Bohemian, too. You'll find her awfully fun." After hiccupping twice, Freddy finished the introductions.

"How do you do." Higgins held out her chair. "Please have a seat."

Eliza placed a cup of coffee in Freddy's hand. "Drink it all. And don't even think about asking for more champagne. Clara will box your ears if you get drunk."

Relieved when Freddy began to sip his coffee, Eliza turned her attention to Aunt Lavender. She noted that her wavy blond hair matched the tresses of her niece and nephew, and she had the same lovely blue eyes. However Lavender looked a good ten years younger than Clara and Freddy's mother. Eliza also was delighted by her daring ensemble: a blue silk suit by celebrated designer Paul Poiret. She read in the fashion magazines that the form-fitting outfit was inspired by men's attire from something called the Consulate period. And while some guests cast disapproving glances Lavender's way, Eliza admired the boldness of the gold and red embellishment on the low-cut bodice, along with the velvet toque that crowned her head. Bohemian indeed,

"Professor, is it true your niece's husband was recently killed in an automobile explosion?" Lavender said. "How tragic."

"I prefer to view it as unexpected," he replied.

"I read about that in the paper," Alice said. "My condolences to your family."

"Thank you. But we are recovering quite nicely from the death." Higgins smiled at Freddy's aunt. "I admit to being something of a fan, Mrs. Stratton. My friend Colonel Pickering took me to see your murals this summer at the Omega artists' exhibition in Bloomsbury Square."

"I was honored to be included. The artists who are part of the Omega Workshops are sure to make an impact on modern design. And it's freeing to use the Greek symbol instead of one's name. I do appreciate your kind words, Professor. Many others have not been as polite."

Eliza laughed. "The Professor's been called many things. 'Polite' has never been one of them."

"Ignore our impudent maid of honor," Higgins said. "Ever since I taught her to speak like a proper lady, her impertinence knows no bounds."

"Hang proper ladies," Lavender said. "I'd much rather spend time with the impudent and the impertinent."

Higgins cocked his head at her. "I hear a touch of Surrey dialect in your speech, accompanied by Queen's College and Bloomsbury. Edinburgh, too."

"Well done. I spend a month in Edinburgh every summer. And I attended Queens College. As for my Surrey intonations, I resided in the county for three years. Molesey, a bit west of Hampton Court." She gave him an approving smile. "So it's true you have the ability to place a person within a few streets of their origin, Professor. A most remarkable talent."

Higgins only shrugged, although Eliza knew he was pleased.

"Have you met the Misras?" Eliza asked. "They're the Indian couple sitting by the fountain. I adore how beautifully they dress. A pity we can't all wear saris."

"Oh, I should love to parade about a London soiree in one. So dramatic." Lavender leaned closer to her. "I've recently acquired a harem outfit from Constantinople. Sky blue gauze and completely transparent." She glanced over at the Indian couple. "I wondered who that striking pair was. I assumed Richard met them when he served in India."

"Actually they're friends of Lady Winifred Ossler."

"I'm acquainted with Lady Winifred. She has a cousin in the Bloomsbury group, the painter Duncan Grant. And she encouraged Lord Ashmore's father to support our work, even though he rather disapproved of us. We cannot thank her enough for that."

"I didn't realize Winifred was on such friendly terms with the old baron," Higgins said.

"She met Baron Ashmore in India years ago when he traveled to the subcontinent to collect antiquities. They hit it off rather well." Her smile turned catlike. "Whenever she came back to England on holiday, she was a house guest here at Banfield."

"Then she's friends with the Dowager Baroness as well," Eliza commented.

"My goodness, no. Why would you think that?"

"She's an invited guest." Eliza was puzzled. "According to Clara, her new mother-in-law invited her. Richard barely knows Lady Winifred."

"Dear Eliza — may I call you Eliza? — in the social circles in which the Ashmores and the Osslers move, friendship has little to do with who is on the guest list. Lady Winifred's husband is held in high regard by Lord Curzon, who is an important man. That makes his friends important. For Lady Winifred to be snubbed would cause a scandal. But you may notice the Dowager Baroness has barely spoken to her. And there are at least four other ladies here who are also receiving a chilly reception from Richard's mother." She raised a carefully penciled eyebrow. "The old baron not only collected art. He collected women."

A swan suddenly thrust its head next to Lavender's arm. As she gave a startled shriek, the swan snatched a leafy green from one of the salad plates before fleeing over the lawn.

"There are far too many birds at this wedding," she said, looking about nervously. "During the breakfast, one of the doves took a piece of bread right out of my hand."

"I wouldn't be surprised if the reception ends with a grouse shoot," Higgins said drily.

"Well, I rather like the peacocks." Eliza gave another raspberry to the peacock who sat just behind her chair. The darling thing had stayed there quietly for the better part of an hour. She suspected this was the same bird who had followed her about since the reception began.

"Stop feeding them," Higgins ordered. "You'll have the whole flock upon us."

"Oh, be quiet. All this fuss over a few birds." She threw her last raspberry to the peacock, who gobbled it up. "There you go. Good boy!"

"I hope Clara and Richard send every single bird off to their estate in Richmond," Freddy grumbled. "I refuse to visit them if any swans and peacocks remain here."

"Ah, there's my sister," Lavender announced. "She's speaking with the wedding photographer. I've been wondering where she is. She looks a bit strained, don't you think?"

Freddy stood. "Mother's probably suffering from another migraine. This wedding has been a bit too much for her nerves. I should see if she's all right."

"We both should." Lavender and Freddy excused themselves and walked over to Mrs. Eynsford Hill.

"How much longer until we can go home?" Higgins asked with an exaggerated sigh.

"Blimey, keep your knickers on. They haven't even cut the cake yet."

"I'm not the only one who's restless. Even the Misras are pacing about."

The Indian couple had been strolling about the lawn for much of the reception. Taral wore a plum-colored jacket and matching turban; Basanti looked enchanting in a coral sari edged with gold tassels. Her shiny black hair hung in a long braid covered by shimmering gold threads. They were accompanied by Lady Winifred, who was nearly as resplendent in a cloud gray satin brocade gown.

"Follow me," Eliza said.

Swallowing the last of his port, Higgins trailed after her. So did the peacock.

Eliza called out Basanti's name, prompting the couple and Lady Winifred to wait until she and Higgins joined them.

Chuckling, Taral pointed at the peacock who stood behind Eliza, his feathers fanned out in full display. "He seems most fascinated by you, Miss Doolittle."

Eliza smiled. "I think he's in love."

"I think he's waiting for more raspberries," Higgins observed.

"It is a most splendid day for a wedding," Basanti said. "The bride looks charming."

Lady Winifred nodded. "Lady Duff-Gordon may be the finest dress designer in Britain."

"I'm happy everything has gone as planned," Eliza said. "I've been looking over my shoulder for the next disaster to happen."

"You should not worry." Basanti patted her arm. "There are so many people here and the servants are watching everyone. It will be fine." She gazed in approval at Eliza. "And your dress is most becoming. You are the maid of the bride?"

"Yes, the maid of honor. And thank you." Eliza loved her gossamer peony silk gown embroidered with lace roses that flowed in a bead-lined chevron pattern. A darker satin sash cinched below the bust. "The matron of honor, Lady Tansy, is over there. She's the one wearing a diamond choker and tiara."

Eliza thought the snobbish viscountess had deliberately showed up the other bridesmaids – and even the bride – by wearing such lavish jewelry. But she seemed in an ill temper nonetheless. As expected, her husband, Lord Saxton, sat slumped in his seat, drunk and leering at every young woman who passed his table.

"Basanti and I are surprised to see those trees." Taral pointed at two odd-looking small trees in large pots standing on either side of the musicians. "They're Indian jujube. I did not think they would grow in such an inhospitable climate."

"They have to be sheltered in the greenhouse most of the year," Lady Winifred said. "The tree is also called the Indian cherry. The late baron loved the fruit."

"I've been told you've visited Banfield Manor often," Eliza said.

"Many times. The Baron was such an intelligent gentleman, and so generous to his tenants and friends. A great patron of the arts. I am hoping his son follows in his footsteps."

"Once again, I must admire the jewelry both of you are wearing." Eliza nodded first towards the dazzling gold necklace, headband, and scalloped earrings of Basanti, then turned her attention to Lady Winifred's ruby bracelet and coiled snake pin, also glittering with rubies.

Both women murmured their thanks.

"When I walked up the aisle during the wedding ceremony, I noticed you were only wearing one earring, Lady Winifred," Eliza continued. "It would be a pity if you lost the other."

Winifred checked her earlobes with a gasp. "You're right. I'm missing one. I remember re-adjusting them in the car because the screws weren't tight enough." She frowned. "I do hope I haven't lost it at the church or out here on the lawn. As you can see, the earring is made of gold and rubies. My husband will not be pleased if I've lost one of them. They were a gift for my fortieth birthday."

"Would you like us to look for it?" Eliza asked.

"Oh, no. I'm sure I'll find it. Perhaps one of the servants has already done so. Some of them remember me from my visits to Banfield Manor."

"Did you know the Smith family? They were members of the staff at Banfield. The organist who played at the church, Thaddeus Smith, spent some time here as a child. The Ashmores paid for his education."

Winifred thought a moment. "Yes, I remember now. His father was a groundskeeper."

"I saw a portrait in the stairway of Richard's father as a young man." Eliza lowered her voice. "It seems Mr. Smith bears a strong resemblance. The same red hair, nose and chin."

Higgins arched an eyebrow. "You're right."

"If you're asking if Mr. Smith is the Baron's natural son, I have no idea. But it wouldn't surprise me or the Dowager Baroness. It's no secret the late Lord Ashmore funded the education of a number of well deserving boys. Mr. Smith should count himself lucky if he was one of them." Winifred touched her bare earlobe once more. "Now I should take my leave of the bridal couple. I must return to London in time to catch the train to Dover. I leave England tomorrow."

"Returning to India?" Higgins asked.

"Singapore first, then Bangkok, Calcutta, and finally Bombay." She sighed. "I can't wait to go home. I've been gone for months. My husband must think I've deserted him."

"Basanti and I owe you much thanks for your kind assistance here in London," Taral said solemnly. "When we return, we would be honored to host you once again in Mysore."

"I look forward to it." She shook each of their hands. "I'm grateful to have spent time with all of you. Enjoy the rest of the day. And please give my best wishes for a quick recovery to the Colonel." With that, Lady Winifred was gone in a swirl of satin brocade.

Eliza turned to Basanti. "In India, are snakes considered good luck or bad luck?"

"Only the best luck, unless you have harmed one." Basanti lifted her long braid by the tassels to show her a serpentine design in gold. "Snakes are the protectors of Indian temples, like the Temple of Parvati in Mysore. Cobras, kraits, and vipers guarded every room—"

Her husband interrupted. "They were all killed when the English looted it."

"To kill a sacred snake brings ill fortune," Basanti said in a hushed voice. "The Curse of the Cobra was brought on when the holy temple was torn apart and taken away."

"Clara is extremely nervous about this curse," Eliza said.

"The groom seems unmoved by her fears." Taral frowned. "He still refuses to part with any of the temple."

"He may change his mind," Eliza said. "Give his bride time to convince him."

They all turned to watch the newlyweds mingle with their guests. Richard looked exceedingly handsome in his red officer's uniform, a ceremonial sword swinging from a scabbard hanging at his waist. As for Clara, Lady Duff-Gordon had outdone herself designing her cream satin bridal gown. The short sleeves ended in embroidered scallops, and a rose-shaped satin bow drew the eye to Clara's tiny waist, where the bodice came to a V. On either side of a gossamer inset, the full skirt flowed down to end in a swirl of embroidered edging. The train dropped a full eighty inches from her shoulders, and a pearl tiara crowned Clara's long tulle veil.

Lord Ashmore's money had been well spent at Maison Lucile.

Excusing themselves from the Misras, Eliza and Higgins walked towards the couple. Eliza's peacock followed, letting out a piercing cry whenever the mood struck him.

"It's tradition for an Ashmore groom to take his new bride into the rose-shaped maze here," Richard was saying to the group. "My great-grandfather had a folly built in the center of the maze. Unlike most other follies, this one is a facsimile of an Indian temple to celebrate his lifelong love of India and its art. Once I take Clara there, I shall surprise my beautiful bride with a family heirloom."

Clara giggled. "I've been told to expect jewelry."

"I hope we can enjoy a little privacy, too." Richard kissed her with passion, eliciting cheers from all the guests.

When Clara spotted Eliza, she rushed over to her. "Isn't Richard wonderful?"

"He seems perfect. And I'm glad you're so happy."

"I was worried at the breakfast, Eliza. Before Richard ate a bite, I made Julian taste every course first. He was such a good sport about it."

"Since the police are in the kitchens, I doubt there was ever much chance of the food being poisoned," Higgins reminded her.

"Thank goodness you and Richard are spending your wedding night here at Banfield Manor. Which means there will be no bombs in cars today." Eliza felt a little more relaxed with each passing moment. Luther North was still at large, but every detective at Scotland Yard knew what he looked like. How could he possibly sneak into this wedding reception unnoticed?

After Clara rejoined Richard, Higgins nudged Eliza. "I see Thaddeus Smith. We should speak to him."

"He looks as gloomy as ever," Eliza said.

"Mr. Smith," Higgins called. The organist turned, standing in almost exactly the same manner that Eliza had noted in the late Baron's portrait. Yes, the resemblance was striking.

When they reached Smith, Eliza gave him a sunny smile. "Such a fine day. We should all celebrate the fact that everything has gone off without a hitch."

"Why should I be celebrating? This isn't my wedding. And the new baron is little more than a stranger to me." He shrugged. "At least he seems a decent chap. To be honest, being at Banfield again makes me rather ill."

"I don't understand," Eliza said. "You told me your parents met and married here. And after the Boer War, the Ashmores were kind enough to rehire your parents."

"Kindness had nothing to do with it. The offer was prompted by guilt and duty."

"But the late baron did fund your education," Eliza said.

"I'm grateful for that. But I've struggled for more than twenty years ever since. I'm five and forty now, with not much to show for it." He stared intently at Clara and Richard on the lawn's far side, still surrounded by friends. "And there's the richest baron in Britain, with a golden haired bride to adore him. Just twenty-eight years old, but he's heir to the Ashmore estates, the art collection, the army of servants who will obey his every whim. Why should life be so carefree and bounteous for him, and so difficult and trying for me?"

"Because he's the 5th Baron of Ashmore," Eliza reminded him.

Smith shot her a shrewd glance. "Is he?" He walked off into the crowd without so much as a by your leave.

"That man bears watching," Higgins said.

"Jack's keeping an eye on all the guests. Especially those who were at the other weddings." A movement in the distance caught her attention. "Looks like Richard is finally taking Clara into the maze. I hope they don't spend too long in there. They're supposed to cut the cake right afterward."

Higgins laughed. "Is food all you think about?"

"No. Sometimes I think about shopping."

They watched as the newlyweds dodged several swans and peacocks on their way over the verdant lawn until they reached the maze. Doves fluttered above the arched trellis entrance as they vanished inside. Eliza breathed a sigh of relief as she and Higgins headed for the tea tent.

"Miss Doolittle?" Taral Misra hurried over to them. "I hope you do not think my wife and I are imagining things. Everyone here was instructed to stay out of the maze. Yet we saw a groundskeeper enter the maze a few minutes before the bride and groom did. The couple were too far away for me to call out to them. It is also very noisy on these lawns. So many people. And all these birds."

"Perhaps the groundskeeper was chasing after the peacocks," Higgins said.

"No. And there is something else." His expression grew positively foreboding. "It is possible I am mistaken. I only saw the man one time at Mr. Farrow's memorial service. But Basanti and I believe the groundskeeper who went into the maze resembled Lady Winifred's chauffeur. The man you call Luther North."

"What? Where's Jack?" Eliza looked around wildly, as if

the Scotland Yard detective would conveniently fall from the sky. "And Detective Ramsey?"

But there were three hundred guests milling about the lawn and tents, and a virtual sea of servants. A musical quintet played from the terrace, and the noise level of the birds had risen to a crescendo. If she called for help, who would hear her? Meanwhile, Clara and Richard had unknowingly entered the maze shortly after the man who murdered Pearl, Winterbottom, and Farrow. Eliza felt such a wave of fear that she started to shake.

"Mr. Misra, ask every man here if he works for Scotland Yard," she ordered. "Find a policeman as quick as you can. Tell them about Luther. And tell them the Professor and I have gone into the maze."

"Yes, yes. Of course." Taral rushed off into the crowd.

A footman carrying a tray of dishes and serving utensils walked by. Eliza grabbed a large cake knife from his tray. Ignoring the fellow's startled expression, she set off for the maze.

Higgins had no choice but to follow her. "We should wait for the police."

"It might be too late. We've got to go now!" Eliza broke into a run. She heard Higgins's labored breathing behind her. When she reached the trellised entrance of the maze, she stopped. The hedge walls were much taller than they seemed when she was sitting near the terrace. She peeked inside but saw only curved paths of stiff greenery. So this was what a maze looked like.

Higgins caught up to her. "Please remember I'm twice your age. I haven't recovered from chasing after you in Blue-gate Fields. Or the explosion that killed Winterbottom."

She pointed at the maze's entrance. "It looks huge."

"And it's also reputed to be one of the most difficult mazes in Britain."

"Clara and Richard don't know what's waiting for them inside. We can't stay out here while Luther does some bloody awful thing to them. We can't!"

"I agree." He took a deep breath. "Let's go in."

As soon as they stepped into the maze, the tall hedge walls towered over them. "Which way?" Higgins looked at the various curving paths.

"Follow me." Eliza darted along the path to their right. She and Higgins went one way, then another, turning right and left until a wall of greenery blocked them.

"We need to start over. Let's retrace our steps." Higgins paused. "If we can."

Frantic, Eliza jumped up and down, trying to peek over the hedges. "If only we could see over the tops of all this bloody shrubbery. Professor, lace your fingers together like this." She demonstrated, then placed both hands on his shoulders and one heeled shoe into the makeshift step of his locked fingers. Eliza boosted herself up, but failed to clear the hedge's top. "It's no good. I can't see over it."

Dejected, Eliza dropped to the ground. Even Higgins looked discouraged. They trudged along for another five minutes, returning to a different path, yet getting nowhere.

They were lost.

CHAPTER TWENTY

"THIS MAY HAVE BEEN A mistake," Higgins announced. "How difficult can it be to find the center of a maze?"

"By definition, a maze is a puzzle solved by exploring its pathways." He frowned. "Which could take hours."

"We don't have hours." Eliza returned to one of the paths that wasn't a dead end.

"Maybe we should figure out how this maze is laid out before we start exploring every opening. I mean it, Eliza. We're running around here like one of those peacocks!"

"The maze is supposed to be in the shape of a rose. One of the paths leads to the right petal shape."

"The blasted maze probably has dozens of paths. We should never have entered it without someone to guide us." He cursed under his breath as Eliza set off down the pathway to their left. "We're already lost. What if we run into Luther, who's probably as lost as we are?"

She snapped her fingers. "You're right. Why should he know how to get to the center of the maze any better than we do? Maybe he hasn't found Clara and Richard. One of us needs to get there before he does."

"One of us? We're both in this maze."

"That's no reason for us to stay together." She pointed at two pathways on either side, both lined with towering hedges. "You take one path, and I'll take the other. This doubles our chances of finding Richard and Clara before Luther does."

"Absolutely not. What if you find Luther? I won't be there to protect you."

She lifted up the six-inch long knife. "I've got this."

"How will you fight off that madman with a cake knife?" Higgins said. "And stop running. You're likely to trip and impale yourself on it."

"Do you really think I've never carried a knife before? And with someone chasing me as well? Blimey, where do you think I was raised? Mayfair?"

"I don't care what sort of improbable childhood you had, we're sticking together. In fact, I advise we stay right here until Jack and his men reach us."

"What if they get lost in the maze? I can't let that monster hurt Clara, not if I can get—"

"Listen." He held up his hand. "I think I hear voices. It could be Jack."

But they were greeted only with the distant murmur of the reception guests.

His frustration grew. "Eliza, if we simply stay here, the police are sure to find us."

"Then we should start yelling for them." Before Eliza could say another word, a terrified scream sounded from somewhere in the maze.

"That sounds like Clara!" Eliza's face paled.

"Clara, Richard!" Higgins shouted. "Where are you?"

Desperate to hear a response, he slowly turned around. Scanning the tops of the hedges, he hoped to see the greenery tremble with the approach of other maze visitors.

"I don't hear a thing now." With a defeated sigh, he looked

over his shoulder at Eliza.

She was gone.

"Damnation! Eliza, where are you?" But he knew exactly where she was, running pell-mell down one of the pathways ... and waving a knife as well.

Hoping she had chosen the path to his right, Higgins darted through the privet arch, hoping to catch her. He'd never been in such a maddening place in his life. The pathway curved, then curved yet again. Although he was a tall man – well over six feet – the hedges were a good foot taller than he was. And they seemed as thick as concrete. All he could hear now were his feet hitting the moss covered paving stones beneath him.

Why would the killer strike again in a maze, especially one as complex as this one? It was far too easy to get lost in the damn thing. But Clara had screamed, which meant the bastard must have found them. Higgins turned down yet another green path. Who would know how to find the folly at the center of the maze? The Ashmore family, of course. And the servants, especially the gardeners and groundskeepers. He stopped.

After the Boer War, Smith's father had been the groundskeeper. He would surely have known how to navigate the maze and might have revealed the secret to his son. Although now it seemed likely Thaddeus wasn't actually the groundskeeper's son. As Eliza pointed out, the portrait of the old baron in the entrance hall bore a strong resemblance to the red-haired organist. If Thaddeus were the natural son of Baron Ashmore, that explained why his education had been paid for by the old man. It might also be responsible for his deep-seated hatred of the family. After all, Thaddeus was born before any of the baron's sons. If he'd not been illegitimate, the title and all the riches that went with it would belong to Thaddeus, not Richard. Was that enough for him to target the latest Baron Ashmore?

The privet hedge that lay before him suddenly shook. "Eliza, is that you?"

"Professor!" Jack's voice sounded from the other side. "Stay there. We'll find you!"

But another voice, one he recognized as Thaddeus Smith's, broke in. "No. Keep walking north until the next fork, then turn left and wait, Professor."

Higgins hurried forward, turning when the path split once again. Within minutes, Jack, Detective Ramsey, and Thaddeus Smith ran around the corner of the nearest hedge.

"Thank God," Higgins said. "I thought I'd be spending the rest of the week trapped in this infernal maze."

"We heard a scream," Jack said.

"Where's Miss Doolittle?" Ramsey looked about. "Did she scream?"

"No, she was with me when it happened. But you know Eliza. She took off down one of these paths, determined to find Clara." He sighed. "She has a knife, too."

Jack and Detective Ramsey exchanged worried glances. "Let's hope she stays lost for awhile," Jack said. "We have to get to the folly before she does. I don't want her hurt by whatever is going on in there."

Higgins looked over at Smith. "I assume you know how the maze is laid out."

"My father taught me how to navigate the maze when I visited Banfield Manor. Follow me." Smith set off through the maze, the other three men close on his heels. The fellow charged down one path, then another, with no sign of hesitation.

"Taral Misra told us he caught sight of a man entering the maze a few minutes before Richard and Clara went in. A man he thought was Luther. Then he informed us that you and Eliza had also entered the maze, which seemed like a recipe for disaster." Jack sounded out of breath. No surprise. They were moving at a near run.

"We didn't have much choice, Jack. Eliza was determined to help Clara and Richard. I don't think it occurred to her that a maze would be so damned mazelike. I couldn't let her come in here alone."

"Which means you both got lost," Ramsey remarked.

"That we did." Higgins threw a look over his shoulder at the winding path behind him. It was as if every time they turned a corner, the hedges closed ranks behind them. "And I'm sure Eliza still is. We'll have to send Mr. Smith after her next."

"Assuming we ever find the center of this thing," Jack muttered. "If these hedges weren't so huge, we'd be able to see the top of that folly. The Dowager Baroness said it's ten feet tall."

"Never will understand the upper crust," Ramsey said. "They build a fancy temple – a Hindu one, at that – then put it someplace hardly anyone can find."

"Makes it more valuable, I guess," Higgins said as the organist now veered to the right. "Smith, how much farther?"

He wondered if they should have trusted Thaddeus Smith. Then again, he'd been with the police when Clara screamed. So who – or what – had frightened the bride so much? A few yards after the last curve, the wall of hedges ended. In the sunlit center stood an elegant white stone edifice adorned with carved elephants. At last. They had reached the folly.

"Clara!" Higgins's gaze swept over the wide grassy area surrounding the small building. All he saw were beds of flowers now reaching the end of their summer bloom.

"Richard and I are in here, Professor," Clara called from inside the folly. "Stay away."

The men threw confused glances at each other. "Are you

both all right?" Higgins shouted.

"Is someone in there with you?" Jack asked. Although the folly was less than twenty feet in circumference, the stone-latticed walls didn't allow them to see inside. Jack and Colin Ramsey began to creep closer. Higgins and Smith followed.

The murderer must be in the folly with the bridal couple. At least Clara was still alive. But was Richard already dead?

"Richard!" Higgins was close enough to the folly that he could see two figures standing next to each other inside. Was the killer holding Clara hostage after doing away with her unfortunate groom?

"I'm here too, Professor!"

Higgins felt a wave of relief when he heard Richard Ashmore's voice.

"Is there anyone else in the folly with you?" he called.

"Yes," Richard replied. "But – but I think he's dead."

At that, the detectives, Higgins, and Smith ran up the three steps of the folly. The newlyweds stood by a large stone pedestal in the center of the temple. Clara had her face pressed against her groom's chest, one eye peeking out in obvious terror. Richard held her close with one arm, while with the other he held out his ceremonial sword.

"What is going on?" Higgins muttered.

The folly had only one entrance, and the latticed walls laced the interior with sun and shadows. No wonder he didn't immediately see the prone figure of a man lying a few feet away. Higgins and Shaw started towards him, but Clara let out a shriek.

"Don't move," Richard warned, pointing the tip of his sword at the floor. "That's an adder. They're poisonous."

A gray snake with a black zigzag pattern down its back lay coiled between them and the Ashmore couple. "Did the snake kill Luther?" Higgins asked, hardly daring to breathe.

"I don't know who Luther is," Richard said, his eyes never leaving the snake. "Unless you mean this poor devil on the floor. He was here when I arrived with Clara."

Ramsey nodded. "That's the suspect we've been looking for, all right."

Thaddeus Smith cursed under his breath. "I wish we had a gun to shoot that adder."

Higgins's eyes had now grown accustomed to the shadowy interior, and he looked down at the unconscious man. With his face turned towards them, Higgins recognized the broken nose and craggy features of Luther North. Even with a poisonous snake a few feet away, he felt relieved. With Luther dead, no one would be murdered today.

"Was he alive when you got here?" Ramsey asked.

"Yes," Clara said tearfully. "We found him on the floor. I thought he was some thief come to steal the jewelry Richard planned to give me. But he had already tossed the case aside." She raised her head to look at them. "He wanted what was in the box instead."

"Box?" Higgins and Jack said at the same time.

"That large wooden box on the floor beside him," Richard said. "Looks like it contained gold coins, a few gemstones." He paused. "The adder was still partially coiled in it when we arrived. The snake must have bit him. The man was unconscious on the floor when we walked inside. He was bleeding, too. I think he smashed his head open when he fell."

"He scared me so much, I screamed," Clara added.

"We didn't see the snake at first," Richard said, "otherwise we would never have come into the folly."

Without warning, the snake uncoiled to its full length. Head now upraised, its black eyes focused on Higgins, Shaw, Ramsey, and Smith.

"Stand very still," Richard said in a low voice. "If it sinks his fangs into you, that venom will act quick."

But the snake seemed bent on attacking whether they moved or not. It shot towards them, as swift as a gray and black arrow. They didn't have time to cry out before a whooshing sound filled the air. Richard had sliced the adder's head off with his sword.

Clara moved first. She threw her arms around Richard, kissing him repeatedly. "You're the bravest man I've ever met. The bravest, the most handsome, the dearest man."

"He's certainly the best swordsman in this group." Higgins knelt down, grateful the blasted snake was dead.

"Let's see about Mr. North." Jack and Ramsey cautiously walked over to Luther.

"Are you sure you're both all right?" Higgins asked the newlyweds.

Richard hugged Clara. "We're fine. But I hoped for a better way to end our wedding."

Thaddeus Smith cleared his throat. "You're both alive. I can't think of a better conclusion. Especially given what has occurred at the past few weddings."

"Hear, hear. I'm just sorry your wedding was spoiled by a death."

"He's not dead, Professor," Jack said. "In fact, he's starting to regain consciousness."

"Maybe the adder isn't poisonous," Ramsey suggested.

"Adders are the only poisonous snakes in England," Richard said. "The gardeners on the estate have been instructed to kill them."

"Poisonous doesn't always mean deadly." Smith nudged the decapitated snake with his foot. "My father was groundskeeper here. He got bit by an adder once. Made him beastly ill. If he survives, that fellow may wish he was dead."

"He can do all his wishing in prison." Jack pulled out a pair of handcuffs from his pocket. He and Ramsey rolled

Luther onto his back and clamped the cuffs on his wrists.

"Liars," Luther moaned. "Everyone lies to me."

"Who lied?" Jack shook him. "And why did you come to the maze?"

Luther began to shudder. Then he jerked to one side and became violently ill. He'd be lucky to survive the next few hours, but Higgins felt no sympathy for the man. Not with the memory of Pearl Palmer being pulled from the Thames with a knife in her back.

"What's this?" Ramsey had been going through Luther's jacket and pulled out a piece of paper.

Jack took the paper from him and unfolded it. "It's a map of the maze," he said. "And there's a note: '*Your share of the treasure will be left in the folly. To escape notice, retrieve it at half past one. The bridal couple are cutting the cake at that time, and no one will notice that anyone has entered the maze. This fulfills our agreement. Our association is now at an end.*'"

"Is there a signature?" Higgins asked.

"No. But whoever wrote this note did indeed lie to Luther. The wedding program clearly states the bride and groom would cut the cake at two o'clock *after* they returned from the maze. Sending Luther here at the same time as Richard and Clara meant he was certain to be caught red-handed with part of the treasure."

"The adder was probably placed in the box as insurance," Higgins said. "The ideal scenario was for Luther to be found dead."

"He might be if he doesn't get medical attention soon," Thaddeus cautioned.

"Mr. Smith, please guide Detective Ramsey out of the maze as quickly as possible," Jack said. "I need more of my men in here, as well as a stretcher. I want the full story out of Luther, and that won't happen if he ends up dead or in a coma."

Smith and Ramsey ran out of the folly.

With a tearful look at Luther North convulsing on the floor, Clara hugged Richard even tighter. "This is all so dreadful. He might die right in front of us."

"Don't feel sorry for him, Clara," Higgins said. "He killed Pearl Palmer. And probably Ambrose Farrow and Clyde Winterbottom, too. He's far more dangerous than any adder. You're both lucky to be alive."

"The note proves he was only in the folly to retrieve that box," Richard said. "Although he may well have done away with us if he hadn't already been bitten by the snake."

Higgins turned his attention to the open box on the stone floor. Several gold coins lay scattered about; he picked one up. He'd read enough of Pickering's scholarly work to know the inscription on it was Sanskrit. But there were no more than eight gold coins in sight. A topaz brooch in the shape of a monkey also lay on the floor and a pearl studded diadem. Having seen Ashmore's Hindu collection, Higgins knew these pieces must be part of the Temple of Parvati. But what was in the box did not add up to anything valuable enough to kill for. If Luther came here to steal from the collection, why not take more?

"It looks like he's stolen some of your pieces from the Parvati temple."

"None of that came from my father's collection, Professor. For one thing, all the gold coins were lost in the Bay of Bengal. And there was never a pearl diadem kept here."

"It's part of that missing treasure then. The treasure Ambrose Farrow hid, and Luther was trying to find."

"I knew that treasure was cursed!" Clara grabbed Richard by the lapels.

"Shhh, darling." He kissed her on the forehead. "We'll discuss this later."

Jack joined Higgins. "I thought the missing treasure was

worth a fortune. What's here would only garner a few hundred quid at most."

Higgins stared down at Luther, who seemed in a desperate state. They'd not get a coherent story from him anytime soon. "He was lured to the folly by whoever does know the location of the treasure. The same person who left the box *and* the snake. Even though the evidence proves Luther killed Miss Palmer, there may be another murderer running free."

Clara's eyes grew wide. "What if he's still here?"

Higgins felt a chill go up his spine. Like Clara, he suspected the killer might be somewhere in the maze.

So was Eliza.

CHAPTER TWENTY-ONE

THIS MAZE WAS DRIVING HER mad. Paths turned into dead ends or circled back on each other. And the hedges were so tall, it was like being lost in a fairy tale forest. If the cake knife were bigger, she'd try hacking her way through the greenery. There hadn't been another scream from Clara, but Eliza didn't know if that was good or bad. Were Clara and Richard even still alive?

Cursing under her breath, she found herself faced with two diverging paths once more. Which way this time? If she had a coin, she would have tossed it. With a sigh, Eliza decided to turn right when a familiar screech rang out from the other path.

Her mouth fell open when a peacock appeared. He emitted another cry upon seeing her, then opened his gorgeous tail feathers with a flourish. This must be the male peacock who had followed her the whole morning. Apparently he had chosen her as his mate.

"Have you come looking for me?" Eliza admired his fan of turquoise and green feathers. "I don't know if anyone has named you, but if you're going to trail after me all day, I must call you something. How about Percy? You look like a Percy to me."

The bird cocked his head at her, giving another piercing cry, Eliza hoped that meant he approved. "I wish you knew the way to the folly." A thought struck her. "Wait a minute. How did you get in here?"

Eliza stared up at the hedges looming over her. She hadn't seen any of the peacocks take flight, so this bird must have walked through the maze like she did. Could Percy lead her out of here? "Percy, show me how you got here." She made a shooing motion. "Go, go!"

Percy instantly folded his tail feathers. Eliza wanted to let out a delighted squawk herself when the bird swept down one of the paths. She ran after him. Eliza prayed he was leading her out of the maze – or to the folly. As they headed along yet another path, something sparkled in the grass. Eliza knelt down and picked up the object. It was Lady Winifred's missing earring.

If the earring was here, Lady Winifred must have been inside the maze before the wedding ceremony began. And only someone who had ill intentions towards Richard and Clara had any business being in the maze today. Eliza stood up, the earring clutched in her hand.

Pickering told them Winifred was a superstitious woman. She'd even admitted it herself. Eliza thought back to the jeweled brooches Winifred wore to the weddings: a ruby snake today, an emerald elephant at Winterbottom's wedding. Eliza had learned these were good luck symbols in India. But Winifred didn't always wear a piece of jewelry meant to bring good luck. A Florentine gold brooch decorated her dress at Farrow's memorial service, and a diamond heart pendant circled her neck at the Winterbottom funeral. Eliza didn't get a good look at the necklace she wore to the Duchess's wedding, but recalled it had a long, sinuous shape. The pendant was likely a snake as well.

Eliza's sharp memory now brought up something Winifred said at the funeral: *Whenever I need good fortune to smile on an endeavor, I take care to wear jewelry in the shape of images said to bring protection.*

She gasped as the truth hit her. The superstitious Winifred wore good luck symbols at the three weddings because she needed all the luck possible to pull off the evil murders she planned.

"I believe that belongs to me," a voice said calmly.

Blimey, she'd been so distracted by the earring, Eliza hadn't noticed that her peacock guide Percy was long gone. And Lady Winifred blocked the path.

The cake knife was still clutched in Eliza's right hand, but she quickly pressed it against her skirt. She hoped Winifred was too focused on the ruby and gold earring to notice.

"You wondered earlier where you'd lost your earring," Eliza said. "Now we know. You left it in the maze."

"I'm grateful you pointed out I didn't have it on at the church. Otherwise I would have assumed it fell off during the reception. That's when I realized I must have lost it in here."

The older woman opened her drawstring bag and pulled out an elegant sharp object. Eliza recognized the ivory handled letter opener as the gift Winifred had given the bridal couple.

"Do you really think you're going to need that?" Eliza's unease grew.

"Do you think you'll need that knife you're hiding among the folds of your dress?"

She held it up. "I hope not. But I'm glad I brought it."

"Aren't you the intrepid young lady," Lady Winifred said with a laugh. "You remind me of myself. Only I know not to get involved in matters that don't concern me."

"My cousin Jack and Colonel Pickering were almost killed. I was involved from that moment on. I only wish it hadn't taken me so long to realize that you shot them But I should have remembered you were at the siege of Mafeking with your husband. I wouldn't be surprised if you had occasion to pick up a rifle there, and probably more than once."

The woman's voice rang with pride. "Oh yes, I fought by his side for months. Plus the soldiers at Mafeking showed me how to use explosives."

"You put the bomb in Winterbottom's car." Eliza couldn't hide her disgust.

"I learned how to rig a bomb with a timer during the siege. Of course, the police never suspected a woman. They did suspect a woman after the shooting at the church, only the wrong one. Such a stroke of luck, Pearl Palmer being a sharpshooter back in America. Scotland Yard was quite dogged in their pursuit of her." "And Pearl paid with her life."

Winifred caressed the letter opener's sharp edge. "I meant the blame to fall upon her for both Ambrose's death and the church shootings. It was a godsend when your detective cousin began hounding Pearl. Then that idiot Luther took it upon himself to stab her."

Eliza listened in vain for approaching footsteps or the cry of her love-struck peacock. Even Percy had abandoned her. "These murders are connected to the missing treasure of the Temple of Parvati," she said. "You've been collecting art and antiquities for years. Especially East Asian art. Who better to be at the center of it all? I bet you're known as the matchmaker for more than arranging marriages. With your knowledge of collecting, you probably matched the sellers of stolen art with collectors willing to pay the price."

"Well done, Miss Doolittle. Ambrose and I worked together several times before he moved to London. Once we saw the opportunity to steal part of the Parvati treasure, I handled the operation from India, and Ambrose oversaw the treasure when it arrived in England. Unfortunately, we had to include Winterbottom and Luther. But they served their purpose. As you did today when you mentioned my missing earring."

She took a step towards Eliza, the letter opener clenched in her fist.

Eliza waved her own knife. "Stay where you are." When the other woman halted, she added, "Pearl said the treasure was hidden in London. You know exactly where it is, don't you?"

Winifred stared at Eliza's knife as if trying to decide how to take it from her. "It's been hidden at my house in Kensington for months. Ambrose was in debt and needed the money, but no more than my husband and I. We disagreed on how to sell off the treasure. Ambrose wanted to dismantle the jeweled objects and sell the gemstones separately. But I knew we'd get a much higher price if we could keep the pieces intact."

"Pearl told me a buyer for the treasure had been found," Eliza said. "That's why Farrow called off his wedding at the last minute. Good thing he did. Otherwise the Duchess would have drunk the poisoned bridal cog, too." A wave of revulsion washed over Eliza at what this woman had done. "No doubt it was easy to pour a bit of poison in the vessel before you made your way into the church. You're an ugly piece of work, you are. Going to a wedding where you intended to kill both the bride and groom."

"As my husband and his fellow soldiers would say, Minerva was viewed as collateral damage. Serves her right for becoming involved with that fortune hunter."

"Did Winterbottom know where the treasure was?"

"Of course. He'd been to my home several times trying to decide which pieces from the treasure he planned to turn over to the British Museum."

Eliza threw a quick look over her shoulder Where in blazes was Higgins? Even it he was lost in the maze, she assumed he eventually would bump into her again. She had to keep Lady Winifred talking until he did.

"Ambrose insisted that everyone who took part in smuggling the treasure should receive what was promised, but splitting the money four ways was not in my plan." She shrugged. "I had to eliminate him. No hard feelings. And early this morning I left a surprise for Luther in the folly, which should distract him and Scotland Yard for some time. I had no intention of returning to the maze at all until you mentioned my earring. I couldn't allow the police to find a piece of my jewelry here. And they would have found it. Now I shall have to hurry if I'm to avoid them."

"You must know the maze quite well." Eliza wondered if she could outrun her.

"When I visited Banfield Manor, Richard's father and I found the maze conducive for romantic assignations. I could lead you through this maze with my eyes closed." Her smile returned, but this time it was chilling. "I intend to escape through a hidden back entrance. Then I need only venture into the deer park and detour to an abandoned cottage at the end of the property. I left my motorcar there."

"No doubt it's filled with boxes of the temple treasure. It's all yours now."

"As you said, I'm the matchmaker. Half the treasure shall be delivered to one buyer tonight, the other I shall transport to Scotland tomorrow. And then I'm off to my doting husband in India. He has no idea my activities involve smuggling. Silly dear. As if we could afford half the jewels we've purchased over the years if I had not dealt with the black market."

"You're a thief and a murderer," Eliza said hotly.

"Which is why I cannot risk you remaining alive."

Winifred moved so swiftly, Eliza saw only a blur before a stabbing pain shot up her right arm. The woman had thrown the letter opener, and her aim was excellent. Letting out a startled cry, Eliza dropped the cake knife. As she pulled the needle-sharp letter opener from her arm, Winifred rushed at her and both women tumbled to the ground.

The air filled with grunts and curses as they began to wrestle. She punched Winifred in the jaw, but the older woman – far more agile and stronger than she looked – smacked Eliza hard and she saw stars. Desperate for an advantage, she grabbed Winifred's hair and yanked with all her strength. So did Winifred, and they both yelled in pain. During their frantic tussle, Eliza heard their dresses rip. And Eliza noticed that a rivulet of blood ran down her arm. If only she could grab the knife she'd dropped. Each time they rolled about on the path, Eliza felt its sharp imprint against her back. But she couldn't free her hands long enough to reach it.

Winifred suddenly straddled her. She grasped Eliza's throat with one hand and squeezed. Eliza fought for breath, aware that Winifred was groping for the cake knife with her other hand. In another second, Eliza was sure to be stabbed. Summoning all her strength, she pulled herself up from the ground and sank her teeth deep into Winifred's arm. The woman screamed.

She flung Winifred off and scrambled to her feet. Winifred caught hold of her dress, but only managed to rip most of her skirt off as Eliza jumped aside. At this rate, she'd end up stark naked. Darting past Winifred's clawing hands, she raced in the direction she hoped led to the exit. Eliza wanted to weep when she met one hedge-lined path after another.

Eliza glanced over her shoulder, hearing Lady Winifred panting no more than ten feet behind her. She increased her speed. Was she going in circles? Was there no end to this maze?

Another choice of paths lay ahead. Right or left? It prob
ably didn't matter. All that mattered was staying ahead of
Lady Winifred. Eliza veered right, praying she could outrun her pursuer. She suddenly found herself surrounded by
hedges. Another dead end.

She spun about as Winifred charged her from behind. The
older woman looked fierce; chest heaving, hair tumbled
about her face, eyes wide with anger. And she gripped the
large knife in her hand. As Winifred lunged for her, Eliza
screamed and threw herself to the ground. She rolled in the
other direction, then got to her knees. Maybe she could
crawl out of here.

But Winifred grabbed her hair and pulled so hard, Eliza's head snapped back. Dear God in heaven, her throat was
about to be slit! Time seemed to stand still. Eliza murmured
a final prayer. Then everything became a blur of green and
blue while the air filled with frantic squawks. Winifred
released her with a shrill scream.

Flipping onto her back, Eliza looked up to see the peacock
attack Winifred. His sharp beak pecked at the woman's face
and his clawed feet scratched at her body.

"Get him off me!" she howled.

When Winifred dropped the knife, Eliza crawled over to
reclaim it. She rose shakily to her feet, but made no attempt
to help the woman.

The bird viciously bit at the corner of Winifred's eye. "I
can't see! Help me."

Eliza briefly considered escaping into the maze. But she
refused to leave her love-struck peacock. Percy had not only
saved her life, he was probably her only chance of ever getting out of this maze. Besides, once he finished scratching
and clawing Lady Winifred, she would be in no condition
to wrestle again. Especially since Eliza once more had the
cake knife.

"Eliza, is that you?" a familiar voice called out from behind a hedge.

She wanted to sob in relief. "I'm in here, Colin!"

Detective Ramsey and Thaddeus Smith burst around the corner of the hedge. They stopped short, alarmed by the sight of Eliza in her torn dress, her arm dripping blood. But they were immediately distracted by the peacock's attack on a screaming Lady Winifred.

Ramsey moved to rescue her. "Don't you dare harm that peacock," Eliza said. "He saved my life. Winifred murdered Farrow and Winterbottom. And she tried to do me in as well."

As if sensing the danger had passed, the peacock abruptly stopped his attack. Winifred collapsed onto the ground, moaning in pain, hands over her bloody face. Ramsey crouched before her with his handkerchief, wiping the worst from her eyes.

Percy strutted over to Eliza, who knelt to welcome him. "You're my hero," she murmured.

The peacock allowed her to gently wrap her arms about his feathered body. A moment later, Higgins, Richard, and Clara appeared behind Thaddeus Smith, who still appeared baffled by what was going on.

"You look awful, Eliza!" Clara cried. "Are you all right?"

"I'm fine." She kissed the peacock, amazed that he allowed her to. "It's all thanks to Percy. Lady Winifred was about to cut my throat when he attacked her."

Higgins slowly walked over to her, as though worried he might startle the bird into defending Eliza once more. "Your relationship with him has progressed quite rapidly. Can we expect the banns to be read soon?"

Eliza giggled.

He crouched beside her. "Your arm is bleeding."

"It looks worse than it is. It wouldn't have bled this much

if we hadn't been wrestling."

"Indeed." His gaze took in her scratches, bruised neck, torn gown, and long tousled hair that had come loose from its pins. "I wish I'd been there to help."

"No need. Percy was watching out for me."

Ramsey stood and pulled Lady Winifred to her feet. He kept an iron grip on her arm, although Winifred was in no shape to fight. "Someone show me the way out of this insane maze. Inspector Shaw needs a stretcher sent to the folly."

"The sooner we all leave, the better," Higgins eyed Winifred's woebegone condition.

"I agree," Eliza said. "After all, Clara and Richard have to cut the cake. And the first piece should be served to Percy."

"You do know the first piece is reserved for the bride and groom," Clara said with a wide smile.

"Not at this wedding. As far as I'm concerned, this brave peacock can eat the whole cake." She stroked the bird's neck, who shut his eyes in obvious pleasure. "Even my piece."

Higgins laughed. "I'll believe that when I see it."

The peacock threw back his head to let out a piercing scream. It sounded like a victory cry to Eliza. Or maybe Percy just realized he was about to eat cake.

CHAPTER TWENTY-TWO

HIGGINS NEEDED A VACATION. HE'D attended four weddings in as many weeks, all of them stalked by a killer. Desperate for a change of scene, he found himself envying Jack Shaw and Lord Ashmore. Both men were about to leave on their honeymoons with their respective brides. The Cotswolds and a first-class train journey to Venice sounded a lot more serene than anything happening at 27-A Wimpole Street. Especially today.

Pickering had returned from the hospital, which naturally called for a celebration. Dinner last night contained as many courses as a state banquet. Higgins had no objection. He was as pleased as Eliza to have his old friend back home, looking as hale and hearty as he did before the shooting. But twelve hours of toasting the Colonel and waiting on him hand and foot was more than enough. However he forgot it was the Colonel's birthday today, which meant Eliza and Mrs. Pearce had scheduled even more feasting, accompanied by two cakes. That he could have tolerated, but it appeared that birthday parties demanded guests. A ridiculous notion, but one which Eliza wouldn't let him override.

The door to his study flew open. "I told you we don't want to be disturbed!" Higgins shouted, refusing to look up from his newspaper.

Pickering put down his own newspaper. "What is it, Mrs. Pearce?"

The housekeeper gave him a benevolent smile. "Detective and Mrs. Shaw are here."

When Jack and his bride entered the room, Pickering got to his feet. "How lovely to see you both."

Sybil rushed over to embrace him. Higgins noticed she took care not to press against his injured shoulder. "Please sit down, Colonel."

"Don't be silly, my dear. I'm perfectly capable of greeting the blushing bride. I only wish I'd been able to toast the two of you at the reception."

"It's not your fault some madwoman turned our wedding into a shooting gallery," Jack said. "Did you know the necklace Lady Winifred wore to Farrow's wedding came from the Temple of Parvati treasure? That's why she tried to kill you."

Pickering shook his head. "A shame I never had more than a glance at it."

"She admitted not expecting to see you at the church that day. Otherwise she never would have worn the stolen necklace. Apparently she had no compunction wearing it around the Misras because Taral never saw the jewels which were taken from the temple."

"What about Luther's role in all this?" Higgins asked the detective.

"According to his confession, Luther stabbed Pearl because she didn't tell him where the treasure was hidden. Of course, the poor girl didn't know. Anyway, both he and Lady Winifred will be tried for murder. And very likely hanged."

"Hand that to me, Detective." Mrs. Pearce took the wrapped birthday present he held. "We're putting the gifts in the dining room."

"There are at least a dozen from Eliza," Higgins remarked. "For all I know, she's popped off to Oxford Street for a little more shopping."

"The dear girl is thrilled to have me home," Pickering said. "And I'm as happy as she is."

Sybil looked around the room. "Where is Eliza?"

"She's getting ready upstairs." Pickering waited until his guests sat down on the leather sofa before reclaiming his own seat. "Eliza has a special birthday outfit she wants to surprise everyone with."

"I hope it isn't a wedding gown," Higgins muttered. He'd seen enough women marching about in wedding dresses to last a lifetime.

"Oh dear, someone's at the door." The housekeeper hurried out of the room.

Higgins put aside his paper. Normally he disliked guests, but he was fond of Jack and his bride. Both of them looked remarkably rested today, especially Sybil whose tailored skirt and blouse matched her always rosy cheeks. Good for them. He wasn't a fan of marriage, but these two were a decent, likable pair and deserved to enjoy their time as newlyweds without the threat of murderers lurking about.

"All set for the motor trip to the Cotswolds?" Higgins asked.

"Can't wait." Jack grinned. "We were lucky a fellow detective at the Yard lent us his motorcar for a week. It's a beauty too: a Maxwell Touring car."

"I wouldn't mind a motorcar of my own," Higgins said. "I quite enjoyed tooling about in Lord Ashmore's Stutz Bearcat."

"Eliza has talked about purchasing one," Pickering added.

"Think of the lovely day trips we could all take if she does," Sybil said.

Freddy burst into the parlor. The young man always seemed

to be out of breath and windblown, even when dressed in a dapper charcoal gray suit as he was today. "Good morning, everyone. Or is it noon already? I've been rushing about so much, I lost track of the time. But I did manage to secure a ripping good present for the Colonel." He bowed his head in the older man's direction, then scanned the study. "I say, where's Eliza?"

"Upstairs," Higgins, Sybil, and Jack said at the same time.

Higgins groaned when knocking commenced at the front door once more. "Just how many people has Eliza invited for Pick's birthday lunch?"

Mrs. Pearce ushered in Detective Ramsey. Higgins thought he seemed a bit too formally dressed for lunch at Wimpole Street. Looked like the young man was out to make an impression. And Higgins knew it wasn't for him. This could be why Eliza was taking so long to get ready.

Freddy and Colin Ramsey exchanged startled looks, as if neither expected the other to be here. "Best grab a seat," Higgins said wearily. "If too many people show up, we'll have to send them to the kitchen to sit."

Freddy plopped down on an ottoman. Colin took a chair on the other side of the room.

"I thought you'd be busy at Scotland Yard, Detective Ramsey," Freddy said. "After all, Luther North and Lady Winifred were only arrested three days ago."

"No need," the detective answered. "Lady Winifred confessed later that day. Then we found the smuggled treasure in the trunk of her car. As for Luther, we had his fingerprints on the knife that killed Pearl Palmer. We didn't need his confession, but we got one anyway. Although we had to wait until the next day when he finally recovered from the snake bite."

More banging on the front door. "Who's here now?" Higgins barked.

He didn't have long to wait as Mrs. Pearce led Taral and Basanti Misra into the parlor. The housekeeper couldn't hide her curiosity at Taral's jeweled turban and Basanti's flowing purple sari. Colin offered the Indian woman his seat, while Taral sat on the piano bench.

"Where is Eliza?" Basanti settled her sari and sash about her.

Before anyone could answer, Eliza swept into the room. A moment of stunned silence greeted her.

She wore a dazzling red sari trimmed in gold. Higgins raised an eyebrow at her bare midriff and uncovered arms. Even more shocking, Eliza's brown hair was neither pinned up nor in a thick braid. Instead it flowed about her shoulders, reaching halfway down her back. He shot a look at Freddy and Colin Ramsey, who stared at Eliza with a mixture of surprise and pleasure.

Basanti clapped her hands in delight. "Eliza, you look most beautiful. And you honor me by wearing the sari I gave you. But let me re-pin the sash so it remains on your left shoulder."

While Basanti fussed with the crimson sash, Pickering said, "My dear, seeing you dressed like that I can't help but recall my many pleasant memories of Bombay."

"It's why I wore it, Colonel. When I took tea with the Misras at their hotel, Basanti showed me all her pretty saris. After she saw how much I loved them, she gave me this. And sandals besides." Eliza stepped back and twirled. The diaphanous skirt and sash swirled with her movements, displaying corded sandals on her bare feet. "Because you spent so much time in India, I wanted to wear it for your birthday."

Higgins hoped Eliza had no plans to wear it on the streets of London. So much bare skin on a proper young Englishwoman would create an instant scandal.

Freddy cleared his throat. "Eliza, perhaps only a woman

from India should wear such a thing. The sari is far too revealing."

"It is a most proper form of apparel," Taral protested. "All my countrywomen dress in such a way."

"I love it." Eliza wore a familiar stubborn expression.

"I love it, too," Colin Ramsey said. He walked over to Eliza and lifted up one of the folds of her sash. "I've heard you're quite the lady of fashion. Perhaps you'll start a trend. I know I wouldn't mind seeing women walking about Mayfair in saris." He winked. "And it looks far more comfortable than those corseted outfits you ladies like to wear."

"Indeed it is." Eliza smiled back at him.

"Although it may not be the best choice for our English winters," Pickering added.

Freddy marched over to Eliza. "You've shown the Colonel how nice you look in the sari. Now please go upstairs and change into something more appropriate."

"I will not," Eliza said. "And I resent you telling me what to do."

"I do not see anything improper with our saris." Basanti sighed. "But he is your affianced gentleman, Eliza. Perhaps you should do as he asks."

"Freddy is not my affianced anything. Even if he was, I wouldn't let him tell me what to do." Eliza smoothed down the silk and chiffon folds of her sari. "If you're going to keep bothering me about it, you'd best leave, Freddy. I won't have you spoil the Colonel's party."

"I'd listen to her," Higgins advised, enjoying the sight of Freddy looking so uncomfortable. "Eliza will have your head if you ruin Pick's birthday."

Colin's smile grew wider. Higgins wondered if fisticuffs would break out between the two men. But another knock at the front door broke the tension.

"Now what?" Higgins asked.

This time it was Clara and her Aunt Lavender who were announced by Mrs. Pearce. With a groan, Higgins got to his feet. They had now officially run out of chairs. Lavender Stratton gave him a gracious nod as she sat in his favorite chair by the Victrola. Clara's aunt looked almost as unconventional as Eliza in a geometric print dress and satin bandanna wrapped about her upswept curls. At least Clara was decked out as expected; she wore one of those ludicrous hobble skirts with a matching navy and white striped jacket.

Clara immediately began to ooh and ahh over Eliza's sari as Basanti described how such a garment should be draped.

"Where's Lord Ashmore and Clara's mother?" Higgins asked Lavender.

"My sister is still resting from all the excitement of the wedding, so I had my driver bring Clara and me here. And Richard is busy finalizing a transaction regarding his collection. He'll be here presently in his Stutz Bearcat. I quite like that car."

"As do I," Higgins said. "Did you say Lord Ashmore is doing something with the collection?"

"Oh, yes." Lavender looked over at Taral who sat listening to them. "I would have thought Mr. Misra would have informed all of you by now."

Everyone turned to Taral. "The day after his wedding," he said, "Lord Ashmore agreed to send the Parvati temple objects back to India."

"He only did that because of me," Clara broke in. "After what happened in the maze, I was quite upset. Poisonous snakes left in boxes, one murderer found at the folly, the other running about trying to kill Eliza! And all because of those dreadful things from the Indian temple. I don't care what anyone says, there *is* a Curse of the Cobra. I told Richard he must get rid of all of it. And as soon as possible."

"He will return all the pieces from the Temple of Parvati

that he has in his collection. But at a price." Taral sighed. "It is a steep price, but my family and the Maharajah in Mysore must pay it."

Basanti went over to her husband. "It is only money. And the Goddess Parvati will surely bless us with good fortune for working on her behalf."

Clara shrugged. "Besides, Richard wants to buy modern art. Picasso, Matisse, Rousseau. And some Norwegian painter called Monk."

"Munch," Lavender corrected her niece. "Edvard Munch."

This sounded like good news to Higgins. Maybe they would all hear the last of the temple and its treasure. "Does this include the treasure smuggled off the ship in the Bay of Bengal? I'm assuming it also belongs to Lord Ashmore."

"Yes." Taral's voice turned cold. "And he refuses to sell that part of the temple. At least not to me or the Maharajah."

"You should be grateful Lord Ashmore has agreed to sell any of his collection to you," Pickering said. "He has no legal obligation to do so."

"Only an ethical one," Taral shot back. His wife quickly whispered in his ear.

Higgins still had questions for Clara. "Then your husband is keeping part of the treasure?"

"I told you, Professor. I don't want a single piece of that beastly treasure near me."

"Lord Ashmore is selling it to the very chaps Lady Winifred planned to sell it to," Colin said. "Both men swore to us they had no idea the pieces they offered to buy had been stolen. We have no way of proving they're not telling the truth. And they're paying an astronomical sum."

Clara clapped her hands together. "Isn't my darling Richard clever? And so handsome. Now he's even richer than before. I plan to buy new furniture for Banfield Manor when we return from our honeymoon. Everything there is so old and dusty. I want modern things."

Higgins wondered just how clever Lord Ashmore was if he was willing to marry such a maddening creature.

Sybil laughed. "Make sure not to toss out any antique heirlooms."

Clara looked down at the diamond sunburst brooch pinned to her jacket. "The only heirloom I care about is this one. Although I never received it in the folly as planned. Not with that deadly snake and chauffeur in there. But Richard did give it to me afterward."

Another loud knocking at the front door caused everyone to look up.

Higgins grumbled. "If that's not Lord Ashmore, I'm going to start turning people away."

But it was the 5th Baron of Ashmore who peeked into the parlor. He looked pleased with himself. "Forgive me for being late, but I had a little difficulty transporting something." He still didn't enter the room. Instead, he merely leaned around the corner. "A gift."

"Please," Pickering protested. "I don't need any gifts."

"This gift is for Eliza," Richard replied. "For being the one who caught the killer."

"Not me." She laughed. "The hero was your lovely peacock."

"Actually, he's your peacock now." Richard stepped into the parlor. Behind him trotted a peacock, his immense tail sweeping the carpeting behind him.

Eliza let out a delighted cry, and the peacock responded with one of his own.

"Percy!" She knelt down and held out her arms. Higgins's jaw dropped when the bird ran over to her, permitting her to embrace him.

"Excuse me, but I do not have a vast estate for this bird — or its tail — to run about in."

"We have the enclosed garden out back, Professor," Eliza said. "Percy will love that. I once owned a canary called Petey. I know all about taking care of birds."

"A peacock is much larger than a canary," Higgins reminded her. "He can't live here."

"Of course he can." Pickering looked on approvingly at Eliza and Percy. "Many households in India have peacocks."

Colin chuckled. "I have to admit he's a handsome animal."

"This is absurd, Eliza," Freddy said. "You cannot keep a peacock as a pet. Wimpole Street is not India, although you'd never know it by the way you're dressed. What if your students tell people that you own a peacock *and* you wear saris?"

"I'm keeping this blooming peacock and my sari." Eliza aimed a defiant look at Freddy and Higgins. "Don't forget Percy saved my life. The darling bird deserves his own little garden. And maybe a tiny room on the first floor. I've a lovely blanket he can sleep on."

Percy threw back his head and emitted five piercing cries.

"By Jupiter, will we have to hear this all day?" Higgins shook his head.

"Luncheon is served," Mrs. Pearce informed the guests.

"The bird is not sitting at the table with us," Higgins warned Eliza.

"Don't be silly. I know that." Eliza stroked the peacock's head. "He can eat in the garden. Only we must make certain to save him a slice of cake. I'm glad Cook baked two cakes."

"As long as I get a slice, too. I'm fond of cake myself." Unlike Freddy, Colin Ramsey seemed amused by the sight of Eliza cuddling the peacock.

Freddy looked even more unhappy with the situation. "This is ridiculous," he whispered to Higgins. "I'm tempted to make Eliza decide between him and me."

"You and Detective Ramsey?"

"Of course not. What is that detective to her? I'm talking about the peacock."

"Maybe you should." In fact, Higgins hoped Freddy did give Eliza such an ultimatum.

As if he knew they were speaking about him, the peacock took a step towards Freddy and Higgins. With another ear-splitting cry, he unfurled his magnificent fan of tail feathers.

Freddy didn't stand a chance.

ACKNOWLEDGMENTS

Our thanks to *The Book of Weddings* by Mrs. Burton Kingsland for its invaluable Edwardian wedding details; to our many loyal readers and fans; and to Dr. Souter, who explained how best to shoot – but not kill – one of our characters.

OTHER BOOKS BY D.E. IRELAND

WOULDN'T IT BE DEADLY
MOVE YOUR BLOOMING CORPSE

ABOUT D.E. IRELAND

D.E. Ireland is a team of long time friends and award-winning authors, Meg Mims and Sharon Pisacreta. In 2013 they decided to collaborate on a unique series based on George Bernard Shaw's wonderfully witty play *Pygmalion*, which also inspired the classic musical *My Fair Lady*. At work on Book Four of their Agatha nominated series, they also pursue separate writing careers. Currently both of them write cozy mysteries for Kensington under their respective new pen names: Sharon Farrow and Meg Macy. Sharon's Berry Basket series debuted in October 2016, and Meg's Shamelessly Adorable Teddy Bear series will be released in May 2017. The two Michigan authors have patient husbands, brilliant daughters, and share a love of tea, books, and history.

Follow D.E. Ireland on Facebook, Twitter, and
www.deireland.com

Printed in Great Britain
by Amazon